SURVIVAL
OF THE
BLOOD

BETH BRISTOW

Printed in the United States of America
Library of Congress Control Number: 2019916575
ISBN: Softcover   978-1-64376-483-2
          Hardcover   978-1-64376-789-5
          eBook   978-1-64376-482-5

Republished by: PageTurner, Press and Media LLC
Publication Date: November 14, 2019

To order copies of this book, contact:
PageTurner, Press and Media
Phone: 1-888-447-9651
order@pageturner.us
www.pageturner.us

"When I find an author who has written a historical fiction work about England and Scotland, I'm in heaven. I just completed Beth Bristow's novel *"Survival of the Blood"* and have fallen in love with Scottish history all over again. This well-researched book is an account of the Cameron clan during the time of Prince Charles and the tragic events of the Jacobite rebellion. *Survival of the Blood* brought the Cameron family to life for me and has left me begging for more."

—Jan Brown, instructor of media specialties

"I am a lecturer of Scottish history. Beth Bristow wrote about historical characters and brought them to life. I felt as if I was there, listening to them, like a fly on the wall. As I read about historical events taking place, I became an observer. I could not put the book down and am waiting for the second one."

—Dick Lucas, owner of The Scottish Armory and lecturer in Scottish history

"I love historical novels, especially about Scotland. As I read *Survival of the Blood*, I could see it all unfolding in my mind. After I read the ending, all I wanted was more. The people in this book are very real and feel like family to me."

—Celena Hyde, Clan MacGillivray

"I've enjoyed reading *Survival of the Blood*. I felt as though I was there in 1745 experiencing the beginning of the uprising. Then, in 1746, the description of the battle was so real I could not put the book down. Thank you for a wonderful read. Can't wait for the next one!"

—Jim Reid, retired army helicopter pilot

Preface

The Clans of Scotland lived the tale, while I've only told it. As I wrote Survival of the Blood, being a member of Clan Cameron, I experienced the anger, sadness and sense of loss the clans felt before, during and after the Battle of Culloden. Over 260 years have passed since that dark day, April 16, 1746 and now, the clans are scattered throughout the world. Perhaps it is genetic memory that draws so many of us back to our homeland. Many of us know the minute we set foot upon Scotland's soil that we have returned home. Scotland is in our blood and we have survived!

There are several references to 'tacksmen' in the book. A description of this word is a person who leases property from the landowner and then subleases that property to another. A 'tacksman or tacksmen' collects rent on the property, takes some for himself and pays the remaining portion to the landowner, all per prior agreement. In fact, such agreements brought about the clearances which began not long after Culloden.

Many of Auntie Mary's cures and plant knowledge in *Survival of the Blood* came from handwritten notes contained in an old book authored by my several-times-removed great-granny, Sophrona who was a midwife and herbalist. Sophrona learned healing skills from her father, who taught her ways to recognize and use plants and common weeds to treat patients. Most of the plants and herbs mentioned in Survival of the Blood grow world wide, with the exception of Bog myrtle which grows in Scotland. I cannot recommend that readers use the treatments that Auntie Mary described in *Survival of the Blood*, however, I do know many of them are still in use today as natural cures.

Yours, Aye,
Beth Bristow

Characters

Ewan Cameron - "I was Janet Cameron's husband and Dunsmuir Cameron's (called "Duny") father. I was not at the battlefield when the fighting took place. Instead I was on my way back from Inverness where I had gone in the hope of finding food and water for the men who had nothing to eat for three days before the battle. I was captured and died from injuries received from British soldiers.

Thomas Cameron - "I was Ewan's younger brother. I died on the battlefield on April 16, 1746."

Gordon Cameron - "I was Ewan's cousin. I left my wife, Elizabeth and our four bairns to fight at Culloden. I did nay agree with the battle and knew we could not win. I died on the battlefield alongside my cousins.

Duncan Cameron - "I also died on the battlefield. Nay, I dinna agree with fighting, certainly naught after seeing the King's Royal Army standing there with their artillery. I died leaving behind my wife, Anne and our two small sons."

Janet Cameron - "I had Gordon's six year old son, Daniel with me when Ewan was captured. We were in the Hielands with no food or water. Surely God protected us and we survived."

Dunsmuir Cameron - Janet and Ewan are my mother and father. Abby and James Dunsmuir are my mother's parents. After the battle, I desperately wanted to know if my parents were alive; and I ran away from my Grandmother's care; eventually, through difficult circumstances I found myself in America.

Elizabeth Cameron and her three sons - "I was Gordon's wife. My sons were forced to watch while the English soldiers violated me one by one, then we were sealed inside the broch and the house was set afire. Aye, the lads and myself were very afraid. We died hoping Gordon waited for us in heaven. It was my last promise to the lads."

Anne Cameron - My two sons and myself were forced to leave Scotland when my husband, Duncan died at Culloden. We escaped to my parent's home in Northumberland, England.

Charles Edward Stuart - "I was known as "Bonnie Prince Charlie". I led the Jacobite army on the battlefield. I wanted to gain the throne in England for my father; upon his demise, I would become King; I desperately wanted to be King of England; my fondest daydream was to see people bowing as I, dressed in my kingly finery and jeweled crown passed by."

Lord George Murray - "I was Charles Stuart's General and led his army on the battlefield. I knew Charles had no experience in leading men in battle, however, I loved Scotland enough to attempt on their behalf to bring a new King to the throne who would treat the people of Scotland fairly. I did not die in the battle, however many times thought it might have been better if I had. William Augustus hunted me with a vengeance as he vowed he would hang me for my 'crimes' of supporting the Jacobite uprising."

Lady Amelia Murray - "I am Lord George's wife. We have five children. I am desperate to leave our home as it is searched every day by English soldiers looking for my husband. I fear our children and myself will be taken prisoners to bring my husband out of hiding."

Abby Dunsmuir - "I am Janet Cameron's, Jamie's and Meghan's mother. I lost my beloved husband, James when he was shot and killed by a troop of English soldiers who wanted my jewelry and our money. I am going to help Lord George Murray escape from Scotland; he must not die at the hand of William Augustus.

Meghan Dunsmuir - "I lost my beloved husband, John MacIntyre when he died in the battle. Our little newborn son, Aaron will grow up without knowing his father."

Jamie Dunsmuir - "I am the son of James Dunsmuir; Meghan and Janet are my sisters and Abby is my mother. Our family has been torn apart by English soldiers who had no concern whatsoever for the people they killed. They had no reason to kill my father!"

Ian Douglas - "I am the son of Anne MacLeod of the MacLeod clan of the Isle of Skye. My father was a Douglas; I inherited his lands and a breed of sheep that thrive in the Highlands. I added to the herd and sold their wool even though the King of England said Scotland could no longer sell wool except to the English who wanted to buy said wool at a low price and resell it for a profit. I delivered my wool via my ship to the continent and sold it myself. I do not agree with England's people profiting and Scotland's people not being able to do the same."

James Dunsmuir - "I was Abby's husband. Together we raised and sold horses to the King's army and private individuals. I died when the King's soldiers shot me because I spoke with a Scottish accent. Abby and I were on our way to visit family in England."

Willie Cameron - "I did naught fight in the battle because I dinna believe Scotland could win the battle; there wasn't enough of us and too many of them. Now, my wife Katie and I have to leave Scotland. There's nothing here for us."

Katie Cameron - "I married Willie so we could make a home for ourselves. I was born in Ireland and left my family to come to Scotland. Willie and I must leave Scotland. We've nowhere to live. I dinna want to, but there's no choice."

William Augustus, Duke of Cumberland; "I am the second son of King George II, Captain General of his Royal Army. I led my men in the Battle of Culloden and, of course, the battle was won. I am now occupied with depopulation of Scotland's Highlanders while I search for Charles Edward Stuart who has a thirty thousand pound reward on his head. I detest Scotland and the people who live there. The country is rough and the people uncivilized. The King's opinion of them is the same as mine."

Introduction

As a new day dawned in Scotland in April, 1746, a long line of weary, hungry Highlanders stumbled across the soggy marshland of Culloden's moor located to the east of Inverness. A few hours later, over two thousand of these Highlanders lay dead on Culloden's battlefield. The men, standing together by clan, bravely fought to their deaths. They did not choose to be there, but fealty to their clan chieftains demanded their presence. Only a few had muskets, rifles, or pistols; the rest carried broadswords or dirks. The men of King George II's British Army were well-fed and well-rested, and they carried both rifles and pistols. After the battle was over, the king's soldiers searched among the bodies, bayoneting the wounded, while mounted dragoons took swords to fleeing survivors. The number of dead Highlanders increased until there were only a few left to take as prisoners.

The Battle of Culloden became known as the last battle to be fought on British soil and was the final chapter in Prince Charles Edward Stuart's attempt to recapture the crown that his grandfather, King James VII, lost when he was deposed in 1689.

The battle still is spoken of at gatherings all over the world. Always the question is asked, "Why did the Highlanders go into battle hungry and virtually unarmed?" *Survival of the Blood* introduces two men, one a trusted friend of Prince Charles Edward Stuart and the other a general in the king's royal army. Together they made an agreement that brought about circumstances forever changing the future of Scotland's people.

The Battle of Culloden was a small skirmish by World War standards, but it profoundly affected the thousands of Scottish men, women, and children who were forced to leave their homeland. Many of them came to the American colonies, where they were called upon, once again, to fight against the king's British Army in the Revolutionary War. They well remembered that bitterly cold day of April 16, 1746, on a faraway moor in Scotland, and this time they were prepared!

Prologue

Two creatures perch on a crumbling boulder at the top of a rocky Highland glen. If seen by mortal eyes, they would appear to be large birds or wild animals waiting for prey to weaken, fall, and die.

One of the creatures is a demonic spirit known as The Dark One. He constructs well-disguised traps for mortals to capture them in a baited net of lies and deceit. The rewards are irresistible: power, money, and pleasure beyond belief. Even though his prey will suffer excruciating mental and physical pain, the desire for more keeps them trapped in the mire. What will it take to be released? Death seems to be the answer, but, as we shall see, it is not.

The Dark One's master, known as De'il, or His Most Evil One, abhors humans. He had no part in their creation and resented the event from the very beginning; so much so that his blazing hatred became the unending fires of hell. The following Scottish poem, likely written by one who knows, is a fitting description. Be warned!

Th' De'il dances on an empty pocket

There's a De'il in every mouthful of whisky
Th' De'il is busy in a high wind.
Th' De'il's guid tae his ain an'
He needs a lang-shanked spain tha' sup's wi' th' De'il!

The second creature is Death. He greets newly separated souls immediately after the expiration of the mortal body. His task is to prepare the soul for the arrival of an escort who will take it to its final destination. Neither The Dark One nor Death will be visible until the moment of dying, and then, depending upon the previously made choices of the newly deceased human, first Death and then one of two other beings will be visible as the soul begins the final passing process.

Another being who might participate in the dying experience is loving and rejoices not in the death of humans but rather in the well-being of their souls. When one of His perishes, Elight, a compassionate spirit of great beauty, arrives to claim the newly separated soul. The healing of the spiritual body and mind begins at that very moment.

Survival of the Blood, by Beth Bristow

Chapter 1

October 1745

Duncan Cameron lay on the ground, the night air chilling the blood that had pooled beneath him. Clad only in a nightshirt, he cursed, "Ye got me, yer bloody thieves, damn ye! Campbell bastards, ye got 'em all!" He tried to sit up, but pain forced him back to the ground. It was morning before his wife found him.

His eyes searching the vacant pastures, Gordon Cameron shook his head. Once he would have been so angry he would have loaded his pistol and gone searching for his missing animals. Now he sat shivering in the cold wind and thought of his empty purse, his empty larder, and his hungry family. What was a man to do?

The gate swung on its hinges when Ewan Cameron kicked it. "Damned Campbells, a curse on ye!" All of his Highland cattle were missing. "Ye'll not keep 'em, yer bloody bastards!"

The next night, Ewan and his brother Thomas, knowing the risks, traveled to Campbell lands to bring back the cattle.

Waiting in the dark by the empty pen, Dunsmuir Cameron listened for the voices of his father, Ewan, and uncle, Thomas. When he heard them shouting, he moved away just in time for the herd to enter the pen. His father and uncle rode on either side behind the black, yellow, and red shaggy-coated herd.

"Th' thievin' damn blackguardin' Campbells! Wha's theirs is theirs, an' wha's mine is theirs!" Ewan cursed as he walked through the herd, scattering hay on the ground.

Thomas grinned as he thought of the empty pen waiting for the Campbells and scuffed Duny on the head. "Aye, they'll be th' ones cussin' us now. *Am bheil thu go mo thuigsinn*, Duny?" (Do you understand me?)

"Aye, Uncle, I do."

Thomas pointed at his nephew. "When yer animals go missin', th' first place ter look is at th' Campbells. None'll know any better abou' stealin' another's animals."

It was almost daylight by the time the two men and Duny made their way to the broch. Duny's empty belly grumbled, and the thought of oat porridge made him walk a little faster, leaving his father and uncle behind. Opening the kitchen door, he dodged the cat on her way out and sat in his chair at the table.

Janet, Ewan's wife and Duny's mother, placed wooden bowls filled with porridge on the table, along with fresh bread, butter, cream, cherry preserves, and baked apples sweetened with honey. Soon, Duny's anticipation was replaced by the comfort of a full belly.

"Duny, yer bed's waitin'. Get along, laddie," his mother said.

Duny climbed the stairs to his bedchamber, pulled the coverlet back, and was asleep before his head landed on the pillow.

"Janet, we'll warm up a bit a'fore we finish sortin' th' animals," Ewan said.

Ewan, Thomas, and Janet pulled chairs closer to the fire. Ewan looked at his brother and wife. "There's four pens o' cattle there tha' belong to Duncan an' Gordon. Thomas, in th' morn I'll ride to

Gordon's broch an' ye'll travel to Duncan's broch. They ha' animals at th' Campbells too."

The next day, Thomas rode south, following a faint path that wound through the valleys of the Highlands. In the distance, stood snow-covered Ben Nevis, visible one minute and gone the next as mist swirled and moved over the peak. A man could easily lose his sense of direction when the mist came in from the north sea and mixed with the fog blowing in from the Atlantic, creating a wet, cool blanket of white swirling with gray. Thomas mumbled to himself, "Blink yer eyes once an' ye'll lose yer marker. Ye could be ridin' south when ye thought it was west ye were goin'."

Ewan rode along the banks of the Lochy River that bordered his lands, Glen Lochy. The river supplied water for three Cameron families on the western side and the Campbell and Mackenzie families on the eastern side. At the gate to Gordon's pastures, Ewan reined in his horse. Water-soaked oat and barley sheaves lay on the ground.

"Dammit, Gordon! Yer grain needs to be in th' barn a'fore th' autumn rains start! If ye dinna do so, ye'll be lookin' for fodder for yer animals an' oats for yer bairns' porridge!" Then a thought crossed Ewan's mind. *Gordon isn't one to leave his work undone.*

Gordon's broch sat on a parcel of rich land placed in his grandfather's care by the Lochiel, Ewen Cameron, chieftain of Clan Cameron. When Ewan passed the barn, he grinned as he thought about the four cousins, Gordon, Duncan, Thomas, and himself, climbing to the top ridge pole in the barn loft and taking turns jumping to the haystack far below. The lads, all schooled by their mothers, could read, write, and do ciphering. Their fathers taught them to care for livestock, plant crops, and manage the responsibilities of a laird. They were handsome lads, each one with a slightly crooked nose, a noticeable Cameron trait.

Gordon, the oldest of the cousins, had married Elizabeth Nelson when he was eighteen and she was sixteen. But lately, he'd lost interest in his daily tasks and caring for his wife and four sons. And Elizabeth was now pregnant with their fifth child.

Duncan, the second-oldest cousin, and his wife, Anne, were known for their hospitality. A Christ's Mass celebration at their home included fine whiskey, ale, and Anne's smoked joint of venison in a savory onion sauce.

Thomas, Ewan's brother, lived with Ewan and Janet at Glen Lochy.

Anne Cameron was born in Northumberland, England, to Lord and Lady Smallwood. Duncan's mother, Martha, also born in England, planned for her son to marry Anne, but Anne's father considered all Scotsmen to be rough and rowdy. When Lord Smallwood learned that Anne wished to marry Duncan Cameron, he flatly refused, saying arrangements had already been made for her to marry an English duke. Anne sent word to Martha, who knew Anne's father would not approve of the marriage. Martha invited Anne to Scotland for a visit, knowing Lady Smallwood would encourage her to accept the invitation. His Lordship was not consulted concerning Anne's visit to Scotland.

Lady Smallwood envied Martha's marriage to a handsome Scotsman, privately wishing that she too were married to a "rough and rowdy" man who wore leather breeches and a coarse linen tunic. Along with inheriting his father's title, land, and manor, Lord Smallwood also inherited his father's harsh manners. A man of few words and no patience, His Lordship believed that the act of lovemaking was for the purpose of procreation, never recreation. Her Ladyship knew he was finished when he removed himself from her embrace and, without a word, returned to his own bedchamber. Once he said as he left her chambers, "Please advise if you do not find yourself with child."

Lady Smallwood was well into the eighth month of her first pregnancy when Lord Smallwood asked if she might be expecting a child. She replied, "You asked only that I advise you if I did not find myself with child." His Lordship looked down his nose at her and left the room.

Anne Smallwood and Duncan Cameron were married while she was visiting Scotland. Lord Smallwood sent a message to his daughter advising that her dowry would be given to her sister and that Anne was no longer a member of the family. A bride of six months when the message arrived, Anne patted her bulging belly and said, "Father will feel differently when he learns he has a grandson."

Ewan Cameron was in no hurry to find a wife. However, he changed his mind when he met a beautiful eighteen-year-old lass who was the daughter of a man who bred and sold fine horses.

Two months earlier. August 19, 1745

At the northern tip of Scotland's Loch Shiel, a sailing vessel put down anchor. A tall, handsome young man held out his hand to his valet, Johnnie Stewart, for assistance in disembarking. "This is Glenfinch, Johnnie?"

"Glenfinnan, Your Highness. The clan chieftains will arrive soon. You appointed Secretary O'Sullivan to contact them, and therefore I—"

"The chieftains," the man interrupted impatiently. "How many have accepted my invitation?"

"Four to six will attend, possibly more. The three you especially asked for, the Cameron, MacDonald, and MacGregor chieftains, will have members of their clans with them. We must have enough food and drink for all, Your Highness." Johnnie smiled. "It's said that music soothes the savage beast. If that is true, perhaps sufficient food and whiskey will have the same effect on the wild and uncivilized."

The man smiled. "The Highlanders are exactly as you describe them. Uncivilized!" He turned to one side and adjusted his powdered wig.

As they walked to a grassy area on the shore, Johnnie said, "Your Highness, I've a suggestion that could make a favorable impression on the men when you speak to them tonight. It's a greeting from the Gaelic language that none but the Highland Scots speak and understand."

"Whatever is it?"

Johnnie smiled, raised both arms in the air, and shouted, "*Slainte!* The men will hear you greet them in their own language."

"Repeat it again."

"*Slainte.* It means 'greetings' in the Gaelic language."

"*Slainte.*" Charles repeated the word several times. "I shall remember *slainte* by recalling a similar Italian word for a greeting, *salve.*"

Charles's plans to dethrone the king of England depended on gaining the support of the Highland clan chieftains, who were the guardians, respected leaders, judges, and jury for a large majority of the residents of Scotland. Tonight, he would gain that support. From all directions the sounds of bagpipes and horses could be heard. "Your Highness, you do remember the Gaelic word of greeting?"

Charles spoke impatiently, "Certainly!"

As the men gathered, each chieftain removed his bonnet, placed it over his heart, and presented himself and members of his clan to the prince. A temporary truce meant there were no visible weapons. But, when the meeting came to a close, should a former wrong become too tempting to dismiss, dirks and sgain dubhs were within reach.

Prince Charles stood with his arms outstretched, "*Salve! Salve! Salve!* My good friends!"

Johnnie, standing behind Charles, frowned and shook his head.

"Let us eat and drink. Then, I will tell you what Scotland's people must do to regain freedom from a king who will tax you to death." Charles raised his voice to a shout. "And then demand that your grieving widow give your burial money to the royal treasury to pay your death tax!"

"Aye! Aye!" the men responded.

Several of the chieftains quietly asked one another, *"Salve? Chan eil mi 'tuigsinnt a canthu sin a-rithist, ma's edo thoil e?"* (Should we ask him to say the word again?)

The MacDonald chief thoughtfully said, *"Salve* may be a greetin' where he's from, but, to me, it sounds like wha' I'd put on a bee sting." The chieftain adjusted his tartan wrapped over his shoulder, touched his clan badge with its Gaelic clan motto, and said, "I dinna know wha' he's sayin', an' I'm thinkin' he did'na either."

The Stuart prince continued, " My friends, please be seated. I've brought haggis, cheese, oatcakes, fruits from Scotland's vineyards and orchards, the very best barley malt whisky from the Orkney Islands, ale, wines, and mead of every variety. You deserve the finest that can be had! Please, eat and drink to your fill!"

Each man was handed a trencher of food and a flask of wine. As they ate, the men spoke of taxes on the sale of goods imported and exported to and from Scotland. The conversation turned to the lack of crops and saleable goods. The chieftains would be sorely pressed to pay the king's taxes when his tacksmen came to collect. Charles Stuart listened intently, nodding his head in agreement.

As the afternoon darkened into twilight, a bonfire was set. By clan, the men gathered around the flames. Prince Charles raised his hand. "Tonight, I speak to you as the great-grandson of King James I and grandson of King James II. I come to offer you freedom from a king who cares not for Scotland or her people! When a Stuart King ruled, Scotland's people had coins, barns with fodder for their animals, and well-fed wives and children! But now, you and yours are hungry. Scotland's lands to the south now are occupied by the English, and they will take more and more until there is nothing left!"

The men shouted in unison and stamped their feet. Charles pointed to the group and lowered his voice. "You have empty purses, aye?"

The men shouted "Aye!"

"Last winter, your hungry families were forced to eat grain

stored for this spring's planting. Now, next winter, there will be no fodder for man or beast. Chieftains, when the king's tacksman comes to your door with his tally of rent and taxes due on properties in your care, what will you give him?"

Pausing, Charles Stuart pointed to a man surrounded by clansmen. "Donald Cameron of Lochiel, you and your family support the Jacobite rebellion. Tonight I seek your support to regain the crown of the United Kingdom for the royal Stuart family!"

Donald Cameron stood and spoke in the lilting accent of the Highlanders. "Aye, Prince Charles! Th' Cameron clan believes in th' divine right of kings, an' we will fight to protect it. Your Highness, we can only offer our brawn. I ask ye, will there be weapons an' men enough to take th' crown?"

"Donald, King Louis of France has promised he will provide funds to support the Auld Alliance between Scotland and France. He has given me his word that gold, arms, and men will arrive as the time draws closer to the uprising. King Louis knows a Stuart King will honor Scotland's agreement with France to support trade and peace between the two countries. At this moment, we have sufficient gold to purchase artillery and ammunition to begin the uprising!"

Charles Stuart held his arms out with palms turned upward. "Men! The royal Stuarts are calling upon you once again to defend Scotland!"

Men lifted their dirks into the air with a shout. Charles Edward Stuart bowed his head, raised it, and said, "Chieftains, I ask for your oath of fealty."

Without hesitation, each one came forward, bowed, and kissed Charles's hand. "Gentlemen, on this date, I, Charles Edward Stuart, raise the royal Stuart standard at Glenfinnan, Scotland."

Twilight became a soft darkness with a bright moon shining over the moors. The evening was mellow and sweet with the fragrance of heather, gorse, and meadow grass. The prince stood in the middle of the circle of men. "King George II plans to destroy the Scottish clans because he believes you are not loyal to him. He considers you to be a threat to his kingship! Mark my word, Highlanders: Soon, you will be fighting to keep your home and lands safe from the English just as the clans who live in the borderlands do now!"

On that night in August 1745, Charles Edward Stuart, the young pretender to the English throne, made many promises to the clans of Scotland. Worried men with empty pockets and hungry bairns listened as he spoke. They believed a Stuart king would provide them with the means to provide for their families.

Many a Scotsman sitting by the warmth of a hearth fire on that August evening felt the cold touch of an icy breath of air. The man would rise from his chair, walk to a window, and search for the source. Some, with a shiver, would make the sign of the cross; others would touch the blade of their sgian dubh. Death and The Dark One hovered over Scotland on that night. Scotland's future and that of her people hung in the balance.

The Dark One hissed, "The Prince spoke with conviction, but he'll not succeed."

Death took a minute to respond. "Meaning ... you have plans in place?"

"Of course! The Scots fighting the English—most enjoyable!

At noon the next day Johnnie knocked on Charles's cabin door. "Good day, sir. Did you sleep well?"

"No, I barely slept at all."

"Your Majesty, the past several weeks have been difficult for you. Shall I serve your lunch on the shore so you can enjoy the beauty of the day?"

"Yes, thank you, Johnnie." Johnnie set a small table on a grassy spot not far from the loch's shore.

As he admired the beauty of the location, Charles smiled. "I've gained the support of the mainland clans!" Charles was in an excellent frame of mind, and Johnnie wondered if he dared bring up questions that concerned him. Interrupting Johnnie's thoughts, Charles said, "Johnnie, you've addressed me as 'Your Majesty.' It is inappropriate to address a prince in that manner. One day, I will be king. Winning the crown for my father can only take place through a win on the battlefield, and it all depends on the loyalty of the Jacobites to the divine right of kings."

Johnnie moved the table out of the way. "Sir, I know nothing about the divine right to be king. Is it to do with religion?"

"No, it is more of a doctrine than a religion. The teaching is that kings, through their bloodline, are chosen by God to rule, and therefore they have religious justification for the power they have as a monarch. Of course, gaining power comes at the expense of a Catholic monarch's chief rivals; nobles and the Protestant church. Both the Protestants and nobles of England are rich, powerful, and seek to depose any Catholic who might have even the most remote chance of gaining the throne."

Charles paused. "I'd like wine, please."

As he poured wine, Johnnie asked, "Your grandfather, King James II, would be an example of the divine rule?"

"Yes. However, the chieftains of the isles no longer believe in divine ordination. I believed they would support a royal Stuart regaining the throne. However, their response when I met with them was very different than what Father and his supporters led me to believe." Angrily, Charles flung the flask away, spilling the wine. Johnnie retrieved the flask, filled it, and handed it to Charles. "I expected their loyalty, but it was ridicule I heard in that thick brogue language of theirs that is impossible to understand."

Both men were quiet for a few moments. Finally, Johnnie spoke. "Then, Your Highness, you were not well received?"

"No, I was not. I failed to secure their support. The MacLeod and MacDonald chieftains said the numbers of men joining the uprising would not be sufficient for a win, and they both said I should return to France and wait for a more opportune time!

"Their reluctance to accept me was based on my arrival in Scotland with only one ship. We left France with two ships. However, both ships were attacked by a British Navy warship, and one of them suffered extensive damage. She crippled back to France while my ship was fortunate enough to enter a fog bank and disappear in the mist."

"Sir," Johnnie said, "There is talk that the English are preparing for the uprising."

Charles nodded. "Yes, I have heard the rumors. However, the majority of English troops are scattered all over Europe. No, Johnnie, idle rumors must not interfere with our plans!"

Then Charles smiled. "Both Mother and Father recommended that I offer you the position as my valet. They knew you would understand why the Stuart family is seeking the throne." Charles sat down and began picking bits of heather from his hosiery.

"Sir, I do understand. My father was chosen to be one of your grandsire's personal bodyguards. Both Father and Mother revered King James and often spoke of the injustice of his removal from the throne. I enjoyed hearing Father speak of life in the royal castle, and no doubt you've heard the same grand stories."

"To be truthful, no! Most of the stories I heard were not grand at all. When one's subjects have turned on them and the result is excommunication, it is not a pleasant experience! Grandfather spoke of those who bowed and smiled to his face, all the while plotting behind his back for the final blow, removal from the throne. The family escaped with little more than the clothing they wore. Mark my word, Johnnie, there are those who hold themselves in high regard, and would not share a crumb from their table with a Stuart. I promise you, they will find themselves begging for crumbs on the streets one day! When given the opportunity to support the royal Stuarts, they failed us! No! I will not abandon the divine right of kings, for to do so

11

would be an affront to the very God who inspires me. I will not return to France, as I am persuaded that my faithful Highlanders will stand by me! They accept me as their own, and the rebellion will begin! The Stuart flag flies over Scotland once more!"

Johnnie started to speak but hesitated. "Johnnie, speak up! You have my permission to do so."

"Sir, it is not my way to offer an unsolicited opinion. However, may I?"

"Speak your mind, Johnnie."

"Your Highness, the path you have chosen will be most difficult. The people of Scotland and England are divided in their loyalties. Do you understand how great the price may be to pursue the crown?"

"Yes, I do. When Father placed my younger brother in the priesthood, I knew he expected me to lead the battle against England for the royal Stuarts. He believes our Jacobite army will force King George II to flee to Germany. The throne will belong to us!" Charles smiled. "John O'Sullivan says the Irish will support us. I am very pleased with my selection of John to be my quarter-master general."

"Your Highness, will Secretary O'Sullivan be joining us this evening?"

"Likely not. He has a meeting tonight with Fort William's general. John is presenting himself as an agent for a German weapons manufacturer. Any information he learns about the munitions stored at the fort will be useful, as we believe the fort will supply the king's army with weapons when the uprising begins. Johnnie, how do you regard Mr. O'Sullivan?"

Understanding Charles' admiration for the man, Johnnie carefully worded his response. "Your Highness, when it comes to your well-being, I trust no one as much as myself. Mr. O'Sullivan appears to be dedicated. However, he is quite boisterous and self-important. What are your plans for him, if I may ask?"

"We must have eyes and ears in many places. John has a

way about him that will serve me well in this regard." Charles continued, "You are quite right about him being boisterous with his booming voice and large girth, but he has gained my trust. John was educated at a very exclusive military academy in Paris where he gained honors in military skills. After hearing of his achievements, I contacted John and found him to be a man with admirable qualities. John believes the kingship must be returned to the royal Stuart family. When I explained my dedication to pursue this goal with a vengeance, he offered to be my generalissimo. Johnnie, do you feel more favorable toward John now?"

Johnnie bowed low and answered, "Your Highness, you are, indeed, an excellent judge of character."

"Ah, yes—I selected you, didn't I?" The prince allowed a small smile to curl the corners of his lips.

Charles touched a holstered pistol hanging from his belt. The pistol, a gift from King Louis of France, had been presented to him when he met with Louis before departing for Scotland. "Charles," the king had said, "I support your venture on behalf of our Scottish friends. They will greet you with open arms, for you will liberate them from the rule of a Hanoverian king who has only the barest of rights to the throne." Charles was especially pleased with Louis' next comment, "You, Charles, are a direct descendent of Stuart kings and have far more blood right to the kingship than the Hanoverian sovereign, whose loyalty is to Germany!"

King Louis spoke of difficulties in dealing with the two Hanoverian kings of England. "George II signed a treaty with me to halt our plans to overtake Germany's capital, but then his army attacked my soldiers! As we retreated to France, we fought an English army that was armed with German weapons. The King of England provides support for Germany with monies from his English treasury. His loyalty is to the country of his birth!"

Charles remembered the concern in King Louis's voice. "If England's financial support of Germany is not curtailed, then one day we shall all find ourselves under Germany's rule. I fear the day, my friend! I will provide both financial assistance and soldiers for the rebellion. With a win, France and England can again be allies, just as France and Scotland are now."

Charles smiled as he recalled his parting comment to the king. "I shall be your strongest ally, Your Majesty."

Johnnie placed a basket with bread, pâté, and sweets beside Charles. "Johnnie, please see if the binding on my wig can be stretched a bit. It is very uncomfortable."

"Sir, I will try. However, if it is too loose, it will move about. Perhaps I can trim your hair a bit closer to your head so the wig has a better fit."

Charles laughed. "I don't want to appear as though I'm a shorn sheep, especially if there is a young lady sharing my bed. Futtering while wearing a wig is most difficult, you see. It takes a third arm and hand to keep the damned thing in place."

"Yes, sir," Johnnie replied, struggling to keep a straight face. "I certainly shall keep that in mind. If you have everything you need, Your Highness, I will return to the ship." Charles dismissed him with a gesture.

Charles Edward Louis John Casimir Silvester Severino Maria Stuart sipped his wine as he gazed at the loch and surrounding high plains that became the Highlands in the distance. Through misty sunlight the peaks were mysterious in their shrouded beauty. Charles smiled to himself as he considered the power he would have when he became king. "Ah, the privileges of royalty!"

Charles closed his eyes and leaned back on his elbows. His thoughts turned to choosing his queen. *She will be skilled in the arts of eros and be elegant, charming, and beautiful, c'est essentiel. We will be the envy of Europe's royal families when we travel throughout the kingdom in our golden carriage. All who see us will bow before their king and queen!*

Charles reveled in the pleasure of his thoughts. He brought out a small locket which held a painting of his lover and cousin, Marie Louise.

We give each other such pleasure; she says my lovemaking is superior to that of her foolish husband, Jules. Charles laughed to himself. *He calls himself a prince. Pah! He is only the prince of a fiefdom with no castles, and his subjects are members of his own family! He is no more than a common lord, whereas I am truly a prince!* Charles thought of Marie Louise and frowned. *What a marvelous Queen she could be. But, she is married!* He considered the situation. *Perhaps the pope will grant her an annulment. When I am king, I will approach King Louis with a proposal to marry Marie. He will want her vast wealth to stay within his control, and as her husband, I will be guardian of her estates and wealth.* Charles mentally counted the great estates in France and Europe that Marie owned or would inherit. He sighed and imagined her languishing from the passion of their lovemaking. *I'll ask Johnnie if there would be a lady to keep me company, perhaps in Inverness.* Charles fell asleep dreaming of wearing a jeweled crown while in a lover's embrace.

Chapter 2

Outside Fort William, Scotland, a horse picked its way through sharp rocks and prickly gorse bushes. Astride the horse, John William O'Sullivan planned his visit with General Shannon Canady. The general, commanding officer at the fort, had accepted John's request for a meeting when John advised he would be discussing a proposal that he knew would benefit them both. John, unsure of the general's loyalties, considered the best way to approach him.

John's father and mother owned a good-sized parcel of land in Ireland's County Kerry. In the spring, he helped his father plow and plant the fields. In the long days of summer, John and his father formed mud and straw into bricks, which were sold in Tralee, the nearest village. Every day John gathered eggs, fed livestock, and swept stalls, pens, and crates. There was a pervasive odor of barnyard about John and his family. His mother milked cows and churned cream to make butter that, along with milk and fresh eggs, were sold to a middleman who made a good profit when the produce was resold for export to England. During cold winter days John learned to read and write. His mother insisted he read out loud to her every morning as she prepared their daily bread and potatoes. Every Saturday morning, John went to the Tralee Chapel to clean the church and polish the silver sacraments. Saturday afternoons, he studied French with the chapel's French priest. He learned to speak and write the language fluently. He was a big-boned, heavy lad with thick arms, well-padded shoulders and a healthy appetite for potatoes creamed with butter, bread with thick slices of mutton, and cheese by the chunk. He watched, but never participated in, arm wrestling and fistfights between other lads of the village. John was not lacking in bravery to fight, but he observed that those who did, both winners and losers, rarely went home without bleeding noses, missing teeth, multiple bruises, and broken bones. Pain was not acceptable to John; he reasoned there was a better way of overpowering an opponent without injury to himself. Surely an intelligent fellow could win by outsmarting the other lad. These thoughts guided John through many of the decisions he would make in the future.

His parents planned for John to enter the priesthood; however, when he told them of his interest in gaining military knowledge, they searched for the best military academy available. They chose one in Paris with expensive tuition, however, they had the means to raise the money to send him. John's father sold the deed to his land to a bank, bringing in enough money for John's tuition and enrollment at the academy. The sale of animals and farm implements provided funds for John's travel expenses, uniforms, and school supplies. When John found he lacked funds to indulge himself in the cuisine of fine Parisian restaurants, he began searching for employment and was hired by a banker who required assistance with collecting unpaid debts. The position was perfect for John. He learned two valuable lessons: The amount to be collected could be doubled, with the difference going into his pocket, and, his size was a definite advantage when he confronted debtors. John continued to add to his girth as he enjoyed French pastries, dumplings in rich broth, and the most delicious of all, rich, dark chocolate torte layered with apricot jam and frosted with thick chocolate crème. His tailor added gussets and let out the seams of his breeches, vests, and jackets. Female friends found him to be amusing and entertaining; however, none wanted to futter him. As one feminine companion gossiped to another, when John slept, he rolled from one side of the bed to the other, thereby trapping an unfortunate bed partner beneath him.

Military life came easily to John. He graduated at the top of his class. He remembered his aging parents' sacrifice and contacted his mother's youngest sister, Auntie Maggie, who agreed to look after them. When John's parents died within days of each other, he sent funds to pay for their burials. Now, he was on his way to Fort William to meet with his Auntie Maggie's oldest son, General Shannon Canady.

When Charles Stuart offered John O'Sullivan an opportunity to join him and a group of men who planned to overthrow England's king, John saw it as a religious rebellion between Catholics and Protestants that could be the means to acquire a fortune for himself. With General Canady's assistance, they could gain control of all of the guns, ammunition, and gold meant for the Jacobite army. Artillery would be sold to buyers for the king's army while the gold would be divided between the two men.

Upon reaching the fort, O'Sullivan presented his credentials to an armed guard who met him at the gate. "Mr. O'Sullivan, the general is waiting for you."

The general greeted John in the European custom, kissing both of his cheeks. "Welcome, cousin. I am delighted to see you!"

Shannon took John's arm and led him to the table where two places had been set. "John! You have made the family proud with your military feats in Paris." They sat at the table as uniformed men brought in silver trays filled with food.

John eyed several desserts sitting on the sideboard: custard pie, fruit compote with cream, and Dundee cake with rum hard sauce. Mouth watering, John swallowed. "General, thank you! But, sir, you have far surpassed me in accomplishments. May I call you Shannon?"

"You may. However, should there be others in our company, I'd prefer that you address me as General Canady."

"I understand, General." The two men resembled each other in coloring, height, and facial characteristics, but then the resemblance ended. Shannon was trim while John was obese. During the meal they discussed John's parents. "I appreciate Auntie Maggie assisting Mam and Da. Did you visit with them?"

"Yes," responded Canady. "Your father and I were chess partners. John, they missed you, but your education was more important to them. I thought them both to be in fairly good health until your father took to his bed, stopped eating, and passed away in his sleep. Then, your mother simply faded away. She no longer wished to live after your father's passing. Their things were given to the poor. However, truly, John, they left very little behind."

"Thank you, sir, for being with them when I could not. You, Shannon, have done very well for yourself. Most impressive!" John made a sweeping gesture with his hand.

Shannon bowed his head to acknowledge the compliment. "You may be wondering how I managed to reach the rather lofty title of general in the king's army when I am nay but a good Irish lad!"

John laughed out loud. "To be honest, I did wonder. Before I came to see you, I did some research and learned that you attended a military academy in London, graduated with honors, and have since led several successful battles on the continent. I also know you received a serious injury in Germany while protecting the borders from the French Army and King George ordered you to Scotland to oversee operations at Fort William while you recuperated."

Shannon laughed. "Mother often remarked on your cleverness." The general stood and moved toward the fireplace.

"Join me here by the fire. I want to hear your plans that will benefit both of us. I am extremely interested."

John followed the general to a pair of chairs beside a blazing fire. Smiling, John said, "There will be an opportunity to generate a very large amount of money! Enough to enable you to pursue the life you deserve, perhaps in Ireland, where you will be able to buy land sufficient to gain a title as a baron or earl. I will return to France and invest in the import and export markets. Shannon, neither of us will generate sufficient funds to support the lifestyle we both deserve without a plan in place."

Looking around the room, John continued, "You appear to be comfortable in your present position, and there's your father's estate, which you will inherit at some point in time."

Shannon shook his head. "Nay, John. Between the Stuart kings and the two German kings imposing taxes upon taxes for landowners in Ireland, there is almost nothing left of my father's fortune! My parents reside in a carriage house because they were forced to sell the great house to pay the taxes."

John's face showed his feelings as he reached over to touch his cousin's hand. "My God, Shannon, I had no idea. I cannot tell you how sad I am to hear it. Well, then, cousin, this opportunity could not come at a better time! Before I say more, I must have your word that what I speak of will not leave this room."

Shannon Canady raised his glass and said, "John, you and I are kin. You have my word." He continued, "Rumor has it that a Stuart Prince is now in Scotland building forces to attempt a coup for the crown."

Reverting to a heavy Irish accent, Shannon smiled and tented his fingers under his chin, "Now, me good cousin, would ye be havin' anythin' ter do wi' it?"

John returned the smile and bowed his head slightly. "Aye, tha' I do! Prince Charlie believes he has sufficient support from the Jacobites, the king of France, and the Catholics of Ireland and

Italy to defeat the king's army, but I believe otherwise." John's smile broadened, and he rubbed both hands together. "Charles has very little battlefield experience. He served under Duke Liria in a border skirmish in Italy, and while Charles led the troops onto the battlefield, the battle was won because of the leadership of a stronger, more experienced man."

General Canady, speaking from personal experience, raised his hand to interrupt John. "John, if a man has any weaknesses, they will become evident during a battle. I suspect that Charles can motivate soldiers to fight, however, when it comes to tactile maneuvers, he does not have the experience to train them. Believe me, this is a serious flaw in a battle commander."

"Exactly, General!" John said. "You have described Charles perfectly. He can recruit men for battle, however, he assumes they know how to fight when they have had no training whatsoever. Charles has almost no battlefield training himself. I learned this when he and I discussed his father regaining the throne. When I questioned him concerning plans to overthrow the present king, I heard about the fine castles his family resided in while they were in England. He has no battle plan whatsoever! Of course, Charles's friends have their own plans, and if I may say so, each one favors saving his own arse while lining his purse." John chuckled and slapped his knee. "And I must include my arse and purse along with the rest of them!" The general laughingly applauded.

"Shannon, there's money to be made in the exchange of military items from one hand to another." Canady nodded. "You have my full attention, John. I assure you, this is not the first time weapons have been bought, sold, or traded in this room." The general made eye contact with his cousin. "John, I definitely want to be a partner in your proposal."

"Excellent! We'll need assistance with moving weapons. How can we best go about locating the right people?"

"I have men in place. All I need from you is information concerning when and where." The general removed his jacket and loosened the cravat around his neck. "Please, John, make yourself comfortable. I often ponder on the plight of our people in Ireland. Dammit, John! Our families are eating potatoes and groats, if they have even that!"

The general pointed his finger at John to emphasize his anger. "Those bastards, the Stuarts and Hanoverian kings, tax every sale made by the Irish to the English middlemen, who double the price and make a fortune! I've no desire for a Stuart to return to the throne. On the other hand, I have no loyalty to King George either. I'm bloody well tired of 'em all!"

"I feel the same, Shannon. It makes no difference to me who sits on the damn throne in England." John refilled both glasses. "I have a question for you, cousin. How was it to follow orders from a German king who could not speak English?"

"It was a bloody insult!" The general wrinkled his nose as if the scent of something odorous were hanging in the air.

John smiled. "You and your fellow officers could not understand him?"

"Nein! We all understood that word!" Shannon rubbed his hands together and said, "John, I would like nothing more than to return to Ireland. I believe I would enjoy overseeing Ireland's export trade. If I had sufficient funds to gain lands and a title, the king might appoint me to such a position." With a thoughtful expression, the general peered into the fire.

"Aye, Shannon, I believe he would. By the way, I've brought you a fine French cognac. You will find it to be very smooth." John rummaged through his knapsack and brought out a bottle. "Shall we enjoy the cognac as we complete our discussion?"

Shannon placed two stemmed glasses with rounded bowls on the fireside table, and John poured each glass half full. They swirled the richly colored liquid and then, after sniffing the fragrant bouquet, sipped it. "Excellent, John, thank you." John nodded and emptied his glass.

"Charles shares all the information he gains with me. Ship-owners in Ireland have contacted him with offers of money and arms. All Jacobites, they are responding to the church's call for support of the Catholic prince. Shannon, I will advise you when and where these arms will be coming into Scotland. When we gain possession, they can be sold to England and the proceeds divided between us. Think about it." John rubbed his hands together as if warming them in front of a fire. "The Catholic Church's financial support of their favored son will add even more wealth to the purse."

John licked his lips, the look on his face the same as when he reached for a fork to consume a plate full of food. "Charles is meeting with the Highland chiefs at Glenfinnan. They will agree to supply men for the rebellion and will ask about weapons. Charles has an answer for them. He will tell them King Louis will send money, arms, and men." John paused for emphasis. "But Charles will not think about the crippled ship that limped back to France, where, you can be sure, the captain relayed the entire fiasco to King Louis."

John refilled both glasses and unbuttoned his collar. "Shannon, if Charles gains the throne for the Stuarts, you and I will be in his favor. If he fails, he'll flee to France or Italy, none will be the wiser, and we can go about our business. Charles believes it is a coincidence that he lost one of his ships to the King's navy, but I believe the king is showing his strength."

"Yes, I agree with you, John. To begin our plan, I'll confiscate all military items coming into Scotland from Ireland or France. Then, instead of turning them over to military ordinance to be counted and identified, my middleman will sell the 'origin unknown' armory to England. Any gold or money will be added to our respective purses. An acquaintance of mine will assist with transporting weapons from Scotland across the English border. He poses as a priest, lives in Scotland's borders, and is a spy for England. John, how will you and I communicate when necessary?"

Laughing, John answered, "The prince is aware you and I are meeting this evening. He believes you are interested in purchasing military equipment from a company I represent in Germany. You and I are having a discussion concerning your weapons inventory."

General Shannon laughed. "How will you keep a straight face when you report back to Charles?"

"I simply imagine my purse full of silver and gold coins!" They both chuckled. "If the prince should happen to see a message from the fort's general requesting a visit, he will be delighted that you have not discovered my disguise. It would be the topic of the evening's discussion!"

The general said, "Do you know of William Augustus, the king's second son? He is known as The Duke of Cumberland and is on duty in Brussels, Belgium, but—" Canady paused. "King George has already placed him on notice to return to London. The duke is twenty-five years old and is a full-fledged captain. Should the king send Cumberland to Scotland to lead his troops and I believe he will, the Bonny Prince had best start looking for a plank wide enough to float his arse all the way back to France, for he will need it!"

John's cake-laden fork stopped midway to his mouth. "The Duke of Cumberland, you say? Charles is desperate to know who will be leading the king's army in Scotland. I've heard of the duke. It's said he cavorts with the devil."

General Canady burst out laughing. "Ah, the duke's reputation precedes him."

John stood. "General, I've enjoyed our time together. Thank you for your hospitality, and insight with overseeing our plans. You and I will gain the spoils of the battle, it's that we will be doing so before the fact, rather than after."

The general took John's hand in his and said, "My pleasure, cousin. Have a safe journey, John."

Perched in a tree outside the military base, The Dark One spoke, "Master will be pleased! Money and power, that's what they want. They lie, steal, cheat, and even kill one another to gain money and power. Master says they trade their souls for money and use the proceeds to buy power!"

Whispering, Death replied, "But they're mortals and forget they have choices. I know of many humans who decide against accepting the bribes you offer, in spite of what you promise in return."

The Dark One shrugged his wings and said, "The ones I've observed lately have not refused!"

Chapter 3

"Halo, *Ciamar a tha thu/sibh, 'S fhada bho nach fhaca mi thu/ sibh*" (Hello, long time, no see), Ewan greeted Gordon.

"Aye, Ewan, good to see ye, cousin."

"Ye'll be well, Gordon?"

"Aye, buildin' a new barn."

"Ye built it next to the Broch?"

"Aye, I wanted to keep th' livestock closer, wha' wi' th' raidin' an' all."

"Ye still ha' yer cattle? Th' damned Campbells stole our livestock a fortnight ago! Thomas an' I got 'em back, though."

Gordon hung his head. "Nay, my cattle an' sheep are gone." He looked into Ewan's eyes. "With th' sheep gone, there'll be no fleece to sell. It'll be a long winter wi'out enough food. I built th' barn an' pens to keep my animals close by, but th' bastards took 'em a'fore I got 'em moved."

Searching his cousin's face for an answer, Ewan said, "Gordon, did ye think about lookin' for 'em?"

Gordon shook his head, " Ah, th' cattle'll be hangin' from a

26

butcher's hook, an' th' sheep'd be on th' other side of Scotland by now. Wi' Elizabeth an' th' babe on my mind, I've not been myself lately." Gordon looked at his feet while he spoke. "Th' last o' my coins went for th' new barn. It'll be a rough winter for us an' th' families livin' in th' village. There's no milk, an' th' last of th' cheese'll be gone by th' end of th' week."

Ewan glared at Gordon. "Damnation, wha' in th' hell is th' matter wi' ye? Yer oats an' barley are layin' on th' ground! Tha's yer family's winter porridge, oatcakes an' whisky! Yer cattle are penned at th' Campbells. I dinna see sheep, but it's likely they're there too. We'll get 'em back! Gordon, get th' lazy village lads to store yer hay an' grain in th' barn. It'll be a wonder if mold has not already set in."

Gordon wrung his hands. "Aw, I've quit carin' about anythin'."

Ewan said, "Yer a Cameron! Get up off yer arse an' get yer work done!"

Gordon stood and placed his hand on Ewan's shoulder. "There's a couple of village men who'll stand at arms for me, an' one of their wives will come in an' cook, so I'll join ye when ye go to th' Campbells. Mayhap I'll get one or two of my animals back, mayhap not. Ewan, sit, an' I'll bring some ale."

Gordon returned with a jug and two tankards. "Gordon, Thomas went to see Duncan about his black cows. They're at th' Campbells too. We'll get 'em in th' dark of night. If we canna see so well, they won't either!"

Holding out his empty cup, Ewan asked, "Ye've heard th' Lochiel is supportin' Prince Charlie? He said he'd not put men or money behind th' Stuart, but he's changed his mind. I'm hearin' we'll be doin' battle in th' spring. Dammit to hell, Gordon, it'll be plantin' time. We need to be in th' fields, not on some bloody battlefield tryin' to outrun a bloody lead ball! When taxes an' rent come due, will th' Lochiel remember no crops got planted or harvested?"

Gordon struggled to put his thoughts into words. "Tha's why I'm sittin' here on my arse! The Lochiel's messenger came by an' said all Cameron men will fight for th' Royal Stuart to regain th' English throne! Bloody hell, I dinna want to fight!" Then he lowered his voice. "It's said Charlie's man on th' battlefield will be Lord George Murray. He has my respect. If we must fight, let it be wi' him leadin' us down th' hillside!"

Gordon stood, "Even wi' Lord Murray, it'll not be enough! Th' English'll be handin' us our arses on a platter. Th' king's army has th' firepower to blow Scotland's Hielanders to th' skies!" Gordon sat down and poured the rest of his ale out. "We'll be dead a'fore we hit th' ground!"

"I'm in agreement wi' ye, Gordon," Ewan said. "We're but a wart on th' hinny of th' English. When a man joins th' king's army, he's paid to serve, an' gets a coat, breeches, shirt, boots, an' a rifle! Besides tha' a wagon wi' a cook has food a'plenty for em. When a Hielander goes into battle, he's wearin' his own kilt an' boots, if he has 'em. He'll carry his own broadsword, an' if he has a rifle, he'll load it wi' gunpowder tha' he brings wi' him. It's damned certain he won't get any coins for his empty purse! If tha' weren't enough, th' Hielander'll ha' naught to eat unless he's brought his own oatcakes!" They both looked down at the ground.

Ewan noticed a gathering of dark clouds around the western high glens. The sunlight was warm, but a chill wind blew down the hillside, bringing leaves from distant trees with it. Gordon asked, "Wha' would we gain wi' a Stuart king on th' throne, instead of a German king? Wha' if th' battle's lost? Blood o' th' clans stainin' the dirt, an' any who live will go to th' hangman's noose, or left to rot in a gaol! Our wives an' bairns'll be cleanin' th' chamber pots of th' English gentry an' warmin' the cots of th' English soldiers!"

Ewan looked over his shoulder before he spoke. "Let's hold off on sayin' anythin' more 'til we hear wha' th' chief has to say about it. Truth is, taxes'll be collected whether we're buyin' or sellin', an' th' money goes to whoever's arse is sittin' on th' bloody throne!"

"Ah, well, there's nay much we can do about it. Come in for a dram an' a bite, Ewan. Elizabeth'll want to send regards to Janet."

"Aye, an' I'd like to see yer lady wife. Janet'll be askin' after her."

Elizabeth sat by the fire sewing a tiny linen gown. She stood to greet Ewan. "Good to see ye, Ewan. Janet an' Duny well?"

Ewan put his arm around her and kissed her on the cheek. "Duny is visitin' James an' Abby in Perthshire. Tha' laddie wraps his mother around his little finger, an' she scolds me when I try to set him straight. It's good tha' he's spendin' some time wi' his grandparents. They'll get him lined out! Are th' bairns all well, Elizabeth?"

"Aye, thank God. My sister is helpin' me wi' 'em."

"Well, then." Ewan pointed to the chair. "Sit yerself down, Elizabeth. I'll fetch th' cups an' whisky. My lady wife has me well trained. If I had ter do so, I could set a fine board for tea an' biscuits."

"Oh, get on wi' ye, Ewan, sit yerself down," Elizabeth responded. "I'll get th' cups an' whisky. Gordon, ye might as well sit as well."

Gordon started to sit. "But while yer up—" Gordon stood again. "Put more logs on th' fire. I felt a cold wind when ye opened th' door."

After Elizabeth left the room, Gordon said, "Sit, stand, put logs on th' fire—yer not th' only one tha's well trained!" Ewan chuckled.

Returning with cups of barley malt whisky, Elizabeth handed Ewan a plate with bread, cheese, and a slice of apple tart. "It'll do 'til ye get home."

"Thank ye, I've not eaten since early morn." Then Ewan asked, "Elizabeth, can ye can spare this?"

She glanced at Gordon, "There's enough in th' pantry for now."

"Thomas an' I'll go huntin', and we'll share wi' ye. Also, we'll be bringin' yer milk cows an' wooly sheep back. Ye ha' my word on it."

Gordon looked at the floor as his wife said, "It's a good man ye are, Ewan Cameron, doin' for others. I thank ye for yer help."

Ewan raised the cup and toasted Elizabeth's good health and that of the babe she carried. When the room darkened, Ewan said,

"By th' looks of things, there'll be rain wi' snow or ice. I'd best be on my way home. Gordon, roust some of yer village men out of their spots by th' fire, an' ha' 'em get th' grain loaded an' to th' barn."

Ewan spoke to Elizabeth. "Take care, Milady. I'll bring Janet to see ye soon. Gordon, when ye can, come down an' we'll get things settled."

"Aye, I'll be there!" Ewan tucked in his tartan when a snell wind blew rain down his neck. "Ah, it's a bonny fine *oidhche mhath* (good evenin') in Scotland," he said to himself. Rain with bits of ice pelted down as his horse carefully followed a path through loose gravel and rocks of the glens.

When he rode into the barn, Ewan saw that Janet had fed and watered the animals and Thomas was not yet home. In the Highlands, autumn brought heavy, dark clouds laden with moisture and wind. It was a taste of the coming winter, when snow fell day in and day out and travel over the high glens became impossible. In the winter, a man fed his animals in the barn, put peat bricks on the kitchen fire, laid logs on the fireplace grate, and enjoyed a cup of his own barley malt whisky. It was a time to repair farm tools, read books, and plan for spring planting.

After hugging her husband, Janet said, "I hoped ye were stayin' at Gordon's for th' night or well on yer way home. This storm'll bring in th' cold, an' there's things tha' must be done a'fore winter sets in."

She brought a meat pie to the table. A wooden board held bread, butter, and a pot of stewed apples. "Thank ye, love. I'm well famished. Elizabeth gav' me cheese an' a slice of tart, but it went right to th' bottom of my belly, an' th' top is very empty. Thank ye, good wife."

"A'fore ye get too pleased wi' yer supper, Ewan, I've a few things to say." He listened while he ate. "There's enough tatties, neeps, carrots, an' apples, but we need meat. We've plenty of cheese, an' there's butter enough to last th' winter."

Janet continued to talk while she patted bread dough into loaves. "I need beeswax, an' honey. When ye go by th' dead tree beside th' south rock wall, look for honeycomb in th' big knot hole close to th' top."

Ewan continued to eat, deep in his own thoughts. Shaking her finger at her husband, Janet warned, "Ewan, ye'd best be payin' attention. Th' whisky barrels are near empty, an' if ye plan to warm up wi' a wee dram when th' snow's up to yer arse, better get th' grain set aside now a'fore it ends up beneath th' grindin' wheel! Speakin' of which, we need oats ground for flour!"

Janet smiled at Ewan when he said, "Surely Thomas could carry out one or two tasks?"

"Yer th' laird, an' it's yer place to assign th' tasks!" Janet winked at Ewan.

"Ah, yer a fine an' fancy lass. I may be th' laird, but th' lady is th' head of th' household! Thomas should be home by now."

"Wi' th' weather he may not turn up 'til th' morrow. Ewan, ye forgot yer knapsack wi' cheese an' bread, so its yer own fault yer hungry." She smiled at him to let him know she was teasing.

"How is Elizabeth?" Janet asked.

Ewan put his spoon down. "She's as pale as th' milk in tha' jug, an' thin. Janet, I heard ye about th' larder. I'll get started on it. We'll be huntin' for Gordon's family too. He's got a good trout stream, an' we'll trade him venison for fish."

"Ye'll be huntin' for Gordon? He canna do his own huntin'? Ewan, wha' is ..."

"He's been sittin' wi' Elizabeth some of th' time, an' th' rest of th' time, he's been stewin' an' brewin' 'bout things. Come, love. Let's move in by th' fire."

When Ewan told Janet how the Lochiel had decided to support Prince Charles's quest for the crown of Great Britain, it felt as if a cold darkness moved into the room with them. He stirred out of his chair, stoked the fire, and placed logs on the grate. Then he spoke, more to himself than to his wife. "In th' past, when th' men o' Scotland were called to fight for Scotland's freedom, they all did so willingly. Whether it's lairds or plain folk makes no difference; we all go when called."

"I dinna agree wi' wha' yer sayin' of goin' when yer called, Ewan. I've heard ye an' Thomas talkin' about th' prince from France, or Italy, or wher'ever." Janet stood. "Yer cup is empty, husband. There's only a few more bottles of whisky, an' we might as well enjoy one of 'em" She poured a full cup for each of them.

"Oh, there's a king in England named George th' Second. Why do th' clans want another man to be king? Wha' could a new king in England do tha' would better things for th' people of Scotland?" She shrugged her shoulders and raised her voice. "Ye must know England will protect her King! They'll do battle wi' Scotland to keep him on th' throne! Wha' right does Scotland's people ha' to decide who rules?"

Janet paced in front of the fire, causing the flames to flicker. "Dinna forget my mother lived wi' English royalty for years an' was related to Queen Anne. I know how much power th' royals ha'! Nay, husband! Why are th' clan chieftains thinkin' about fightin'? When good Queen Anne was on th' throne, she signed th' Act of th' Union, which brought Scotland an' England together under one ruler. So, now th' chieftains are goin' against it?" The expression on her face was between anger and tears.

Ewan cleared his throat. "It's nay a battle for Scotland to ha' her own king, an' it dinna go against th' Act of th' Union. It's about bringin' in a new king to replace th' German king. Donald Cameron will decide wha' th' clan does, an' he's the chief, aye?"

"Aye!" Janet made no effort to hide her impatience. "I know him well. He collects part of every coin ye earn!"

Ewan shifted uncomfortably in his chair. Carefully choosing his words, he said, "Donald is a Jacobite, an' he an' other Jacobites ha' pledged their support to remove th' Protestant King George, so they can replace him wi' a Catholic Stuart. Th' man they want to be king is James Stuart, th' grandson of th' deposed King James's son. It's James's son, Charles Edward, tha' will be leadin' th' battle. There's three men known as pretenders to th' throne, Charles Edward Stuart an' his father an' grandfather. If King James had not been removed from th' throne by th' English Parliament, then his grandson James an' great-grandson Charles would ha' succeeded to th' throne because the Jacobites believe it is their divine right. Instead, a Protestant from Germany, who is barely related to th' Stuarts, was brought in to be king. An' now his son, George th' Second, sits on th' throne. It's proof of how much th' Protestant parliament hated th' Catholic Stuarts an' th' power they ha'. Th' Hieland chiefs are bein' courted by Prince Charlie. He wants their support for th' uprisin'. At first, th' Lochiel refused to be a part of th' rebellion, but now he's promised loyalty to Charles Stuart! From wha' I'm hearin' about Charlie, it seems to me he's cut out o' th' same fabric as his sire an' grandsire, but I'm thinkin' his piece was th' end of th' bolt an' th' weaver ran short on some of th' threads!"

"Ah, so ye ha' doubts of yer own, hum?"

Ewan answered, "Aye, I do. When th' Lochiel calls a gatherin' of th' clans, he'll tell us more. He believes, as do many Hieland chiefs, tha' a Catholic Stuart has th' right by bloodline to be king of England an' th' king from Germany has no right to th' throne. This is part of th' reason for th' uprising. Th' Protestant English aristocracy stands strong against th' papacy. They dinna want a mortal man in Rome tellin' 'em wha' to do, an' they'll go against any Catholic who tries to take th' throne. See, Janet, they believe tha' James Stuart an' his son, grandson, an' great-grandson, Prince Charles, all three bein' Catholics, answer to th' pope instead of God."

Ewan finished his explanation by saying, "It's th' reason Parliament banished th' Stuarts from England an' they lost th' kingship." He pointed to his wife, "Yer relative, Queen Anne was a Protestant Stuart. When she died, another Protestant, George th' First, was chosen be king, then his son, George th' Second, inherited the crown when his father died."

Thinking he might help Janet understand, Ewan said, "We pay little attention to th' politics of England. There's two groups, th' Whigs an' Tories."

"Aye," said Janet. "I've heard of 'em."

"Whigs are known as 'Whiggamores,' Gaelic for horse-drovers. 'Tories' means nothin' more than 'Irish robbers,' an' they're always suspect in any ill doins' in England because they support Catholic Jacobite beliefs. Th' Whigs, those in Scotland an' England who dinna want a Catholic king, are strong enough to overpower th' Tories, an' tha' brought about where we're now, wi' a Protestant king who has only a wee bit of th' royal bloodline. Do ye see, my love?"

Then, after a pause, Ewan looked at Janet and said, "Why'd I ask ye to understand, when I'm questionin' it myself? A man born in Italy, livin' in France, speakin' Italian an' French an' not one word o' Gaelic, wants th' Scottish Hielanders to help him sit on th' English throne. It makes even less sense now than it did a'fore!"

After retiring to their chamber, Ewan held Janet close to him, "I love ye so very much. More than anything in th' world, I hold ye most dear."

"Ewan, I feel th' same for ye, an' I pray to God tha' we'll be safe from harm. Come to bed, husband."

Ewan caressed Janet, marveling at how quickly he responded to her soft, willing flesh. Later, lying in each other's arms, Ewan said, "After our lovin' I welcome sleep, but for some reason, tonight I'm uneasy. I dinna know why."

"Ah, yer need a toddy, to ease yer mind." She brought warmed honey and whisky to Ewan, who emptied the cup, turned over, and soon was asleep. Janet tucked the down-filled comforter around him, and sat in a chair by the fire. She considered Ewan's description of politics, religion, and how the two seemed to cause so much trouble. *Mayhap we should sail to th' American colonies!* But then they'd be facing another uncertain future. She closed her eyes, and thought of a field of bluebells, wild roses with a soft scent, and ...a field full of men calling out in pain, or lying silent and dead. The Cameron plaid covered bodies lying side by side. Opening her eyes, she tried to banish the vision from her mind. But she knew that this vision, like others that came unbidden to her, had not yet happened. The bed chamber's small paned window looked out over fields where a light covering of snow sparkled in the pale moonlight. The evenings were cold enough to keep fires burning. *The Hielands are more than beautiful,* she thought. *They become a part of one's heart. If I were a man, I'd go to battle and fight for Scotland too.*

Her thoughts returned to the time when she was a child living in a different part of Scotland. Picking up her brush, she sat in front of the fire and began brushing her hair until it reflected the hearth light like a piece of russet silk woven with threads of cinnamon and amber.

Chapter 4

Janet Dunsmuir was born in the gentle rolling hills of Perthshire, Scotland. The hills were not high and bare, and the valleys were not the deep gorges that held water as the land did in the Highlands. Her parents, James and Abigail Dunsmuir, raised fine horses. James's reputation was so well known that buyers for his horses came from England, Scotland, and France. Late one night, Ewan Cameron returned home after a day of searching for horses to purchase. He'd heard of James Dunsmuir's animals in Perthshire and decided it would be worth the trip to have a look. Ewan's herd of Highland cattle provided meat, hides for leather, and milk for cheese and butter. The brawny animals could pull a plow and wagonloads of produce, but they were slow and cumbersome. Ewan wanted horses that could pull wagons loaded with hay and grain to market. His crops were always substantial. After giving his tenant farmers their share, as well as paying the Lochiel his portion, and setting aside enough for himself, there was plenty left to sell. He packed a knapsack with oatcakes and flasks of ale. "Thomas, I'm goin' to Perthshire lookin' for horses. I'll return within a fortnight.

If ye'll work on th' wagons while I'm away, an' if I can find th' horses we need, we'll be ready for th' fall market. I hope to sell enough grain to pay for th' horses an' ha' a bit left over."

When he reached Perth, Ewan stopped at a tavern to rest his horse, quench his thirst, and find food. After buying a pint of ale, he was handed a plate for food. The barmaid gave him directions to James Dunsmuir's broch and invited him to spend the night at the inn next door. She looked at the handsome fellow in a linen tunic and leather breeches, with a tartan thrown over his shoulder and fastened at his waist with a silver pin. Slim and tall with broad shoulders, he had blue eyes and brown hair. She smiled at him. "Will ye be needin' a bit o' company, Milord?"

Ewan looked her over and saw a lass who was missing several teeth and wore a stained gown. When she leaned over to whisper in his ear, he caught a whiff of sour breath and unwashed body. "No, fair lady, thank ye kindly. I must keep to the road."

When Ewan rode onto James Dunsmuir's land, he whistled when he saw the broch built into a hillside, surrounded on three sides by a water-filled moat. At the front gate, he was met by a man-at-arms who asked his name and business. "Ewan Cameron, here to purchase horses for my land to th' north an' west of here. I'd like to meet James Dunsmuir, if he's agreeable."

"Leave yer dirk an' sword wi' me." The armed man stood with arms outstretched, waiting for Ewan to comply. This was customary when a man was not known, and Ewan did not expect otherwise. James Dunsmuir met Ewan at the door, invited him in, and bade him to sit by the fire. He handed Ewan a flask of ale and said, "If its horses ye need, I keep a stable of brood mares as well as stallions an' geldings, an' they're all bridle trained. Many of my mares will deliver foals in th' spring. Might this be wha' yer lookin' for?"

Lifting his cup and emptying it, Ewan said, "I need horses that can pull wagons loaded wi' produce to market an' also be saddled for a rider."

James filled Ewan's flask again. "I ha' 'em, an' I'll take ye for a look. My price is fair, an' my animals are healthy an' trained to work as well as bein' fine tae ride. I also raise Deerhounds. If ye dinna know 'em, they're great dun-colored beasties tha' are guardians for sheep, cattle, an' horses. Take a look by yer side. One of my bitch's pups is lyin' by yer right boot. His name is Bran. Ye've heard of Finghal? He was a giant of a man an' had a huge deerhound he called Bran. This pup is th' biggest of th' litter, so we've named him Bran."

Ewan nodded. "Aye, I've heard of Finghal. He was of Machrie Moor, an' it's said he'd boil half a cow for a meal an' gi' th' bones to his dog." The young dog stayed by the side of Ewan's chair throughout the evening meal. Ewan, who usually paid no attention to dogs, found himself noticing the animal, who responded with a wag of his tail.

James watched the two studying each other, "Ah, young Bran has selected ye to be his owner."

Ewan looked at the dog. "Does this dog understand wha' I'm sayin'?"

James chuckled and said, "Of course he does!"

Ewan patted the dog on the head and was rewarded with a paw placed on his boot. "James, will ye be payin' me to take this mongrel, or will I be payin' ye?"

James thought a minute before responding. "Ewan, I'm prone to trust th' judgment of my dogs. I'll be giftin' him to ye, providin' ye buy one o' my horses."

Along with fine horses and dogs, James and Abigail had two daughters and a son. The oldest, Janet, had golden red hair and green eyes, while the younger daughter, Meghan, had her mother's blonde hair and hazel eyes. Their son, James Andrew, had dark hair like his father and his mother's light brown eyes. Janet was a tall lass, looking almost eye to eye with her father. Her mother said she inherited her height and red hair from Mary, Queen of Scots, who was a distant ancestor.

Janet's father, ill pleased with those suitors who came to court his eldest daughter, sent them on their way. One was lazy and looked at the broch, animals, and fields with a wary eye; another was a whore-monger with bastard children scattered over the countryside, and a third had nothing but an empty purse and boots with holes in the soles; this one asked about the size of Janet's dowry. Janet's father declined his blessing on all three marriage proposals, and possible husbands went out the door. Abigail wondered where a suitable husband would be found; Janet was eighteen, already an older maiden.

Chapter 5

Abigail Dunsmuir grew up in Queen Anne's royal court. Queen Anne, the daughter of the deposed James Stuart II of England, was a staunch Protestant who gained the respect of many of the residents of Scotland and England. Even the Catholic families of the two countries were tolerant of her rule. The queen's first cousin, Beatrice, was her closest friend and lady-in-waiting. Beatrice provided support when the queen's husband, Prince George, who was lazy and without ambition or judgment, drank to excess. Prince George was aware of the queen's feelings toward him; he occupied her bed only long enough to get her with child. After seventeen pregnancies resulting in two sons and three daughters born alive and then dying soon after birth and twelve stillborns, the queen announced that she was dismissing the prince, who returned to his native Denmark. But the queen was distraught. There would be no sons or daughters to inherit the throne when she died. When Beatrice married, conceived a child, and tragically lost her husband, all within the space of a year, the queen welcomed Beatrice to her court. After Beatrice's daughter, Abigail, was born, her godmother, the queen, vowed to provide for her should her mother be unable to do so. On Abigail's fourth birthday, the queen gifted her a rocking horse with a leather saddle trimmed in silver. Delighted, she hugged and kissed the queen.

"I love you, Auntie Queen," she said. None other than Abby would dare to address the queen in such a manner. "Next year, may I please have a real pony to ride? I shall practice on this play one."

Abigail was a beautiful child who dearly loved tending to and riding the queen's horses. She rushed through her lessons in the royal nursery and then ran to the stables to help the stable master curry the horses. Once, while dashing down steps to the garden, she bumped into the queen's table while Her Majesty was having morning tea. A teapot crashed to the ground, and fruit tarts went flying through the air. After making sure Abigail was not hurt, the queen asked her to sit down, called for more tea and cakes, and asked where she was going in such a hurry.

Abigail curtseyed and said, "Oh, Your Majesty, may I please go? Golden Lady is about to foal, and I do so want to be there to see the new colt. I just know she is going to foal today. Please, may I go?"

Smiling, the queen took Abby's hand and said, "Go, my child, but walk slowly. When the foal is born, come and tell me if we have a mare or a stallion to add to our stables. Please do that for me."

Abigail nodded, grabbed a tart from the tray, and walked slowly around the hedge. Then she ran as fast as she could to the stable path. For her sixteenth birthday, the queen presented her with a pair of chestnut mares, perfectly matched with white stars on their foreheads. Abigail named the horses Morning Star and Evening Star. The animals were carefully groomed, trained, and ridden, every day.

When young James Dunsmuir traveled to Holyrood where the queen's stables were located, he intended to purchase several animals. Instead he found himself to be far more interested in

Abigail, who knew horses as well as he did. Beatrice, aware of the stable courtship, favored James over the foppishly mannered gentlemen of the court. James was always well groomed in clean breeks, with his hair combed back and neatly tied with a ribbon, but he paid little attention to the goings-on of the court. During long dinners, James would eat his fill and then leave as soon as possible. He could be found in the stables talking with the queen's master of horses. Often Abigail would leave the table as well; she could be found grooming a horse or mixing grain for the feeding bags. Both Queen Anne and Beatrice noticed Abby had little time for the gentlemen of the court. They all paid her a great deal of attention, but Abby's mind clearly was elsewhere.

The queen and Beatrice, over tea, discussed Abby's prospects for marriage. "Bea, I'm hardly one to give advice on choosing a husband. When I married the Prince of Denmark, supposedly a man with manners and upbringing, I believed I would be assured of a good bloodline for our children. Instead, he was little more than a common sot, with defective seed, who could not manage to sew a crop that would grow into maturity! I wasted my time with him, and I'm glad he's gone! You, on the other hand, married for only a year but loved your husband, and he returned your love. Still, my dear, you suffered greatly when he died leaving you with a child to bring up without a father."

Between bites of cherry tart, the queen remarked, "Is marriage such a fickle thing? If so, I would advise our Abby to remain single until she has wisdom enough to choose a husband who will give her healthy children, remain sober, stay alive, and not leave her a grieving widow. What say you, Bea?"

Beatrice, who admired the queen's ability to put her thoughts into words, said, "I'd agree with you, Anne, but for one thing, Abby understands men better than you might think. She declines favors offered by the court's dukes and earls, some married and some not. Not long ago she told me of an experience she had with one eligible young man, and I had to wonder if he had any pride left when she finished with him."

"Hmm," responded the queen. "Tell me about it."

Bea brought the sherry decanter and two glasses to the table between their chairs. "Might as well get comfy, Anne. It's an entertaining tale." Bea poured sherry while she talked. "The young gentleman—you'll know of whom I'm speaking—is Gordon Lovat, the son of Lord Lovat, who will one day inherit his father's title and lands. Young Gordon is considered to be a particularly good catch, him being the lord's only heir. He decided to court Abigail and gave her a beautiful gold and emerald necklace. Abby thanked him, but it didn't change her attitude toward him one bit."

The queen held out her glass for more sherry and chose a cream-filled ginger cake from the tea trolley. Between bites she said, "I'm sure the young man thought when she accepted such an expensive gift that he could proceed with courting her, don't you think, Bea?"

"I said the very same words to her. She smiled and said I needed to hear the rest of the tale."

"Pray then, cousin, continue," the queen said as she selected a custard tart sprinkled with cinnamon.

Beatrice sighed. "Last week he asked her to accompany him on a walk through the garden. You know how Abby is, Anne. Instead of flirting, she looked Gordon in the eye and said, 'Sir, I've made other plans, but you are welcome to join me if you wish. I suggest you change your silk pantaloons, hose, and satin slippers for breeks and boots, for I am going to the horses' stables. Otherwise, it's quite possible you'll slip and fall in the shite! How would you feel about that, sir?'"

The queen began laughing and clapped her hands. "Well, Bea, what happened then?"

"Young Gordon pulled out his linen handkerchief, wiped the perspiration from his face, and stood there. It was obvious he did not want to follow her into the stables!"

43

Both women laughed as they wiped away tears rolling down their cheeks. Beatrice filled the glasses again while the queen wiped her sticky fingers after eating a honeyed mincemeat pastry. "Bea, I'll not worry quite so much for our Abby after hearing how she taught the Lovat lad a lesson in courting. If one really cares for someone, they had best be ready to walk through shite, if that is what it takes to capture her heart."

"She has excellent manners. She can pour tea beautifully," Beatrice said. "And Abby loves pretty gowns. However, it's clear to see that above all, she loves her horses!"

Queen Anne said thoughtfully, "We've not discussed Abby's frequent companion, James Dunsmuir. Everyone is talking about him." Beatrice nodded her head in agreement. "As Abigail's godmother, I will see to her best interests by speaking with the young man. I want to know who he is, where he comes from, and where he will be going when he leaves here. I'll not be having him dally with Abby if he's returning to a country wife waiting with a bevy of bairns."

"Yes, I agree. Please do find out all you can about the man."

Members of the court watched while Abby and the handsome young Scotsman talked and rode together. They gossiped that he might be a possible suitor for her, but his clothing was plain, and he did not converse well. He smiled and bowed to the lovely daughters of earls and dukes who fluttered their eyelashes and fans at him, but it was easy to see he was being polite. Who was he to think he had a right to be talking with beautiful Abigail, whose mother was cousin to the queen? Queen Anne sent an invitation to James to join her for tea in her private quarters. He wondered if she was considering him to be an assistant to her master of horses or perhaps even for a position in her royal guards. If so, he'd be honored, but would have to plead for a pardon on behalf of the land in his care and his responsibilities to the folk who depended on him to manage those lands. He would be sorely tempted by such an offer, as it would mean he could see Abby every day. He hoped they would have a future together. He dared not think beyond that.

The queen and James sipped tea from dainty cups. She filled a fragile plate with cakes and handed it to James, who carefully balanced the plate on his knee. He sat on the very edge of his chair waiting for the queen to speak. Smiling at him, Queen Anne said, "Mister Dunsmuir!"

"Please, Your Majesty, I am James."

The queen nodded her head and continued. "Abigail's mother and I have observed that you and our Abby are spending quite a bit of time together. With that in mind, I must explain her background so you will understand who she is. During Abigail Simpson's early years, she lived in the royal nursery meant for the children of the king and queen of England. Abby has been the only child in the royal household. I dearly love that young lady and her mother, Beatrice, who is my cousin. You see, James—" the Queen's voice trembled. "I was unable to bear a child who would live past the day of its birth, and even though I prayed for an heir, none survived."

The queen's eyes filled with tears as she explained how Abby had become very dear to her, almost as her own child. "Sir, if you have intentions toward Abby, then I must ask you to tell me about yourself, your family, and your reason for being here. Have you a wife who is waiting for your return? If you do, then fair Abby is not to be played with as you would other ladies of the court. She is my beloved niece, and I will have no harm coming to her. Remember, young man, I am the queen, and I can either give or deny permission for you to see her."

The queen stood and walked over to the window. James carefully placed his plate and cup on the table, dropped to one knee, and said, "Your Majesty, may I speak?"

"Yes, sir, please do. You have my full attention."

James stood. He waited until the queen returned to her chair before he seated himself across from her. James, dressed in his

Dunsmuir plaid woven of fine wool, with a silver broach holding the pleated tartan over his shoulder down to his waist, said, "Your Majesty, I'd like to put yer mind at ease where Abigail an' her mother are concerned."

"Proceed, James."

"I inherited my sire's lands near th' town of Perth. Our family home was built by my grandfather. I ha' a sister, Margaret, who is married to John Buchanan. They live in northern Scotland close to Dornoch. My father an' mother attended court when your father, King James, was crowned."

The queen looked at James with a question on her face. "Aye, Your Majesty, my mother an' father were invited to th' coronation of your father. They told me about th' ceremony an' how pleased they were to ha' been invited to attend. Mother, ye see, was a Stuart, a relative of King James. I've known of yer family for as many years as I'm old."

"Your mother was a Stuart before she married your father?"

"Aye, Your Majesty, she was a Scottish Stuart."

"Very well, very well, please continue."

"Thank you. We lost our mother when Maggie was only twelve. While she was well cared for by household staff, they couldn't take th' place of her own mother."

"No, I'm sure that is true. You say she is married?"

"Aye, Majesty. When she was seven years old, an agreement was made for her to marry John Buchannan, whose father owned a portion of land borderin' our da's land. Margaret said not a word about marrying a lad she did'na know, but I felt sad for her, wi' no mother." James spoke quietly; the queen could see he had very tender feelings for his sister.

"Your father," the queen asked softly, "he raised both of you by himself?"

"Aye, he did. It must ha' been difficult for him. Shall I continue, Yer Majesty?"

"Yes. You see, James, to me your life seems to be one with strong family ties, and I am quite envious. Your father, is he still alive?"

James shook his head. "Nay, but he gave life a good run while he lived. Father did'na remarry; he said there'd be no other for him."

The queen interrupted with a comment. "Your father was a decent and good man, and you are like him."

"Thank ye, Majesty. It's been over a year since he passed, an' I've spent th' time learnin' th' business of bein' a laird. If I can breed an' train horses to sell, an' grow th' fodder to feed 'em, buyers'll come, purchase my animals, an' tell others. Majesty, yer horses are th' finest I've ever seen. With your permission, I hope to purchase two animals, a stallion an' a mare, to begin th' blood line on my lands in Perthshire."

Pleased, the queen responded, "James, as my kin, you are most welcome here. You may be surprised to know that many a distant relative arrives with a hand outstretched asking for lodging, food, and coins. On the other hand, you have not, at least to my knowledge, mentioned our kinship to anyone, even Abby or Beatrice. With my blessing, you will find the horses you wish to buy in my stables. I will speak to the master of horses about my discussion with you. You shall have, at a fair price, the animals you deem to be best for your needs. Now James, tell me, what do you think of our fair Abigail?"

James said, "Present company excepted, Majesty, Abby's th' fairest lady in th' court, an' she dinna put on airs or care for those who do."

The queen smiled and nodded her head. James continued, "I'm th' same; I care not for foppery. When Abby an' I are together, we talk about horses an' ways to improve th' blood lines. She's wise when it comes to knowin' how to mix their fodder so they'll grow strong an' healthy, an' I believe she'll be th' same wi' her bairns. I want to wed Abigail! Will you gi' yer blessing?"

"I will, most willingly. The two of you must advise Beatrice immediately. She will want Abby to have a court wedding."

Smiling at James, the queen continued, "There will be many gifts if the wedding takes place in the palace, and I should not be surprised to find a fine pair of horses amongst them! But I must warn you of what to expect when the nuptials are announced. More than one member of the court will look upon you as being less than a suitable husband for Abigail. Remember, James, as my kin, you can hold your head high. I shall rather enjoy sharing the news of our kinship with the lords and ladies of the court."

James bowed low before her. His voice husky, James said, "Beloved Queen, I'll always be at your service."

After James left the room, the queen wiped tears from her eyes and thought of her perfectly formed babe who had lived only a few hours; he could have grown up to be like young James, intelligent and mannerly. "I shall give my blessing and love to Abby and James; they both are my kin."

The next afternoon, James asked Abby to ride with him to the field where the newest foals were with their mothers. When they reached the foal's pasture, they stopped by a tree that stood near a small creek. With his sgian dubh, James whittled a heart into the trunk of the tree. He carved "J + A" inside the heart. "Abby, will ye miss yer mother if I asked ye to marry me an' live in my home away from her?"

Abby smiled and said, "I'll miss Mother, of course, but this is the way of daughters. They grow up, meet husbands, marry, and leave their childhood home to become wives and mothers. Yes! I will marry you. I'm anxious to be your wife and to start our own herd of horses."

"Och, Abby." James smiled. "At least ye ha' th' order of things right. First ye'll marry me, an' th' horses are second. I'm relieved to hear you speak so!"

The two laughed as they walked together, arms linked. "Your mother needs to know of our plans, an' the queen hopes we will be married in the castle."

"Mother will want us to be married in the castle, and so do I."

The day before the wedding, Abby and her mother sat together as Beatrice sewed tiny silk-covered buttons down the back of Abby's wedding gown. "Ah, the top two buttons are a bit crooked. I'll resew them so it's just right."

"Oh, Mama, it doesn't have to be perfect. The crooked ones will keep the straight ones looking nice, don't you think?"

Beatrice smiled. "You are so like your father, my dear. It's time you knew more about the man who would have loved to walk beside you down the aisle on the morrow." In her lap underneath the satin was a small wooden chest.

"I've waited a long time for this day, and I'm pleased you've found someone you can love as much as I loved your father." She opened the chest, brought out a leather bag, and handed it to Abby. "Your father left you these things."

Abby loosened the tasseled cord and opened the bag, emptying the contents into her lap. There lay ten gold coins, ten silver ones, and a lock of light brown hair. Eyes glistening, Beatrice smiled. "He was a fine man, Abigail. Every time I see you smile, I think of him. When you toss your head, place your hands on your hips, and shrug your shoulders, I see a shadow of your father standing there. You do not favor him, but you have his ways. He would be proud of you and approve of your James. I've not spoken of him to you because it pains me even now to do so. His name was Andrew Simpson. We loved each other dearly, and out of that love, you were born. Abby, your father was an unusual man. He had visions of things that were yet to pass. I did not believe him when he said he would not live to see our babe born and handed me this box. He said the contents could be used if needed, but if not, it should be put aside for your dowry. Now, dear daughter, because of our beloved queen's generosity, everything is as he left it: a gift to you, from your father."

Tears flowed down Abby's face. "Oh, Mother, thank you for telling me about him. I understand how difficult it is for you to speak of him."

"My dear, we have much to be thankful for. I have loved and been loved, and now you have a man who loves you. I ask for nothing more."

Abigail's gown was made of ivory silk, and she wore a pearl necklace and pearl earrings gifted to her by the queen. James was handsome in his black velvet jacket with a Dunsmuir plaid tartan draped over his left shoulder and pinned to his kilt with a Dunsmuir clan badge. He wore a bonnet of black felt trimmed with an eagle's feather and a sprig of Scottish heather. Queen Anne smiled when she introduced James as a relative. After seeing everyone's faces, she said it was a time to rejoice: an English lady was marrying a Scottish gentleman, and the marriage of the two was symbolic of how the two countries could live together, side by side.

Their wedding night was spent in the king's chambers. James whistled softly when he saw the suite of rooms with its gilt furnishings. In an adjoining room a table with soap and linens sat next to a large porcelain bath tub. Abby and James sat talking about the wedding, the guests, and Queen Anne's wedding gift, a pair of Shropshire horses, until they were interrupted by servants carrying pitchers of hot water.

"God's nightshirt," James exclaimed. "Abigail, can ye swim? I surely hope so, for otherwise ye'll drown in tha' tub filled wi' water."

"Yes, James, I can. But the tub is big enough for two, and surely you would take care that I'd not drown!"

James took Abby's hand in his and said, "Love, do ye know wha' to expect this night? I want to please ye, but I fear the first time will not be as pleasurable for ye as it will be for me. Later, I hope that ye too will receive pleasure when we make love."

"Oh, James, I do know what to expect. I've spent as much time in the stables as you have. While I do not expect you to mount me from the back as horses do, I certainly understand the entire process from start to finish. I am anxious for this part of being husband and wife to begin, and my curiosity is about to overtake me. Let's proceed on, shall we?"

She began by helping James out of his shoes, hose, and kilt. Surprised that he had nothing on under the kilt, she smiled and said, "Now I know what all the ladies mean when they chatter about what is worn under the kilt. Why, it's nothing at all!"

James grinned and asked, "Wha' do I do wi' this?" when Abby handed him a button hook. Turning her back to him, she explained how to maneuver the hook around the button and slide it out of the loop. After a few minutes had passed and only half a dozen buttons were undone, Abigail said, "James, let me see if I can slip it down without having to undo the loops."

But it was impossible. There was no way to get it up or down without each loop being loosened from its button. "Stop shaking, James! I am standing perfectly still. Get on with it, husband!" Finally the last button was undone, and she stepped out of the gown. She removed petticoats, a corset, and chemise and finally stood completely naked. James could do nothing but stare with a foolish grin on his face.

After the bath they dried each other and sat on the edge of the bed. James stood and said, "We can take th' rest of th' supper wi' us on th' morrow."

She looked at him. "James, come here, please. I think you need some encouragement."

"Aye, wife, I suppose I do."

Later, Abby said, "It was just as I hoped it would be. I did not know how everything would fit together, but it does." Caressing his chest, she spoke softly. "I am glad you took the time to be sure I was ready. Even though there was pain at first, the rest of it was wonderful. James, I am hungry. Are you?"

"Aye, I am. Let's have th' rest of the food, shall we?"

Giggling, Abigail said, "I like being married. If I do something that does not please you, say so. On the other hand, I will certainly tell you if there is something that you need to do differently. You can count on that, husband." James brought her close to him and began kissing her, starting at the tiny pulse at her throat and not stopping.

Early the next morning, with a cart full of gifts, James and Abby began their journey home. Abigail's mares, Morning Star and Evening Star, pulled the cart, and the couple rode the Shire horses. In the cart was a gift from Cook, a wooden box filled with pots of jam, pickled onions, packets of seeds, and a book of handwritten recipes. After good-byes, it was time to go. When Holyrood Palace was out of sight, James said, "We'll stop only to feed, water our animals and rest. By the second day, we'll be close to home."

"Our home, James! Mother and father did not have a home. They lived in a tiny room above a grocer's market in York. They were married only a year before Father died. Queen Anne knew Mother was alone and expecting a child, and she was very generous when she offered Mother a place in her court and an apartment in the castle. Mother took great pleasure in decorating and furnishing the rooms." Abby spoke softly, "Still, the apartment did not belong to her. I did not know until she spoke of it how much she wanted to have her own home. James, she is so pleased that I will have one."

"Hmm, Abby, would Beatrice consider living nearby if we built her a cottage? Do ye think she would?"

Abby thought before answering. "No, I cannot think of Mother anywhere but near the queen. She'll never leave her side."

They talked as they rode. "James, what do you prefer to eat? Is there a food you do not like? Tell me about the house. I want to know everything."

"In Scotland, we call a home or house a *broch*, th' Gaelic word for shelter. It'll be good to ha' a woman in th' house again. It's not in order, but when I left, I was thinkin' only about buyin' animals. We'd best stop, ha' a bite of supper, and feed our animals." James pulled off the road into a stand of fir trees. Abby brought out the food basket while James fed and watered the horses and gathered wood for a fire. Abby set out bread, butter, cheese, and apples and they sat beside the fire drinking wine from flasks.

As they ate, James answered Abby's endless questions. "Ye asked about meals? I usually ha' burned porridge, washed down wi' ale. I'm no particular, but I remember Mother setting out platters, an' pans of food. She had household help an' ye'll be needin' some help as well, but until I can get things in place, can ye make do?"

Abby thought about Cook's box with the book of recipes. She hoped it'd be helpful. As of now, she could make a pot of tea and spread jam on oatcakes, and that was it. She slowly nodded her head.

They woke before dawn. James kissed the tip of Abby's nose. "By th' day's end, you'll see the bridge tha' leads to my broch. Oh, sorry, Abby—I mean *our* broch."

They traveled all that day, and as the sun was setting, James pointed. "Abby, there's the bridge." She could see the faint outline of an arching stone and timber bridge with a rushing burn passing underneath. Then there was the house that would be her home. Built of thick blocks of chiseled stone, the broch had two fireplace chimneys which towered above the slate roof. They crossed the bridge and rode into a cobblestone courtyard. "I'll feed an' water th' horses. It's too late to unload th' cart tonight. We'll leave it in th' barn."

"James, I'll help." Together they put out fresh hay and oats in the mangers and stalls.

"You have no hens? What do you do for eggs?"

"I dinna cook anythin' tha' uses eggs, Abby. We'll get some chicks from the village."

"Good, we'll put the coops by the haystack."

James smiled at her. "Yer already th' lady o' th' barn," he teased. James opened the door to the broch and turned around to face Abby, who was waiting on the steps. "Enter, Milady. My home's yer home, an' all tha' I ha' is yers."

Abigail crossed the threshold and looked at a room with a fireplace at either end. She shivered and pulled her cloak around her shoulders. The room was dark, cold, and smelled of dampness and charred wood. While James brought in firewood, Abby looked at the kitchen. Two smoke stained windows shed dim light on a table covered with pots, pans, wooden bowls and plates.

James built fires in both fireplaces while Abigail moved two chairs closer to the fire. She found one lamp with oil; it was enough to chase away the shadows. They shared the last of the bread, butter, and wedding cake sitting in chairs by the fire.

"Wife," James said, taking Abby's hand, "I'll manage our money from th' sale of horses an' crops so we can provide for our needs. I want th' tenant farmers livin' on these lands to ha' a roof over their heids an' enough to feed their families as well. They'll help wi' th' plantin', tendin', an' harvest, an' I'll depend on 'em for their strong backs an' willin' hands. It's a good way of livin', an' I hope ye'll take to it, Abby. It'll not compare wi' castle livin', though."

Abby smiled. "Husband, I married you to be by your side. I'll not walk behind you or go in a direction of my own. I'll be the best wife I can, but like you, I'm learning. You won't find meals to compare with your mother's cookery. I've cooked only a little, and the castle cook said it went to the hounds."

The look on James's face made her smile. "If you're willing, and do not die from starvation, I'll get it all mastered sooner or later. Let's talk about children. It was lonely for me as an only child. I'd like to have, oh, two boys and two girls? They'd be company for each other. If you agree, we could begin tonight, hum?"

James responded with enthusiasm, "Aye! We can! Abby, in Scotland, th' Gaelic word for children is *bairns*. It's a term of endearment. An' aye, two lads an' two lasses would be grand, especially if they favor their beautiful mother. I'm not too sure about my looks; I suppose I ha' no given it much thought."

"To me, James, you are most handsome."

Abby woke at dawn and went downstairs. The house had long been without a lady, Abigail thought. The barn, with its ropes, scythe blades, tools, and farm equipment hanging neatly on the walls, was better organized and cleaner than the broch. She swept up pieces of bark, sawdust, and dry leaves that led to a wood pile by the front door. After filling both grates with wood, she fanned embers to get the fires burning. At one end of the room, a beautifully carved cabinet held dishes, goblets and yellowed linens. She admired an ornate silver tea service sitting on a burlwood table. Everything was covered with a grimy layer of smoke and dust, together with the markings of mice and the remains of their meals. In the kitchen, she looked at a pan on the cluttered table. It had burnt food in the bottom. A family of mice nesting in the peat basket scattered when she looked in the basket. Was there a tabby cat somewhere? If not, there soon would be! Their morning meal would be leftover oatcakes with jam; the larder had nothing but a box of moldy apples.

James called out, "Abby, ye did well wi' th' fires in th' great room. I'll get th' kitchen fire goin'."

Soon the tea kettle was steaming, and their first day at home had begun. After eating, Abigail began cleaning the kitchen. Cook had included several cakes of soap in the box, along with directions for more. The soap, scented with fir tree sap, made the kitchen smell fresh and clean. As she scrubbed with a boar's-hair brush, her hands became rough and chapped. But when she stood back to admire the gleam of shiny copper pots and pans hanging from iron hooks above the kitchen fireplace, she was pleased. Outside the kitchen door, she found a small garden with rhubarb, berry vines, parsley, and some overgrown rose bushes. Next year it would be her vegetable garden. But what could be done about the bare larder for now? Abby wondered where one could purchase vegetables and fruit. When James brought two pheasants and a rabbit into the kitchen, it did not occur to him that Abby did not know how to prepare them for cooking. *I'll think of something*, she thought as she dug out Cook's recipes. There were cookery directions for roasted meat, meat pies, and stews. Roasting a pheasant seemed easy enough, but preparing it sounded very difficult. After reading Cook's notes, she concluded that foods were boiled, baked, salted down, or smoked and it should be easy to decide from the four choices how to prepare what one had on hand. Apples and rabbit would be baked while potatoes would be boiled; that was simple enough.

Several days later, after a particularly unappetizing meal of burned meat served with sticky oatcakes, James remarked that cookery was difficult for him too. He saw the look on Abby's face and hastily added that he certainly could not do as well himself. James arranged for Mrs. Whyte from the village to help in the kitchen twice a week. She made cheese, bread, and butter, but otherwise, Abby was on her own. James's dogs snapped at each other for the best spot next to the kitchen door, where nearly every day food was thrown out.

One frosty morning, Mrs. Whyte arrived with a cart filled with food for the larder. There were carrots, onions, turnips, parsnips, potatoes, and sacks of dried peas and beans along with baskets of apples and pears. Abby watched as Mrs. Whyte dressed and cooked fresh meat. When James asked for a second helping of baked pheasant, she smiled. Preparing flour paste for pies was easy, and she discovered the same recipe made dumplings for meat stew.

James's and Abby's babe was born on their first anniversary. She was beautiful, with curly golden-red hair. "I'd like her name to be Janet Anne, if it pleases you, James."

"Janet Anne Dunsmuir! We'll send word to yer mother an' th' queen."

"James, I'm sad."

"Sad, why?" James looked at Abby; she had tears running down her cheeks.

"Oh, James, Mother and Father were married less than a year when he died, leaving her with child. Except for Auntie Queen, she was alone when I was born. I had no idea of the pain she bore, first losing her husband—and then, when I was born, he was not there to ... Do you see, James? Do you?"

James nodded. "I dinna carry our babe for many months, but all th' same I shared in ever' moment of it. Aye, I see why yer sad. On yer birthday, we'll send a gift wi' a note to yer mother expressing our thanks to her for giv'in ye life."

Chapter 6

Abigail found that many of the medicinal treatments she used for horses also worked for people. Her knapsack contained feverfew, yarrow, oil of camphor, oil from boiled sheep's wool, ointments, salves, and potions. Abby knew ways to knead the belly of a laboring woman so the babe would be born head first. After the delivery of a fine bairn, the father always asked what he could do in payment for her services; she would ask, "Will you help James plant and gather in the harvest?" She always got a heartfelt nod of the head.

As James' reputation of raising fine horses grew, a steady stream of buyers came from near and far. When a buyer from Ardou Brewery in Edinburgh purchased a pair of matched Shire geldings, he explained the brewery could now deliver ale and spirits to taverns and pubs in southern Scotland and northern England. "I'll be back next fall to buy four more geldings if ye ha' 'em. The brewery owners will pay extra for horses trained to pull loaded wagons."

James nodded. "I ha' two pairs of yearlin' Shire colts not yet trained to th' bridle, but they can start any time."

The two men talked as they walked to the pasture where the young animals were penned. "Your animals are bigger an' stronger than elsewhere, James. To wha' do you attribute th' difference?"

James, who always warmed to the subject of talking good horse flesh, said, "I believe th' horses ye've seen elsewhere came from breedin' a Shire to a different breed of animal. Here's wha' ye should see in a purebred Shire horse. You'll want th' head of th' animal to be long an' lean. Their eyes will be large an' bright, an' they'll ha' attentive ears. Look for a shoulder which is deep an' wide, an' th' chest will be wide as well. Th' Shire horse will ha' a muscular back, an' th' hindquarters will be long an' wide. They're proud animals an' will no' respond to beatin's or beratements! Those responsible for 'em must understand tha' they're smart an' will listen for commands. Talk to 'em as they're being put to th' bridle. Then they'll be calm an' know wha' is expected of 'em." James pointed out each feature on young horses. "Notice th' featherin' on th' legs; it should be free of tangles, briars, or matted hair. This confirms th' animal is well cared for."

"James, now I've a better idea of what to look for, and I'm ready to buy." He handed James a bag of silver coins. "Here's compensation for your time in trainin' my employer's horses. We ha' a gift for you, a cask of our finest ale. Thank ye for preparin' these animals for th' work we ha' for 'em."

James now had over two hundred leather bags full of gold and silver coins. "Abby, we've coins enough to bring in some help. I'm thinkin' a cook, housekeeper, two cleanin' lasses, an' a man to help wi' th' horse operation. There'll be folks in th' village who'd be willin' to accept room, board, and a little wage."

Abigail was delighted. "I've a surprise, James. At Christ's Mass time, a new bairn will be born. I've no morning illness, but sometimes I want nothing more than to sit for a while with my mending. Perhaps one of the new lasses could watch Janet a bit. She's beginning to walk and gets into everything.

James smiled widely as he said, "A Christ's Mass bairn! We'll ha' a laddie, I'm thinkin'."

They stopped at the village church, where Father Benjamin sat outside in the sunshine. "Good day, Father. How does th' day find ye?"

"Ah, well, indeed, an' you, your lady an' bairn?"

"Blessed, Father, very blessed. We'll soon be welcomin' a new lad or lassie, an' Lady Dunsmuir is in need of household help an' I can use a fellow to help wi' the horses. Would there be folk from th' village?"

Father Benjamin thought a minute and said, "Aye, if it's a cook ye need, an' a man to manage yer barns an' animals, Farley an' his Bess would be my pick. Farley's th' one who fashioned a horse-drawn rake to gather up cut hay."

"Aye, he's a good man!"

"Sir, ye'll not find a better cook than Farley's Bess. Her rabbit pie is th' best in th' village, an' her loaves of bread coolin' on th' windowsill are always temptin' some youngster to lift one an' run. To be truthful, I may ha' fetched a couple of 'em meself," Father Benjamin said with a chuckle. "Though I'd always leave a coin or two for 'em."

Bess wagged her finger at James when he asked her to be the cook for the household. "Milord, I'll manage th' broch as well as th' kitchen! You'll ha' a clean broch an' good meals. We'll bring alon' th' McDougal twins, Ellen an' Meg, to help. They're hard-workin' lasses."

"Aye, Bess, there's two rooms by th' kitchen, one for ye an' Farley, an' th' other'll be for th' lasses."

With the help settled in, it was time for fall cleaning of the broch from top to bottom. Abby threw out the rushes and scrubbed and swept the floors.

"Now!" she declared. "There'll be no spitting or pissing in the corners, and all dogs, excepting Bran, will stay outside!"

Abby and Bess gathered berries, fruit, peas and beans for drying. Bess saw to the grains to be milled into flour and prepared butter and cheese enough to last until spring. Carrots, parsnips, and turnips were covered with hay and left in the garden until a hard frost. They packed kale and cabbage in a wooden barrel with a brine of salt and vinegar. Abby sorted apples to store some in crates and others to be sliced and dried in the sun.

Abigail's babe was born the day before Christ's Mass. He was a strong, healthy lad with dark hair like his father's. James held his son and said, "If it be God's will, he'll take my place when th' time comes. Let's name him. Wha' think ye, wife?"

Abby thought for a minute and said, "If he's called James Andrew, it'd please mother."

"Ah, then James Andrew it'll be. We'll christen him wi' tha' name, but he'll be called Jamie."

Abby taught her children to read, write, and do numbers. In the queen's court, the prettiest women quickly found husbands, but the ones who could converse well, read books, and play chess made the best marriages. When Jamie inherited his father's lands and business, he would have the skills he needed to be the laird. Crop planting required planning with some pastures set aside to be fallow for the season. A quarter of the barley crop would be for whisky, to be doled out to ease the bone-chilling dampness of long, cold winters. Hay for fodder went to mangers in barns, and oats were ground for flour, rolled into flakes, or cut for porridge. Always, James put aside a third of the bounty for the villagers, who also gleaned in the fields after the harvest.

Jamie learned the business of raising and selling prime horses. Meghan, a year younger than Jamie, hoped to find a suitable husband before she was her older sister's age. Janet at eighteen, was a beauty, and while there were several young lads who came to buy horses, of them all, Ewan Cameron was by far the most handsome. The Cameron clan plaid was always a part of Ewan's attire. His breeches of tanned leather came from the hides of his Highland cattle, and his woolen shirt had buttons fashioned from the horns of the animals. At the Dunsmuir broch, Ewan was treated as a valued guest welcome to dine at the high board with the family. He usually emptied a platter passed to him and took no notice of the plates sitting next to him. But what he lacked in table manners, he made up for with after-supper stories. Often the villagers and members of the household staff joined the family for the evening's entertainment. One evening, as whisky and ale were being passed around, Ewan began speaking in the ancient Gaelic language. "*A bheil gaidhlig agat/agaibh?*" (Do any of ye speak th' Gaelic?) Several heads nodded, but many did not.

"I'll tell th' story so all can understand. It may be tha' th' men of Scotland'll ha' to fight again someday, an' there's history tha' tells how it's done an' why. My tale is about a great battle at Bannockburn, a tiny village surrounded by low, marshy fields, lying toward th' western hills at th' foot of th' Hielands. Th' marshlands of Bannockburn are wi'in ridin' distance of Stirling Castle. It's there tha' Bruce's army of seven thousand men won a great battle over King Edward II's army of twenty thousand men. Think of it, lads! Th' English had almost thrice as many soldiers as wha' th' Scots had! Yet, over four hundred years ago, bravery won out. But I'm gettin' ahead of th' tale about a braw man who had th' sight to see an' take back wha' belonged to th' Scots but had been taken over by th' English.

"Th' Bruce began planning to take back Stirling Castle from King Edward late in th' year of our Lord, 1313. Robert, ridin' his great Shire horse, met with th' king's men, who gloated to themselves as they looked at th' man who wanted to fight th' king's army on th' Stirling Plains. They later told th' king how easily th' battle would be won an' said they could take over even more Scottish lands to th' north! Th' Bruce traveled th' Hielands, th' lowlands, an' th' east an' west coasts of Scotland, carryin' a wooden cross wrapped in white linen stained wi' blood. He gathered th' clan chiefs around him. 'Tis th' Fiery Cross,' he said, 'stained wi' th' blood of Scotland's men, who died for naught! We're not free men in our own country!

Will ye join me to bring our own Stirling Castle back to its rightful owners, th' people of Scotland?"

Ewan stood, pulled his broadsword from its scabbard, and held it high. "Th' Bruce brought together th' men o' Scotland to fight th' battle." As the men in the room stood and cheered, Ewan accepted a whisky-filled silver quaich from James. Holding it in both hands, he emptied the cup, turned it over, placed a kiss on the bottom, and continued his tale. "Th' Bruce knew how to train his men to fight. First, he separated 'em into three groups an' made certain tha' each man had weapons to fit his abilities. Those who had experience wi' th' bow an' arrow were his archers, an' their bows were fashioned from th' wood of th' ash tree, tempered an' water cured so it'd send an arrow, trimmed wi' goose feathers, on its way, true an' straight. Men who arrived on horseback were given tempered an' sharpened blades, bound wi' sinew to seasoned straight poles. Men on foot carried heavy broadswords an' deadly dirks."

Moving to the center of the room, Ewan said, "Some of th' Bruce's fightin' men were nobles. Others were knights, landowners, an' tenant farmers. Together they were kin, wi' th' Bruce as their leader." He began naming the clans who fought. "Th' Cameron, Campbell, Chisholm, Fraser, Gordon, Grant, Gunn, MacKay, MacIntosh, MacPherson, MacQuarrie, MacLean, MacDonald, MacFarlane, MacGregor, MacKenzie, Menzie, Munro, Robertson, Ross, Sinclair, Sutherland, an' Stewarts."

When a sharp wind howled around the corners of the broch. James held up his hand as he stood to place more wood on the fire. There was no need to ask for silence; the room was so quiet that everyone jumped when a log burned in two and fell on the grate. Ewan loosened his plaid and wrapped it around his waist. His eyes looked into the distance, seeing in his mind the battlefield, the men holding their broadswords, and the war horses ready to take their riders into battle. Using his arms, he held an imaginary shovel to show how Robert had the men prepare the far side of the battlefield by digging holes in the ground and then covering them with twigs and leaves, leaving no sign. "On th' morn th' battle began, th' English advanced onto th' field, an' th' Scots, marchin' behind their pipers, moved toward 'em. Th' skirlin' of th' pipes carried all th' way from th' front line of th' Scots army to th' ears of Edward's army. It was as if th' very souls of th' Scots th' English had killed through th' ages were crying out through th' sounds of those bagpipes! Then, th' battle began! Th' Scots sent th' first arrows, an' th' English answered wi' their own. Men on th' front lines of both sides fell, but neither side gave ground. As th' day neared its close, Robert searched for a way to turn th' tide. It looked as if th' English had th' advantage. But when night fell, th' English battalions changed their location. Th' Bruce, familiar wi' th' lay of th' land, realized tha' King Edward had moved his army onto a small marshland bounded on three sides by water. Th' Bruce knew this could even th' score."

Ewan moved his chair to the center of the room and sat down. He handed his empty cup to Janet, who filled it and handed it to him as all waited for Ewan to resume the tale. Only the crackling of the fire broke the silence.

"Th' great English horses cloaked in heavy chain mail were trapped in th' marshy ground an' unable to get to dry land. Th' king's soldiers, weighted down wi' armor, were easy targets because they too were trapped in mire. King Edward saw tha' he was beat an' lay beside his dead horse 'til dark. Then he crawled in th' muck on his belly an' made his way to an English camp located in th' border lands. No one knows why th' king made such a foolish move of his men to th' marshy land. Robert th' Bruce an' his army won th' battle, an' th' English were driven back to th' border lands between Scotland an' England."

Ewan stood and looked at each man in the room in turn. "Our fathers an' their fathers before 'em fought to defend Scotland, an' it's likely tha' we'll be called to do so again. Th' people of Scotland are paying th' highest taxes of all in th' kingdom. I say, we'll fight again!" For a brief moment, the room was quiet. Then the men stood and shouted, "Aye!"

Janet stood and spoke to the young man who stood before her. "Sir, I admire yer loyalty to Scotland. But there's th' signin' of th' Act of th' Union in 1707 which brought together Scotland an' England under one ruler. My mother was there when good Queen Anne signed it into law. Yer sayin' we'll fight England again?" Ewan turned to Janet and saw that she was fair to look upon, with her long, red hair shining in the firelight and her green eyes on nearly the same level as his own. He answered her question. "Th' king's army took possession of lands tha' belonged to Scotland's people. When th' Bruce had th' means to take back those lands, he did so. We're still fightin' to hold our borders an' lands from England takin' 'em over."

"Sir, Robert prepared himself an' his army to meet th' king's army on th' battlefield. Had it been otherwise, th' battle would ha' been lost. Ye believe th' men of Scotland will fight again? Th' Bruce is long dead. Where's th' man who'll take his place?"

Ewan shook his head as Janet continued, "If there's such a man, he'll best prepare his army as Robert did, as th' odds'll be no different, I'm thinkin'."

"Aye, lass, I agree wi' ye."

After a restless night, Ewan asked James Dunsmuir if he could court Janet. When James consented, Ewan gathered a bouquet of fragrant heather and wild roses and placed them on the high board at Janet's place. He politely passed food to her and waited for her to fill her plate and return the platters to him before filling his own. For a hungry Highlander, this was truly a display of manners. When James spoke with Janet about Ewan's request, she asked, "Wha' did ye say, Da? Tha' I'm a wretched lass? Wha' did ye say?"

James chuckled at his daughter's anxious questions, "Aye, I told him all tha' an' he still plans to court ye! Lass, I like th' man, for he tells things th' way I see 'em. Tell me if yer not happy wi' it, an' I'll send him on his way, but there may not be another like him."

"He's a wondrous storyteller, and I'll welcome his attention."

Two weeks later, they were married in the village chapel. The ceremony included a melding of Clan Dunsmuir with Clan Cameron. Using his sgian dubh, Ewan pierced the skin on Janet's thumb, bringing a drop of blood. Then he cut his thumb in the same manner and pressed the two together, wrapping the plaid of the Cameron clan around their two hands to signify the joining of the two clans by blood. After a wedding feast, Ewan and Janet began the trip to Glen Lochy with three mares, a stallion, and one half-grown deerhound. Janet's dowry was a leather bag with twelve gold coins; Ewan told her to put it away for safekeeping.

Ewan and Janet Cameron spent their first night together on the Highland moors beside a burn cascading down from snow melt on the high glens above them. Ewan told her that the deep, abiding love of a husband and wife took time. He spoke of the bairns they would have. He described how his broch looked out over glens and valleys, pastures and rivers. Ewan lifted Janet to his lap and wrapped his woolen plaid around the two of them. Joining together for the first time on a rocky hillside in the misty coolness of the night was a memory that they both would have all of their lives. Janet would remember the sweetness of the lovemaking and Ewan's patience with her. Ewan would never forget the fragrance or smoothness of her skin. It could not have been any better a night for making love.

Chapter 7

Stretched out on a short bed with a thin mattress, Charles Stuart felt the sharp ends of straw poking through the mattress covering. "Johnnie, come here!"

"Yes, sir?"

Charles sat up. "Why is the bedding so crude here?" Sitting on the bed's sideboard, Charles pointed to the sway in the middle of the bed. "If I were to entertain a lady in this bed, it would hardly hold the two of us."

"Sir, I am sorry. I will search for other accommodations on the morrow. At the least, I will request another mattress for your bed. Your Highness, the bedding may be typical for this inn. Mine is exactly as yours."

The prince gestured impatiently. "Never mind. If the inn's owner realizes he is accommodating the future king of England, surely he would provide the finest room he has! We are staying here only because I expect several Irish ships to come into the Inverness Port. John is in Fort William to learn if the British Navy is patrolling the area. If so, we'll need to get word to the captains advising them to seek another port. O'Sullivan is providing an invaluable service for me. I could say he is worth his weight in gold. However, considering his girth, there is not likely that quantity of gold to be found in this part of the world. Johnnie, might I impose upon your good nature?"

"No imposition, sir. How may I be of service?"

"It has been several months since I left France," Charles said. "There's been no opportunity to court any of the fair ladies of Scotland. I've observed several who are quite lovely, even if their clothing is plain. Would you search for a comely lady to share my bed for a few days?"

"Sir, if you will give me some idea as to your preferences, I shall begin looking."

"I am easily pleased," said Charles. "A younger lady, one with all of her teeth and a shapely body, will do. I don't mind a fragrance as long as it is unlike a sheep."

Johnnie stifled a smile. "Yes, sir, I understand. Perhaps our landlord could make a recommendation. Will you be paying the lady for her favors?"

"I am very accomplished when it comes to lovemaking and she should be paying me!" Charles winked. "Let me say this; if I am pleased, there will be compensation."

"Very well, sir."

"Johnnie, when you speak to our host, ask about a different mattress and a bed that can support two people. I cannot imagine making the last thrust in lovemaking and finding my lady and myself on the floor, the two of us suffering from puncture wounds caused by straw!"

"Certainly, sir. I will see to it immediately."

"Thank you, Johnnie."

John Stewart returned to his windowless room, which was just big enough for a cot with a thin straw mattress, a rough wool coverlet, and a table with a water pitcher and bowl. Johnnie was weary of packing and unpacking Charles's extensive wardrobe, combing and cleaning his wigs, brushing his velvet jackets, and washing his underclothing. It all took considerable time. Then there were the long nights he spent hovering nearby while Charles met with friends and supporters. As the hour grew late, Johnnie reminded Charles of the next day's appointments. "Yes, Johnnie, I must be up and about early to meet with the Duke of Morris. We have a most interesting agenda to discuss." The evenings ended with Charles listening to accolades from visitors who hoped to benefit if he became the king of England. "Dear friends, I depend upon your financial support as the royal Stuarts pursue the crown. Please note the box on the table for contributions. Your financial support will mean a sure gain of the kingship. Be assured Father and I will remember your assistance."

After leading Charles to his bed chamber, Johnnie helped him undress and don his night shirt. The next morning, Charles always looked in the collection box on the table. Once, among the coins, he found a playing card, the nine of diamonds. If it had significance, Charles, not being a gaming man, did not know what it was. He tucked the card away. Perhaps its meaning would become known to him.

Now, Johnnie searched for a comely woman who had teeth, did not smell like a ewe, and would be willing to share the Prince's bed for a fortnight, with or without compensation. Johnnie considered Charles' appearance when he removed his wig and took off his finery. He was a tall man with a paunch and considerable body hair while the hair on his head was thin. The prince perspired profusely, but when dressed in finery and doused with cologne, the man could smile, tell a grand story, and charm the very underdrawers off most women. *Interesting*, Johnnie thought, *how the ladies find him so attractive.* Then he smiled. *From what I've seen, he's no better endowed than most men; perhaps it's his royal blood that enchants them!*

He descended the inn's narrow stairs, and knocked at a door on the first floor. A woman with dark hair, very blue eyes, and a mouth full of teeth opened the door and smiled at Johnnie. "Please, Milady, is your father in?"

"No, he's away just now. But please, come in." She led him into a small, nicely furnished room. "May I offer ye a cup o' tea?"

"Yes, thank you." She left the room and returned with a tray with a teapot, two cups, a china dish with warm sultana buns, butter, and jam. As she poured the tea, she smiled at Johnnie. "We are most honored to ha' Prince Charles stayin' wi' us. Is there anything I can do to assist ye?"

"Two things, Milady. As the prince's valet, I am aware that he has delicate skin and the mattress covering on his bed is very coarse. The sharp ends of straw protrudes through the mattress covering. His Highness is asking that he be provided another mattress, preferably with feathers or down. Would you be able to assist with this?"

"Oh, I do apologize, sir. Apparently the maids have switched the mattresses. Usually that bedroom has a lovely feather mattress and a down-filled comforter as well. Aye, I shall see to it immediately. What is your second need, sir?"

"Before I continue, my name is Johnnie Stewart, and I am at your service. His Highness is used to the company of lovely ladies, such as yourself, Milady. As of late, the prince is suffering from a lack of companionship and has asked me to inquire on his behalf if there is a lady who might be interested in spending time with His Lordship."

Smiling, she handed Johnnie a cup of tea. "A sweet bun, sir, wi' jam?"

"Yes, thank you."

The bun was delicious, the tea hot, and the lady most interesting. Johnnie made himself comfortable on the cushioned chair across from her. "May I ask your name, Milady?"

"Yvonne, an' my father owns this hostelry."

"Yvonne—is that French, Milady?"

"It is. My mother was raised in France, you see."

"Will we be meeting your mother?"

"Ah, no." Yvonne's smile faded. "She is no longer wi' us."

"Oh, I am very sorry."

"Thank you. Father was a sea captain, an' he traveled far an' wide. After meeting my mother, he fell in love with her, married her, an' brought her to Scotland, where his family's business, this inn, is located. I'm afraid th' story is rather dreary after that. Father inherited th' inn, an' after I was born, Mother's health declined until she passed away several years ago. I took her place managing th' financial affairs of th' business. Father misses th sea an' would return; however, he feels a responsibility to me."

"Do you have friendships with gentlemen, Milady?"

"Aye, I do," she responded, looking Johnnie in the eye. "I ha' th' means to live my private life as I choose. To answer yer unspoken question, I'd be most interested to meet Prince Charles. I feel certain I can comfort him in his loneliness. I believe in life, love, an' all tha' goes wi' it."

"Excellent! Now, if I may be so bold, please, milady, allow me to look at you."

"Of course, Johnnie." To his surprise and delight, she loosened the top of her gown and lowered it to her waist. She was very well endowed, and Johnnie, who usually did not respond to the attributes of the fair sex, found himself aroused and somewhat breathless. "Milady, may I?"

"But of course; I would expect you to be sure I am worthy of entertaining th' prince."

Johnnie cupped the full breasts in his hands and kissed Yvonne, who led him to a velvet settee. "Johnnie, my dear, you must be very, very certain of your choice for His Highness."

Later, after making arrangements for Yvonne to meet the prince in her dining room for supper, Johnnie returned to his room, quite pleased with his efforts to find the right lady for His

Lordship. Perhaps some of the more tedious aspects of his position as the prince's valet could be overlooked, at least for the time being.

His thoughts were interrupted by a knock on the door. "Yes?"

"Sir, it's about your bed." Johnnie opened the door to find two maids holding a mattress and a comforter. "Please allow us to make yer bed for ye; our mistress has instructed us to do so."

"By all means." Johnnie watched while the straw ticking was removed and replaced with a plump mattress. Over the mattress they placed a soft knitted covering and then spread a comforter on top. Last, a pillow with an embroidered cover was placed at the head of the bed. "Our mistress says to tell you she's most pleased to make your acquaintance."

Smiling, Johnnie said, "Please express my appreciation to her and tell her, likewise."

Chapter 8

Late that afternoon, Johnnie helped Charles into his brocade evening coat with black velvet breeches, white hosiery trimmed with black ribbon, and a white shirt with black velvet trim. His wig was arranged in rows of round curls in front and over his ears, with a black ribbon tied queue at the back. He smelled of spicy cologne.

"Milady, I am Prince Charles Stuart, lately of France and presently of Scotland." After bowing low, Charles smiled at Yvonne, who bowed and extended her hand to him.

"Your Highness, I am pleased to make yer acquaintance. Father an' I are ardent supporters of th' royal Stuarts."

Charles kissed her hand and breathed in the scent of her floral perfume. "Thank you for your invitation to supper."

Yvonne smiled while the prince admired her revealing blue velvet gown and ample bosom. "Your Highness, it is a privilege to share your company this evenin'. My name is Yvonne. Please, this way to th' dinin' room. There will be just th' two of us, an' perhaps later on, ye will allow me to play th' harp an' sing for you."

"Delightful, my dear, absolutely delightful!" Charles escorted her to the dining room, where a low fire was burning, taper sticks in silver holders glowed on the table, and the delicious smell of food wafted on the air. "Highness, Cook prepared my favorite, roasted capon served wi' a white wine. Then we will have a beef ragout an' a red wine. Our third course will be lettuce wi' boiled eggs, dill, an' pear served wi' honey mead, an' dessert is raspberry jam cake wi' a sweet wine. After dinner, we'll sit by th' fire an' share a French cognac, which I hope you will enjoy."

Charles could hardly contain his excitement. "Superb, absolutely superb. I am very pleased, and you, my dear, are very lovely. Johnnie tells me your mother was from France. May I ask where?"

"Paris, Milord. She was raised in th' Visitandine convent on th' Rue de Bacq."

"A convent! Well, my dear, this is the beginning of an interesting story. Here you are, which raises some questions?"

"Your Highness, Mother was abandoned at th' convent when she was a babe. Th' nuns raised her in th' church an' expected her to become a servant of God. But fate intervened, an' she met my father, a bawdy sea captain."

"Ah," Charles said, laughing. "Your father surely is most charming to woo your mother away from her home and future in the convent."

"Oh," she said, "he's a rascal, an' Mother fancied him. Even today, though he is hardly a young man, Father is still very popular wi' the ladies. He is courtin' one this evening, I believe. Her husband is in Germany on business, an' Father will keep her company—at her invitation, of course."

"Your Highness and Milady! Dinner is served."

Charles lifted his goblet of wine and said, "To a lovely and delightful lady."

Yvonne bowed her head. "To a most charming man who will

be king. I'm pleased to be of service to you, Your Highness." The glasses were emptied and replaced with tankards of amber ale. China plates with bread and creamy cheese topped with slices of cucumber were placed in front of the couple. Then, as the meal progressed through the white meat, red meat, and vegetable dishes, more wine, ale, mead, and finally cognac were served while the two sat by the fire. Yvonne spoke softly to Charles. "Sir, if I may, I will play an' sing a song for you. It is called 'Love, a Garden of Delights.'"

Charles, wishing he could unbutton the top of his breeches, said "Thank you, my dear. It has been a while since I've had the pleasure of the company of a beautiful lady, and there's entertainment! I shall enjoy this."

Yvonne slowly strummed the harp strings and sang about a maiden who observed a prince as he admired her beautiful garden. A stream flowed through the garden, and when the prince saw the maiden's lovely face reflected in the water, he became so enamored of her that he asked if she would allow him to make love to her there beside the stream. The song described how the prince dipped his fingertips in water and slowly caressed the maiden until her passion met his own. The song ended with her singing about the sensations she experienced when the prince made love to her in her garden of delights.

The candles were burning low. Full of food and spirits, Charles unbuttoned his jacket and motioned for Yvonne to join him on the settee. He kissed her and said, "My dear, I have a great desire for you. May I?"

"Sir, your pleasure is my pleasure." She began undressing and finally stood in front of Charles clad only in her stockings and chemise. He loosened his breeches, more than ready to make love. She positioned herself on the settee so that he could avail himself of her. After entry and several thrusts, he shuddered and said, "Thank you, my dear. I must return to my room to see to tomorrow's schedule."

"Of course, sir." After the door closed behind him, Yvonne poured the rest of the cognac in her goblet and lit a small clay pipe filled with an aromatic tobacco. *Royalty or not,* she thought, *tha' was a quick one!* Then she frowned. *He's a man of many words an' few strokes! When he comes to dinner again, I shall serve only two meat dishes an' wine. Charles is one who does not perform well when there is plentiful food an' drink. But his valet ... well, as Mother would say, Oooh la la!*

Chapter 9

Thomas's horse galloped through the fields. In Ewan's courtyard, he shouted, "Ewan! I've brought Duncan!"

When Ewan saw the lathered horse and Thomas still astride supporting a man's body, he said, "My God, wha' happened?"

Duncan lifted his head. "Th' bloody thievin' Campbells stole my cattle, Ewan! Th' bastards shot me!"

Ewan asked Thomas, "Is he hurt bad?"

"It'll be a fight to keep his leg. Duncan heard th' cattle bawlin' an' decided to ha' a look. He dinna ha' a gun wi' him, but he went on anyway. There he stood in his nightshirt, wi' not even a rock to throw! Duncan yelled at 'em, and one of 'em took a shot at him. Th' ball went in th' fleshy part of his leg an' out th' other side. He went down, an' there he lay 'til Anne found him th' next mornin'. She sent Duncan for Janet to work on him. Ewan, they got all of his animals."

They carried Duncan into the broch and set him in a chair by the fireplace. Ewan called, "Janet, come quickly, lass."

Duncan tried to stand when Janet came into the room. He grimaced as he lifted himself out of the chair to greet her; then he fell, pulling the chair over as he went down. Janet motioned for Ewan and Thomas to carry him to the kitchen table, where she began removing his clothing. His leg was swollen from his ankle to his groin. The entry wound above his knee had yellow pus around the edges. A large wound covered with dried blood covered most of the back of his leg above the knee. As Janet examined his leg, she saw the lead ball did considerable damage to his upper leg. When she poured warm salted water into the wound on the front of his leg, the water did not drain out the other side. Duncan was sweating and shaking. "Ewan, pour whisky down his gullet, a bit at a time."

Ewan said, "Duncan, lad, I'm sparin' a dram or two o' my best whisky so yer leg can be worked on. Now, help me by swallowin' it."

Duncan's eyes were closed, but he opened his mouth. Ewan poured the liquid slowly so Duncan could swallow. "Duncan," Janet said, "Ye'll need to bite down on this bit of leather."

"Aw, Janet, I'd jest as soon ha' th' whisky," Duncan said, raising his head.

Janet smiled. "As ye wish. We'll keep spoonin', an' ye keep swallowin'. "Ewan, ye an' Thomas each hold down a shoulder, an' we'll get on wi' it."

She held Duncan's leg in one hand and a thin hot poker in the other. Taking a deep breath, she pushed the metal through the wound until she could see the tip coming out the other side. There was a gush of black blood, pus, and bits of flesh from the opened wound. "Duncan, th' worst is done." As she talked, she pulled the hot poker back through the injured leg.

Duncan cried out, "Let me up, let me up!" He sat up and started retching. Finally, he lay back, and Janet placed a wet cloth on his forehead. "It's not hurtin' as bad," he said. She placed a poultice of boiled willow bark and feverfew on the wounds, wrapped the leg in a clean linen cloth, and held out her arm. "We'll take ye to th' chair by th' fire an' prop yer leg up. I've a cup o' tea wi' a bit of whisky an' honey waitin'. Are ye feelin' any better?"

"Aye, lass," Duncan said. "It was tortuous at first, but now it's not painin' so much."

By morning Duncan was feeling better. Janet removed the wrapping on the leg and examined it. "Duncan, Thomas can take ye home. I've instructions for Anne to care for yer leg. Duncan, rest wi' that leg propped up, do ye hear me?"

"Aye, Janet, I will. I'd dip it in barn muck if yer said ter do so."

Several days later, Gordon arrived. "*Slainte*, Ewan."

"Good to see ye, Gordon. Tell me about th' crops. Did ye get th' lazy louts to help ye?"

"Aye, I did. All th' hay, oats, an' barley are in th' barn. Ewan, thanks for bitin' off a piece of my arse. I had it comin'."

"Ah, cousin, ye may need to do th' same for me sometime. How is yer lady wife?"

"She's better."

"Good! We're goin' to Fort William to see if any of our animals show up on th' block. Th' Campbells may try to sell 'em; there was no fodder tha' we could see. Thomas, saddle th' horses, an' we'll be on our way."

After the three cousins left, Janet and Cook began wrapping cheese and butter for the winter's larder. Janet filled a stone crock with cream; the cream would thicken and sour for bread dough, giving a good tart flavor to each crusty loaf.

Duncan, walking with a cane, met Ewan, Gordon, and Thomas at the gate. On the way to Fort William, the four cousins talked about horses and cattle. The Jacobite rebellion was in the back of everyone's mind, but no one brought it up. In Fort William, the barn was crowded with men from Glasgow buying beef animals to butcher and sell, people from the Isles buying sheep and goats, and wives purchasing live hens, geese, and ducks. After looking over the selection of animals and making sure none of theirs were on the sale block, the cousins went to the adjoining pub and ordered tankards of ale. As they doffed one after another, they talked about the raid.

Duncan spoke first. "Ewan, can we can get to th' Campbell's place, retrieve our animals, an' get out wi'out anyone gettin' shot?"

Ewan answered, "Thomas an' I got in an' out wi' our animals, an' no one took any notice."

"Ah, now lads, we must be very careful when dealing wi' th' Campbells," Gordon said softly. "Dinna think they wouldn't cut yer throat if they had a chance. They're murderers, th' entire lot o' 'em! Ye know th' story, aye?"

"Aye," Duncan said. "But, ye'll tell it anyway, so get on wi' it."

Gordon tipped his cup and started the tale. "Th' good MacDonald clan of Glencoe welcomed a Campbell army regiment into their home when th' Campbells told how they'd been turned away from quarters at Fort William because of bad weather an' no beds available. It was February, snow was flyin', an' th' Campbells enjoyed th' hospitality of th' MacDonalds for several days. They had meals fittin' for guests an' were entertained wi' th' pipes, songs, an' story tellin'. Then, on th' last night before th' Campbells were to leave, th' MacDonalds enjoyed their whisky an' ale all evenin', but th' Campbell's drank very little. Th' tipsy McDonalds went to their warm beds on tha' cold night."

Gordon mimicked a MacDonald man walking around the table, holding on to keep from falling. Several other men in the tavern took notice of Gordon's tale and began listening. One man whispered to his companion, "Tis th' tale of th' bloody Campbells. Listen well Willie MacDonald, an' be glad it was a'fore yer time."

"I ken it well; it's a tale tha' ever' MacDonald bairn hears a'fore they even walk."

"Shortly after midnight, a Campbell man slipped into th' MacDonald chief's bed chamber, slit th' man's throat, stripped his wife of her clothing, carried her down th' stairs, an' threw her out into th' night where a ragin' blizzard was blowin'. She was'na found 'til th' next day, lyin' a few steps from th' broch's front door. Th' poor naked lass died of th' terrible cold."

Every man in the pub shook his head in sorrow at the thought of a fine wife dying before her time. Gordon continued, "But she was a braw lass, an' before th' Campbells threw her out, she called out to warn th' rest of th' clan. Several of 'em heard her cries an' hid, but still, thirty-eight MacDonald men, women, an' bairns, were murdered."

Gordon pulled out his 'kerchief and wiped his eyes. "Lads, th' blizzard was still ragin' th' next day, an' many of th' clan who escaped froze to death. A goodly number o' 'em were mothers wi' sucklin' babes. To this day, folks say th' ghosts an' ghoulies o' Glencoe wait for a Campbell to get caught out alone. I'd be stayin' away from Glencoe, if my name were Campbell."

"Aw, a Cameron'll not be a'feered of a Campbell," Thomas said. "One night, I'll sneak over, take a look around, an' then we'll make our plans."

"Good lad," Duncan said. "Let's ante up coins for Thomas to warm Elly's bed for th' night."

Thomas grinned. "Aye, tis somethin' to take my mind off th' Campbells!"

They handed him silver pennies and agreed to meet after Thomas looked things over. Several days later, after a late-night trip, Thomas described the layout of the Campbell broch, barns, stables, fields, and pens. "Ewan, if there's any watch at all, it'd be from th' barn where they can see th' sheep an' cattle pens. Th' sheepfold is by th' barn under a big tree, an' behind th' barn is four pens of cattle."

"Two nights from tonight, th' moon'll not come up," Ewan said. "That'll be th' night we go. Th' Campbells will look for us on a full moon night, but on a dark night, they'll drink an' fall in their beds. If there's a watchman, he'll be soused along wi' 'em."

That night, Ewan and Janet talked about Gordon and Elizabeth. "Janet, I want to see if there's enough food in the larder for Elizabeth an' th' bairns."

"I'll go wi' ye. I'm worried too."

"Good, lass, I'll saddle th' horses, an wake ye at dawn; we'll need a bite of food along wi' us." Janet woke before Ewan, dressed, and went to the storeroom to select a piece of soft blue woolen material. She wrapped the fabric in parchment paper and placed it together with cheese, bread, apples, and a flask of wine in her knapsack. She selected rose hips and herbs and tied them in a small cloth bag. In the larder, she gathered dried beef, potatoes, onions, carrots, and filled a lidded flask with thick cream. She was waiting when Ewan came down the stairs. She chided, "Shall I saddle th' horses as well, Milord?" He grinned and gave her a slap on the backside.

When they reached Gordon's broch, Janet found Elizabeth lying in bed, awake and pale as the linen sheet she rested on. Janet took her hand. "Elizabeth, I've brought some things to help ye get ready for th' birth of your bairn."

Elizabeth said, "Oh Janet, I'm fearful for th' babe. Several fortnights ago, I thought labor was comin', but it did'na."

Janet placed her hand on Elizabeth's belly and felt the child move. "Th' babe is hungry! Ye must eat to feed him! Is Sarah still here?"

Elizabeth answered, "Nay, she's home. Gordon brought Bridy MacMartin in from th' village to help."

Janet found Mrs. MacMartin in the kitchen preparing food for the morning meal. "Are ye called Bridy?"

"Aye, I am," she answered.

"Bridy, pay attention while I prepare milady's meal so ye can do th' same when I'm not here." First, Janet dropped several pieces of dried beef into boiling water. Then, in another pot of hot water, she added oats with a bit of salt and stirred in honey. She spooned the thick mixture into a wooden bowl and poured cream from her flask over the top. She poured beef broth into a cup and placed it all on a serving tray. She motioned for Bridy to follow her up the stairs to Elizabeth's room.

"Elizabeth, Bridy'll be fixin' yer meals. I want yer to eat wha' she brings to ye. Ye'll feel better, an' it's good for yer babe."

While Elizabeth ate, Janet and Bridy went downstairs. "Milady, there's no cream in th' cold room. Where'll I find th' dried beef yer used?"

"I brought it wi' me, Bridy. We'll see wha' ye need, an' I'll make certain ye get it." A quick inspection of the larder was as expected: there were a few potatoes and two rabbits. The oats barrel was nearly empty. Half a wheel of cheese and a wooden bowl of butter sat on the shelf. Angry, Janet bit her tongue as she saw Elizabeth slowly coming down the stairs. "I'm feelin' better, Janet."

"Good, go sit by th' fire, dear. I'll bring a cup of rose hip tea for ye."

"Do ye ha' a good midwife in th' village to help ye wi' th' birthin'?"

Elizabeth thought for a minute and said, "Since ol' Annie passed on, there isn't any I know of."

"Then I'll be here, so dinna worry," Janet said. "When ye feel yer first pain, or th' waters break, send for me. I've brought ye a gift for th' new babe."

Janet handed Elizabeth the packet with fabric for a blanket. "Thank ye, Janet. It's most appreciated." Uneasy about the empty larder, Janet wondered why Gordon was failing to see to the needs of his family. There must be a reason; it could not be good.

Ewan and Gordon stood outside in the courtyard. "Ewan," Gordon said, "Yer plan to go to the Campbells in th' dark of th' night is a good one."

"Gordon, I'll warn ye ahead of time, wi' Duncan being shot on his own lands, we'd best be prepared!"

Both men turned when they heard Janet speaking loudly to Elizabeth. "Now, get yer rest, an' ask Gordon to do th' heavy things. He'll not mind helpin', aye, Gordon?"

Gordon looked at his boots and muttered to himself. He was to follow them to Glen Lochy after his animals were fed and the children were in bed. On the way home, Janet said, "I'm very angry wi' Gordon. Th' larder is bare! Why is he neglectin' his wife an' bairns? If he's drinkin' or whorin', then he'll answer to me for it! I'll not ha' a Cameron cousin runnin' 'round wi' his breeks down to his ankles while his family's starvin'. Ewan, wha' do ye know about this?"

"Simmer down, lass. Gordon's in trouble wi' me over th' same thin'. I've chewed his arse up one side an' down th' other. We're all goin' to help th' family, an' tha's th' way it is."

Ewan saw the set to Janet's mouth and the glare in her eyes. He could remember one other time when she had that look, and he truly hoped this was not going to be a repeat.

Chapter 10

Ewan, Thomas, Duncan, and Gordon sat at the kitchen table. Janet placed tankards of ale and a platter of cheese, bread, and apple tart on the table. "I'll send oatcakes an' ale wi' ye tonight. It's cold, an' there's no tellin' how long ye'll be gone."

"Janet, wha' we really need is whisky to keep our spirits up," Ewan said.

"I think not, husband. It's my opinion tha' when one drinks whisky, his spirits may go up, but his common sense goes down." Then she smiled and said, "No whisky 'til th' deed is done."

She turned to Gordon and said, "When I'm called to help birth yer bairn, if I dinna see food in th' larder an' meat hangin' in th' cold room, ye'd better be sayin' yer prayers. I'm not havin' ye sittin' around on yer bollocks doin' nothin'! Do ye understand, sir?"

Gordon pulled his cap out of his pocket and wadded it into a ball. "It's my own doin', an' ... well, I'm a sorry lot."

Janet crossed her arms across her chest. "Gordon! Yer lazy!"

"Aye, I am."

Janet shrugged and pointed her finger at him. "I'll send eggs, vegetables, an' apples wi' ye, an' yer cousins will bring meat. Tha's all I care to say to ye for now, Gordon Cameron!"

Ewan, Thomas, and Duncan stared at the two, one looking at the floor, and the other standing with arms folded, tapping one foot. "Janet, I gi' my word, I'll do better."

"Good! I'll be holdin' ye to it!"

As Ewan said, it was a dark night. When cold began creeping into the room, Thomas put more logs on the fire. They listened to the wind whistling around the broch. Bran roused himself from his place in front of the fire and made his nightly rounds, going from room to room, sniffing as he went.

Janet noticed Duncan limping when he walked. "Does it pain ye, Duncan?" Janet asked.

"Aye, lass, it does."

"Take off yer breeks, an' I'll ha' a look."

"Nay, lass, I ha' nothin' on underneath."

"Duncan Cameron, get yerself in th' kitchen an' roll them breeks down 'round yer ankles! I'll be seeing not one thin' I ha' not seen before, an' yers is no different, I'll wager." Janet was pleased to see the leg was healing well.

At midnight, the four men were ready to leave; Bran trotted alongside Ewan's horse. Janet watched until they were no longer in sight. She found herself thinking of the night when Duny was born. As always, she wondered why there had been no more bairns; it seemed likely there would be no more. Elizabeth Cameron had four children and was expecting her fifth. Janet thought that in his wisdom, God knew what was best. She placed more wood on the grate, wrapped herself in a warm robe, and settled down to wait.

A fortnight before, Meghan and her new husband, John McIntyre, had come to visit. Meghan explained how their father was in considerable pain from two broken ribs on his right side and a cracked right knee after a fall from a horse he was breaking to the saddle. She smiled as she told about their mother splinting his leg and forbidding him to climb the stairs.

Janet said, "Ah, he'll do as mother says, he's learned it's for his own good. Now, why did ye not send word th' ye were marryin'? We'd ha' made th' trip."

Megan hugged Janet. "It all happened so quickly that only Mother, Father, Jamie, and Duny were there—and the priest, of course."

"Hmmm," Janet wondered out loud. "Is there somethin' ye'll be telling' me?"

Meghan put her hand on her sister's arm. "Not what you're thinking! Your marriage to Ewan was the same. John needed good horses, and Father had them. He didn't plan on meeting me or a marriage!"

"Megan, ye look just like our mother; ye ha' her colorin', an' ye sound very English, just as she does." Meghan smiled, pleased at the compliment.

The next day, John and Ewan talked. "Ewan, I'll bring Duny home for ye."

"Nay, John, th' way things are in th' Hielands, Duny had best stay wi' James an' Abby."

"Aye," said John, "I know of wha' yer speakin'. Th' MacIntyre clan ha' promised support to th' Bonny Prince. I've only a few coins to do plantin' next spring, an' it's nay enough. I dinna want to fight, but ... there's no choice."

"Aye, I feel th' same an' so does Thomas. I'm nay convinced we'll win."

Unable to sit still, Janet decided to milk the cow, who waited patiently while she placed the wooden bucket, pulled up the milking stool, and started milking. The cow turned her head to look wonderingly at Janet, who usually had a gentle touch. "There, there, my bonny." She patted the cow's side. "I should'na milk when I'm worried."

She found four eggs to boil and add to the stone crock with vinegar and salt. The brine preserved the eggs; with bread and cheese they were a good supper on a cold winter's night. It took all spring, summer, and fall to prepare for winter. Butter, cheese, taper sticks, soap, and medicines had to be in the larder in sufficient quantity to last through the long winters until the next spring's plants and animals were again producing.

"Poor Elizabeth. With four bairns and a fifth on the way she barely could keep up with things, an' she had no help from Gordon!' Janet's anger grew as she considered what Gordon should be doing instead of feeling sorry for himself. Then, she heard the muffled sounds of men calling and the bawling of cattle. Gordon, Thomas, and Duncan were on horseback, driving the cattle and a flock of sheep, with Bran moving back and forth to keep the flock together. Behind the sheep, Ewan rode with two lambs in his arms.

After the animals were penned, the men sat down at the kitchen table, tired, hungry, and smelling of cow dung, sweat, river water, and ale.

"Who'd ha' thought th' Campbells'd sleep through it?" Ewan said with his mouth full.

After eating, they went into the great room and pulled chairs up to the fire. Ewan petted Bran and said, "Good dog, Bran, good dog." Bran took the beef bone Janet offered him and carried it to his place by the hearth. "Bran knew wha' to do when th' time came. He brought th' sheep through th' river, up th' banks, an' kept the flock together. He's a bonnie fine dog, he is."

Ewan sat back and brought out his pipe. Outside a heavy rain pelted down, and the wind found thin spots in the chinking around the windows. "Lads, there's a storm comin' in. If we'd waited 'til tonight, we'd not ha' 'em home."

Janet said, "Pray tell, Ewan, wha' happened?"

Ewan grinned and said, "Nay, wife, ye promised us whisky when we got back! Fetch th' whisky. Then we'll tell th' tale."

Janet went to the cellar and brought up two bottles of whisky. Pouring a cup of the amber liquid for each man and one for herself, she waited.

"We crossed th' river, an' all was quiet. Thomas held th' horses while we walked to th' first pen an' began layin' a trail of hay to th' outside o' th' pen an' down th' hill to th' river. Th' animals started out th' gate, but we'd put down too much hay! They wanted to stop an' eat while we were tryin' to get 'em out of th' pens."

Gordon continued the tale. "We led 'em to th' river, an' th' beasties came right along. Most were on th' other side a'fore we started movin' th' sheep."

As Janet poured more whisky into everyone's cups, Ewan smiled and said, "Bran did'na bark even once. I pointed to th' sheep, an' he knew wha' needed to be done. Two lambkins were still in th' pen, I picked 'em up, an' Bran kept th' sheep movin' to th' river. We herded th' whole lot of 'em out of th' water on th' other side. Damned if it didn't work just th' way we'd hoped!"

"Gordon's lost two sheep, three lambs, an' part of his cattle herd, but then, he thought all were lost." Duncan scratched his head. "We got most of my cows an' one bull. They're all thin from lack of forage. It's best to not move 'em again 'til they've settled down."

Ewan looked out a window, "Wi' th' rain, there'll be no sign of our comin' and goin."

The four cousins napped: Thomas in his chair, Duncan with his leg propped up on a footstool, and Gordon and Ewan on a rug in front of the fire. "Janet, I need to start home around noon," Gordon said.

She looked at him. "I've food for ye to take to yer family. Gordon, it's not for yer tha' I'm sendin' it. As far as I care, ye could do without! It's for Elizabeth an' th' bairns. They're my kin, an' I'll not be havin' 'em go hungry!"

Gordon heard the impatience in her voice. "Janet, we've th' cattle now, an' I'll butcher one o' 'em."

Janet nodded. "See tha' ye do." The sky darkened; snow and ice mixed with rain began falling. Janet placed wood on the fire, sat down in her chair, picked up her mending, and said a prayer of thankfulness. Soon she too was asleep.

At noon, she woke Gordon. He gave her a hug when she handed him the basket of food. "Gordon, I'm expectin' yer to keep yer word on stockin' yer larder. Dinna put it aside to sit an' ponder on!"

"Ye ha' my word on it, Janet."

"Call for me when Elizabeth's labor starts. And, Gordon, shore up. Ye've got family to provide for."

As she watched, Gordon and his horse disappeared in snow blowing across the moors. After Gordon left, they began sorting out the animals. Ewan grinned. "The Campbell's won't get out in this weather. They'll stay to bed 'til spring!"

Duncan said, "If we'd waited one more day, we'd not ha' 'em."

The next morning Gordon returned with a wagon full of hay to replace what his animals had eaten. He handed Janet several bottles of cherry brandy.

"Well, Gordon, how be things?"

Gordon responded, "Very well, very well." He handed her the bottles. "Elizabeth made th' brandy last year. She mixes a bit in her cakes and gives th' bairns a spoonful when they're fussin'.'"

"Well, thank ye, thank ye very much."

Duncan arrived soon after Gordon. "Janet, Anne made this for ye." He handed her a tapestry rolled and tied with ribbon. "She did the needlework for takin' care o' my leg. We'll always be grateful."

Janet loosened the ribbon, unrolled the fabric, and saw a beautiful scene that she immediately recognized: Glen Lochy, complete with rock wall, gate, and rosebushes in bloom. "Oh! Duncan, it's beautiful!" She hung the cloth over the fireplace and then stood back to admire it. Janet sighed as she admired the beauty of the gift. It would be a family heirloom.

Chapter 11

As Christ's Mass approached, Janet planned a celebration. After chapel services, there would be a meal and an evening of festivities. Ewan always gave a silver coin to each head of household, and there would be a basket of food for every family. She counted twelve families and an additional ten for widows and single men, including the stable keepers, watchmen, and Father Benjamin. There was a knock at the kitchen door. "Aye?" she called out.

A man's voice said, "I've a message for Lady Cameron."

Janet opened the door. "I'm Lady Cameron."

"Milady, th' Laird is askin' tha' ye come for Her Ladyship."

"Aye, go on ahead. I'll not be far behind."

"Thomas," Janet said as she gathered things she needed, "Please bring in pine boughs for th' doors and windows, an' ye'll need to help Cook finish th' baskets."

It was afternoon when Ewan and Janet rode into Gordon's courtyard. Janet hurried up the stairs, where she found Gordon sitting by the bedside, holding his wife's hand. He motioned for Janet to step outside the room. Whispering, he said, "Elizabeth delivered th' babe an hour ago. Th' poor wee lassie never drew a breath."

Tears ran down his face. "Elizabeth is bleedin'. I've done all I know to do. Thank God yer here! I canna bear losin' our bairn an' Elizabeth too."

"Hand me my bag." Janet examined Elizabeth, noting that her breathing was slow and shallow. She looked up when Ewan came into the room. "Ewan, bring a pan of hot water, clean cloths, an' a bottle of whisky. Quickly now, dinna dawdle."

She pulled back the blankets and drew in her breath at the sight of blood pooling beneath Elizabeth's hips. Carefully raising Elizabeth's legs, Janet saw the torn opening to the birthing canal with blood pouring from the tear. She shouted, "Ewan, get yerself up here wi' th' water, salt cellar, an' whisky. Gordon, fetch Elizabeth's sewin' box, now!"

Ewan brought a pitcher of water, salt, cloths, and whisky. Janet lifted Elizabeth's hips, placed a clean pad beneath her, and began speaking softly. "Elizabeth, there'll be more pain, but it won't last long. Gordon—" Janet bumped into him when she reached for the water. "Move out of my way, cut a piece of thread, an' bring it to me wi' a needle!"

She poured whisky in a cup and held it out to Elizabeth. "Drink this, an' then I'll mend th' damage done when th' babe was born."

Janet pulled a chair closer and motioned for Gordon to sit. "Ewan, go downstairs an' see if wood needs to be put on th' fires— an' bring me a cup of tea."

As he sat down, Gordon remembered that he had a threaded needle in his hand and handed it to Janet. She drenched the torn flesh with warm salt water and began stitching. There was so much blood that it was difficult to hold the needle, but the flow slowed as she sutured the torn flesh. She completed the repairs with only a few drops seeping through the stitches. Before the task was finished, Gordon left the room, tears running down his face. He found Ewan in the kitchen filling the teapot with water.

"My God! I must tell her tha' our babe dinna live."

"Gordon, ye ha' four fine lads. Remind her of 'em."

Janet sighed with relief when she examined Elizabeth; the bleeding had stopped. "We'll get ye in a clean gown."

Elizabeth opened her eyes. "My babe?"

"Elizabeth, we'll talk in a while."

Elizabeth said no more while Janet changed her gown and bedding. Elizabeth's breasts were dripping milk; Janet wished she knew how to stop the flow. In the hall outside the room, she spoke with Gordon. "Tell her th' babe did'na live an' reassure her tha' her lads are well. She'll be sad, but when she's able to care for her bairns she'll feel better. I'll speak wi' her about what she can do to keep another babe from happenin'. Ye can still be a husband to her, an' she can be a wife to you."

Gordon sat on the edge of the bed and took his wife's hands in his. "Elizabeth, our babe was so tiny an' beautiful, but she did'na live. She must be named; wha' name would you choose?"

"I must hold her just once, Gordon. I must." Softly crying, Elizabeth said, "Bring her to me so I can know the name that belongs to her."

"Aye, Elizabeth, I'll be back." The little body, dressed in a white christening gown, was wrapped in the blue woolen blanket that Janet gave Elizabeth. Gordon placed the babe in Elizabeth's arms and then pulled the blanket back so she could see the tiny, perfect face. "Oh, she's so beautiful. Did she not breathe?"

"Nay, she didn't, Elizabeth."

"Oh, th' darlin' babe looks as if she's asleep," Elizabeth said. "Her hair is th' color of a golden rose. It'll be her name, Rose."

"Aye, it fits her." He began thinking about preparing a wooden box and cross to be marked with the name Elizabeth had chosen and considering the words that might be said for the little one who could not live.

Janet was concerned about Elizabeth. The stitched area had to be kept clean. She instructed Bridy and her helper, Lucy, to warm fresh water daily, add salt, and dip a clean cloth into the water to wash between Elizabeth's legs. Later, the stitches would need to be removed, not too soon and not too late. Janet walked to the horse barn, sat on a wooden bench, and cried until she could cry no more. This is where Ewan found her. "Janet, are ye ill, lass? Oh, my dearest!"

Ewan picked her up and sat down on the bench, cradling her in his lap. As he murmured in a gentle voice, she said, "Oh, Ewan, th' stitchin' I did to stop th' bleedin'—I've never done it before. Th' bleedin' stopped, but was it th' best thin' to do? I pray Elizabeth'll not sicken from it."

Ewan spoke to her softly in Gaelic. *"Tha gaol agam ort."* (I love ye, lassie.) He smoothed her hair with one hand and pulled her head down to nestle in the crook of his neck. "Now, now, there's no more ye can do. I'd nay like to be in Gordon's place. He has to bury his bairn an' somehow comfort his wife. He's barely up an' on foot himself."

Janet stood and shook the hay from her skirt. "I canna say about Gordon, but a'fore long, Elizabeth'll be up an' busy wi' her brood. Young Daniel's a good laddie. He'll be laird one day, an' a fine one, I'm certain."

"Janet, lass, ha' ye ever known of a man whose spirit has a sickness—" Ewan paused to choose his words—"like a body can?"

"Hmmm," Janet said. "Canna say tha' I ha', but then, I suppose it could happen."

"I've cursed Gordon up one side an' down th' other, but he's quit carin'. He's not interested in th' lasses, an' he's never been lazy, but he's not himself! When I saw his grain crop lyin' on th' ground, molderin', I knew somethin' was wrong. Yer' harpin' on him has done as much good as anythin'."

Janet managed a small smile. "That's my way, Ewan. Ye'll be knowin' yerself."

"Aye, it is, lass."

Bridy placed a kettle of pea soup on the table. She brought out wooden bowls, spoons, fresh bread, butter, and wine. "Thank ye, Bridy. This is a good supper," Janet said. "After we eat, we'll take a look at th' larder an' see wha' we need."

She was surprised to find a brace of pheasant, a box of salted fish, and venison in the cold room. "Good! He's kept his promise!"

Bridy pointed to a shelf holding wheels of cheese and blocks of butter. "Milady, we're all workin' to get caught up. Th' cattle'll not freshen 'til spring, an' there's no garden. But some o' us from th' village are sharin' wha' we ha' wi' th' laird an' his family."

"Good!" Janet exclaimed. "Yer laird would share if there was a need."

"Aye, tha' he would, Milady, an' has."

Bridy and her helper, Lucy, waited for Janet upstairs. She instructed them in keeping Elizabeth and the bedding clean. "Ye'll need to take out th' stitches in four or five days. It'll be painful, but nothin' like she's already suffered. There's rose berries downstairs; pour hot water over a spoon full of th' berries an' let it steep for a while. Add a spoon of honey an' whisky an' gi' it to her twice a day. Ye both ha' birthed bairns, an' ye know how it is to get back on yer feet after th' birthin'."

"Aye, we'll take good care of Milady. She's been good to help us too."

The next morning Rose was laid to rest in the Cameron cemetery in the village kirkyard. A wooden marker reading "Rose Cameron, b. 23 Dec 1745, d. 23 Dec 1745, One of God's Angels" was at the head of the tiny grave.

Chapter 12

They traveled slowly through ice and snow. Janet listened while Ewan spoke of how life in the Highlands had changed since his father's time. She asked why the clans fought and stole animals from one another. "When th' King forbid us to sell our wool, we lost our way of makin' a livin'. England can buy wool from us and sell it at a high profit, but we'd nay make profit enough to pay back our cost. I brought in Hieland Cattle to breed an' sell, but I still struggle to pay the Lochiel his rent an' taxes. Stealin' has become a way of life for many o' th' clans. Most of us—"Janet interrupted. "Ewan, why do ye allow th' clan chief to ha' th' last word on wha' you do or dinna do?"

"Janet, I support th' chief an' th' clan, as I know tha' if I died tomorrow, ye an' Duny will be taken care of. Th' men swear an oath of guardianship for a man's widow an' his bairns."

Janet understood Ewan's loyalty to the clan was more about her and Duny than about the clan chieftain. When they reached home, Thomas was waiting for them. Janet told him of the stillborn, and he shook his head. "Th' Lochiel's messenger just left. We're to meet at Glenfinnan two days after Christ's Mass for a gatherin' of th' clans. Yer news is no better than mine."

As they warmed in front of the fire, a thought occurred to Ewan. "Janet, yer wantin' to know more about medicines an' treatin' sickness? On th' way to Glenfinnan we'll stop at Auntie Mary's cottage at Stronabaw Glen, an' ye can stay a couple of days wi' her. Auntie's taken care of th' Camerons, MacDonalds, an' their lot for many a year. Her da was physician for one of th' kings, an' her mother was a healer. Auntie Mary learned wha' she knows from both of 'em."

"Would she mind havin' me there?"

"I think she'd be pleased to ha' yer company," Ewan replied.

Ewan considered the clan gathering and dreaded it. He knew he did not want to fight. He did not believe a battle for the throne could be won. He did not believe in the Catholic Stuart enough to fight for him, but if Donald Cameron ordered it, he'd have to comply.

The next morning dawned with a hard wind blowing snow into deep drifts. Janet smiled as she went downstairs; a fresh scent of fir boughs freshened the great room, and fires burned in both of the fireplaces. She made a cup of tea, and her spirits lifted as she thought of the Christ's Mass celebration. Snoring, Thomas sat by the fire. Touching his shoulder, she said, "Thomas, are ye well?"

He opened his eyes. "Aye, I was just takin' a wee nap after feedin' th' animals."

"Thank ye for gatherin' in th' boughs."

"Cook filled th' baskets, an' I added a bag of sweets to each one."

Janet smiled. "I do so love to see th' bairns an' their families enjoying themselves! I'm grateful we can all be together an' hope we always will."

The day went by quickly. By the middle of the afternoon, the light faded to gray and then turned dark. Families began gathering in the village chapel, where candlelight made the chilled air feel a little warmer. Splendid in his white robe with gold satin trim, Father Benjamin began the evening service. He spoke of the Heavenly Father's gift to all people: his beloved son, Jesus. After the service, everyone gathered at the Cameron broch admiring the glowing candles and fir boughs tied with red yarn. After all were seated, the food was served. There was roasted venison, baked trout with lemony sorrel, and stewed rabbit with vegetables. Two platters held salty and sweet ham and a brace of baked pheasant. Wheels of cheese, bread, butter, fruit preserves, minced meat pies, and apple tarts flavored with cinnamon were at both the high and low boards. Wine was served at the high board where Ewan, Janet, Thomas, the priest, the village tacksman, and his family sat beside a piper who traveled through the countryside. Ale was served to the villagers, and everyone looked forward to the evening's entertainment.

After the meal, the head of each household brought his family to the high board, where they acknowledged Ewan, Janet, and Thomas. Ewan expressed his appreciation to each man for the year's service by giving him one day of the week to hunt and fish on Cameron lands. Thomas handed out the baskets, and the evening's entertainment began. The bard, Robbie MacMartin, tuned his harp and brought out his wooden flutes. When he plucked single string on the harp, the room grew silent. Speaking in Gaelic, he sang while strumming the harp strings, "*Failte, Ceud mile failte, Feasgar mat. Slainte mhor agad!*" (Welcome, good evening and good health to all!) Then, plucking the strings, he began to sing. He sang about the Little People of Scotland who did not have weapons to protect themselves, so they moved underground to live in caves deep inside the hills and glens. The bard told how they came out at night to finish the day's work after the farmers and their wives went to bed. The bard looked at his audience and said, "For payment for their good deeds, th' little folk were partial to cream an' honey wi' a good servin' o' whisky."

Then the song began again with the words sung loud and clear, "Ohhh, on a cold winter's night, a dram o' whisky was th' cost, on a cold winter's night, a dram ... o' whisky ... was th' cost. Now tha' my song is finished, Ohhh, a dram o' whisky is my cost, a dram of whisky is my pay." Soon, the bard had cups of whisky sitting in front of him. Everyone watched as he downed one after the other. His fondness for spirits was well known, and some said he could sing better after havin' a few drams. Others said the singing did not get better, but after everyone else had several drams, he sounded better.

Robbie smiled at his audience and began the next story. "Once upon a time, there was a king who was turned into a warty frog by th' spell of a wicked witch. Wi' a kiss from a beautiful maiden, he turned back into royalty." The bard sang, "So, lads an' lassies, next time yer see an ugly frog, blow th' wee creature a kiss, for th' frog may be yer next king, or mayhap, th' king may be yer next frog. Hooch, yer frog may be yer king an' sit upon th' throne in England!" Everyone laughed and raised their cups in a toast to Robbie.

He blew several notes on his flute and began a playing a well-known tune. The beat and pace increased, with the listeners tapping their feet and clapping their hands. After a lengthy round of applause, the piper began playing. Dancing began with the pipes, fiddle, and flute playing jigs and reels. Couples held hands and formed a circle, with each one taking turns meeting their partner in the middle. After the dance was completed and everyone was seated, the room grew quiet. All eyes went to Ewan, dressed in full Highland attire, as he walked to the far wall where two pairs of swords hung crossed upon each other. He carefully lifted the swords from their place. Walking to the center of the room, he placed them crossed on the floor as he prepared for the traditional Scottish sword dance, one of ritual and battle skills. He bowed to the onlookers and then called to the piper. "Piper, play th' ancient call to arms!"

The piper played the first notes of "The Gillie Callum" as Ewan lifted his arms over his head. Then, with his forefinger touching his thumb on each hand and the rest of his fingers extended out, he began by slowly leaping between the crossed blades, never looking down. As one foot hit the floor, the other was lifted high, moving into the next space between the swords. He passed between the blades, keeping his body straight, and then placed one hand on his waist, the other hand still in the stag horn form. Thomas walked to the center of the room, bowed to all, and entered the dance. The music increased in tempo as the two men twirled and jumped over the blades lying on the floor. It was a defiant dance, one of no accidental moves or misplaced feet. The swords were sharp, and both Ewan and Thomas knew that each had to follow the other's movements as well as his own. Just as on the battlefield, two could not occupy the same space and survive. Should a sword be touched, it was a bad omen; the man could expect to be wounded in an upcoming battle. If a sword was hit more than once, it meant that the battle would be lost. Finally, Ewan jumped from the circle, and Thomas did the same. Neither one had touched the blades. Both bowed to applause and toasts to their good health.

At midnight they all went outside. Father Benjamin asked for God's blessings and gave thanks for the blessed babe Jesus. He prayed for the people of Scotland to have peace and prosperity in the New Year. After saying good-byes, each family made their way home.

Chapter 13

Two days later, at dawn, Ewan, Janet, and Thomas left Glen Lochy well protected by four men-at-arms. They traveled through snow and ice covered valleys and hills. After dark, they reached Stronabaw Glen. Ewan knocked on the cottage door and called out, "Auntie Mary, it's Ewan an' Thomas Cameron. Are we welcome here?"

A door opened, and a small round face peered up at them. "Ewan Cameron! Why ha' ye not been here a'fore now? I helped birth ye, an' this is th' thanks I get! Look at ye, Thomas. I'm thinkin' your mam must ha' dropped ye on yer heid; yer standin' there lookin' like a dunce. Speak up, lad! Say somethin' for yerself."

Seeing Janet, the face broke into a smile. "Well, bless my soul! Ewan, is this yer lady wife?" Mary looked Janet up and down. "Oh, my! She's a darlin' lass. Now, th' three of ye come in an' sit. Dinna stand or ye'll surely knock a hole in me good thatched roof, as tall as ye all be."

Mary reached for Janet's hand and led her to a cushioned chair by the fire, "Sit yerself down, my dear, an' I'll get ye a cup o' tea. Ha' ye ha' supper? Then I'll set th' table."

The two brothers sat on a couch that looked as if it could collapse any time. Mary placed what might have been a tea set for fairies on the table and poured tea for the three visitors. "Drink yer tea, th' three o' ye, an' I'll get a bite o' supper." They sat by the crackling fire and drank the spicy tea. Ewan and Thomas closed their eyes.

Fighting sleep, Janet went into the kitchen, where Auntie Mary stirred peas porridge in a kettle hanging from an iron hook over the kitchen fire. "Mary, I'd help, but I'm so sleepy. Th' tea was sweet, an' I did'na know I was tired until I drank it."

Mary patted Jane's arm. "Well then, lassie, I may ha' put a bit too much St. John's Wort in. But I thought ye all needed a wee bit of rest a'fore ye continue on."

"Ah, Ewan an' Thomas will be goin' on after they've eaten, but ... if ye'll ha' me, I'd like to stay wi' ye 'til' they return."

"Aye, I'll be glad for yer company. It's lonely here on th' moor, wi' only th' sheep an' mouser cat to keep me company." Mary placed wooden bowls, spoons, a block of cheese, and a plate of warm bannock buns on the table.

"Mary!" Janet exclaimed, "Bannock buns! Ye dinna know we'd be here."

"Ah, well, I'm used to bein' called out anytime o' th' day or night, an' I always ha' food set back so I won't be troublin' th' lady of th' house for summat to eat while I'm sittin' up wi' a patient. Buns an' a dab o' butter can be a meal, if need be."

Janet smiled and said, "Aye, I've left home to help wi' a birthin' an' did'na ha' time to eat. No one thought to offer me a bite, so I left home hungry an' returned hungry." Janet continued, "Mary, I'm here to ask for yer help. I know ways to wrap a broken bone an' treat cuts an' such, but it's not enough. Ewan's cousin's wife, Elizabeth, birthed a stillborn an' nearly died afterward."

Concerned, Mary spoke. "Ye say Elizabeth was th' mother? Which one of th' Cameron cousins did she wed? Let's see now, besides Ewan an' Thomas there's Duncan an' Gordon; I delivered 'em all."

"It's Gordon. They ha' four healthy bairns, but havin' one every year an' her being poorly most of th' time, it was no surprise when the babe was stillborn." Janet waited for Mary to speak.

"Lass, sometimes a babe will be born tha's not meant to live. Ye know ye can't get upset when somethin' such as this happens. Folks look to yer for strength, an' if yer bawlin', how're ye goin' to help 'em?"

"Well." Janet searched for an answer. "It was because of Elizabeth bein' kin tha' I felt sad. Will ye tell me how to help people, please?"

"Of course, lass. I'll teach ye wha' I've learned from my father, who was a physician in th' king's court, an' my mother, who gathered herbs an' made her own salves, potions, an' ointments. There's one drawback to learnin' this time of year: it's nay th' growin' season. Lass, wha' are ye called?"

"Janet. I'm from Perthshire, an' my father breeds an' sells horses. I met an' married Ewan when he came to buy horses." Janet smiled as she said, "He was, an' still is, a handsome fellow."

"Aye, all of th' Cameron lads are handsome fellows, my dear, even wi' their crooked noses, they are!"

"We ha' a son, Dunsmuir, who's stayin' wi' my family while my father's broken leg mends."

"How old is th' laddie?"

"He's fourteen. We wish for another bairn or two. If it's God's will, it needs to happen a'fore I'm past bein' able to bear children."

Mary peered into Janet's eyes. "I can help ye. There's things ye can do tha' will help ye get wi' child an' other things tha' will help one who is wi' child an' did'na want to be. Did Ewan tell ye his family an' my family were th' dearest of friends? There's a fine table in th' great room in yer broch." Mary paused to look at Janet.

"Aye! Mary, it's th' most beautiful piece of furniture there."

"I'm pleased tha' ye think so," Mary said. "Father gave it to Ewan's parents. When my mother died, Da built this cottage. There was no room for th' table, an' he knew it would be of use in th' Cameron broch."

Janet sighed. "Mary, ye may understand wha' I'm speakin' about. It's different in th' lowlands. I did'na understand 'til I married Ewan tha' his clan chieftain, Donald Cameron, owns him, his dirk, sword, pistol, an' th' very broch we live in."

Janet sipped her tea and spoke more to herself than to Mary. "But that's as it is, an' I must accept it." She looked at Mary. "Ewan knows how I feel about him followin' th' clan chief into battle." Janet sighed.

Mary nodded her head as she stirred the porridge. "I dinna agree wi' loyalty to a clan. I think th' clans will come to an end a'fore long. Th' English king dinna take well to 'em."

"Come along, lads! Yer supper is ready. Ye say they'll be leavin' afterward? It'll be a cold ride for 'em."

"Aye, they're to be in Glenfinnan by midnight." Janet called out, "There's hot porridge waitin'."

Ewan was the first to head for the kitchen. "Auntie, where's th' wash pail? Ye always pinched my ear if I did'na wash my hands a'fore supper."

"Aye, Ewan, th' water pail's here, an' soap too. Thomas, get yerself in here an' tuck yer shirt in yer breeks. Wash yer hands an' tidy yerself up. I'll not be havin' great oafs such as yerselves makin' sorry company for this grand lady who accompanied ye."

Janet smiled when both Ewan and Thomas moved quickly to the water pail, Thomas stuffing his shirt in his breeks. The two men sat at the table as Mary crumbled oat cakes into bowls before pouring in the pea soup. They looked like two boys minding their manners at the table, knowing if they didn't the consequences would be boxed ears. Janet and Mary ate their soup sitting by the fire. After they finished, Mary brought out a fragrant cake wrapped in greased paper. It smelled wonderfully spicy. "Th' laird gifted this to me, an' I wondered wha' I'd do wi' it. We'll ha' some, an' I'll pack several slices in yer knapsacks."

Mary looked through the window. "Lads, must ye leave

tonight? Th' snow's deep an' still fallin'. Ye could be here by th' fire, warmin' up wi' a wee dram."

Ewan stood. Then, realizing his head was nearly touching the ceiling rafters, he sat down again. "Auntie, th' Lochiel called us, an' we must go." Taking her hand in his, he said, "Donald is goin' to lead us to fight for Charles Edward Stuart, so Scotland can again ha' a Stuart king on th' throne."

"Ewan." Mary took his hand. "Could ye leave this be? I ha' a dreadful feelin' about it."

"Auntie, we've been fightin' th' Redcoats since th' clock started tickin'. It's time to settle it!"

"Lads, ye could go to th' new country across the sea. My cousin Patrick an' his wife, Martha, did. They sent me a letter sayin' there's more land than anyone can believe. They settled in Carolinashire, I believe. Would ye gi' it a thought, lads?"

Ewan shook his head. "Auntie, th' colonies ha' th' same king we do. Those who go to America can't get away from payin' taxes to th' crown. Mark my word, there'll be a battle when they grow weary of it!"

Ewan and Thomas wrapped their cloaks around their shoulders. "We'll put wood an' peat blocks outside th' door for ye."

Mary looked up at Ewan, who towered over her. "Auntie, yer just as beautiful as ye was when I was a lad." Bowing low, Ewan kissed her hand.

"Ah, get on wi' ye, laddie." Thomas opened the door and took a step back when wind and snow blew into the room. The fire flickered, and the room darkened. "Lads, must ye ..."

"Auntie, we must!" After the front door closed behind them, Mary cleared the table, sat down, and patted the chair beside her. "Yer from Perthshire. Where is it?"

"A long day's ride from Edinburgh. Th' land lies gently wi' hills an' rivers. It has meadows an' grasslands, an' th' weather is not as harsh as in th' Hielands."

"Mayhap I'll travel to tha' part of th' country some day. Let's bed down tonight an' start out fresh in th' morn." Mary opened the door to a small bed chamber off the kitchen. A table with a pitcher of water, a drying cloth, and a worn book of psalms sat in the corner. Janet washed her face, put on her gown, crawled into bed, and pulled a down-filled coverlet over her. Soon she was toasty warm and drifting off to sleep until she thought to look for a chamber pot. She found one tucked under the edge of the bed. "Dear God, keep 'em safe. Bless us all."

Early the next morning, she woke to the sound of pots and pans banging in the kitchen. "Janet, are ye awake?"

"Aye, I'm dressing now." She could see drifts of snow almost to the window ledge, and it was still snowing. "Mary, ye mentioned a cat an' sheep. Do they need to be fed?"

"Aye," said Mary. "After a bite, we'll feed 'em." They sat down to bowls of oat porridge, bannocks, jam, a pitcher of cream, and a pot of fragrant hot tea. The tiny kitchen was warm and cozy.

Janet nodded. "Ye managed th' brothers well last night. Here ye are, a tiny little lass tellin' 'em to get their hands washed an' Thomas to tuck his shirt in. Ye ha' spirit, Mary, an' a way of gettin' folks to mind ye."

Mary shook her head and said, "When yer an ol' lady, ye can say wha' ever ye wish an' no one pays any mind to it."

"Nay, Mary, ye've earned their respect, an' they listen to ye!"

After finishing the last of the tea and bannock buns, Mary brought out a sack of oats. "I'll stir up oatcakes for th' lads. They'll be hungry when they get back."

Mary stirred together handfuls of ground oats along with honey, salt, and water. She pressed the dough into a flat, round cake, put it in an iron pan, and placed the pan on the grate. "Janet, get yer cloak an' mittens, an' we'll go to th' barn. There's a rope tied to th' door latch so we' won't wonder off onto the moors."

As soon as Janet stepped outside, she grabbed the rope. Inside the barn, it was almost warm; the snow banked against the walls

106

outside kept the warmth of the animals inside. Mary picked up a large black and white cat. "Good mornin', Miss Mouser Cat. I see ye ha' a full belly. Good lassie ye are!"

A dozen white sheep with black muzzles and feet bleated and waited expectantly. "Ye ha' eaten all tha' I put out for ye yesterday, two of ye ha' already lambed, an' it's not long 'til th' rest of ye'll be havin' yers, so I'll be puttin' out hay along' wi' th' grain." Mary turned to Janet and motioned toward the hay stack in the corner behind boards.

"The grain'll make healthy lambs, an' th' hay'll fill th' ewes' bellies. Th' same is true for breedin' women. Their babes need to be fed too." Janet remembered how thin and pale Elizabeth was. With so little to eat, it was no wonder the babe was stillborn. She placed the blame on Gordon, the lazy lout!

Mary pitched loose hay into the feeding mangers. She placed cracked oats, and wheat in chicken coops with a fat hen in each one. "Janet, love, look for eggs, will ye?"

Janet felt around in the nests, disturbing the chickens, who started clucking. That started the sheep bleating. "Mary." Janet had to yell to be heard above the racket. "There're two eggs. Wha' will ye do wi' 'em?"

"Two ewes are fresh, and I'll make a puddin' wi' milk, eggs, an' a wee dram of brandy. Then, my dear, we'll ha' puddin' wi' our tea an' biscuits!" As they finished the chores, Mary talked. "If yer carin' for a babe born a'fore it's supposed to, ye can gi' th' bairn ewe's or goat's milk if there's not enough mother's milk. Same if th' babe's mother dies. Put your finger in th' babe's mouth an' drip milk down your finger so th' babe can suck an' get th' milk. Many a little one who's too tiny to suck at their mam's teat will live if ye'll drip milk into their mouths every two hours. Rub their little throats an' they'll swallow for ye. They'll be cryin' while yer getting' started, but once they get a taste of warm milk, they'll quieten' down. I'm chilled an' need to go back to th' fire. Let's bring Mouser Cat in wi' us. I've a wee mousy chewin' on my flour box."

Mary tucked the cat into her cloak and opened the door to a wall of blowing snow. She found the end of the rope, and they walked until they bumped into the corner of the house. The cottage was toasty warm. It was twilight and not yet noon. "Ah, our oatcakes are fare th' well done, an' I see tha' we'll be needin' a bit more light than th' lantern. I'll make up some button lamps. I've neglected makin' 'em, wha' wi' one thin' an' another."

"Button lamps?" said Janet.

"Aye, my gran taught me how." Mary brought out two shallow clay saucers, spread a thick coat of rendered fat in each one and threaded twine through the holes of two round bone buttons. She twisted the twine into a wick, tucked the two loose ends underneath the button, and placed the button on top of the fat. Then she lit the wick, which had absorbed fat from the saucer. Janet was fascinated, "Mary, this gives off a good bit of light."

Mary was pleased with Janet's praise. "Come, sit, an' we'll ha' a bit o' tea. Now, lass, wha' has troubled ye in carin' for folks?"

Janet looked as if she were about to cry. Mary patted her on the hand. "Now, shore up, lass. By th' time yer leave, ye'll feel better."

"Elizabeth, Gordon's wife birthed a stillborn, an' I did'na know wha' would dry up her milk tha' came in when she held her wee dead bairn. She was bleedin', an' I did wha' I could to stop it. Then—" Janet paused to sip her tea. "Th' clans go at one another over things."

"Aye, lass, if I had a coin for ever' wound I've doctored or lead ball I've dug out, I'd go on a sailin' ship to America!"

"I thought as much, Mary," Janet said. "Duncan was shot, an' th' lead ball went all th' way through his leg. It happened when th' Campbells were roundin' up his cattle an' on their way to makin' off wi' 'em. Duncan was tryin' to stop 'em an' did'na even ha' his boots, let alone a pistol."

Janet and Mary both shook their heads at a man who tried to stop cattle rustlers unarmed. "Lack of common sense, I'd say," Mary thought out loud.

Janet agreed, "Aye. Duncan went down an' lay there 'til Anne found him th' next mornin'. When Thomas brought him to me several days later, I dinna think I could save the leg. He was feverish, an' th' leg was red from his ankle on up. I heated a steel poker an' ran it through th' hole to th' other side. It opened up th' scab so th' festerin' could drain out. Before long, he was up an' able to walk on his leg, but it still pains him, an' he uses a cane. What would ye ha' done, Mary?"

Mary started to speak, but Janet continued. "There's more—feverish bairns tha' canna tell ye wha' is hurtin'. An' I've heard of a sickness where people have scabbed sores on their skin an' are bleedin' from their bowels, an' all those who had it died. It's said tha' sailors bring th' sickness, but others say it's a plague from God."

While Janet spoke, Mary watched as emotions moved over her face. She knew Janet had the caring soul and touch of a healer; once she knew how to diagnose and treat illnesses, she would be much sought after. "Mary, I can set a broken bone, but treatin' burns is somethin' I know nothin' about. One of Duncan's lads caught his nightshirt on fire standin' too close to th' fire, an' he was in terrible misery 'til th' burns finally healed. Even then, they left great red scars tha' pain him." Janet looked Mary in the eyes. "An' there's more."

Mary stood and said, "Well, lass, I can see we've got our work laid out for us. I'll put the teapot back on th' fire an' let it warm up a bit. Here's a ginger biscuit, an' dinna forget there's puddin' for later." Mary pushed the ashes to the back of the oven, placed a peat brick on the fire, and set the teapot on the grate; soon it was steaming.

"Let's ha' our tea. Then we'll get started on th' list of things tha' troubles ye. I believe I've answers for everythin' except one, an' tha's th' body sores an' bleedin' from th' bowels. For tha', I'd be lookin' for a priest to say th' last rites, an' tha' is all ye can do." By the time they finished their tea, the light in the room was a little brighter, with a faint glimmer of sunlight.

Mary opened the front door. "Ah, a bit o' sunshine! It'll not be snowin' for a while, but look at th' western sky, lass. See tha' bank of low clouds?"

"Aye, I do." Janet shielded her eyes from the vast whiteness of the snow. "An' I know wha' it means. More snow, an' if we're blessed, only snow an' no wind."

"Might as well get settled in for th' day, love," Mary said. "We'll ha' a fine time sortin' out all of my dried leaves, stalks, flowers, an' roots. I'll send packets of things wi' ye. Ye canna get 'em now, an' ye'll need 'em. Let's sit here by this chest, for it has most everythin' we'll need. First things first, Elizabeth's birthin' injuries. Wha' did ye say ye did to stop th' bleedin'?"

"I stitched up th' torn place like ye'd mend a tear in breeks."

"Hmm," Mary said thoughtfully. "I could do no better! Did ye wash th' area well a'fore an' after th' stitchin'?"

"I did."

"Good lass!" Mary said.

Janet continued, "I used warm salted water, as I know salted water can help wi' healin'."

"Aye, an' I'll tell ye some more healin' things. One of 'em is bog myrtle. Do ye ken it?"

Janet thought and then shook her head. "It grows only in th' Hielands, an' water boiled wi' it has th' strength to take soreness out of cuts an' wounds. After th' bog myrtle has soaked in water, dry it for a poultice. Bathe th' injured area wi' th' bog myrtle water. I'll show ye wha' th' dried plant looks like. It grows into a bush, an' th' smell of bog myrtle is very strong. Folks like to cut bits of it for a sick room. It smells fresh and clean. Here's the dried leaves. Take a whiff. Ye'll not find any bugs on this plant, for they dinna like th' smell or taste of bog myrtle. Some folks use it to get rid of crawlin' things in th' broch. When ye gather the leaves, boil some in a pot wi' water an' strain it off, savin' it in a glass flask. Then, spread th' leaves to dry in th' sun. When it's dry, be sure to keep it dry, for it'll

110

ha' an awful stink if it gets wet." Mary chuckled. "To be truthful, all plants an' their parts will be a stinkin' mess if they aren't well dried, so ye'll spend as much time gettin' things ready to keep over th' winter as ye do in gatherin' 'em."

She continued, "Witch hazel water is wha' I use for birthin' injuries. Boil th' bark an' leaves of th' plant in rain water an' save th' water. It's very soothin' an' will make swollen, tender places less painful. There're times when a mother who has had several births will tell ye about tender areas in her hinny, if'n ye know wha' I mean? Men can ha' tha' too. Dippin' a clean cloth in witch hazel water an' washin' th' sore part will cure th' problem. Another thing about witch hazel: Rub th' tea steeped from th' bark on a bruise or spider bite. It'll take away bleedin' under th' skin an' th' itch an' burnin' of th' bite. I use dried witch hazel bark to make a tea to drink when my joints get to hurtin'. To find witch hazel, look for a bush or small tree tha' blooms in th' wintertime or a bush tha' in th' summertime will ha' leaves, flowers, an' fruit all at th' same time. The witch hazel flower will ha' four petals colored dark yellow or red. Strange thin' about witch hazel—if yer lookin' for water underground, say a place to dig a well, a forked twig of th' shrub'll bend toward th' water if ye hold it in both hands an' walk over th' ground."

Janet was looking at Mary with a puzzled expression. "Did I hear ye right? Th' twig'll bend toward water in th' ground?"

"Aye, ye heard right! It works, but ye'll ha' to see it for yerself to believe it. An' a word to yer: Dinna tell anybody how ye know. They'll be thinkin' yer a witch!"

Mary continued, "To make deliverin' bairns easier, lay yer heid on th' mother's belly to listen for th' sound of th' babe movin' around. If there's no movement, then ye best prepare for a stillborn. Sometimes th' babe is far enough down tha' movin' sounds canna be heard. If th' mother is carryin' a stillborn, then her body will get rid of the remains wi'out ye havin' to do anythin'. Make her as comfortable as ye can, and when ye tell her tha' she can ha' another babe, hope yer tellin' th' truth. If there's somethin' out of th' way or lyin' wrong inside, it can happen again. If it happens more than once, be wary of tellin' th' woman to keep tryin'. Somethin' is not workin' right, or mayhap th' man's seed is weak. If you think this is th' problem, tell th' husband to hold off for several weeks; it keeps his fluid thick an' strong."

Mary patted Janet's arm. "While we're talkin' about it, I'll tell ye how to get yerself wi' child again."

Mary smiled at Janet, who blushed and smiled back. "It's not about reaping th' harvest, love. It's about gettin' th' garden spot ready an' th' sowin' of th' seed. Dinna couple an' go to sleep. Lift yer hips up on a pillow so th' seed can reach yer womb, an' dinna wash yerself until th' next mornin'. If ye want a lad, eat honey an' cakes. If ye want a lass, take a spoonful of vinegar wi' water. Now, I dinna know why it's this way, but it is."

Mary shook her finger at Janet. "Watch for yer cycle of th' moon. It'll be exactly on th' half time since ye last cycled an' will cycle again. Mark th' days down. It'll be fourteen days since yer last bleedin' tha' ye will be th' most likely to get wi' child. Tell yer man tha' ye need him, an' lead him to yer bed wi' makin' a bairn on yer mind. I promise he'll rise up to th' occasion." At this, Mary laughed, and Janet blushed even more.

"I thought couplin' was enough. I really do want another bairn, an' I know Ewan would like one too."

"Aye, I'm sure he would. Men do like th' sowin' of th' seed. For some, it's th' best thin' they do." Both women smiled.

"Back to birthin' an' complications. To stop a milk flow, bindin' th' breasts is best. It'll be painful for a couple of days, but drinkin' tea made from willow bark will help. Trim several pieces off a strip of bark, an' let th' pieces steep in a teapot wi' hot water. Sweeten th' tea wi' honey, as it'll help keep fever from th' breasts. Janet, remember to ha' honey in yer cupboard always."

"Mary, I need to write these things down."

Mary went to a small cupboard and brought out paper, quill pen, and ink. "I'm pleased tha' ye want to make a record of wha' I'm tellin' ye. Ye'll be my apprentice, wha' say ye?"

Janet smiled, stood, and hugged the older woman. She had to bend over, and Mary had to reach up to pat her on the shoulders. "About Duncan being shot in th' leg—ye cauterized th' entire path of th' lead ball. That's somethin' I would not ha' tried, but it did th' trick. While th' treatment was harsh, still, it was th' most healin' thing ye could do. Th' hot poker seared th' flesh an' kept it from bleedin' so it'd heal from th' inside out, so ye did very well for th' man. Ye asked wha' would ha' helped wi' his pain? I'm thinkin' a tea made from dried leaves of th' feverfew plant, an' maybe a poultice of the bog myrtle plant. It takes down swellin' an' helps wi' fever.

"Janet, I ha' a strange thing to tell ye about treatin' festerin' places on th' body, an' I dinna know why it works. I heard it from my mother who treated a sailor wi' a shark bite. My father said th' only way to save his life was to amputate th' arm. Mother, who grew up a sea captain's daughter, said she'd try one more thing, which was puttin' a moldy bun on th' wound. My father said he did'na know whether to laugh or question mam's wits. Ye may find this hard to believe, but mam said she saw it wi' her own eyes. She placed th' bun wi' green mold on th' wound an' wrapped a cloth around' it. A day later th' swelling had gone down, an' th' red streaks up his arm were fadin' away. Then, she replaced the bun wi' another moldy bun. Th' wound healed, an' the sailor kept his arm. Mam said it was somethin' her da knew about, but he did'na know why it worked. I've not done it myself, but I'd try it if nothin' else works. We dinna ha' to understand th' whys an' wherefores of it. Say it's God's miracle an' let it go at tha'. Healers, known as 'th old ones,' knew th' use of all plants an' trees. My mother knew many of their teachin's an' told 'em to me."

Janet was writing it all down. "I hope this makes sense when I need it. I canna think why anyone'd put a bun, moldy or otherwise, on an injury. This sounds like one of Ewan's tales of throwin' salt on th' fire to rid th' broch of evil spirits."

Mary smiled. "As I said, Janet, sometimes we'll do things tha' turn out well. But other times, they don't! Yer need to know how to ease pain because it helps th' patient heal. Keep dried rhubarb on hand. It's th' stalks I'm talkin' about, not th' leaves. Here, see this? It's rhubarb dried an' ground to a powder. Put a spoon full in a teapot after heatin' th' water. Let it steep an' gi' th' tea to yer patient wi' some honey, but dinna' add any cream or milk."

Mary opened a pack of folded parchment paper, revealing a small amount of fine yellow powder. "This is goldenrod pollen. It's good to put on festerin' cuts an' wounds. It works best when it's fresh from th' flower. As winter goes along, it did'na work as well." Mary paused to think what she would talk about next. "I want to tell ye about St. John's Wort. It's for high-strung an' sleepless folks. I mix th' dry, ground-up leaves an' stalks wi' tea an' let it steep for a little while. I'd say a small spoonful for a grownup an' less for a bairn. Here's some dried St. John's Wort. See th' flower petals? It ha' yellow-green leaves wi' some black spots on th' underneath side of th' leaf. Th' flowers are yellow an' ha' five petals. Pick th' flowers, th' leaves, an' smaller parts of th' stems an' dry 'em. St. John's Wort is good for girls an' women who are startin' their monthly cycle an' ha' some misery of pains. Make a weak tea of th' plant parts an' add a spoon of honey to th' cup. Sometimes, when I'm workin' to help somebody who's too upset or distraught to let me get on wi' it, I'll make up a pot of th' St. John's tea an' insist tha' we all sit down an' ha' a cup. It helps me as much as th' patient, an' if we all ha' a little nap, so much the better."

Mary shrugged. "Sometimes th' healer needs a bit of healin' too, ye know? My St. John's Wort tea tha' I made for th' three of ye Cameron folk night before last put everyone to sleep, so I made it a bit too strong. Some plants make a stronger tea than others, an' how ye dry it can make a difference."

Mary held up a stalk with tiny flowers. Janet said, "I know this plant. It's feverfew, an' it grows in my kitchen garden. I usually dry it and mix some with water when I need it."

Mary said, "One more thing about feverfew: Ye can use it to start up a lassie's monthlies again, if it needs to be done. Ye'll be knowin' wha' I mean?"

"I do." Janet made a note. "Wha' would be th' dosage, Mary?"

"I'd say a heavy dose, say two heapin' spoonfuls of leaves an' stems to a cup of water. The leaves an' stems ha' more strength than th' flowers do, an' th' dried stems ha' even more. I'd gi' a dose three times a day. Are ye keepin' up, Janet? I'm wantin' to make a trip to th' chamber pot. Would ye make another pot of tea? And did'na use any St. John's Wort, for I'm about asleep now."

"Aye, Mary, me too. I see it's snowin' again, an' I'm thinkin' a wee nap might be good for both of us. Wha' say ye?"

Mary nodded in agreement. Janet picked up her cloak, which was drying by the fire, and spread it on the floor. "Mary, this time I'll sleep by th' fire, an' ye rest on yer good bed." Soon both slept. Snow swirled and gathered into deep drifts. The little stone cottage with rounded corners and thatched roof was warm and snug.

Chapter 14

Donald Cameron of Lochiel sat alone in a darkened room, whisky glass in hand, brooding about the events which had caused him to change his mind and embrace the Jacobite uprising. Only a few months ago, he sent Charles Stuart a firm, resounding "No" to his invitation to join the rebellion and clearly told him why. At the time, Donald believed his reasoning was well justified. Now, God help us all, he had given his word to support Charles in th' uprisin'! The grandson of Sir Ewen Cameron and son of John Cameron, young Donald listened when his grandsire and father discussed clan matters. Donald, the eldest son, knew one day he would be the clan chieftain. His brother Archibald aspired to be a physician, and a third brother, John, wanted enough lands to raise sheep and cattle. When Donald learned Charles Stuart had asked for and was denied support from the great chieftains of the Isles, he understood why. Charles arrived with one ship, seven men, and a small purse. The MacDonald chieftain and the MacLeod chieftain looked Charles over and saw an immature and inexperienced young man with the barest of military experience and no financial backing. When he promised support from the King of France, they did not believe him. Donald recalled the sinking feeling in the pit of his stomach as he listened to Charles relate how his two ships were attacked by the British Navy; one was damaged to the extent that it lost its cargo. The other carried little more than a few muskets, swords, and some French gold coins. Yet Charles, determined to move forward, insisted that there would be no better time to begin the uprising.

It was a weak beginning and Donald was amazed that Charles did not grasp the seriousness of the lack of military supplies, men, and money. Donald thought of his family's steadfast commitment to the royal Stuarts. Were they all blinded by their desire to have a Catholic Stuart on the throne? As he poured more whisky in his glass, Donald recalled the dwindling supply of coins in his treasury. Last winter he had to send hungry members of his clan away with less than they asked for. In payment of rent and taxes, his tacksman brought him rabbits, pheasants, and trout instead of coins. The divine right of kings was the only reason Donald had reconsidered his position regarding Charles Edward Stuart. As Catholic Jacobites, he and his family believed that God chose a man through the royal bloodline to be king. It was a Biblical principle. Would a man not support God's own word? Would he be a traitor to his church and beliefs? He pondered on promises made by Charles to rectify the poverty experienced by most of the clans. As did many of the chieftains, Donald suspected Charles made promises because he coveted their support for the uprising.

When James of Scotland, the son of Mary Queen of Scots, was crowned king of England and Scotland, it felt as if Scotland's son was on the throne. But soon, King James became angry with Scotland's people as he thought they were disloyal to his kingship. He unwisely made an alliance with the king of France to export only England's products to France, thereby eliminating Scotland's primary source of income. Donald recalled at one time, his grandsire believed he had the king's support. King James promised a ship to deliver Scotland's wool to the continent. His grandfather assured other clan chieftains there would be buyers for all of the wool they could produce and a ship to deliver the wool to market. But when the ship did not materialize, stacks of wool filled the loading dock until they were forced to sell to England's dealers at a low price. Then, Scotland's finest wool was resold to markets in Spain, France, Italy, and Germany at a high profit for the English middlemen. His grandfather said he would never again place his trust with a Stuart king. Now, two generations later, a Cameron chief was once again providing support to a Stuart who aspired to be king. Donald struggled with his decision to support Charles Stuart.

Earlier, Donald had been very vocal about his fears. His brother, Dr. Archibald Cameron, was sent as an emissary to tell the Stuart prince of Donald's decision to remove himself and his clan from the battle for the crown. Charles knew he could not proceed further without the support of the most powerful clan chieftain in Scotland. Charles, well aware of his persuasive abilities, was so certain that he could change Donald's mind that he stated, "Let me face Donald. I will reassure him and bestow upon him the power and respect that will belong to him when a Stuart sits upon the throne." Charles Stuart had no doubt that he could bring Donald Cameron to his knees in allegiance to him. Donald's own brother told him it would happen, and it did!

As the clock ticked away the minutes and hours in the room, Donald recalled the meeting between the prince and himself. Earlier, Donald had asked John, his younger brother, how he felt about supporting Charles. John responded that he would not support Charles's ambitions. He urged Donald to write his refusal in a letter and send it rather than telling Charles of his decision face to face. John knew his brother well; they both were raised by parents who believed that God, in His infinite wisdom, appointed a man to be king through his bloodline. John's fears were substantial.

He was afraid that Charles would persuade Donald to change his mind and support the prince and the rebellion. But Donald insisted that he tell Charles Stuart to his face that his plans were doomed. Donald's meeting with Charles went exactly as John had anticipated. The prince spoke eloquently, full of praise for Donald's achievements and the regard that other chieftains held for him. Even after listening to Charles's compliments, Donald still spoke his mind and strongly advised Charles to return to France to await a better opportunity. Charles, well prepared for Donald's response, replied there would be no better opportunity than the present. He explained that the majority of the king's royal army was on assignment in Europe, leaving only a few sparse and newly formed regiments in England and Scotland. Charles pointed out that these inexperienced soldiers would be no match for the ferocious Highlanders on the battlefield.

Charles knew exactly what to say to bring Donald to his knees. He placed the responsibility for a failure on Donald; if he withheld support, it would be Donald's fault if a royal Stuart perished at the hands of the king's soldiers in the attempt to regain the throne. Charles said, "Lochiel, with the few friends I have, I will raise the royal standard and proclaim to the people of Britain that Charles Stuart has come to claim the crown of his ancestors—to win it or to perish in the attempt. The Lochiel, whom my family often told me was our most loyal supporter, has declined to join me, and thus he will be as responsible as the king's soldiers in deciding my fate."

The Cameron chieftain recalled the guilt and sadness he experienced when he heard Charles's statement. He bowed before the prince and said, "Nay, I share yer vision an' fate, an' so shall every man over whom God has given me power. I gi' my word that th' Cameron clan will be with ye, whether it's marching to battle or on th' battlefield itself." Charles Edward Stuart, with his eloquent words, successfully won the support of a chief so powerful and influential that others would follow without question. Donald, the

Lochiel, chieftain of the Cameron clan, covered his face with both hands and wept.

Now, the rebellion could begin! Like the sound of the bagpipes, the word carried on the winds blowing through all of Scotland. Loyal men would rally behind their chieftains to fight for a new king of the United Kingdom. The Dark One smiled and spoke to Death, who was close by. "I am fascinated with watching humans struggle with making choices. They are so shocked when their choice leads to a destination where they do not want to be. It is interesting that they still continue on, even though they could turn around at any time and go back. They forget they always have a choice, even to the very end of the road."

Death replied, "We've discussed this before, and I'll say it again. You belong to the one who is known to be the master of disguise and deceit; he can make the wrong path appear to be the right one. I understand why humans forget about their ability to choose. They may not realize they have chosen the wrong way until it's too late!"

Laughing, The Dark One said, "Ah, Master's ability to deceive is the best of his gifts!"

Chapter 15

Ewan and Thomas sat beside other Cameron men around the fire. While they waited for the chieftains to speak, they speared chunks of smoked boar, wrapped bread around it, and washed it down with ale. Donald Cameron waited until the men were through eating before he spoke. A sgian dubh was tucked into his woolen hose, and a sporran made from the hide of a silver fox hung from a leather belt at his waist along with a broadsword in a heavy silver scabbard. He moved to the center of the circle, drew his broadsword, and held it over his head. "Men of Scotland, yer clan chiefs ha' gathered ye to this place because of th' oppression of England's King George. Our bards tell of our history of fightin' to keep our freedom. Well over five hundred years ago th' Arbroath Declaration was written." Donald raised his voice to a shout:

"That so long as one hundred Scots remain alive, we would never submit to the English; for it is not for glory we fight, for riches or for honours, but for freedom alone, which no good man loses but with his life."

"Th' Act of th' Union was signed in 1707 sayin' Scotland an' England would share th' same ruler. Queen Anne was on the throne then, an' she, bein' th' daughter of a Stuart king, treated th' people of Scotland fairly. She had compassion for our people th' Hanoverian king will never ha'. England's king controls th' sellin' of goods, an' we cannot sell our wool. This is not wha' William Wallace an' th' Bruce fought an' died for! Will their fight for Scotland's rights be for naught?"

Donald threw the broadsword's point to the ground, where it pierced the earth and swayed from side to side. "I say nay!"

Leon MacDonald stood and spoke. "Donald Cameron, ye ha' spoken wi' Charles Edward Stuart. Do ye trust him? Look around ye, Donald. Ye see none here of th' MacLeod clan of Skye, an' there be others who'll nay do battle. Some say a battle'll not be won an' there'll be a high price to pay if we lose. I ask ye, Donald Cameron, why should we gi' more when we've lost so much?"

"Chief MacDonald, yer concerns are well founded," responded the Lochiel, who raised his voice and pointed to those gathered around him. "Men, th' king of England must recognize tha' Scotland's people ha' earned their rights an' privileges. We pay taxes to keep our country safe an' depend upon th' king's royal army to protect Scotland as well as England. But why should we pay higher taxes than th' English, an' why are we not treated as equals able to sell our goods as th' English do? Th' king is punishin' th' Scots an' we are sufferin' because of it!"

Donald raised his flask and shouted, "To Scotland, an' those who ha' gone before us." Every man rose to his feet and lifted his flask high. "To Scotland," each one shouted.

"Prince Charles Edward Stuart is callin' th' clans to join him in a battle tha' will bring th' royal Stuarts to th' throne. When th' king's royal army is defeated, we'll carry Bonnie Charlie into London on our shoulders, where his father, James, will be crowned th' rightful king! Th' battle will be won just as Prestonpans was won in September of last year. Th' bloody Redcoats were no match for th' Hieland fightin' clans. We won th' battle wi' only thirty men lost. Aye, th' victory was sweet! We captured th' royal army's arsenal wi' gold coins, rifles, an' ammunition. Our Jacobite prince is seated at Holyrood Palace in Edinburgh!"

Donald called to the chiefs and their clans, "Cameron, Campbell, Chisholm, MacDonald, Fraser, MacKenzie, Chattan, MacIntosh, MacLean, Gordon, MacIntyre, an' Stewarts of Appin, ye represent yer clans as well as th' many smaller groups of families tha' live on yer lands an' are under yer will. All of us will be called to fight in wha' I believe will be th' last battle fought on Scotland's soil." The men stood and cheered.

William Fraser stood. "Donald, my question is one tha' we all need an answer to."

The Lochiel gave him a nod. "Aye, William, ask wha' ye will."

William moved out of the circle of men and stood in front of the Lochiel. "Will Lord Murray be leadin' us in th' battle or will it be Prince Charles?"

"Lord George," said the Lochiel.

John MacIntyre, Ewan's brother by marriage to Janet's younger sister, stood. "My kin believe th' English will be ready for this battle. They'll remember their loss at Prestonpans. Will we ha' men an' arms to meet th' Redcoats on th' battlefield?"

"Th' prince says he's bringin' military men from France wi' artillery. Charles also says th' French king is sending gold to buy guns an' ammunition. We'll be carryin' enough firepower to defend ourselves."

Donald Cameron sheathed his sword and pointed to Ewan and Thomas Cameron. "Those two men are my kin. Another clan stole their cattle an' sheep, an' a Cameron was shot on his own land tryin' to protect his family an' animals! We fight among ourselves for food to feed our families! England's men ha' lands, livestock, food, an' money while we scrabble rocky glens an' valleys to provide for our wives an' bairns an' th' English'd take tha' away if they could!"

Donald shouted, "Long live King James. God save King James an' his son, Charles, th' Prince of Wales!"

Many of the men stood and repeated the words while some remained seated. "What say ye, men? Will ye sit on yer arses while th' bloody English steal everythin' from under yer nose?"

Looking around the circle, Donald waited. Men looked at one another, waiting for someone to speak. The Stuart of Appin clan chief stood. "Donald, I'm speaking to ye as a chief, one to another. I'm a Stuart, an' Charles is my kin. Plain speakin', I ha' doubts about him leadin' th' uprising. Aye, he's a Stuart by blood, but he was raised in Italy. He says he's a Scotsman, but th' truth is, he first set foot on Scottish soil a few months ago. Donald, th' prince is not well thought of by many who know him. Some of my kin say neither Prince Charles nor his father ha' th' followin' they claim they do. It's said Charles has no battlefield experience but he thinks highly of himself. Some of my family who travel in France say th' French will look th' other way when th' time comes for 'em to support Charles. Donald, I fear th' Hielanders are bein' asked to do battle for a man who dinna understand wha' he's doin' an' we're goin' into a battle tha' can't be won."

Alexander MacDonald, of Clan MacDonald from the eastern part of Skye, stood and spoke. "I hear th' Appin Stuarts' concerns, but I dinna believe we ha' a choice. It's either pay high taxes an' starve, or go to th' battlefield! We'll join wi' Donald Cameron an' support Charles Stuart. My cousin, Leon MacDonald of th' outer Isles, is speakin' against joinin' th' battle because he says a loss of lives will not benefit Scotland. I feel th' same, but like Donald, I've grown weary of th' bickerin' for food between th' clans. If a Stuart king will change things for th' folk of Scotland, then we'll fight!"

The talking continued through the night into the early hours of dawn. Bottles of ale were passed around, and more were brought out to replace the emptied bottles. The MacDonald chief brought his clan's piper, a MacIntyre man, and the McDonald bard into the center of the circle. The piper was a fierce and formidable man with a full beard, long hair, and his great Highland bagpipes on his shoulder. The bard spoke. "Th' English dinna take well to th' sound o' th' pipes. I say, let th' pipers play an' th' English be damned!"

A cheer went up from the men. "Lads, I've words for ye, an' then our piper will play th' tune tha' goes wi' the words."

"Ye brave men of Scotland,
Will give yer all,
Will give yer all,
Ye call yerselves Jacobites
Pray tha' ye dinna fall,
Dinna fall.
Hold high th' banners,
When th'
Fiery cross ye see,
Come to th' battlefield,
An' fall in line b'hind me,
For I'll play th' march,
To lead ye on,
Lead ye on.
Oh, men of Scotland,
Pray tha' ye dinna fall,
Dinna fall.
If saved ye be,
Then, Scotland will be free,
But if ye fall,
Scotland's lost her all,
Lost her all.
Brave men of Scotland
Pray tha' ye dinna fall!"

The piper began playing; the keening sounds swirled around the men standing by the dying fire. As he played, smoke from the fire mingled with blowing snow. Falling moisture fell on the faces of men who wiped it, along with tears, away. Donald Cameron bade all good night, loosened his tartan from his waist, and wrapped it around his body to shelter him from the wet snow. He lay down on the damp ground. Ewan and Thomas did likewise, one on each side of the chief.

Death and The Dark One sat on a rocky hill above Glenfinnan that night. Death passed a skeletal hand in a wide sweep over the group. "All but a very few will die."

The Dark One grinned, long fangs glistening. "Hmm," he whispered. "Think of it: Charles Stuart and William, Duke of Cumberland, both pampered sons of kings, related by blood, will be leading the armies on the battlefield. Charles was taught to pray in great cathedrals, but all the time, his thoughts were on gaining the throne in England. William could have believed in God, but he was taught that God does not exist. Now, between the two of them, Scotland's people will be destroyed. Master will be very pleased!"

Early the next morning, Donald said to Ewan and Thomas, "Bring twenty animals to Inverness when th' time comes. Th' Prince's man will oversee th' slaughtering an' preparing th' meat for th' men. Cameron wives are to send oatcakes, bread, an' cheese. I'll send a man wi' th' fiery cross likely in March or early April. If a clan man chooses to not join me, he'll be named a traitor, both to me an' th' prince.

The Lochiel turned to Ewan. "Yer lad is old enough to do battle, an' I'll expect ye to ha' him wi' ye."

Ewan answered, "Duny is wi' his grandsire in Perthshire. Janet's father fell an' is not yet over his injuries. Duny is helpin' wi' th' horses 'til James is well again."

"Aye, it may be tha' we'll need several of those fine animals tha' James Dunsmuir raises. Ask wha' James could spare for us, will ye?"

Nodding to Donald's request, Ewan hoped as the chieftain considered the horses, he would forget about Duny. Ewan took John MacIntyre by the arm and led him away from the group of men. "John, how are ye an' Meghan farin'?"

"Meghan is expectin' our first bairn." John lowered his voice,

"Ewan, I'm sorely tempted to take her to th' colonies. Would ye blame us, Ewan, if we did?"

Ewan shook his head. "I'd not blame ye, but I'll remind ye tha' th' man who is king of England is also th' king of th' American colonies. If ye go to th' Americas, how long will it be before they rebel against th' tacksmen who collect rent an' taxes for th' same king tha' we're payin'?" Ewan shook his head. "Th' American colonies ha' great shippin' ports, an' there's crops growin' on lands as big as Scotland. Th' king'll want all of that tax money, an' to be sure he gets it, he'll send his men to collect it."

"My God! " John exclaimed. "We're damned if we go one direction an' dead if we go another!"

"A word, John: dinna openly disagree wi' th' rebellion." He touched the younger man's shoulder. "Ye can think as ye will, an' no one need know."

The Lochiel's greeting to Ewan and Thomas was, "Remember my words about traitors!"

"Aye, Donald, we'll not forget," Ewan answered, but he knew that neither he nor Thomas would name a clan member who did not go to the battlefield. "We'll ha' th' cattle in Inverness several days before th' men gather."

Donald placed his hand on Ewan's shoulder. "Yer fealty to me is noted. I'll convey my appreciation of ye to Charlie Stuart; he'll see to it tha' yer rewarded for yer efforts."

The two men started the trip with empty bellies. The horses had no grain, and the snow-covered moors had no grazing. Quiet Thomas, who usually said very little, reined in his horse. "Ewan, why dinna we prepare for th' trip home? We ha' no food an' th' horses ha' not been fed for two days. Wha' is th' matter wi' us?"

Ewan shook his head and said, "Mayhap we've too much else to think about. We'll stable th' horses, find food an' a place to lay our heids in Fort William." They both rode on, thinking about the fears expressed by those chieftains who dared to speak out.

Chapter 16

Janet listened to the storm raging outside. Puffs of wind blew down the chimney, causing the fire to flicker. She closed her eyes and slept. As she slept, she dreamed about a windy moor and a rider on a black horse. He held an English flag and carried a fiery brand that cast a blood-red glow over Highlanders lying on the moor, dead or dying. She reached to pull her cloak around her and woke with a start; she knew she had experienced something that was yet to come. When Mary came into the room she caught her breath when she saw Janet's face, "Janet, lass, wha' is it?"

"Oh, Mary! Sometimes I ha' dreams about things that are yet to happen, an' sometimes it's about things that ha' already happened. Th' dreams tha' ha' not yet happened are fearful."

Mary nodded. "Aye, child, yer one tha' has a cursed blessing—or a blessed curse, I know not which. It's called *Dha Shealladh*, th' second sight. Keep it to yerself. Some think it's witchcraft, an' it's naught."

"Mary, yer th' only one besides Ewan tha' knows about it."

Mary asked, "Can ye speak of wha' ye saw?"

Janet answered, "Th' Jacobite uprising an' dead Highlanders."

Mary shook her head. "We'll help those we can, an' those we canna help, we'll say a prayer. There's naught to do about wha' our men do, except wrap up th' injuries they gi' one another!"

Mary sat at the table and selected a drawer marked "Boneset." "This powder is good to get a fever down, an' some say it helps ease pain in th' bones. Use a good pinch to a cup of hot water an' let it steep for a few minutes. I dinna use it much because boneset tea will cause loose bowels, an' patients dinna need tha' along wi' th' pain. It looks like a common weed, with long leaves tha' taper to a point. Dry both leaves an' stems an' grind 'em into a powder as fine as ye can make it. Collect fresh rain water to use in medicines an' tea. Dinna use or drink water that's been left standin'. Always wash yer pots, pans, an' drinkin' cups in hot water wi' soap. It's like yer clothin'. Yer want to be clean, inside an' out. Rain water is as clean as God can make it by runnin' it through th' clouds an' rainbows."

Mary chucked and said, "That'd make a good tale for th' faeries, now wouldn't it? I ha' a wee story for ye. Saint Bride was a beautiful lass who planted flowers all over Scotland. She gathered seeds an' scattered 'em to th' four winds. It's said her favorite plant's flower is th' same color as her golden hair. Th' plant starts blooming in early spring an' blooms until frost. The bees love it, an' it's one of th' most healin' of all plants because it's blessed by Saint Bride herself. A drink made from steepin' th' dried leaves in hot water will be a tonic for th' early mornin' sickness of a woman wi' child. But tha' is not all. Pick th' leaves in early spring, an' use 'em chopped up wi' green onion or wild garlic. It's tasty wi' a leg o' spring lamb. My father made a golden wine from th' yellow blossoms. A hot drink can be made from th' roots when they're dried an' ground. Do ye know what th' name of this plant is?"

Janet shook her head. "Why, it's th' dandelion, th' most common of God's wild flowers!" Mary rummaged through the packets and drawers. She found a dried plant that had a center stem with tiny branches. It appeared to be prickly. "Ye know this one?"

"It's heather?" Janet was no longer sure after looking at so many stalks, leaves, and flowers.

"Aye, it is. Did ye know Hieland heather can be brewed into ale? It makes a man a man! Drink th' ale an' there's no stoppin' th' laddie chasin' a lassie around the bed chamber. I canna' speak for this, even though I've recommended it. Mayhap I need to remember tha' since I've not heard otherwise, it must be workin', as th' lads are too busy to stop by!" Mary laughed and waved the bit of heather in the air. "Just think, lassie, every Scotsman drinks water tha' has flowed through th' Hielands covered wi' heather. No wonder they're so lovey!"

She stood up and stretched. "I'm thinkin' a bowl of tattie soup wi' some bread an' cheese will fill the empty spot in my belly. What say ye?"

"Mary, how do ye ha' time for all of th' things ye do?"

"Oh, I make good use of th' long summer days. Look under th' table. See th' wooden crate? There's tatties, carrots, neeps, an' onions. Fetch me two tatties and an onion, an' get th' pitcher of milk from th' cool box in th' bed chamber."

Janet rummaged through the box, selected two potatoes and an onion, and placed them on the kitchen table. Mary talked while she was peeling, chopping, and making the potato soup. "I ha' some other things to speak wi' ye about. Write 'em down if ye will, but ye'll remember when th' time comes. When there's a mortal injury or wound, ye can gi' poppy syrup to ease th' pain of dyin'. Be careful to not hasten th' death along by givin' too much! But then—" Mary shook her head and looked into Janet's eyes, "I've had a few broken bodies surprise me by livin' when I did'na think it was possible, so dinna use th' syrup 'til yer sure!"

Mary placed the milk, potatoes and onion in an iron kettle and hung it over the peat fire. "Lass, always take a look at yer patients. Are they thin an' weak? Are their eyes cloudy or a little yellowish? A good strong drink of tobacco water will rid one of worms tha' get in th' bowels. A woman birthin' a bairn in a cottage where there're bairns wi'out enough food will ha' a hard time. She'll ha' a frail babe. Do everythin' ye can to get food in th' house. A hungry mam can't make milk for a bairn if she's naught to eat herself."

While Mary sorted through packets, Janet thought of Gordon and Elizabeth's larder and wondered how many evenings the bairns and Elizabeth went to bed hungry. Mary added salt and chopped parsley to the pot and set out bread, butter and cheese. Janet ladled the chowder into two wooden bowls, and the women sat down to eat. Janet thought how simple the meal was and yet how tasty. The tiny room was neat and tidy and yet cluttered with things that Mary had collected through the years. "Mary, watching ye in th' kitchen is a lesson by itself. I canna tell ye how delicious this is, an' ye put it together wi' hardly any effort."

"Janet, does yer chapel ha' a bread shelf?"

Janet thought for a minute. "Nay, but any who ha' a need can ask Ewan or me."

Mary replied firmly, "Some folks ha' pride, ye know. Ewan is th' laird, an' he's to see to it tha' there's a place in th' chapel where bread, oats, barley, an' flour is there for those tha' need it, so they can get it wi'out havin' to ask!" Janet nodded in agreement.

"Let's talk a bit about men. They dinna ha' th' patience tha' women do an' may not see how others are farin'. It's th' way God created us. Our men fight battles, an' they're stronger than we are. But sometimes a man will misuse his strength."

"Aye, I've seen it myself, Mary. Ewan's never raised a hand to me—an' he'd not. Sometime he'd ha' to lay down his heid to sleep, an' I'd be standin' over him wi' my iron pot in my hand."

Mary laughed out loud. "Aye, Ewan an' Thomas were raised to respect their mother, an' likewise their wives. It's th' men who empty th' whisky an' ale flasks an' be mean an' no good tha' beat their wives an' bairns. Dinna get involved in their fightin' yerself. Go to their clan chief or th' laird an' tell him about it. But lass, be sure tha' th' laird ye tell is not one of th' blackguardin' bastards himself, or ye mi' find yerself on th' wrong end of th' strop. Speak wi' Ewan about it; he'll know how to advise ye."

Mary spoke with a sad voice. "Too many women an' bairns ha' broken bones because of mean husbands an' fathers. I've been known to give an extra heavy dose of boneset tea to th' man." Mary chuckled. "If he's shittin' on th' chamber pot, at least he's not beatin' on his wife or bairns."

Mary handed Janet a packet with boneset plant leaves. "Some men ha' all sorts of troubles wi' their male parts. Ye'll see balls tha' are swollen an' sores on their cocks. This is wha' they get when they've been lyin' wi' whores. I treat 'em by pourin' raw whiskey over th' sores. When it stops burnin' an' they're through cursin', tell 'em to put their cocks away an' keep their breeks on. Then I set husband an' wife down an' ha' a hearty talk wi' 'em. I tell th' man tha' if he does nae want his male part to rot off, it is best to keep it in his breeks, except when he's at home. Then I tell his wife to take a look at it a'fore takin' it in, an' if there're sores or red spots, tell him nay." Mary smiled and said, "Wi' ever'one drinkin' all tha' good heather water, it's no wonder th' breeks are goin' up an' down, up an' down." Both women giggled.

"Father always said he could tell a Frenchman from an Englishman just by th' smell of 'em. The Frenchman smells of sweat, piss, and perfume, an' th' Englishman smells of horses, shit, an' perfume."

Janet laughed. "I'll write this down. It'll be of great help to me should I be called upon to treat patients from France an' England; I'll be able to tell which is which just by takin' a sniff."

Mary chuckled. "Lass, there'll be times when takin' a sniff is th' last thin' ye'll be wantin' to do. There's somethin' else yer need to know about, an' that's men who lie wi' other men. They can get th' same kind of clappy disease as if they're wi' a whore."

Mary nodded her head up and down at Janet's look of disgust. "If yer wonderin' how a man manages wi' another one, they use th' bowel openin' like a woman's birth openin'. Don't waste time thinkin' about it. I'll say this about it, ye'll not see tight bowels in a man who fancies tha' he's a woman."

As she talked, Mary put away the tiny drawers of dried herbs, flowers, and plants. "Many physicians use blood lettin' to cure illness. My father was one who did. But I've watched strong men die from loss of blood, an' I canna think tha' losing more blood is goin' to heal any sickness. Besides, I've seen too many suppuratin' wounds after bein' cut by a physician's dull knife. I'd ha' to see a cured man walkin' away from a pannier full of blood a'fore I'd want to try it. Just gi' me my herbs, salves, ointments, an' teas. I may not be able to cure ever' one of my patients, but I dinna gi' 'em more sore places either. Janet, always boil yer knives an' implements in hot water before usin' 'em. Dinna ask me why. I think it's to do wi' th' heat making th' knives sharper so they cut easier. My mother said to do this, an' I'm in th' habit of it.

"There'll be times when ye'll be called in to treat a sickness tha' is not of th' body but of th' heid. My mother told me about a young girl who heard voices in her heid. Her family brought her to mother for help. Mother said she told th' family she only tended to illnesses of th' body, not th' spirit. She sent 'em to a priest. Mayhap someday, we'll understand ways to mend sick minds as well as we know how to mend broken bones now."

Janet thought of Ewan asking if Gordon's troubles could be a sickness of the mind. "Janet, we dinna know enough about th' body to understand how th' heart beats. We know it does, but wha' keeps it beatin'? When ye think about it, our bodies are a miracle of creation, an' only God knows how they work! Someday, lass, ye'll be teachin' this to yer daughter, an' she'll teach her daughter. Best to write it all down, love, so ye'll remember everythin'."

Mary walked to the window, where the light was growing dimmer by the minute. "I'm thinkin' some dumplin' soup would be good for supper. Ye'll not ha' tasted it; Father said it comes from Germany. It's good for when a body's sick, or on a cold winter night when there's nothin' for th' stew pot. Tell yer why it's one of my favorites: it takes four things to cook a pot full, an' ye'll ha' 'em in yer larder."

Mary got out a wooden bowl and emptied a full cup of flour in the bowl. Then she added a good pinch of salt and one egg. She blended the flour, salt, and egg until it was crumbly. Then she poured a pitcher of milk in a kettle. "Yer can use cow's milk, goat's milk, wha'ever yer ha'. Let it heat 'til ye see bubbles around' th' sides of th' pan, but not boilin'. Then slowly add th' flour crumbles an' let it simmer. Keep stirrin', add a bit of butter, an' then sprinkle some parsley in. It's good for wha' ails a body."

They sat down to bowls of the soup. Janet was surprised at the rich flavor of the broth, and the dumplings were tender and good. "Mary, this could be made when th' larder was nearly bare."

"Aye, an' I've added a bit of carrot or a tattie or neep."

Mary cleared the table while Janet wiped out the bowls. "Do ye pare away th' fat from th' meat of a goose? Many throw it away, but it's th' best I've found for my ointments. It's a soft fat an' dinna smell too bad. Rendered goose fat will make a gentle soap when mixed wi' lye. I add a bit of rose water tha' I make from dried rose petals, as I like th' smell of roses. It's good to wash babes too. For a salve, I mix in bits of mint an' rub it on chests. Then cover th' chest wi' a piece of cloth; it'll clear out a bad cough. Another one of my cures comes from sheep's wool. If ye've handled sheep's fleece, ye'll know tha' it has a rich oil tha' is healin' for sore, dry hands. Boil th' fleece, scoop off th' oil, an' save it in a glass jar if ye ha' one, as it'll soak through a clay pot. About belly aches tha' won't go away, I dinna always know wha' causes 'em. I ask my patient if they ha' loose or tight bowels first. If tha' is not th' problem, then I tell 'em to eat only white food, milk pudding, creamed tatties, or the dumplin' soup for a few days to see if tha' helps. For a sour belly tha' is announced by belchin' and stinkin' air, mix two spoons of black burned breadcrumbs or powdered charcoal in a cup of milk.

134

"In th' cold of winter, when we dinna bathe, we ha' itchy skin from th' wee lice an' fleas. Ye'll see little blisters an' red places. Look in th' crotch area first. Tha's where th' little bugs get started, in th' hair of th' privates. Proper bathin' an' washin' hair on th' heid an' body, usin' plenty of soap, helps. There's many who believe they'll catch their deaths of cold if they bathe in th' winter, but I tell 'em to put a pot of water on th' grate, strip down, an' use tha' nice warm water to wash every part wi' a bit of th' goose grease soap. I always carry it wi' me when I go doctorin'. It's good for washin' festerin' places.

"Next comes th' part tha' none ever takes well to," said Mary. Janet waited, wondering what she had to say. "I tell 'em tha' washin' th' bed clothes ever' week an' dryin' them outside is good. Tell yer patients to throw th' fur coverlets out of th' cottage. They ha' more fleas an' lice than ye can count. Use good wool blankets, an' if they get buggy, take 'em outside an' soak 'em in a pot of water an' yer strongest lye soap. Throw out th' rushes on th' floor. If ye ha' dogs or cats in th' broch, they'll be bringin' in fleas, an' then when th' floor is not swept all winter long, th' hoppin' fleas will be everywhere. I sweep my floor every morning, an' sometimes I sprinkle some bits of fir bark around. Th' wee mites dinna like th' smell. In th' meantime, ye'll be treatin' bug bites. I know of two things tha' will take awa' th' sting. First, rendered lard mixed wi' sulfur tha' ye find at a spring. Ye'll smell it before ye see it, for it smells like th' worst of rotten eggs. If ye find such a place, mark it in yer mind an' scrape up some of th' yellow or green powder—it comes in handy when yer' doctorin'. The second thing is a bit of gunpowder mixed wi' lard. Put a pinch of either one on th' itchy places an' rub it in."

Mary chuckled. "If yer patient's a lady, she'll not be pleased, for smellin' like bad eggs or gunpowder is nay goin' to attract th' gentlemen. But then, tha' mayhap be good, as they likely gave her th' bugs to start wi'!"

Janet couldn't help but laugh. "Mary, yer very wise. Ye know how to treat people as well as curin' their sicknesses. How can I ever thank ye?"

"It's easy, love," Mary responded. "Just name yer little bairn after me. She'll be a darlin' babe, wi' yer red hair an' green eyes, an' I'd be honored to ha' Ewan an' Janet Cameron's second born carry my name."

Tears filled Janet's eyes. She covered the small, work-worn hand with her own and then reached over and kissed Mary on her wrinkled cheek. Mary smiled. "When the time comes, I'd like ye to ha' my cabinets of herbs an' plants, an' th' tools I use. I'll tell th' parish priest about it."

Janet nodded and found her handkerchief to wipe her eyes. "Now, back to our work. If yer patient has a sore throat, canna' swallow or eat food, an' is feverish, mix up half a cup of warmed rain water, two spoons of apple vinegar, an' a spoon of salt. Ha' th' patient hold th' mixture in their mouth an' swish it around good, lettin' a tiny bit go down th' throat. If it's a bad sore throat wi' knots swollen up under th' ears, take a look in th' patient's mouth. Yer may see yellow spots at th' back of th' throat. For th' cure, mix up boneset leaves an' stems wi' water, boil it, an' let it cool. Ha' yer patient drink th' tea an' then drink hot water wi' honey an' whisky mixed in. Put 'em to bed, an' pile on th' blankets. Build up th' fire. When th' patient starts to sweat, ye know they'll live. If they dinna sweat, ask a body to go for th' priest. Remember tha' I said to use honey wi' th' whisky! I ha' cured some bad festered places wi' honey. If ye can spoon honey into th' back of th' patient's mouth an' ask 'em to not swallow for as long as they can, it'll help. Lass, always keep a pot o' honey around; it'll cure just about anything except syphilis, an' it might help wi' tha'. I think I've told ye everythin' I know, an' yet, I know I've forgotten things."

Janet looked at Mary. "Come with us when we go home. I'd love to spend more time with ye, and ye'd be most welcome."

Mary smiled. "Ah, lassie, I love my wee cottage. I'm used to being alone an' dinna think I'd be good company in a big broch wi' people around."

Janet understood how well Mary managed being alone. "Who comes by to see if ye need anythin'?"

"My great-nephew, Andy Stuart, comes by to bring hay an' tea. He's an Appian Stuart an' is a supporter of Prince Charles. Andrew claims kinship wi' th' prince an' thinks he'll be a duke or earl when th' Stuarts take over th' throne in England. I tell him to not count his lambs before th' ewes ha' been wi' th' ram, silly lad!"

"Mary, it's this takin' over th' throne tha' Ewan an' Thomas ha' gone to Glenfinnan about. They think I dinna know, but I do."

Janet thought about her own garden of healing herbs and plants. "I wonder how many plants I've pulled an' thrown away 'cause I dinna know wha' they are."

"Many of th' wild plants an' flowers ye'll need will'na grow in a garden. They're like th' folk of Scotland; they want to grow in a place where they're free."

Mary began separating leaves, stems, stalks, seeds, flowers, tree bark, and roots into separate piles. She carefully tore parchment paper into good-sized pieces and began wrapping each pile in paper. "Oh, I nearly forgot. If yer wantin' to make a nice stew wi' a pigeon or pheasant, no need to get out yer slingshot or pistol. Just soak some grain in barley whisky an' spread a goodly amount on th' ground. Th' birdies come in to eat th' grain, an' when they get to sittin' an' lookin' around, yer can walk out an' grab 'em. Easiest way of bringin' in meat for th' table tha' ye ever saw!"

Janet sat with her mouth open. "Mary! Ha' ye done this?"

"Aye, of course I ha'! Do ye think I'd be tellin' ye to do somethin' tha' I ha' not done myself?" She had a twinkle in her eye and a smile on her face. "Ye'll want to try it, if for no other reason than to see th' wee birdies feelin' their whisky, aye?" Janet laughed until tears ran down her face.

Chapter 17

E wan and Thomas stopped at a Fort William tavern where a piper and fiddler played as if all were well in the world. "Thomas how's yer coin stash holdin' up?"

Thomas brought out a well-rounded leather pouch. "I've enough to keep us from bein' pitched out th' door."

After purchasing ale, they were invited to help themselves to food on the counter. Ewan filled a trencher with stew and buttered bread. Thomas heaped a thick slice of ham, boiled tatties, pickled partridge eggs, and bread on a wooden plate. They emptied their flasks of ale and bought more. The fiddler began playing "Molly, Me Darlin' Girl."

Thomas and Ewan sang along, "Molly, me darlin' girl, I'm comin' home to ye, wi' a longin' in me. Will ye lay me down an' love me darlin', for I'm goin' to ha' to leave ye."

As he sang, Ewan's eyes stung with unshed tears. When the song finished, the barkeep brought tankards of ale for the brothers. "Yer both Camerons, aye?"

"Aye," they answered together.

The man said, "I'm a MacIntyre, an' my good wife is a Cameron. A more lovin' or bossy lass ye'll nay meet. Are ye comin' or goin' to th' gatherin'?"

"We've been, not yet made up our minds on wha's best."

After eating, they returned to the stable, where hay was piled in the manger next to their horses' stalls. With full bellies, they settled down, covered themselves with their plaids, and slept. Awaking before dawn, they saddled the horses and were riding when the first light of dawn appeared.

"Thomas, after a night's sleep, how're ye feelin' about th' gatherin'? Sometimes, brother, I know less about wha' ye are thinkin' than I would a Campbell, an' they dinna think much about anything."

Thomas scratched his head, cleared his throat, and spoke, "Yer right, I dinna talk much, but because I dinna tell everyone wha' I'm thinkin' does'na mean tha' I can't. It's just tha' I dinna care to tell most of th' time. Besides, brother, yer clatter is enough for both of us, sometimes too much!"

Working hard to keep a straight face, Ewan looked at Thomas. "Thomas, that's th' longest set of words I've ever heard ye say at one time. Be ye all right?" Ewan smiled and reached over to punch Thomas.

"Aye, I am." Thomas drew a deep breath. "While ye was talkin' wi' th' men, I played cards wi' Donny MacDonald, Leon MacDonald's youngest, ye ken?"

"Aye, I know Donny. Did he win any coins off ye, Thomas?"

"Nay, I paid for our supper last night wi' th' winnin's."

"Wha' did th' lad ha' to say?" asked Ewan.

Thomas lowered his voice and said, "I thought Donny was playin' th' fool wi' me, but I dinna think so now. We were playin' 'One Up On Ye' when Donny pulled out th' nine 'o diamonds an' said, 'This card's cursed, do ye know?' I told him I did'na an' asked him to tell me about it. If I'd of known wha' he'd say, I'd not ha' asked."

Ewan snorted. "Aw, little brother, yer a big lad now. No need to be a'feared of th' dark—nothin's got ye yet."

They both remembered how Thomas would beg Ewan to go up the dark stairs to the bed chambers while he would wait at the bottom of the stairs to see if something got Ewan. "Ewan, yer did'na help any when ye said ye saw a witch ridin' a broom goin' in our bed chamber. I use tae' ha' nightmares about it, no thanks to ye, sorry brother tha' ye are!" Thomas lifted his bonnet, smoothed his hair, and continued, "Donny said Queen Mary played a card game called Comette, an' whoever had th' nine of diamonds would win th' game. Donny said th' nine of diamonds was known as th' Curse of Scotland 'cause people gambled away their purses bettin' on it."

"Thomas," Ewan said, his eyes closed and impatience in his voice, "I've heard nothin' tha' scares me. I think Donny was a'foolin' ye, aye?"

Thomas shook his head. "Wait 'til ye hear th' rest. Donny said he could tell th' outcome of th' battle we'd fight against th' Redcoats by lookin' at th' playing cards. I told him I did'na believe so, but he said he could. He shuffled th' deck, an' I cut th' cards. Then he said, 'Take a card from th' deck.' I did an' held it to my chest. Donny said, 'Yer card will show th' king of England.' I looked at th' card, an' it was th' king of hearts. I told him what th' card was, an' he said, 'King George attracts th' ladies, so he's th' king of hearts.' Then Donny said, 'Pull another card'. So, I did, an' held it so only I could see tha' it was th' two of spades. He said, 'How many are sitting here lookin' at each other?' I held out th' card, th' two of spades. Then, he said, 'Draw another card'. I did, an' this time it was th' nine of diamonds. He said, 'If ye ha' th' ace of diamonds, Scotland'll win th' battle, an' Prince Charlie, who wears diamonds on his fingers, will be our new king. But, if ye ha' th' nine of diamonds, it's our death. Those wi' th' sight ha' already told of th' man who'll lead th' English troops havin' a pack of cards wi' him. It's said he'll pull th' nine of diamonds from a deck of cards, turn it over, an' write two words on th' back, "No quarter," which means tha' all Hielanders will be killed on th' battlefield.' "'Donny,' I says, 'Wha' card do ye think I ha?" He says, 'I did'na know, but I know th' card called th' Curse of Scotland has told th' future before. Thomas, if ye ha' any other card, pray tell me, for I'll be very happy if ye do.' Ewan, my heart was poundin' when I showed Donny th' card; he said, 'Then it's done!'"

Ewan put his hand on Thomas's arm. "Now, Thomas, dinna let a card game scare ye. Mayhap he had th' cards stacked in some way tha' ye dinna see."

"Nay, Ewan. I've played cards in th' pubs, an' I'd know. If ye'd seen Donny's face, ye'd know wha' I'm meanin'. He was a'feared too. Do ye ken wha' I mean, Ewan?"

Ewan's look of disbelief was replaced with one of concern. "Aye, Thomas, I do. I surely do."

"After th' nine of diamonds came up, Donny threw th' deck in th' fire. He dinna want to put 'em in his pocket. Do ye think a deck o' cards can tell th' future?"

"I've never been one to put stock in fortune tellin' an' th' like," Ewan answered, "but I can see why yer unsettled about it; I'd be too."

Chapter 18

Mouser Cat was under the table with a gray mouse pinned down with one paw. Now that she had her prey, she could enjoy the catch. The mouse was a toy to be played with before it became her meal. The cat appeared to be bored and inattentive to the mouse that was lying between her paws. She looked at Janet and Mary and ignored the mouse as its slowly crawled away. After the mouse was a short distance away from the cat, it began to run. But at the last minute, the cat extended one paw and pulled the mouse back to her. Each time the mouse tried to get away, the cat would retrieve it. Finally, it was too much for the mouse, who went limp. The game over, Mouser Cat carried it to the mat beside the fireplace and began her meal.

Mary remarked to Janet, "There's a lesson to be learned from tha' cat an' mouse. It's a bit like th' king of England bein' able to collect taxes an' tellin' us here in Scotland wha' we can an' canna do. We're like mousey an' think we can crawl away, but it's not so. There's no gettin' away after all."

"Aye, th' question is how does mousey get by wi'out bein' a meal for th' cat?" Janet answered.

Earlier Mary had fallen in the kitchen. Had it not been for the table, she would have fallen to the floor, and as it was, she hit her head on the corner of the table. "Are ye sore from yer fall, Mary?"

"Aye, my knee hurts, but my heid bounced right off th' table." Mary chuckled. "It'll take more than a bang on wood to dent my heid."

Janet pulled a chair closer to the fire. "You stay here by th' fire, an' I'll feed th' animals. I'll pour ye a cup of tea wi' a bit of St. John's Wort."

"I believe I will." Mary sat in the chair while Janet made tea. She brought the tea to the table by Mary's chair.

"I dinna know I was so tired. I think it's th' short days an' stayin' in th' cottage overlong. Mayhap I need to get myself up an' get outside."

Janet pulled the curtain aside and looked out the frost-covered window; there was only blowing snow to be seen. "Nay, ye stay here. Rest an' sleep for a bit."

"Janet, use th' rope to guide ye to th' barn an' back." Janet wrapped her cloak around her head and shoulders and stepped into the bitter cold air. The wind had died back, leaving deep snow drifts between the cottage and the stable door. She wished she'd thought to bring the broom to sweep the snow aside as she made a path through the snow, opened the door, and stepped inside the stable.

In the dim light, she could see no sheep, stalls, or mangers. The building was bare except for shapes lying on the hay strewn dirt, some covered with blankets and others wrapped in shrouds. Dizzy, she closed her eyes and stood quietly; she heard voices, very far away, but could not understand what they were saying. There was a strong odor of death and decay. The air was warm, and even with closed eyes she sensed a brightness outside. Janet dared not open her eyes; perspiration dampened her skin. She waited, hoping to hear familiar sounds; instead she heard Mary's voice. "Put 'im in th' far corner, away from th' rest."

She waited. Then with her eyes still closed, she took a deep breath and felt chilled air fill her lungs. Her face became colder, and she smelled the scent of animals and chickens. She heard a ewe calling to her newborn lamb. Janet opened her eyes; the animals were waiting for their hay and grain. Hands shaking, she looked for eggs in the hen coops, put grain in the coops for the chickens, and pitched hay from the manger onto the stable floor. It took a few minutes to comprehend the vision. It was of something that had not yet happened; she thought about the shroud-wrapped bodies, the warmth and brightness of spring or summer, and the stench of death. Chilled, she felt her way back to the cottage, where the fireplace was crackling with a warm, bright fire. Mouser Cat was washing her face after finishing her meal, and Mary was asleep in the rocking chair, snoring. The vision, while disturbing, did not seem to be about anyone or anything familiar. She breathed a sigh of relief.

Chapter 19

Ewan and Thomas stopped at an empty crofter's cottage. "Thomas, we'll not reach Mary's cottage a'fore night fall. If we use wha' light there's left to settle in, th' storm might clear out around dawn. There's wood to build a fire, room for th' horses to come in out of th' cold, an' some hay for 'em in th' manger."

Thomas agreed. The two men sat by the fire, drinking from flasks of whisky. "It's peaceful here, Ewan. I might gi' some thought to movin' to a cottage, only I'd want to stay year round an' dinna care if I saw a body or not."

The brothers started teasing one another. "Ah, now Thomas, ye'd get to missin' Elly, an' surely ye'd want to see me an' yer sister-in-law?"

"Aye, I ken wha' yer sayin' about Elly an' Janet, but as for ye, once ever score o' years would suffice!"

The wind stilled at dawn. Ewan opened the door to a wall of snow. "We'd best sit this out. Course, it could get worse. What do we ha' to eat?"

Thomas looked in his knapsack. "Oatcakes an' cheese."

Ewan checked to see what he had. "I've bannock buns an' oats for the horses. We'll wait." Ewan threw several logs in the fire pit and leaned back against his saddle. "Thomas, I'll stop at Gordon's broch on th' way back. He's not wantin' to leave Elizabeth. He needs to know wha' could happen if he refuses."

Ewan handed Thomas a bannock bun. "We've our share of problems too. There's barely enough coins to pay this year's taxes. I've saved seeds for plantin', but we'll need to be here to do it! Who'll help us if there's no hay in th' barn an' no food in th' larder? When th' time comes to plant th' crops an' bring in th' harvest, th' villagers will help, but if there's no crops to bring in, they'll not stay!"

Ewan looked at his brother. "Thomas, yer not bad off bein' a single man. Ye ha' no worries about keepin' a roof over yer heid or feedin' yer family."

Thomas responded, "Now, Ewan, dinna think I don't worry, for I do!"

Ewan, unaccustomed to hearing his brother speak of such things, heard the sadness in his voice. "If I met a lass an' wanted to get married, I ha' nothin' to offer her. Ye ha' th' family home an' all tha' goes wi' it. I'd be unable to come up wi' a crofter's cottage as fair as this one. What'd I do? Ask my lady wife to share a haystack for a bed wi' me? Dinna think yer th' only one who thinks about things. I've not married a'fore now 'cause after lookin' th' lasses over who ha' a dowry, I'd just as soon stay single! Any I've seen, I'd ha' to put out th' light a'fore I kissed 'em."

Thomas grinned, and Ewan chuckled. "Now, Tom, when th' light's out, ye dinna think wi' th' heid on yer shoulders. It's th' other heid yer thinkin' wi'."

"Speakin' of which—" Thomas's smile widened—"I might stop to see Elly on th' way, to see how she is."

Ewan poured more whisky in their flasks. "On th' way back from Elly's, stop at Duncan's an' ask if he can spare an animal or two for Inverness."

Thomas shook his head. "Nay, Ewan, he can't care for his animals or even climb th' staircase wi'out help!"

"Damn!" Ewan cursed. "I dinna realize it was tha' bad."

Ewan scratched his head and thought back to when Duncan and Anne were married. "Anne's th' daughter of an English lord. I'd reckon she married Duncan wi' a good dowry."

"Ewan, ye talk when ye should be listenin'! Anne had no dowry when she married Duncan. Her father disowned her because she married a Hielander. He's since forgiven her, but there was no dowry. When Duncan an' Anne's first laddie was born, Anne's father sent word he'd set aside fifty gold coins for his grandson, providin' he was sent to him to raise."

Ewan was shocked as he listened to Thomas' words. "How'd ye know?"

"I usually stop at Duncan's to break up th' ride from Elly's. I always enjoy visitin' wi him an' Anne. He makes a good malt whisky, an' Anne always has an apple tart tha' she serves wi' a sharp cheese. Now there's a treat, good cheese wi' apples. Ye'd think cream'd be best, but cheese is my favorite."

Ewan shook his head. "Thomas, why did ye not say somethin' a'fore now? I'd ha' helped Duncan if I'd known."

"Just as ye ha' yer ways, Ewan, so does Duncan. He has his pride," Thomas responded. "He'd not ask for a handout, aye?"

Ewan said, "Aye, I'm th' same. Say, Thomas, we could always cross th' border an' steal a couple of animals. None'd be th' wiser, an' we'd sell 'em at Fort William an' gi' Duncan th' money. Nay." Ewan paused. "Now tha' I think about it, we'll naught do tha'."

The Dark One, overhearing the conversation from his perch on a lone tree outside the cottage, considered the man's words. "For a moment I thought the human, who was so angry when his own cattle were stolen, was planning to carry out the same deed. But at the last minute, his conscience overruled his plan."

The demon pulled at his long, pointed ears. "Damn, damn! His idea was excellent! There are times when I can thwart a human's better judgment, but as for the conscience they all have, unless

147

they deliberately choose to ignore it, there's little I can do." Then he stroked his pointed chin and smiled as he went on, "But once they ignore it, they'll do it again!"

By noon the sun shone with a thin, watery light. Ewan turned north as he left the cottage; Thomas went southwest. Late in the afternoon, he reached Mary's cottage. She insisted that Ewan and Janet not leave until after supper. But after eating, Ewan pushed his chair back and yawned. "Ewan, it's too late to start out."

"Aye, Auntie, it is." He stretched out in front of the fire while Janet slept in the fireside chair. The next morning, Mary handed Janet two knapsacks, one filled with food and the other with all the packets and notes Janet had carefully written. "Ewan, yer did a smart thin' when ye married this lassie. Bring her to me this spring, an we'll go a-pickin' flowers an' plants."

"Aye, I will, Auntie."

On the way to Gordon's broch, Janet waited for Ewan to share his news, but Ewan said he'd wait until they could sit down together. When they reached Gordon's broch, Ewan took Gordon aside. "We'll be goin' to Inverness when th' date is set."

"When th' time comes, I'll join ye."

"You've put my mind at ease, Gordon!"

January snows were added to by more in February. It was a cold and wet spring; an icy rain driven by a bitter north wind fell almost every day in March. On the last day of the month, the Lochiel's messenger arrived. The battle would take place in April. The Scottish army would gather at Culloden's Field on 15 April, 1746. Janet questioned his plans when he separated out cattle to deliver to Inverness. When Ewan did not answer, she knew he was not ready to tell her. After supper one evening, he remarked that the days were beginning to lengthen and asked if she would like to walk with him.

As they walked down the path, Janet noticed the rose bushes beside the rock wall had tiny green leaves. "Ah," she said, "I've never been so happy to see a bit o' green. After th' winter we've had, I'm ready for green grass, flowers, an' fresh air. Soon we'll open th' windows an' doors an' sweep out th' dirt an' dust of winter."

Ewan bought her hand to his mouth and kissed it. "Dinna open th' windows an' doors just yet. Look to th' north an' west, lass; there's dark clouds. There's be more snow comin'. Nay, love, winter's not yet over." Ewan pointed to the high glens. "Th' snow lies thick up there."

"Aye, it does, husband. Please, get on wi' wha' yer wantin' to tell me."

Ewan cleared his throat. "I've waited to tell you about th' upcomin' battle, as I needed to be wi' you in th' comfort of our home for as long as I could a'fore I spoke to ye about it. Dinna think I'm doin' this because I want to, for I don't! I've given thought to sellin' everythin' an' goin' to th' colonies in America or elsewhere. But I keep comin' back to not wantin' to leave Scotland. When Thomas returns from carryin' th' fiery cross, we'll deliver twenty animals to Inverness to feed Charlie's army. Some of th' animals are ours, an' some are Gordon's." Ewan spoke with great tenderness. "Janet, lass, I'll return home! I'll go wi' tha' in my mind."

"Ewan, I knew ye'd be leavin' when ye came home from th' gatherin'. I've been preparin' for it, just as ye ha' prepared yerself. Nay, I dinna accept yer leavin', but I'll listen to wha' ye ha' to say, an' then I'll begin doin' wha' I must."

Ewan hugged her. "I love ye, lass. Dinna forget it. Th' Cameron wives are to send bread, cheese, an' oatcakes for th' clan, an' one of Charlie's men, a Mr. O'Sullivan, will see to th' provisions after we deliver 'em to Inverness." He looked into her eyes. "We'll meet at Culloden's Moor in mid-April. Donald says Charles has a large number of men who'll join us. I know they say ammunition an' artillery will be there, but to my mind, we'd best take our own. Lord George Murray will lead th' Hielanders on th' battlefield. When I heard he'd be in charge, it raised my hopes. He led th' battle tha' won Edinburgh for Charles. I've not heard any say but good about him."

Ewan took Janet's arm and began walking back to the broch. He opened the kitchen door and waited for Janet to step inside. "A cup of tea, Janet—would ye make one for me?"

"Ye know I'd do anythin' for ye tha' I can." She looked at Ewan's face and shook her head. "Ewan, wipe tha' sorrowful look off yer face; I can hardly stand to see yer lookin' like ye lost yer last an' best friend. Surely it's not as bad as ye claim, aye?"

"Aye, it is, an' worse! Th' king increased taxes on th' lands around Fort William, sayin' th' owners had th' extra protection of th' king's army nearby an' they should pay for it. Th' tax was to provide provisions for th' military, but after King George took his portion, there was little left. Th' fort's ordered their soldiers to take wha' was needed from land owners, be it animals, fodder, or th' contents of a full larder wi' th' full protection o' th' king! Ye'll nay know th' man by name. Wha' happened to him an' his family is a shame an' disgrace. Brian MacDonald had a fine broch, close to th' fort. He made a livin' buyin', tradin', an' sellin' good Hieland cattle. I bought my animals from him. If Brian had a fault it was bein' outspoken in places when he should've been listenin', but that's th' MacDonald way of doin' things."

Janet threw up her hands. "And yer sayin' th' Camerons dinna do th' same?"

Ewan smiled. "No, lass, I'm nay sayin' tha', for we do. But Brian was in th' wrong place to speak his mind. He was havin' a pint at th' inn when he said he was not sparin' any more provisions to th' red-coated English soldiers."

Ewan paused to drink from his cup. "Ewan, I'm thinkin' there won't be a happy endin' to this tale, aye?"

"Aye, but it'll help ye know th' reason why there has to be a day of reckonin' between England an' Scotland. One evenin' Brian was late comin' home after deliverin' a load of barley. He had a purse full of coins an' a belly full of ale. Horses an' wagons were in his courtyard, an' when he walked into th' broch, th' bloody Redcoats were emptyin' out his larder. A servin' girl lay on th' floor in th' kitchen, an' th' poor lass lived just long enough to tell Brian tha' his wife an' bairns were safe in th' attic. Brian drew his pistol an' shot one of th' soldiers a'fore he was overpowered an' tied to th' kitchen table. Then th' sorry bastards cut his balls off an' told him they'd be cookin' 'em for supper to ha' along wi' th' cheese an' bread they filched from his larder! One of 'em said 'Keep yer mouth shut, or ye'll be wi'out yer cock!' Before th' soldiers left, they burned his barns to th' ground, an' his cattle an' horses perished in th' flames. Brian held his pistol to his heid an' pulled th' trigger."

Ewan saw the look on Janet's face. "Th' MacDonalds want revenge, but how can a clan, even though th' numbers are many, take on th' king's military?"

Janet shook her head, "They can't. Ewan, I've heard ye talkin' wi' Thomas an' yer cousins, an' I know ye ha' doubts about th' bloody prince. I'm questionin' Donald sendin' Cameron lads into a battle tha' won't be won. I dinna think th' pretendin' prince has th' wits to win a battle!"

Ewan nodded his head in agreement. "Donald says there's somethin' about Charlie pullin' at his wig as if it's not big enough for his head. Mayhap if he did'na have such a high regard for himself, it'd fit better, aye?"

Janet met Ewan's smile with one of her own. Ewan lowered his voice. "Ye'll be safe here 'til th' battle is over. Ye'll not need to go lookin' for food. Feed th' animals at night, an' there's plenty of fodder an' water in th' barn. Keep a low fire, enough to take th' chill away. I've thought of takin' ye to Anne's 'til I return, but there won't be any soldiers nearby 'til th' battle is over. Th' women o' the village will go to family elsewhere. Th' men will join us fightin'."

Ewan shook his head. "Janet, I should ha' told yer earlier, but I forgot. Megan's wi' child, an' John took her to be wi' James an' Abby. He dinna want to leave her alone."

"Ah, James will go too. I'm glad Megan will be wi' Mother."

"Janet, if th' battle is lost, when ye hear of it dinna delay. Take

Prince an' ride to Duncan's broch. Then ye, Anne, an' th' lads cross th' border to England, where ye'll be safe wi' Anne's family. Did'na go to your parents' broch! It might be in th' middle o'things. Later, ye might be able to make th' trip."

"Ewan, should we bring Elizabeth an' th' bairns here?"

"Gordon seems to think she'll want to stay home. She feels safe there."

"I'll welcome their company if she changes her mind."

"I've not made efforts to bring Duny home, as th' Lochiel would ha' him fight wi' me."

Janet squared her shoulders. "Ewan, Donald would put Duny by yer side, an' he'd be no more than a target. Ye've some fightin' experience, but Duny's only fired a pistol at a rabbit." Janet looked at Ewan and placed her finger under his chin, bringing his face up so that his eyes were looking into hers. "Tell me wha' ye think will happen. I want to know."

Ewan's voice was husky. "I think it's going to be a bloody fight, wi' th' clans fallin' to th' king's army. I tell ye, th' win at Prestonpans is small compared to fightin' for th' throne in England."

"Well, then," Janet said, "I'll nay waste time cryin'. It might be one of my oatcakes or a slab of cheese tha' gives ye strength to stand yer ground on th' battlefield."

Time passed, with dark, icy days and long, cold nights. There was no spring melt, and snow clouds clung to the high glens. Ewan reinforced the courtyard pens and built new mangers inside the barns for his cows about to calve.

Chapter 20

"A slender crosslet, formed wi' care,
A cubit's length in measure due,
Th' shaft an' limbs be rods of Yew,
Whose parents in Inch-Cauilloch wave
Their shadows o'er Clan Alpine's grave
An', answerin' Lomond's breezes deep,
Soothe many a chieftain's endless sleep.
Fast as th' fatal symbol flies,
In arms th' hits an' hamlets rise,
From windin' glen, from upland town,
They pour'd each hardy tenant down."

Crossed and bound with sinew, charred yew branches were wrapped in cloths bathed in the blood of a lamb. The fiery cross was a call to battle for the clans. Thomas's task was to take the cross to every Cameron broch. If the battle was lost, the English would take their lands and families to do with as they wished. When the Highlanders met Thomas at their gates, the men left newly tilled fields or sheep folds with shears in their hands. Some came from barns where newborn foals lay beside their mothers. They were all bound by blood to follow their chief's direction.

When Thomas reached John MacIntyre's broch, John took the cross. "When I'm done, Thomas, it'll go to th' MacDonalds."

On April 10, Ewan kissed Janet good-bye, mounted his horse, and caught up with Thomas herding the cattle to Inverness. Around his neck, Ewan wore a cross Janet had fashioned from long, fine hair of his Highland cattle. His horse pulled a cart filled with oatcakes, cheese, bread, and bottles of ale. They both were armed with pistols, ammunition, sharpened dirks, and broadswords. Because there was no grazing for the animals, they stopped at farms along the way to ask for fodder. Each time they were queried, "Are ye taking 'em to market?"

Ewan's answer was, "Nay, they're to feed th' clans fightin' for a Stuart king to take th' place of England's German king."

Some replied, "I'll pitch out hay for 'em. Then ye come in for a dram an' a bite."

Others said, "Be gone wi' ye!"

Three days later, the two brothers herded the cattle into Inverness, where they met Duncan, Gordon, and Mr. Hay, who informed them he had orders from John O'Sullivan to accept the cattle for slaughter and the wagonload of food. He advised the meat and food would be transported to Culloden's field and dismissed the men with a wave of his hand. Uneasy, Ewan and Thomas said nothing. Thomas muttered under his breath when the thought of a playing card, the nine of diamonds, came to mind. The narrow road from Inverness to Culloden's field was deeply rutted by horses, wagons, and men traveling to the battlefield.

Chapter 21

When Ewan and Thomas reached Culloden's moor, men gathered around them, "Ha' ye any to eat? We'd settle for oatcakes, anythin'."

"Aye, we ha' some. There'll be more on th' way," Ewan emptied his knapsack. "Here lads, bread an' oatcakes. Be ye settlin' in for th' night?"

The answer was, "Nay, we'll be marchin' to Nairn, an' we've had naught to eat since two days ago!"

Ewan introduced himself. "Yer goin' to Nairn?"

"Aye, we leave at dark. Th' prince says we'll ambush th' Red Coats while they're drinkin' an' sittin' around th' fire. It's a bloody waste of time lookin' for their camp in those snow-covered hills. We've a long walk ahead o' us, lads! If we dinna find 'em, we'll march back an' do battle on th' morrow! Bloody hell!"

While Thomas handed out the last of the bread and oatcakes from his knapsack, Ewan spoke to the men. "Lads! Two days ago, we delivered twenty head of animals an' a wagon load of food to Inverness. They'll be butchered an' sent here alon' wi' bread, cheese an' oatcakes."

Edward MacGregor, standing beside Ewan, quietly said, "Ewan, ye'd not know it, but John O'Sullivan, th' prince's right-hand man, decides who gets wha'. If th' food was comin', it'd be here by now. It'd take part of a day to kill, butcher, an' pack th' meat an' th' rest of th' day to deliver it. No need to keep th' bread an' cheese 'til' they were finished wi' th' meat. It ought ter be here by now. Nay, lad, there'll not be anythin' comin' from Inverness."

"Jesus wept, Edward!" Ewan said. "There's enough meat to feed every man on this moor! Where is it?"

Edward MacGregor gazed into the distance and said, "Mayhap we'll run across it on our way to Nairn."

Ewan stared at the man, unable to grasp his meaning. "When'll they hand out th' guns an' ammunition?"

Edward stared at Ewan. "Guns an' ammunition? There's none to hand out."

"No weapons?" Ewan asked.

"Nay, they've gone th' same way th' food did."

The truth hit Ewan hard. He looked for Thomas. "Thomas, there's no weapons or food! Those of us who brought rifles, pistols, gunpowder, an' lead will be armed. Those who didn't will be wi'out! Th' food we brought for th' men has gone elsewhere!"

Ewan paced back and forth. "I'll ha' a word wi' th' Lochiel. Then I'm goin' to Inverness to look for somethin' to feed these men. How in th' hell can we fight wi' empty bellies?"

Ewan crossed the field to a farm house and knocked on the door. A woman opened the door and asked what he wanted. He replied it was a matter of urgency and he needed to speak with Donald Cameron. She motioned for him to come in and wait in a long hallway with several closed doors and one standing partially open. The smell of roasted meat wafted through the air. If the men outside knew there was food here, there would be a mutiny.

He sat on a chair outside the room with the open door and waited. A man with a pronounced lisp spoke. "Lord George, in

Derby, you gave me no choice but to withdraw from England!" The voice became louder. "We should have proceeded on to London and seized the throne. But you advised we must return to Scotland, and against my better judgment, we turned back!"

"Charles," another voice answered, "You will recall tha' we had no ammunition, and th' king's army had us surrounded on three sides. You knew there was no choice but to retreat. You agreed to it."

"Do not use that word in my presence! We did *not* retreat. We merely withdrew to wait for a better opportunity, Lord George!"

Ewan realized he was overhearing a conversation between Charles Edward Stuart and Lord George Murray. "George, must I remind you of who I am?"

Lord George Murray did not respond right away. He recalled the doubts he had when he heard Charles Stuart would lead the Jacobite rebellion in Scotland. Before the rebellion began, Charles sent the duke of Perth to Lord Murray to offer him the position of field commander in Charles's army. Lord Murray advised the duke that he did not believe Charles could win the rebellion. Murray declined the offer; he knew the risk of a hastily-thrown-together uprising. He believed there was an extremely high probability that Charles's plans to overthrow King George II would end in failure. Lord George loved Scotland, but he hated the high taxes and resulting oppression forced on Scotland's people by King George. He reconsidered Prince Charles' offer and wrote a letter to his brother, Charles Murray, advising that his loyalty to Scotland forced him to think first and only of Scotland's people. He wrote, "If this young pretender has even the thinnest of chances to free Scotland from England's oppression, I must for all conscientious reasons join the Stuart cause."

Lord Murray accepted Charles's offer to join the Jacobite uprising and received the commission of lieutenant-general in the prince's army. While he pledged his loyalty to Charles Edward Stuart, it was because of his love for Scotland and concern for her future that he accepted the offer. The prince and O'Sullivan completely ignored Lord Murray's expertise and advice as they planned the uprising. John O'Sullivan advised George Murray that his opinions would be considered if they were in written format and delivered to him for consideration. There would be almost no opportunity for Lord George to speak directly to the prince.

Lord George, a natural leader of men, readily gained the confidence of the Highlanders. They knew of his courage during the 1715 uprising and the win at Prestonpans. Lord George was familiar with the Highland way of fighting. When Charles, following the advice of Secretary O'Sullivan, criticized the fighting methods of the Highlanders, Murray intervened on their behalf. After Lord George led the Jacobite troops to victory at Prestonpans, he believed he had earned the right to speak directly to Charles. Now, on 15 April 1746, Murray had serious concerns about the next day's battle. He had to make the reasons and need for a change of plans known to Charles, and this would be his only opportunity to do so.

"Your Highness, I bow to your royal ancestors, who were kings of Scotland an' England. It is because of their loyalty to Scotland tha' I am here. Sir, I too am bound by loyalty to Scotland." Looking around the room, Lord Murray said, "Charles, I do not see your valet, nor O'Sullivan. Will they be joining us?"

"No," the prince replied. "Johnnie is overseeing preparations for my coronation wardrobe. The fabrics I've selected have just arrived. John is attending to business elsewhere."

Lord Murray stood and addressed him directly. "Charles, I must formally advise you of my concerns about th' upcoming battle an' my recommendations to rectify, at least to some extent, those concerns. My recommendations may be contrary to th' opinions of some. However, even so, sir, I am under obligation to speak out. If I do not, it would be against my written agreement wi' you to provide counsel regarding these very matters. Sir, I strongly advise you to immediately move th' Highlanders an' all others who are willing to fight in this battle to th' hills facing th' Nairn River, away from Culloden's moor."

Charles turned his face away from Lord George.

"Your Highness, I ask tha' you give this your attention. It is not too late! Culloden's flat, boggy moor is unsuitable for th' Highlanders, who are far more accustomed to makin' a charge down a hillside. It is, however, ideal for Duke Cumberland's men an' horses! Sir, if th' duke had selected Culloden's field for th' battle, he could not ha' chosen a site tha' would better meet his needs! If our army relocates to th' hills, we could lead a charge tha' would place th' Highlanders at a small advantage. Even so, sir, th' odds are still against us."

Lord Murray spoke directly to the prince. "Th' king's royal army has heavy fire power, wi' a massive supply of ammunition." Lord Murray raised his voice. "Sir, by all military standards, we are going into battle unarmed! Th' small amount of artillery gained from th' English Army at Prestonpans was depleted during th' invasion of northern England. At last count, we ha' less than a dozen cannons an' even fewer cannon balls!"

Lord Murray held out his hand, index finger pointed at Charles. "Your Highness, th' Highlanders are unarmed; most of them came here thinkin' there would be weapons waitin' for them. Sir, you asked if I know who you are. Yes, I know who you are! But, many of th' men who are going to battle for you do not know you. They gathered here after being told by their clan chieftains tha' there would be weapons an' food waitin' for 'em. But Your Highness, not only are their hands empty, their bellies are as well!"

Charles sipped from his water glass.

"Highness, I am accustomed to leadin' men into battle. But if they do not ha' adequate weaponry, th' outcome is predictable. There must be a reason for th' lack of weapons an' food. I intend to find out wha' tha' reason is. Th' men believed they would have weapons!"

"Lord George!" Charles pushed back his chair, stood, and shouted. "You are directing unfounded suspicions toward my secretary and perhaps even myself!" Charles struggled to get his lisp under control. "Mr. O'Sullivan tells me you are argumentative and question his directives."

The prince folded his arms across his chest and let out an exasperated sigh. "Your mannerisms are the same toward me! I well understand John's reluctance to deal with you, and for this reason, I must take full command of the Jacobite army. You may lead the troops out on the field on the morrow; however, they will wait for my order to fire the first shot. Lord Murray, of all that we are undertaking here, is there anything that meets your approval?"

Charles peered into Lord Murray's face, eyebrows raised and lips pursed.

Lord Murray calmly replied, "Your Highness, I agree wi' you on sendin' a regiment of men to find Cumberland's camp at Nairn. Th' long walk will be well worth it if we ha' th' advantage of a surprise attack. It would gi' us a win, which we sorely need. Sir, in th' interest of saving th' men needless walkin' as we search for th' English campsite, I urge you to send scouts on horseback who will report back on th' English army's whereabouts. We can then follow their directions to th' site."

"I think not, Lord George. There's not sufficient time."

Even though he knew Prince Charles would not want to hear him speak of the man who would lead the king's royal army into battle, Lord George said, "Charles, do you ha' knowledge of Th' Duke of Cumberland?"

"Yes, John O'Sullivan has fully advised me of Cumberland's military history." Charles Stuart looked away from George Murray, picked up his fork, and began clinking the tines against his wine glass.

"Allow me to share a little more of William Augustus's experience an' background wi' you. He was th' commander in chief of all British, Hanoverian, Austrian, an' Dutch troops at th' Battle of Fontenoy, an' he learned well from that experience. We've all felt th' heat from th' fire he's been breathin' down our necks for th' past month! A spy in th' king's army tells me th' duke has trained his troops in tactics especially for fighting th' Highlanders. Sir, he is interested in one thing: ceasing Jacobite uprisings once an' for all. He will not rest until he has accomplished it."

Charles laid the fork aside, picked up a spoon and began tapping it on the table. "Your Highness, if you are to gain possession of the throne for your father, your every action an' thought must be centered on winnin' tomorrow's battle! If you do not accept military guidance, then th' misfortune of your decision will fall upon th' poorly equipped Highlanders! Your inattention to th' very things tha' matter th' most cause me concern! Have you walked Culloden's moor from one end to th' other? Are you knowledgeable about th' terrain where th' battle will take place? Where will our army be positioned? God forbid, but if there's no choice but to call a retreat, what is your plan for th' men?"

Charles Stuart picked at a loose button on his jacket.

"Charles! You must consider these questions. If the enemy charges our army, how will we counterattack wi'out breakin' formation? Wh' if they call a retreat? Will we pursue or let them depart? I do not know your plans, an' in th' absence of John O'Sullivan, I must ask you personally."

Prince Charles pushed his chair away from the table, stood, and turned his back to Lord Murray.

"Your Highness, th' men are fightin' amongst themselves. Many of them ha' left th' battlefield to search for food. They need food before they go into battle. Sir, most of them are not armed! Where is O'Sullivan wi' th' artillery an' ammunition you promised th' clan chiefs?"

Prince Charles faced George Murray. "George, you are repeating yourself! Listen to me. Yes, I know the men are leaving the campsite, but they will return, eager to do battle. I spoke to them earlier, promising them the spoils of the battle, and they cheered me, George!"

Charles picked up a china cup and set it down so hard that it broke into pieces. "Lord George, muster the troops, and let's be on our way to Nairn. I believe weapons and food supplies will be arriving at any moment. As for the battle site, what matter is it where the battle is fought? Or how the troops form their lines or manage a retreat, be they English or Scots? I cannot be concerned with every small detail of this military action. I have full respect for Secretary O'Sullivan and his military expertise. He selected the battle site, and you would do well to regard him as I do."

The prince looked at George Murray. "As a military man, Lord George, you should be jubilant about our accomplishments. With far less men and artillery than the royal army has, we are now in position to gain a victory for the royal Stuarts and Scotland!"

Charles approached Lord George and put a hand on his shoulder. The two men looked eye to eye at one another. "I must correct you, Lord George. When you assume that I have not studied our opponents and their methods of warfare, you are very wrong. I assure you that when we go to battle on the morrow, we will face an army of uneducated English lackeys who first picked up a rifle two days ago and now call themselves soldiers! Their fine red coats with the brass buttons mean nothing when it comes to bravery. Let me remind you how we saw the backs of their coats flapping against their arses when they deserted the battlefield at Prestonpans! There were many who said we would not win, and yet we did! You have made the mistake of underestimating me again, Lord George Murray!"

Lord George chose his words carefully. "Sir, th' hungry an' weary men sittin' outside in mud are not th' same as th' strong an' ready men tha' fought at Prestonpans. Tha' battle site was far different than th' marshy bog here. You speak of English lackeys an' their rifles? I can only wish our men were as well armed! Perhaps th' grumblings of the men's bellies will sound loud enough tha' th' English soldiers will turn an' run, thinking there is a new weapon being readied!"

"George, this is the same thing you were ranting on about earlier. Do you have anything else to speak about?"

"I do. Ha' you looked out th' window? Hell! Th' field is naught but mud, wi' standin' water everywhere."

Charles shook his head and with a voice full of sarcasm said, "George, surely you, the great and well known military officer, have fought battles in less than desirable conditions!"

Ewan stood when a red-faced Prince Charles Edward Stuart came marching down the hall. Ewan could not help but stare at the prince's wig; his ear protruded on the right side, and his left ear was hidden by the edge of the wig. Ewan thought, *I wish Janet could see this. How she'd laugh.*

Another door opened. Several chieftains, including the Lochiel, sat at a table with the remains of a meal in front of them. From the doorway Ewan asked, "Donald, I'd like a word?"

The Lochiel nodded and stepped out of the room. "Yer takin' my time, Ewan. We're drawin' out th' battle lines."

"Donald, ye asked us to bring animals an' other provisions to Inverness. We left it all there as ordered by Mr. Hay, who said he'd be deliverin' both food an' meat here. But where is it?" Ewan spoke quickly, afraid that Donald would walk away before he finished. "There's neither food nor weapons. If I can buy oats an' water in Inverness, we can stir up brose for th' men to gi' 'em strength. But, th' weapons? I can do naught about tha'."

Donald, perspiring, searched for his handkerchief. Placing his hand on Donald's shoulder, Ewan waited for a response. The chieftain wiped his brow and said, "Many of th' men are goin' to Nairn to make a surprise attack on the Redcoats. I'll need ye here to keep peace amongst th' ones who remain."

"Donald, listen to me!" Ewan tightened his grip on Donald's shoulder and peered into his eyes. "They're hungry! It would'na take much to give 'em enough to do battle."

"Ewan Cameron, you heard my orders! Unhand me now!"

Ewan turned, walked out of the house, and found Thomas sitting with others of the clan. Quietly he asked, "Thomas, our horses—where are they?"

"Tethered at the edge of th' field. Wha' did Donald say about ye goin?" Ewan motioned for Thomas to walk with him. "I'm going against his word, but I'll bring back wha' I can find for th' men an' see my suspicions either put to rest or dealt wi'. Come wi' me, Thomas!"

"Ewan, ye'll not make it to Inverness an back a'fore daylight. I'll stay here wi' Gordon an' Duncan."

Ewan told Thomas about the conversation he had overheard. "I sat in tha' broch' at th' edge of th' field an' listened to Charlie an' Lord George arguing. Lord George said tha' Hieland men are not used to fightin' on flat land. Th' prince told Lord George tha' he'd be given' th' orders to start th' battle."

Ewan placed his hand on Thomas's shoulder. "If Donald asks, tell him tha' I'm at th' trenches wi' a sick belly. I'll be back wi' wha' I can find, if no more than oats an' water."

"Godspeed, brother." Thomas's words were not heard, for Ewan was already on his way. That night, on horseback, Charles Stuart and Lord Murray led a troop of Highlanders to the snow-covered hills surrounding Nairn. They found no signs of the Duke's army, and the weary men turned around to walk the twelve-mile return trip to Culloden's moor. Exhausted, they reached the battlefield where no warm fires burned and there was no food. It would be only a few hours until they would muster for battle.

Death looked at the men gathered on Culloden's field, some barely past the smooth faces of childhood. He considered the battle about to take place. 'If I could feel sadness, I would do so knowing their lives will be taken from them.'

The Dark One, perched beside Death, clicked his claws and smiled. "Today the events will take place! There's one more task to do."

He pointed toward the sky. Skimming just over the tops of the trees, a handsome raptor flew with wings spread wide, showing his chestnut, white, and black feathers. The bird paused just above the head of The Dark One. "You called, sir? It has been a long time. How may I be of service to you?"

"Clamhan, this is a special day for you and your kin. There will be flesh, more than you can consume, and after you provide a service for me, you have my permission to partake of the feast. One of mine needs the use of your eyes and knowledge. While he is not yet aware that you will be of assistance to him, with time, he will learn to rely on your ability to hunt and kill. Serve him well, my beautiful Kite, and a great gift will be yours."

"As you wish, sir. Who requires my services?"

"William Augustus, the man who leads the king's troops. You will be able to communicate with him, and he will answer you in the same manner. It will take time for him to accustom himself to using your skills instead of relying on his own, but eventually the two of you will become as one. Stay close to him, and keep yourself hidden from the sight of others."

"I am your servant, Dark One; many times you have provided sustenance for me and my offspring, and I am indebted to you." The great bird silently flew away, seeking the one he was to join with.

Chapter 22

Nairn, a small fishing village on the shore of the Moray Firth, lay northeast of Culloden's field. On the night of 15 April 1746, The Duke of Cumberland and selected members of the king's army spent the evening and night at the Nairn Public House and Inn, celebrating The Duke's twenty-fifth birthday. On their way to Nairn, The Duke and his men were within a stone's throw of Prince Charles, Lord Murray, and their men. They passed in the night; neither knew of the other's presence. The Jacobite regiment returned to Culloden, tired, and in despair when they did not find the enemy. In comparison, the king's men ate, drank, and rested well after an evening of celebration.

Earlier that day, William Augustus had traveled to Culloden's field alone. He surveyed the lay of the land, noting the prevailing winds from the south. With his troops facing north, the winds would blow over their heads and into the faces of Stuart's army. He walked through dense heather and gorse in the boggy marshland, the watershed for the great Culloden and Assich Forests. He made note of a low rock retaining wall. It would slow down the prince's men, if they got that far. William appreciated the selection of this particular field. It was, in fact, the only level ground to be found in the area. There was not a better location for the king's royal army to do battle with the prince's Jacobite army. The Duke of Cumberland maintained the strictest of discipline in his camp by rewarding those who met his standards and discharging those who did not. After studying the aggressive charge of the Highland clans, he trained his troops to carry out a unique way to bring down a Highland soldier. The famous Highland charge, with one hand holding a sword high and the other holding a shield over the heart, was not easy to overcome; however, it left several vulnerable areas on the Highlander body. Cumberland taught his soldiers to ignore the Highlander standing directly in front of them and instead bayonet the man to the right, whose torso was unprotected from the side. The man on one's left would be doing the same, aiming for the Highlander to his right. Cumberland's men learned to trust their fellow soldiers, and every man knew exactly what to do. Each soldier defended himself, protected his fellow soldiers, and stood fast. There was no need to discuss a retreat. It would not be necessary. They practiced aiming a rifle at the center of the forehead for one perfect shot; then, with a pistol, they aimed a similar shot at the man behind the one who had just fallen. After a soldier discharged both his rifle and pistol, he would exchange places with the soldier just behind him, gaining time to reload both pistol and rifle so he could replace the soldier who by now had emptied both of his firearms. Soldiers who mastered this skill received an invitation to attend the duke's birthday celebration, where there would be food, drink, and ladies to entertain, a highly esteemed reward.

William Augustus was not a handsome man. Because he was fond of rich food and drink, he had a paunch and a double chin beneath his long face. His eyes were black and piercing. He favored wearing a full wig at all times. Considering his size, he carried his weight well and possessed uncommon strength. He had no trouble mounting his horse or walking an entire day alongside his troops. William had few interests other than military matters; his objective was to do battle and win.

Inside the inn's tavern, the men gathered around their commander. "Sir, a salute for your twenty-fifth birthday," a young soldier called out.

William nodded and shouted to the barmaid, "Bring ale for all, and keep it coming! Men, I salute you!" William raised his tankard. "I praise you for your hard work. Captains, lieutenants, and soldiers, you stand proud to represent His Majesty, King George II."

One young soldier spoke up. "Milord, sir! We're prepared to meet our opponents and know what to expect from them. But sir, we know little about Charles Stuart. What can you tell us about him?"

William emptied his tankard of ale and nodded to the soldier. "Corporal, it is always important to be aware of your opponent's strengths. When they are known, you also will know his weaknesses. There is not a remote chance that Charles Edward Stuart will win the battle on the morrow, and I'll tell you why."

Cumberland eased into a chair and began his story. "Charles is the last and only hope of the Catholic Stuarts to regain the crown. Believe me, the prince is desperate."

The Duke of Cumberland held his flask out to be refilled. "I want," he told the serving girls, "These men to have their fill of drink and food. You are serving soldiers loyal to His Royal Highness, King George."

The duke continued, "Charles grew up in Italy, spoon-fed by his parents that it is his divine right" to be the king of England. In other words, through his bloodline, he believes himself appointed by God to be the succeeding ruler. Somehow, the prince's father, James Francis, managed to gain the support of France's King Louis, who we know seeks control over Germany and her people. Charles Stuart, with the help of his father, planned a rebellion that would be financed by King Louis and the Church of Rome. We became aware of the plans when a loose tongue in Louis's palace sent word to us confirming Louis's agreement to finance the Jacobite uprising."

William continued, warming to the tale concerning his initial meeting with Charles Stuart. "Several years ago, I traveled to France to gain information. I was not known there, could speak French fluently, and blended in with the king's military men."

The duke emptied his tankard and called out to the serving girl. "Wench, bring all of your malted whisky." He gestured to the group. "You must try this whisky. It is unlike any other because it is made from only one grain, barley."

The Duke drank the whisky brought to him and held his cup out for more. The serving girl smiled at him as she was filling the container, but when she looked into his eyes, she caught her breath. It was as if she had caught a glimpse of the darkness at the bottom of an underground cavern. Her intention had been to invite him to join her and her three companions in an evening of pleasurable futtering; however, she was unable to speak even one word.

The duke rearranged himself in his chair, crossed his legs, and continued with full cup in hand, "I was invited to attend an officers' gathering at the palace. I arrived in a borrowed uniform and joined a group of men on leave from Marseille. We were discussing the latest firearms, body armory, and the use of horses on the battlefield when the conversation was interrupted to announce a visitor, 'His Highness, Charles Edward Stuart, Prince of Wales and son of James, the next king of England!' Immediately, Charles was the center of attention. He greeted us and asked that each one of us introduce ourselves to him. Not wanting to draw attention to myself, I stood beside the last two officers in the line. Charles bowed and acknowledged each man. When it was my turn, I said only my given name, 'William.' As was the fashion, I clicked my heels together and bowed as I was speaking. It was just enough to obscure what I had not said. Charles stood in front of me, touched the lapel of my borrowed jacket, and asked if I knew the tailor's name. I responded in French that I did not know the tailor's name. Charles said he would have a tailor prepare a similar uniform for himself, exchanging velvet for the woven wool."

The duke laughed. "The son of James, the next king of England, was more interested in the fabric and cut of my jacket than he was in establishing a relationship with French officers who likely would be sent to the British Isles to provide support for him when he led the Jacobite uprising! You ask what I think about the man we will face on the battlefield? I wager he has not taken the time to walk over the field where his troops will be forming battle lines."

He stood. "Lads, Charles's field commander, Lord George Murray, is a foe to be reckoned with. Murray, in spite of all of his battlefield experience and expertise, will not be giving the order to fire the first round tomorrow. The prince himself will be giving the order."

William Augustus smiled as he spoke. "Lord Murray would have the good sense to get on with the battle, while Prince Charles will not be able to find his arse with both hands!"

This drew loud laughter and hoots. The duke smiled and raised an eyebrow. "Our Jacobite friends say the Highlanders are short on weapons and food. If Charles Stuart ignores Lord George's advice—" Cumberland raised his cup in a toast—"there'll be a quick end to the battle, with little loss of lives to the king's royal army!"

Everyone raised their cups and cheered. "A question, Milord?"

"Yes, Lieutenant?"

"When you met the prince, did you think you might one day face him on the battlefield?"

William, with wisdom gained in his early years, responded with a wry smile. "Every person you meet has the potential to be an enemy. Yes, I had a premonition that I would one day meet the prince in battle. Tomorrow, it will take place, and lads, I am ready!"

Several scantily dressed young women joined the group. That night, they provided an age-old service for the men of the king's royal army. All but The Duke of Cumberland engaged in the taking of sexual favors from the women. He observed the activities, but his thoughts were focused on winning the battle. By midnight, the men were asleep. Early the next morning, after a meal of freshly baked bread, ham, boiled eggs, butter, and jam, they mounted their horses and made their way to Culloden's field. On the way they compared the sexual talents of the women who had entertained them the night before. It was a night they would remember. They arrived at the battlefield well-fed, rested, and in good spirits.

At daybreak Ewan rode into Inverness. A stable boy pitching hay from a wagon looked up as Ewan rode by. "Is there food at th' inn?"

"Aye, ye can eat for th' price of a pint. I'll see to yer horse for ye, sir." Ewan paid for a tankard of ale and filled his plate. His next task was to find a cart to carry oats and a barrel of water.

Thomas woke when he heard men cursing as they were pushed away from a smoky fire by others seeking warmth. Seamus Cameron, a gray-bearded man from the lands north of Loch Laidon, held up his hand. "I've tack bread an' water, as far as it'll go." Men holding out their hands, gathered around him.

Seamus turned to Thomas. "Even tho' Donald said we'd nay need ter bring weapons, never ha' I gone in tae battle wi'out my broadsword an' targe. Th' prince told Donald there'd be artillery enough for all of th' Hielanders. So then, lads, where th' bloody hell is it? Where's th' food? I dinna go to th' Glenfinnan gatherin'. Wha' did th' Lochiel say, Thomas?"

Thomas respected Seamus; he always lent a hand to any who needed to borrow a good bull or some fodder toward the end of the winter season. "Donald told Ewan an' me to deliver cattle on th' hoof an' oatcakes, cheese, an' bread to Inverness, an' we did tha'."

Thomas looked over his shoulder. "Ewan's gone to Inverness about provisions. If any asks for him, say he's sick at th' trenches."

The men looked at one another and nodded. Seamus made a sweeping gesture with his hand. "Where's th' thistle, lads? Do ye see our lovely thistle growin' in th' field? Where a thistle will nae grow, a Hielander ought not to be! Gi' me a bonny hillside, where th' pointy leaves of th' purple flower grow, an' I'll show ye a place where a Hielander can do battle. Lads, where th' bonny thistle is nae, I dinna wanna be."

Seamus leaned down on his haunches and spoke to the men. "Last night one of th' MacDonald lads said there was a fight between th' Clanranald an' Glengarry men of th' MacDonald clan. They were rollin' around an' fightin' on th' ground, each one cursin' an' blackguardin' th' other. Th' Clanranald MacDonalds sided wi' their kin, while th' Glengarry MacDonalds were standin' by their man. Before long, all of 'em were fightin'. Most of 'em gathered up their belongin's an' left! It bein' dark, none knew who left an' who stayed."

The Cameron men shook their heads and muttered to themselves. One was heard to say, "If we ha' th' good sense God gave a jackass, we'd be hightailin' it out of here."

The men began pacing back and forth as they waited. Dark clouds covered the sky. Then a pounding downpour began. Soon it was mixed with ice and snow. The clan chiefs directed their clan members to begin battle formation. As the Highlanders formed lines, they struggled with moving their mud covered boot-shod feet.

Thomas was armed with a broadsword, targe, and pistol. Duncan carried a musket; his sword was sheathed at his side. Gordon had a pistol and a sword. Had they not brought their own weapons, they would have been empty-handed.

Chapter 23

At noon, the Argyll militia, part of the king's royal army, entered the battlefield. They sighted in the cannons and positioned the heavy artillery. The Highland army was ordered to muster weapons and stand at attention. The Duke of Cumberland, astride his horse, surveyed the waterlogged marshland. He did not feel the cold wind blowing or the sting of ice pellets striking his face. But he did become aware of a voice in his ears. Unsure where the sound came from, he looked over his shoulder.

I am here to assist you, sir. Look to your right, at the top of the bare tree. You will see me. I will be your eyes to see from afar and will protect you from those who would harm you. Look for me; I will always be close by. To speak with me, clear your mind. Then think those thoughts you need me to know. I will answer in the same fashion.

William Augustus's eyes found the tree and widened at the sight of the great bird sitting in the very top. *Sir, I await your direction.* William heard the bird's thought and responded, "Where is Charles Stuart?"

The bird left his perch and flew over the field. *He is to the back right center of the lines, sir. He sits on a white horse, and the Cameron Lochiel is to his left. If you will look, sir, you will see the Stuart standard.*

"Yes, I see it. Do you have a name?"

I am known by the Gaelic name of 'Clamhan,' meaning 'scavenger,' one that is always hungry.

William laughed. "I value your assistance, Clamhan. Who sent you to me?"

When it is time, he will make himself known to you.

The first line of the Highland army formed; the Atholl regiments stood on the right flank, followed by the Camerons of Lochiel, the Stewarts of Appin, and the Frasers, MacIntoshes, MacLeans, MacLachlans, Farquarharsons, Stuarts, and MacDonalds. Thomas, Duncan, and Gordon stood together, next to their Cameron kin. Eleven cannons were in place; they would be fired if the damp powder would ignite. The royal army in three regimental lines advanced and then halted as the dragoon regiments moved to the outside of the lines. Six pounder guns were placed behind the royal army's front lines, and the mortars stood in a battery behind the big guns. Standing three hundred yards apart, the two armies were in position to begin the battle. The king's soldiers loaded their muskets and covered them with moisture-proof thin leather cloths. The Highlanders had nothing other than their wet tartans to protect their loaded rifles and pistols. Many would not fire at all.

Both armies were in place. Charles Edward Stuart had yet to call the first shot. At one o'clock, cursing under his breath, Lord Murray gave the order to fire the first round, giving a small advantage to the Jacobite army. The Highlanders fired on the royal army's officers surrounding The Duke of Cumberland. In response, the royal guns aimed and fired at the prince at the back of the right flank. The Highland chieftains, fearing for Charles's life, quickly moved him out of sight. The royal army began firing into the Jacobite lines using ball and grape shot. Casualties mounted quickly; grape shot, consisting of nails, sharp-edged metal pieces, and shards of glass, severely injured whomever it hit. Writhing in their own blood, the men fell. The next line had to step over the bodies of their fallen clan members before they could aim and fire their weapons. The newly formed front line of men was even closer to the royal army's deadly weapons.

The voice spoke, *The prince has left the battlefield. However, the Lochiel remains. If you will look at the man mounted on the gray horse, just behind the third line of Highlanders, you will see the Cameron chief. The cannon smoke is heavy; look carefully.* "Yes, Clamhan, I see him." The voice continued, *I will cause his horse to rear, which will bring the Lochiel's right side into view for a clear shot. Then I will cause the horse to rear again, bringing his left side into view. Carefully aimed shots will wound him, giving cause to leave his Cameron clan on the battlefield.*

Cumberland called for a marksman and instructed him in what to do. As William watched, the great bird flew over the Lochiel's horse. The animal reared and raised his front hooves off the ground. The marksman aimed and fired, hitting the Lochiel in the right ankle. The bird hovered over the horse and rider, waiting to give the marksman time to reload his pistol. Then it gave a loud shriek, causing the horse to lunge a second time, bringing the Cameron chieftain's left side into view. The marksman aimed and fired; the lead ball entered Donald Cameron's left ankle. Sobbing, he guided his horse off the battlefield. The Cameron Highlanders were without their clan chieftain, Donald Cameron. on the battlefield. "Thank you! I am impressed with your abilities," said Cumberland. The great creature responded, *It is my pleasure to be of service to you, sir.*

"Clamhan," William thought, "Why are you here?"

Sir, a most devoted companion admires you and wishes for your success in all that you do!

Duncan, Gordon, and Thomas saw their clan chieftain leave the battlefield. The three cousins stepped over the bodies of their clan members and moved forward. Gordon was the first to collapse, mortally wounded when a musket ball penetrated his skull. Duncan died when he aimed at a charging Redcoat whose bayonet pierced his left side, spilling out his intestines. Thomas lay dying, muscles protesting, when his neck was broken by a swinging broadsword held by another Highlander. The three lay side by side where they fell. The MacDonald clan held back their advance, hoping the first line of the Redcoats would weaken so they could begin a charge. Only a few front-line royal soldiers fell. The ranks quickly closed as soldiers moved forward to fill the positions of the fallen men. The first and second lines held firm. Less than fifty royal soldiers were dead.

Culloden's field was filled with the sounds of the living, cursing and shouting, and the dying, moaning and begging for help. Resorting to fighting the way they knew best, the Highlanders shouted battle cries and ran, broadswords in the air and targes held across their chests. As predicted by Lord Murray, the choice of Culloden's field, with its flat, boggy ground and deep mud, severely hampered the Highland army. When the wind blew clouds of arid gunpowder and cannon smoke into their eyes, they blindly shot their fellow soldiers. Finally, the two armies were within an arm's length of each other; fierce hand-to-hand combat took place. When the Highlanders lifted their heavy-bladed broadswords to bludgeon their foes, their opponents fired pistols or lunged with bayonets, either one inflicting a fatal wound. The Highlanders' thick leather shields deflected a sword's thrust, but a lead ball penetrated the leather to find its mark. When a dulled dirk could not penetrate the heavy woolen coats worn by the Royal Army, it was discarded; then fisted hands became the only weapon some had. Wet gunpowder would not fire, and many died still grasping their weapons. They fell line by line. Charles Stuart escaped to safety with the surviving clan chiefs not far behind. Field Commander Lord Murray stayed on the field until he was nearly alone. Two thousand Highland men died during the battle that lasted less than an hour. Those wounded but still alive suffered even a worse fate when the royal soldiers followed Lord Cumberland's command, written on the back of the nine of diamonds playing card: "Give no quarter." With cries for mercy on their lips, they were shot or run through with a bayonet.

Well done, sir, very well done. You have defeated those who sought your father's throne!

William closed his eyes. "Please express my gratitude to the one who is my benefactor. I am most pleased with the outcome."

I shall do so, sir. Perhaps soon, you will be able to speak with him yourself.

Chapter 24

E wan's belly cramped as he threw up its contents. Exhausted, he lay on the stable floor and slept. After waking, he returned to the inn, where he ate bread and butter and drank watered wine. Less nauseated, he rode to the holding pens and spoke to a man pitching hay into the pens. "Where's th' Hieland animals I brought to this pen?"

"I dinna know."

Angrily, Ewan said, "Mr. Hay was to deliver th' meat to Culloden's moor!"

The man nodded his head. "Aye, he say he was leavin' by boat an' asked for help loadin' supplies. I sent him to th' capt'in at th' port."

Ewan shook his head. "He took th' meat by boat?"

"Mayhap so, mayhap nay." The man winked, "Mr. Hay was gamin' an' futterin' one o' th' inn whores th' night before. He could've traded th' meat for boat passage, or mayhap a bit o' cuddlin'. Ask th' butcher down th' road."

He pointed to a small stone building with an attached barn. "That'd be th' butcher's shop."

The butcher looked Ewan over. "I'm busy."

Ewan said, "I brought ye twenty head of Hieland animals. Do ye know wha' happened to 'em?"

"Aye—well, fer some of 'em, anyhow. They was kilt, salted, an' boxed." The butcher shrugged his shoulders. "A man named Hay did th' ordering, an' I know no more than th' crates of meat left here two days back."

"The meat should ha' been at Culloden's moor a'fore I left, then! Do ye know where th' crates went?"

"When meat leaves my shop, as it does ever' day of th' week but Sunday, it's no business o' mine where it goes. I was paid my price for th' killin', skinnin', an' butcherin'."

"Who paid yer fee, sir?"

"It was paid by Mr. Hay. I'm done tellin' ye. There's others waitin'."

At the Inverness dock, Ewan asked, "Where'd I'd find th' log of boats leavin' this port?"

He was directed to a building where a counterman answered his questions. "A boat wi' a cargo matchin' tha' description left from here. Th' loadin' ticket says there were twenty-six crates of artillery an' ten crates o' meat."

The counterman looked at the paperwork. "Th' boat had a captin, two mates, an' th' gentleman who paid th' boat's fees. They shipped out at four o'clock on Tuesday, wi' no destination listed. Th' boat likely went to Dundee or Leith. By th' looks of her cargo, I'd say it's meant fer th' king's army, wha' wi' there bein' both guns an' meat."

Ewan nodded. "Ha' ye any word of th' battle takin' place on Culloden's field?"

"Aye, a rider came by a while ago an' said th' battle's done."

"It's over?"

"Aye. Th' king's army finished off wha' was left of Charlie's army."

Ewan steadied himself. "Th' English won th' battle?"

"Aye." The boat master looked at Ewan's face. "Be ye well, laddie? Sit yerself down. Yer white as chalk. Do ye ha' kin fightin'?"

"Aye, I do—my brother, cousins, an' clan."

The boat master handed Ewan a cup of whisky. "Wha' does a win for th' English mean, laddie? Will they take wha' we ha' left? We pay taxes on th' taxes! Th' bloody king of England must ha' a treasury full of coins by now."

Ewan finished the whisky; it might not be as they'd heard. The only way to know was to return to Culloden. "Sir, I'm grateful. Wha' do I owe ye?"

"Keep yer coins. It may be th' last ye'll ha' when th' English finish wi' us."

As Ewan left Inverness, he prayed, "Father, watch over those on th' battlefield, be they alive or dead. If dead, welcome 'em into heaven, for they've fought bravely. If alive, give 'em strength to stay alive 'til they can be helped."

He concentrated on guiding the horse over the ice-covered path. Reaching the western edge of the fog-shrouded, icy moor, Ewan tethered his horse and began walking in the direction of faint voices. Scavenger birds pecked at the eyes and wounds of both dead and alive men on the battlefield. Heavy with carrion, they made no effort to fly as he moved through them.

"Kill any who are still alive and stack them for burning. Search their clothing for things of value; some of them have pocket watches an' coins. Keep whatever you find. Take any artillery, swords, and dirks to the wagon." The voice belonged to an Englishman.

If he kept a distance from the voices, the thick fog would hide him as he moved about the field. He stepped over bodies clad in Frazier plaid, then McDonald, and then Campbell. He could hardly put his foot down without stepping on bodies. He did not stop even though he recognized many of the open-eyed faces. No one was left alive. The Camerons would be next. He found a shred of Cameron tartan and then another. Here was a leg. There were a foot, a hand, and a torso wrapped in the Cameron tartan; the head was missing. Heart pounding, he found a body face down in the mud; when he turned it over, he looked into Gordon's face. Beside Gordon lay Duncan and Thomas. Gordon had a shot to the head. Duncan died from a gaping wound in his side, and Thomas's head was nearly severed. He cradled Thomas's body in his arms, silent sobs wracking his body. He felt as if his heart were going to explode; the physical pain of it caused him to stand and gasp for air. He could not leave them lying there.

He found a length of flattened iron used as leverage to move a piece of artillery and used it to dig a grave for his kin. When he pried a flat stone and a smaller chalky rock out of the ground, he set them aside to fashion a marker for the graves. It was a terrible thing to search the bodies of his family, but anything he could take back to their families would be cherished. In a leather bag around Gordon's neck, Ewan found a few coins and a drawing of Elizabeth and their bairns. Duncan had a few silver coins in his sporran; a bloody leather pouch with several coins and a wooden cross lay on Thomas's chest. Tears slipped silently down Ewan's face. The crosses were made by their father and given to each son on his sixteenth birthday.

Sounds made by English soldiers' women laughing and talking among themselves carried as they searched bodies for loot. He shuddered at the terrible noise of the great scavenger birds flapping their wings when they finished consuming one body's soft tissue and moved on to the next. The voices were closer; he was running out of time. Ewan placed the three bodies in a shallow grave, covered them with remnants of their tartans, and spread dirt over them. He whispered, "Father, they're good men. Bless 'em."

On the flat stone using a chalky rock he scratched the name Cameron. He placed the stone on top of the grave and crawled away just as the first soldier came into sight. He crawled to the edge of the field and mounted his horse, remembering the starving, weary men he left the night before. They went to the battlefield, knowing it would be their last day on earth.

Ewan needed time to clear his head before he returned home. He found a sleeping room at the Inverness Inn, removed his clothing stinking with the smell of blood and death, drank the two flasks of wine in his knapsack, lay down, and slept. While he was sleeping, a light-filled mist gathered around him. He could see distant shapes. Thomas called out to him, "Ewan, th' bloody English soldiers killed Gordon an' then Duncan. When I turned to help 'em, one of our own swung his sword at an' English soldier an' hit my heid so hard it broke my neck."

Ewan replied, "Thomas, ye lost yer life fightin' for Scotland, not th' selfish man who wanted to be king."

Thomas nodded and walked away, the mist closing behind him. Then the mist parted again, and Gordon came to him. "Cousin, see to it tha' Elizabeth an' th' bairns dinna come to harm."

"Aye, Gordon, I'll do as ye ask."

Gordon turned and walked away, and again the mist swirled. A third time, the mist parted, and Duncan walked, straight and sure without a limp, toward him. "Ewan, help Anne an' th' lads to safety. Promise ye will, cousin, will ye?"

"Aye, Duncan. I promise ye, it'll be done."

Then Ewan drifted into a restful sleep, knowing his cousins and brother were at peace. The next morning, he found a shop where he bought clean clothing to wear home. He was not yet ready to begin the trip; he knew he could not answer the questions that Elizabeth and Anne would ask. Priests and ministers usually were at the sidelines of a battlefield. When Ewan noticed a priest walking down the stone path toward a chapel, he called out, "Father, were ye at Culloden?"

The priest answered, "Nay, but Father Timothy was. He's inside at th' altar. Been there since he returned."

"Do ye know—"

The priest interrupted. "It was a massacre! Wi' th' English soldiers burnin' th' bodies, we can only hope th' clan chiefs recorded th' names of those who fought, else who'll know who died?"

Ewan shook his head. "Families will know a'fore long. Could I ha' a word wi' Father Timothy?"

Chapter 25

Astride his horse, urging the animal to hasten away from Culloden's Moor, Charles Edward Stuart reflected that he had not fired his pistol or drawn his sword. He was disappointed that he had been unable to fire even a single shot; however, his men had urged him to move out of firing range for his safety. As he rode, he considered the outcome of the battle. *Blame for losing the battle must be placed where it belongs: with George Murray!* He began to consider his options. *It is not unusual for a rebellion to experience a setback. For the sake of the many who support me, I shall not forsake my mission.*

Briefly, the thought that a second attempt could not succeed crossed his mind. The distant sounds of battle well behind him, he guided his horse through the forest and began formulating plans. When a cold wind blew around him, he searched for his overcoat but then remembered leaving it behind because it would have covered his splendid uniform. In his leather knapsack, he found a flask of wine and several biscuits. He ate and drank while reassuring himself he had no choice but to leave the battlefield when he did. Before long, Charles was joined by several men, John O'Sullivan among them. "Charles, Lord Lovat's castle is close by. We can rest and refresh ourselves. His son fought for you on the battlefield, and while I am sad to say the lad lost his life, he fought a good fight. We must express our gratitude to Lord Lovat."

The group of four men rode southward following the shores of the Ford of Failie. "Your Highness, what are your plans now?" John O'Sullivan hoped to keep Charles occupied with something other than the loss on the battlefield.

"John," Charles responded, "I must think of my men. Please get word to them to meet me at Invergarry Castle, near Fort Augustus. If there is sufficient support, we can regain what has been lost and proceed onward."

"By all means, sir, I will see that a message gets to ..."

John O'Sullivan hesitated for a moment, cleared his throat, and continued, "Ah, the—those chieftains who survive."

The group approached a well-protected broch. "Halt! Who be ye?"

"Prince Charles Edward Stuart, Master John O'Sullivan, Father Allan MacDonald, and Ned Burke. We will lay down our arms."

"Approach the courtyard an' leave yer artillery." Lord Lovat met them at the door. "Ye'll stay only 'til dark. I canna risk th' ire of Cumberland's troops, should they discover ye under my roof. Charles, I've given ye my son, my only heir, an' I ha' nothin' else for ye!" Charles noted they were given only tea. He was hungry and asked for food, but none was served. In the late afternoon, they were handed their weapons and observed until they were well away from the castle.

The night was spent in a misty, cold ravine with no fire. Ned Burke, a former house servant, was well prepared with an extra blanket and knapsack of food, but because he believed the prince would ask for the food and the others would do without, he said nothing. Charles, with no coat, blanket, or food, asked Ned for the blanket and then inquired if anyone had food. Later, in the dark, Ned shared oatcakes with the others. At dawn, they were on their way to the castle. Charles, riding behind the rest, thought of what he would say to the men who would meet with him. He would begin by asking for their continued support. A return trip to France should raise necessary funds to continue the uprising. Charles searched his knapsack for a stray biscuit but found only crumbs. Thirsty, he emptied his flask of wine. Still wearing the same clothing he had worn to the battlefield the day before, he wished for fresh underclothing.

Charles Stuart could not fathom the battle had not been a win for the royal Stuarts. The crown in London did not belong to his father, and he was not second in line for the kingship. He began deflecting blame away from himself. *I had reasons to delay calling for the first shot, but George Murray defied my orders!* Charles was aghast at Murray's insubordination. *I left the battle only because my officers insisted that I do so! The lack of food and weapons was the fault of suppliers! Certainly, they will be held accountable!*

He thought of Murray asking that the battle site be moved from Culloden's moor. Was it really as unsuitable as George Murray thought?' "John, ride with me," Charles called out.

John reined in his horse and waited for Charles. "John, is there a reasonable answer for the lack of weapons and food yesterday? I recall you telling me to not concern myself with it and I, being occupied with other matters, followed your direction."

"Charles, there is a strong possibility the suppliers could not deliver the food and arms if they were not available."

"Were they paid with our funds?"

"No, payment was made by our supporters in Ireland."

"I'd like more information on this, John."

"Certainly, if the opportunity presents, certainly."

"John, do you continue to feel Culloden's moor was the best battle site?"

John turned toward Charles and said, "Of course!" He twisted the reins in his hands as he searched for reasons to support his decision. "Wasn't it remarkable how unstable the English army's cannons were because of being precariously balanced on wet ground? You saw yourself how they frequently misfired."

"Yes," Charles said. "That was a lack of preparation on their part."

"Correct," replied John as he wiped perspiration from his forehead. "Also, many of the clan chieftains were able to retreat because the field was flat and open."

John reached out and touched Charles's arm. "Charles, what is your opinion of the location?"

"As you said, John," Charles responded. "The field was easily vacated when it became necessary."

In heavy fog Charles and the four men with him searched for the high turrets of Invergarry Castle, but as they rode by the area where the castle should be, they were unable to locate it. When the fog lifted they backtracked and were dismayed to find themselves within a few feet of the ruins of the castle. The Duke of Cumberland and his men had destroyed the building as they traveled to Fort Augustus after the battle. Charles was at a loss for words when he surveyed the total destruction of what had once been a handsome fortress.

"John, is there cognac or whisky?"

"Your Highness, I did not bring any with me. I have some wine, and of course you are welcome to it."

"Thank you, John. Please bring it to me." Charles was beginning to see, as well as feel, the effects of the loss at Culloden. "We will seek sanctuary at Donald Cameron's home, Achnacarry House. It will be standing where it has always been, in the shadows of the High Glens."

Traveling south and east, they followed a trail leading to a clearing in the foothills of the High Glens. In the middle of the clearing, a barn stood near the burned ruins of what had once been the great and impressive home of the Cameron chieftain. Inside the barn they found Donald Cameron lying on a pallet, unable to walk. Charles asked, "Donald, where are your men?"

"Th' king's soldiers emptied th' house an' then set fire to it. As for my men, th' few left are in hidin'. They come at night wi' food an' to bandage my wounds."

"Donald, I'll not forget your loyalty to me."

"Charles, I remain yer friend an' will always be grateful tha' ye led th' battle for th' royal Stuarts. If ye return to France, I'll follow."

The Lochiel lowered his voice. "It's best tha' I leave Scotland."

After dark, they traveled to Glen Pean, where yet another Cameron owned a still-standing broch. They were offered beds and food and stayed as long as possible, hoping they would hear from the remaining Jacobites. It was here that a letter was delivered to Charles from Lord George Murray. In this letter, Lord Murray expressed profound anger at the devastating results of the battle. He stated the loss was due to John O'Sullivan's incompetence and Charles Stuart's support of O'Sullivan's ill-advised plans. The letter also included Lord Murray's resignation. Charles handed the letter to John O'Sullivan. When he finished reading, Charles said, "John, I am aware George Murray harbored ill feelings toward you, but he is also blaming me for supporting your battle plans!"

O'Sullivan responded, "Sir, you and I made plans for the uprising together. We discussed every step from start to finish. Yes, there were unforeseen circumstances, but it is to be expected. Murray's comments are no surprise to me. My advice is to accept his resignation and send the bastard on his way."

Charles read and reread the letter. Would he allow one man to divert the plans of the royal Stuarts? There was still the hope that France might send a ship with guns and ammunition. Then he could move forward, this time with John O'Sullivan as his lieutenant general. But Charles was no longer the handsome prince seeking the throne for the royal Stuarts. Instead, he was a hunted fugitive with a thirty-thousand-pound reward for his capture. Now, rather than reassembling his army, his thoughts turned to who could be trusted to not reveal his location for the reward.

When Charles asked John about his plans for the future, John shook his head. His shoulders sagged, and his face became the epitome of sadness. "Charles, the funds you promised me have not been forthcoming. I have not requested compensation for my own expenditures during your campaign, and believe me, sir, they were considerable."

Charles responded, "Yes, John, I am aware of that. But as you well know, when one goes into battle, the outcome is not guaranteed. I too am without funds, and I must ask King Louis for reimbursement of my expenditures. Surely he will remember that I pursued the uprising with his encouragement and my efforts were made on his behalf."

Charles added as an afterthought, "I must get in touch with my tailors. It seems my coronation robes will not be required for the time being."

Charles waited for what he hoped would be O'Sullivan's approval of his plan to ask the king of France for compensation. "Your Highness," O'Sullivan said, "No one can say what the king's reaction to your request for compensation of expenses would be. You will be approaching him with empty hands and without the glory of winning. I think he might not ... well, sir, the outcome is not predictable, is it?"

"No," Charles said. "One never knows how another will react."

Having abandoned his powdered wig shortly after the battle, Charles smoothed back the few hairs on his head. "Returning to my question, John, what are your plans?"

"Sir, it was my hope to be by your side managing military affairs as your father assumed the kingship. However, now I shall have to consider any options that come my way." Taking out his handkerchief, John wiped his eyes and continued. "With the shortage of funds being what they are, I must find a way to provide for myself. For now, I will stay with you to assist in any way I am able to do so. My future plans ... I do not know, sir."

John O'Sullivan refrained from patting his vest pocket, where he kept a banking receipt in his name for close to a million pounds. He had more than sufficient funds to purchase a large parcel of land and begin a business in France. For now, he felt an obligation to stay with Charles, and his plans would have to wait.

The king's royal army pursued Charles with a vengeance. Even in the outer Isles, he was constantly in danger of being discovered. Flora MacDonald of the Isle of Skye took pity on Charles and disguised him as her maid, Betty Burke. Later, while in France, Charles described the discomfort he felt when he wore the coarse clothing of a servant. Both Charles and O'Sullivan stayed with the MacDonalds of Kingsburgh's family on Skye for a short time; however, even in a fairly remote area, Charles knew he could be found.

Finally, Charles, disguised as a common sheep herder, boarded a boat carrying animals for market to the Scottish mainland. O'Sullivan also boarded the boat, paying his fare and that of his herder, who stayed with the animals below deck. The boat, headed for the port town of Mallaig, was overtaken by the English navy and searched for a tall man who spoke English with an Italian accent. No one took any notice of a commoner in rough brown clothing who was below deck on his hands and knees in the sheep pen, scooping up droppings. At Mallaig, Charles took shelter in caves, empty crofters' cottages, and haystacks out on the moors. John supplied him with food when he could. Charles was cold, hungry, and without weapons to defend himself. He thought of nothing but his own misery; it didn't occur to him that his circumstances were similar to those the Highlanders faced at Culloden's moor.

Finally, Charles Stuart and John O'Sullivan traveled back to Borradale, Scotland where, nearly a year earlier, he, along with seven companions, landed with aspirations to secure the throne for his father and ultimately himself. A French frigate provided passage for John O'Sullivan to Norway. A British navy ship received word that Charles Stuart might be a passenger and pursued the French frigate to the point of firing upon it. Finally, with borrowed funds, Charles bought passage on the ship *L'Heureux* bound for France. He boarded on 19 September, 1746, and stood at the ship's railing looking toward Scotland. It is said that he lifted the tattered Stuart flag, waved it once, and then, as fog moved over the ship, disappeared into the misty, damp coolness of the morning. Charles Edward Stuart, in his quest for the throne, left behind a broken society that would never be the same again.

A romantic story of a fugitive Highland prince who, out of loyalty to Scotland, endured great hardships began to develop, and Charles became both a hero and legend in Scotland. Just as the surviving Scottish Highlanders could no longer own lands, wear their clan plaids, or play their beloved bagpipes, Charles Edward Stuart's life was forever changed by the failure of the 1745–1746 rebellion. The loss resulted in the formal abandonment of the Stuart claim to the British throne.

In France, Charles renewed his relationship with his cousin Maria. For a while, he was honored and addressed as "the future king of England"; however, eventually King Louis and members of the French society grew weary of Charles's constant demands for attention and funds. When King Louis advised Charles it was time for him to return to Italy, Charles refused and continued to petition the king for funds. When the king declined, a petulant Charles became angry and sulked. After months of this, patience sorely tried, the king asked that a writ of excommunication be prepared for Charles, who, when he learned of the document, chose to ignore it. One evening as Charles was on his way to the opera, his carriage was waylaid and the writ was handed to him. After being escorted to France's border, he was provided with a horse, ordered to leave France and not return. Without a permanent home, Charles traveled in Europe. He searched for a release from the torment and frustration he felt. He consumed alcohol to excess, and his female companions bore the brunt of his anger. Charles, an extraordinarily persuasive man who might have been the king of England, suffered from severe depression. He married, but before long his wife left him. Charles had one child, a daughter, Charlotte, who was born out of wedlock. After ignoring her for years, at the urging of his brother, a cardinal in the Catholic Church, he finally legitimatized her.

When the pope declined to recognize Charles's royal status with funds, his depression deepened, and he continued to drink. After suffering multiple strokes, on 31 January, 1788, Charles Edward Stuart died, in the very village where he was born on 30 December, 1720. His daughter, Charlotte, terminally ill herself, was by his side when he died.

Death listened to the man's labored breathing. Choking on his own body fluids, he was in excruciating pain. A priest was on his way to the man's bedside to administer the last rites, but before he arrived, a violent seizure gripped the man's body as he desperately gasped for air. His physical body, wasted and ill from years of excessive alcohol and symptoms of venereal disease, finally succumbed. Death spoke to the newly released spirit. "Ah, there you are! I'll be with you until your escort arrives. He'll be along soon."

Death, waiting for the activity expected when a spirit of importance such as this one came along, looked around in anticipation. Thunder resonated from heavy, dark clouds in the sky. Lightning bolts crashed from one hilltop to another, and the sharp tang of sulphur hung in the air. The Dark One had arrived. "Thank you, Death. I appreciate you watching over my friend here." The newly released spirit looked from one to the other. "I thought the pain would stop when I died! Who shall I complain to about this? Another thing: I'd kill for a cup of cognac."

"Yes," The Dark One hissed. "I know you would; you've done it before for less. No, my friend, you have work to do. Here's your rags-and-bones cart to pull along behind you. I'll help you get the harness adjusted, and then it's off to hell with you, my friend."

The Dark One paused and said, with a horrible attempt at a smile, "I do owe you a debt of gratitude for all of those innocent men who died because of your spectacular lack of care for them."

Reaching into thin air, he brought out a bottle and a cup. "Here you are," he said as he poured the fragrant cognac into the cup and handed it to Charles, "This should suffice to express my appreciation. Oh my! I almost forgot!" The Dark One howled with laughter as he watched Charles attempt to drink the liquid, you have no means of swallowing drink now, do you Charles? You will be thirsty for the rest of eternity! That, my friend, is truly hell!"

Chapter 26

Ewan was troubled by knowing his brother and cousins owned firearms but rarely carried or used them. An Act of English Parliament in 1715 made it illegal for clansmen to carry firearms. Those who did carry firearms invited their clan chieftain's ire when the English government, suspecting a possible uprising, conducted an investigation into the clan's affairs. Only a few men in the Cameron Clan had battlefield training. Ewan thoughts of these things as he entered the chapel where he found the priest on his knees at the altar. "Father Timothy?"

The startled priest stood. "Aye."

"Were ye at Culloden? I've lost my brother an' cousins there. It'll be my task to carry th' news to their families, an' I've no answers for their questions. Wha' can ye tell me?"

"Aye, I was there." The priest looked into Ewan's eyes. "I see yer a Cameron by th' plaid pinned to yer bonnet. Wha' is yer given name?"

"Ewan."

"Aye then, Ewan Cameron, put away yer plaid, an' dinna wear it again if ye want to stay alive! Sit yerself down, an' I'll tell ye th' tale." The priest looked thoughtful. "I watched th' battle through a veil of smoke an' rain. I'll tell ye, th' royal army's cannons were on uneven ground sittin' in mud, one side higher than th' other. Those of us on the sidelines dodged cannonballs meant to fall in th' Jacobite lines. This was th' only fault th' king's army had!"

Father Timothy placed his hand on Ewan's arm and said, "I'm in need of a cup o' tea, an' mayhap a bite of somethin'. Will ye join me?"

"Aye, Father, forgive me. I'm not thinkin'." The two men walked through a garden and up several steps into a room where two chairs sat on either side of a fireplace with a cheerful evening fire burning.

Father Timothy called out, "Sister, is there a cup o' tea, an' mayhap a bite to eat? We've a guest, an' by th' looks of him, he needs a good cup o' tea."

A nun appeared at the door. "Ah, Father, when I last looked, ye were on yer knees at th' altar. There's tea, bread, cheese an' apple tart. Father Timothy, if ye wish, I'll prepare a meal. Ye've naught eaten for I dinna know how long."

"Sister, wha' ye've offered will suffice. Ewan, here's a plate. Help yerself."

After they ate, the priest filled two glasses with whisky. "Now, I'll tell ye wha' I know." Father Timothy clasped his hands and began. "Those of us standin' on th' sidelines could see th' Hielanders were blinded by smoke from th' king's cannons. They were shootin' into their own lines! When their weapons failed to fire, we saw 'em throw their pistols an' rifles to th' ground. There was no dry gunpowder to replace th' wet. Then, all they had to fight wi' was their dirks, swords an' fists. Several had rocks in their pockets an' they threw 'em. Near as I could tell, th' Highlander cannons dinna fire at all."

Father Timothy pulled out a handkerchief and wiped his eyes. "I've never seen anythin' like it, an' I hope never to again. I tell ye, th' sound of so many men dying' in th' little time it took canna be told in words!"

"Father, my own brother died at th' hand of a Cameron who drew back his broadsword, brought it down, an' hit him instead of th' English soldier he aimed for."

"Ewan, how do ye know?"

"Ye'll think I'm daft. He came to me in my sleep an' said th' hit was meant for a Redcoat."

The priest nodded. "Aye, Ewan, yer nay daft, I've heard folk speak of such before. Besides me, there were two other priests an' a Presbyterian minister standin' at th' edge of th' battlefield. Wind an' rain blew across tha' Godforsaken field as if th' De'il himself was there."

Father Timothy and Ewan crossed themselves. "Lord Murray told us to depart quickly if th' king's army won, as they'd show us no mercy."

Father Timothy looked into Ewan's face. "Laddie, are ye sure ye want to hear this?"

Ewan nodded. "I must." Ewan spoke more to himself than the man sitting across from him. "I was to be there by th' side of my brother an' kin when th' battle began, but th' men were starvin'. I left th' night a'fore to search for th' food we left in Inverness. I learned tha' th' meat an' food meant for Charles's army went elsewhere, I suspect to th' king's army. Our men fought wi' empty bellies! By th' time I returned to Culloden, th' battle was over. My brother an' two cousins were lying where they fell, an' I dug a grave an' buried th' lads. It was little I could do for 'em."

Ewan stopped to wipe tears. The priest filled the glasses again. Ewan drank deeply, and Father Timothy refilled his glass. "Ewan, Scotland is no more."

"Aye, when a German became king, he dinna care if we live or die."

"Aye, laddie, I've heard th' same from folk in th' parish." The priest continued, "Th' Stuarts asked me to say th' blessin' for Charles a'fore th' battle. They all believed he'd win King George's crown. But after I took a look at th' king's army, all regimental, orderly, an' armed, I knew no Stuart would be sittin' on th' throne!

"About noon we heard th' piper playin'. Then came th' Hielanders, about five thousand of 'em, marchin' behind him. Then came th' drummers of th' king's foot soldiers as they marched to th' field. We were told th' prince would call for th' first shot, but finally Lord Murray did. It appeared th' prince couldn't decide wha' ter do. When th' English fired grapeshot of nails an' shards o' glass, our men started fallin'. Th' air was smoky, an' when th' wind died back, a heavy fog settled in. When it was all over, th' English solders shot any who were still alive. I heard th' king's army numbered eight thousand, an' well trained they were! When one soldier fell, another stepped forward to take his place. Ever' one o' 'em was armed wi' rifles, swords an' pistols.

"In less than an hour Th' Duke of Cumberland claimed a victory if ye can call killin' unarmed, weak, an' hungry men a victory! Th' English said they killed over two thousand Jacobites, wounded th' same number, an' took a thousand prisoners. Those of us watchin' knew they killed all th' wounded where they fell. Th' duke's lieutenant told us th' royal army lost fifty men, an' three hundred were injured. Charles Stuart left th' battle after th' second round of shootin' got too close to him. Th' Cameron chief was shot an' left th' battlefield. On th' way back to Inverness we all knew there'd be a price on all Hielanders' heids. Th' king's soldiers will deal harshly wi' traitors, an' any found will be put to death."

"How do ye know th' Lochiel left th' battlefield, Father?"

"We saw him leave. Lord Murray was th' last to leave. It's said he's sick at heart. He loves Scotland, he does."

Ewan looked at the priest. "Father, yer dedicated to th' church. Ye canna understand wha' it means to lose wha' ye hold dear, even yer belief in God. Th' lives of th' clans will never be th' same again."

Ewan started to stand but stopped when Father Timothy held up his hand. "Ewan, I do understand! I'm my father's third son an' my only inheritance was my name, which I gave up to become Timothy, one of th' apostles. When I was born, Father pledged my

196

life to th' church. I understood tha' was my callin'. It was nay a question of whether I did or dinna want to be a priest. It was nay up to me to decide, just as it was not yer choice to belong to th' Cameron clan. Laddie, dinna lose your belief in God! Ye canna trust people, but God? He's th' same from th' beginning to th' end. Put yer trust in him. Ewan, God's plan for ye dinna mean ye'd die in th' battle. He's other plans for ye."

Ewan brought out his leather pouch and placed a handful of silver coins on the table. "Bless ye, Ewan. Ye'll be in my prayers."

"An' ye, good Father."

Chapter 27

Weary, Ewan had to rest before he started home. After stabling his horse he walked to the tavern, drank a cup of whisky, and fell asleep at the table. The owner shook him awake to ask if he wanted a bed. Ewan followed the man to a room, sat down on the bed, removed his boots, and lay down. He was asleep before he could pull the coverlet up. He slept that night and part of the next day.

When he went downstairs, he was surprised to see people sitting at tables, some wiping away tears and others with dazed looks on their faces. "Ye mourn for those who died at Culloden?"

"Nay," the tavern keeper said, "ye'd not know."

"Then wha' is it?"

"We've been visited by a De'il ridin' on a black horse." The tavern keeper pointed to the path in front of the tavern. "Someone, or somethin', came to town ridin' a black horse."

The barkeeper crossed himself and continued, "He murdered any man, woman, or bairn who crossed his path an' then rode away. Several men rode after him but could nae follow his trail. It's as if th' De'il himself came in! It could ha' been th' one they call Th' Butcher, but none saw his face. Now, we've got th' dead to bury. Is there no end to it?"

Sitting alone on the top branch of the cemetery's lone tree, The Dark One's face twisted into a terrible smile. "He does my bidding without question. Master will be very pleased." The spirit preened the wiry hairs hanging from his face. "Death should be along soon."

The Dark One looked around. "Ah! Here he is. Are you pleased with the harvest I've reaped for you?"

Death responded, "It is not for me to be pleased one way or the other. I am completing my assigned task. It's a pity you missed the light show after the killings. Your competition lit up the entire universe with His grand and glorious light. You did not reap even one soul out of this, so what did you gain?"

"No," said The Dark One, "I did not. However, all of the demons in hell are celebrating because there are fewer of those who belong to the competition left behind to complicate things!

I am very pleased with my friend. Now he is known as 'The Butcher.' As for the light show, Death, you know I always avoid those performances. I get no pleasure from watching Him gathering in souls, and I detest bright lights! Death, my friend, I've planned an even greater harvest yet to come. Perhaps you'll need some assistance!"

Pulling his hood back with a bony hand, Death turned to face The Dark One. His silver eyes reflected The Dark One's shadow as he spoke. "Dark One! No point in wasting your compelling ways on me. Unlike the humans you prey upon, I am immune."

When Ewan left Inverness, he hoped to ride as far as the Glens before he stopped. After the sun set, a sliver of moon rose in the east. He stopped, dismounted, and took a deep breath of the clean, fresh scent of growing heather and sage. The quietness of the night had a calming effect on his troubled soul. *Dear God, I love this land. Father, gi' me strength for wha' lies ahead. In Jesus's name, I pray. Amen.*

He would tell Elizabeth that Gordon had died bravely. He would offer safety to her and the bairns until she could go to her family. Then, he and Janet would go to Duncan's wife and see that she and the lads were safely delivered to the borders.

Ewan rode on through the night; by daybreak he was on the high pastures of Gordon Cameron's lands. Cattle and sheep grazed in the fields. The barn was empty, and the horse and cart were gone. It was likely that Elizabeth and the bairns had made their way to Glen Lochy. His heart lifted when he reached the northern edge of his lands. He stabled his horse and walked to the door. Janet opened the door, and simply said, "Thank God, yer home."

She took his arm, led him into the kitchen, and pulled out a chair for him. "Elizabeth an' th' bairns are here. After ye left, I went to see about 'em. I knew she'd be hard pressed to manage alone. I brought 'em here, mayhap as much for my own good as theirs. It gave me somethin' to worry about other than ye, husband."

Janet stood by Ewan's chair and put her hand on his shoulder. "Before ye say so, I know ye've terrible news, but we must hear it. Eat, an' then ye can get on with it."

He thought he was not hungry, but then he smelled the stew that she ladled into a trencher of bread. When Janet brought out bread, cheese, and more ale, Ewan said, "I'm thankful for food to be eaten in my broch wi' my wife." Overcome by the horror of the past days, he wiped away tears.

"Bear up, Ewan. When yer ready, we'll call Elizabeth, an' she can decide about tellin' th' bairns. Her oldest laddie, Daniel, helps wi' feedin' th' animals an' takes care of his younger brothers. He's just six years old, but he seems much older."

"Ah, well." Ewan sighed. "We'll get on wi' it."

Janet called up the stairs, "Elizabeth! Ewan's home, an' there's news."

At the bottom of the stairs, Ewan held his arms out to her, "Gordon, Duncan, an' Thomas died on th' battlefield. I buried 'em there. Thousands perished; only a few were taken prisoners."

"Gordon said he'd nay return," Elizabeth said. "I argued wi' him, but he shook his head an' said, 'It'll not be'. I'll grieve for th' loss of him, but I must think about our bairns, as he would ha' done if I'd died birthin' our last babe."

Softly, Ewan spoke. "Elizabeth, ye an' th' bairns will be safe here, but not for long. Janet an' I will take Anne an' her lads to th' border. While we're away, gather wha' ye must ha' to travel. When we return, we'll take ye an' th' lads to Perthshire, where Janet's family and Duny are. It's closer to yer family home in Aberdeen."

Elizabeth wiped away tears. "We'll be ready. Ewan, do ye know if any of the clan survived? Wi' th' threats th' Lochiel made, I suppose they all fought."

Ewan said, "I dinna believe any o' th' clan are left, except for me an' I was in Inverness tryin' to find somethin' for th' lads to eat when the battle began. Th' Lochiel was injured an' left th' battle early on. Afterward, th' king's army cleared th' field of bodies. There'd be no way of knowin'."

Ewan and Janet went to their bed chamber to gather a few things. They chose woolen breeks, tunics, heavy woolen stockings, boots, and dark cloaks. As Janet took off her skirt, petticoat, and chemise, Ewan's breath caught in his throat. "Love, yer beautiful standin' here. I canna take my eyes from ye."

"Ewan, is there time for us to ..."

"Aye, we'll make time."

Afterward, in Ewan's arms, Janet said, "Several nights ago, as I slept, I saw a battlefield strewn with slain men where they'd fallen, clan by clan. Three Cameron men lay side by side, covered wi' th' tartan. I did'na see who they were, only tha' there were three o' 'em." Janet sobbed. "Ewan, I knew ye'd come home, while Thomas, Gordon, an' Duncan would not."

"Janet, I disobeyed th' Lochiel's orders, or I'd be in th' ground too! Th' night before th' battle, I went to Inverness searchin' for food. There was not so much as an oatcake for th' men for two days before th' battle started."

"How could tha' be? Wha' happened to yer cattle an' th' cart full of food?"

Ewan shook his head. "I asked th' same questions an' got no answers; no one knows where th' food went. There were no weapons either. There's someone behind all this, but I dinna know who."

Ewan paced the floor. "I buried my brother an' cousins on th' battlefield wi' th' English soldiers right behind me. At least I know they'll nay be picked at by birds or thrown on a heap an' burned! I can't bear to think about it just yet."

Janet shook her head. "Ewan, ye took an awful risk to put them to rest."

"It's nay over. Th' next day, in Inverness, there was a massacre. They say it was done by th' De'il who rode a black horse. I'm wonderin' if it was Th' Duke of Cumberland. He's called 'Th' Butcher' after th' way he's ordered th' killin' of th' Hielanders. Janet, get dressed an' pack th' food. I'll ha' th' horses saddled by th' time yer finished."

Janet and Elizabeth filled knapsacks with oatcakes, cheese, and bread. "Janet, could Daniel come alon' wi' ye? I want him to see his cousins before they leave Scotland. I fear they'll not meet again."

Janet considered Elizabeth's request. "There's little time to get Anne an' the bairns to th' borders, but I think Ewan will agree to Daniel comin' along."

"It'll be a comfort to him to be wi' his uncle Ewan."

Janet found Ewan in the barn, standing by the stall where Prince, Thomas's horse, stood. "Are ye ready, Janet?"

"Aye, I ha' a question for ye. Could Daniel come wi' us? Elizabeth wants him to say good-bye to his cousins. It's not likely their paths will cross again. Wha' say ye, husband?"

"I've thought about takin' Elizabeth an' th' bairns wi' us, but, if they come along, we'd need two more horses an' a cart would be better for th' little ones. I'm hatin' to leave 'em behind." Ewan turned away, but not before Janet saw tears in his eyes. "It's best they stay here. Daniel can come along an' take turns ridin' wi' us. Th' English soldiers will be movin' slowly as they'll plunder an' burn ever' broch, cottage, an' village they come to. Horses pullin' wagons loaded wi' booty must move slowly over th' hills an' glens."

Ewan continued, anger in his voice, "Oh, they'll be festive, drinkin' our whisky an' ale an' eatin' food they steal from our larders. Wi' full bellies an' soused heids, it'll be several weeks a'fore they reach Glen Lochy. All th' same, Elizabeth will need to be very watchful. Fetch Daniel an' we'll be on our way. See tha' he's wearin dark clothin'."

When she walked through the kitchen door, Janet's eyes were drawn to a corner of the kitchen where a peat basket sat underneath an iron kettle hook hanging on the wall. She had a fleeting feeling that gave her a chill, but she pushed it away. She quickly collected the tapestry of the broch, Ewan's mother's silver spoons, and a teapot containing twenty gold coins, twelve silver coins, and a silver cross with a closed circle said to have belonged to Saint Andrew. She placed them in a space behind a loose stone in the fireplace wall. *For safekeeping*, she said to herself. *They'll belong to Duny one day.*

"Elizabeth, we'll take Daniel wi' us. There'll be no need for ye to leave the broch. Ewan's filled th' mangers wi' hay, and there's water for th' animals. I've brought in peat bricks for th' kitchen fire, but keep it low. Ye dinna want th' smoke gainin' th' attention of any around. There's firewood by th' door; if ye build a fire, do so after nightfall when th' mist is heavy. Be very watchful. If someone's on th' path, Bran'll let ye know. There's a loaded pistol under our bed, if ye need to, use it! "

"Janet, I'll pray for yer safety. When ye return, we'll travel wi' ye to yer parent's broch, then mayhap th' lads and I can get on to my family in Aberdeen."

Janet hugged Elizabeth and prayed Gordon had not gotten her with child again before he left. As Elizabeth hugged Daniel, she said, "Daniel, mind yer auntie an' uncle. Tell yer auntie Anne an' cousins tha' yer mother greets 'em."

Elizabeth buttoned his jacket, placed his cap on his head, tucked his mittens in his pockets, and placed him in front of Janet on the horse. She secured his knapsack behind the saddle.

Chapter 28

Elizabeth sat her three younger sons, Thomas, Brian, and Joseph, around the table for supper. She spooned oat porridge over buns spread with jam and filled cups with milk for the three lads, who sat quietly waiting for their mother to join them. "Lads, yer da is watchin' over us. Daniel's visitin' yer auntie Anne an' her lads a'fore they're off to England. Someday we'll go visitin', an' ye can meet 'em. One is named Mark, an' th' other is Timmy. They'll be about yer age."

"Mam, will we never, ever see Da again?"

Elizabeth spoke softly to her sons. "Nay, ye won't, but he'll always be here wi' us in spirit. Tha' means th' part of him tha' loved an' cared for us is here."

They looked at one another and smiled. "I told ye Da would'na leave us," Thomas said.

"Eat yer porridge, lads, an' then' we'll be goin' to bed early. I'll tell ye one story, an' tha's all. Then ye'll be nice an' warm in yer beds, an' we'll all—"

Elizabeth and her sons jumped at the dog's loud warning bark.

Then they heard a gunshot followed by a howl. "Quick, lads—in th' larder, back in th' far corner under th' empty sacks."

Elizabeth poured water on the peat fire and snuffed out the single candle on the table. She followed her sons into the larder and joined them huddled in the dark corner beneath the grain sacks.

They heard the front door crash to the floor and then shouts as the soldiers entered and began going through each room. When they reached the kitchen, one shouted, "They're here somewhere. The tea kettle is warm."

Elizabeth heard the larder door open. A soldier shouted, "Here's meals for a week!"

Elizabeth heard the sound of boots walking in the room. "Take it to the wagons. There's venison, and plenty for a feast!"

"There'll be a whisky cellar," the captain said. "Ah, here's a trap door. Help me, lads."

Carefully, Elizabeth placed her arms around her sons. Two of the men climbed down the ladder and carried up bottle after bottle of ale, wine, and whisky. One soldier walked over to the pile of grain sacks and kicked it, hitting small Joseph in the head. He yelped and stuck his fist in his mouth, tears coming into his eyes. The soldier began pulling the sacks away and uncovered Elizabeth and her children. "Come, lads, see what I've found! It's a bitch and her whelps."

The soldier kicked Elizabeth. "Up with you and your brats."

The captain ordered, "Tie them together. Wait, the wench is not bad to look at—a little scrawny, but we'll see if anyone wants to futter her before we burn the house with 'em in it."

Several of the soldiers stepped forward. One picked Elizabeth up and flung her against the stone wall; she slumped to the floor. Her sons were tied together with a rope. Their faces were tearstained; Joseph's breeks were wet with urine. Thomas cried out when the soldiers ripped his mother's gown away and began using her, one after the other.

The soldiers loaded everything they could find into carts and, as ordered, fired the timbered roof of the broch. As sparks fell to the second floor, it began burning. One of the soldiers carried a burning brand to the basket of peat blocks in the kitchen. He tied a rope around the children and their mother, wound it around the iron hook, and pulled it tight. After taking one last look at the smoke-filled room, he walked out the door. His pockets held jewelry and a bag of coins plundered from the upstairs bedchamber.

Flames and smoke filled the kitchen. Elizabeth's body fell to the floor when the rope burned through. Joseph cried out when his breeks caught fire. Thomas held his brothers in his arms, and they stood together as the flames gathered around them. As he caught his last breath, Thomas looked up and saw a light coming toward him. *Mama, look*, he thought.

Aye, lad, I see it too. Thomas, give me yer hand. I am here beside ye. He heard his mother's voice speaking to him as he passed from this world to the next. *Brian an' Joseph, here we are. Thomas an' I are waitin' for ye. Come along, lads.*

The soldiers closed the barn with the animals inside and set fire to the timbered structure. Finally, they killed the shaggy cows and calves in the pens beside the barn, leaving them where they lay.

Death waited for the four newly freed spirits. They would not have long to wait until their angels arrived. The spirits of Elizabeth, Thomas, Brian, and Joseph Cameron hovered in the sky. Death greeted them, "Come along, all of you. Be not afraid; the worst is over. Elizabeth Cameron, you and your sons are known by the Holy One, and all of you are precious to him." The heavens parted, and four angelic beings appeared. One of the angels spoke. "I am called Elight. Welcome, dear ones. We were watching as you comforted each other. Elizabeth, do not sorrow. Your husband and baby daughter Rose wait for you. Thomas, Brian, and Joseph, you will greet your father and little sister, and those of you who are here shall be together." The angel smiled, and the four felt a cleansing of their souls and bodies. She said, "Look, you have bodies that seem the same but are not. Never again will any of you feel pain or sadness. This is our Father's promise, and He waits for you. Come. I will show you the way." Death watched as they gathered together and departed through the glowing heavens bright with every color of the rainbow.

The Dark One sent a message by a large black bat. "Death!" The flying creature shrieked. "The Dark One asks that you refrain from expressing what appears to be pleasure while you wait with souls until they depart for heaven. He feels he is being cheated of equal time. He's sent me to ask you to carry out your tasks without the emotions, or he will have to speak to his master about it!"

Death shook a bony finger at the bat. "Remind your superior that I am a free spirit! Neither he nor his master has any control over me. If I prefer the light to the dark, that is my choice!" The bat circled around Death and then flew away, looking back over his wing as he went.

Chapter 29

Rain filtered through thick tree branches, quieting sounds of their horses moving through underbrush. "Janet, I'll be close behind ye. Keep Daniel quiet, an' be on guard."

Janet nodded as she guided her horse around a thicket of brambles. Ewan saw Prince's ears perk up and then heard the faint sound of horses moving through the forest behind them. He rode forward and motioned for Janet and Daniel to dismount. In single file, they led the horses to a fog-filled ravine. Ewan whispered, "Pull yer cloak over yer heid. Yer red hair is like a beacon. Whoever is out there is a ways behind us. When they come to th' crossin', pray they go to th' left, not down th' ravine."

Janet found a place beneath a briar bush where a small animal had nested, birthed, and raised young. There were tufts of fine hair and a round bed made of leaves and moss. She held Daniel close and silently prayed when she felt the rhythm of horses' hooves on the ground. When she wrapped her black cloak around both of them, they blended into the shadows beneath the thorny bushes. Ewan climbed a tree at the edge of the path, crouched down, and pulled his cloak around him. In the mist, he blended with the bark and branches. He watched as a troop of English soldiers approached.

The captain called a halt a few feet past the tree where Ewan hid. "We've lost their trail. I doubt they could make a way through those briar bushes; they're somewhere in this forest. They may have doubled back to seek a different path. Ah well, makes no difference. If we're unable to find them, another troop will. The duke will be pleased that we burned Ewan Cameron's house with its occupants. Think back to the Culloden battlefield. The Cameron clan stood in the first row of the Highland clans, just behind the bagpipers. Speaking of which, by God, those bloody instruments make an unholy racket! Our regiment was quite a distance from the front lines, but the wailing of those bags of air was still too close. I personally think they should stick the long-necked, racket-making bladders up their Scottish arses and see if they can fart hard enough to play a tune!"

The men all laughed and responded with shouts. "Ah, lads, we're still on Cameron lands. This map shows another broch quite a distance from here. Let me see. It belongs to Duncan Cameron." The captain looked around. "We'll stay to the left, it appears to be on higher ground. Once we're out of the forest, we'll stop to enjoy Ewan Cameron's whisky and larder. Those of you who futtered the lady of the house can tell us all about it. Lieutenant, lead on."

Once the last soldier was out of sight, Ewan dropped to the ground. He knew Elizabeth and the bairns perished when the broch burned, but he could not do anything about it now. Behind a thicket of brambles the horses stood quietly. Janet and Daniel peeked out from behind the briars. Whispering, Ewan said, "We'll take th' path through th' ravine."

Janet asked, "Ewan, did those soldiers pass by Glen Lochy?"

"Quiet."

They made their way through burns, rocky ground, and thick undergrowth.

Just before dawn, they reached the outer fields of Duncan's broch. "Janet, when I reach th' barn, ye start across th' field. If there's Redcoats, return to th' forest as quickly as ye can. If I'm caught, Anne an' th' lads are in danger too. So save yerselves, however ye can."

By the time Ewan reached the barn, the sun was above the horizon. He caught a glimpse of Anne scattering hay for the animals; she looked up, waved at Ewan, and ran to meet him. Janet and Daniel rode into the barnyard; Ewan led them all inside. "Anne, Duncan died in th' Battle. Later, I'll tell yer wha' I know about it. On our way here, we hid from a troop of English soldiers. I overheard 'em talkin'. Janet take Daniel inside, gi' th' lad a bite to eat an' come back to th' barn."

When she returned, Ewan placed his arms around her and Anne. "Elizabeth an' th' lads died when th' Redcoats burned Glen Lochy."

Anne gasped, and Janet cried out. Ewan continued, "They may stop before they reach here but they know where Duncan's broch is and are on their way!"

Anne wiped her eyes. "I'll plan to leave after sunset. There's an abbey on the Scotland side of the border where the children and I can rest. Then we'll cross the border and ride on to Father's lands."

Ewan raised his voice. "Nay! Anne, dinna ye hear me say how close the soldiers are? Ye canna manage both Mark and Timothy on one horse."

"Ewan, I'll pull a cart behind my horse, and the lads can ride amongst the things I want to bring with us."

Ewan shouted as he grabbed Anne's shoulder. "Dammit, Anne, gather wha' ye must for yerself an' th' lads, an' we'll go! Anne, I promised Duncan I'd see to it tha' ye an' th' lads are safe. I'll always bear th' pain of tellin' Gordon th' same an' not doin' so!"

Anne looked into Ewan's eyes. "He asked this of you?"

Ewan nodded.

"Do you know where he lies?"

211

"Aye, I buried all three, side by side, on Culloden's moor. There's a marker wi' th' Cameron name."

"Bless you, Ewan. Janet and Ewan come with me," she said. "I've a bottle of Duncan's best whisky. We'll drink to three grand men who gave their lives for Scotland, and may they be remembered for it! We'll also think of Elizabeth an' her bairns, God bless their blameless souls." Anne filled cups with whisky, and they drank, remembering those who were no longer with them.

Janet prepared food while Anne ran upstairs to gather clothing for herself and the boys. She placed Duncan's clan pin, his mother's wedding ring, coins and clothing in a bag in her knapsack. Then she hugged Mark and Timothy.

"Lads, we must go."

"Mama, where're we goin'?" Timmy asked as he looked at his mother's face.

"Later, I'll tell you."

The three walked to the barn where Ewan, Janet, and Daniel waited. "Anne, carry wee Mark wi' ye. Timothy will be wi' me. Janet, ye'll ha' Daniel."

"Ewan, there's no need for the three of you to place yourselves in more danger. I could saddle another horse for Timmy and—""Anne, I ga' my word! Say no more!" They stopped at the last gate while Anne looked back at the hill where the broch stood. She nodded, wiped away tears, nudged her horse into a trot, and did not look back. She held Mark close and wept for her fatherless sons.

Timothy asked, "Uncle, why's Mama cryin'? Mama, dinna cry. We'll find Da!"

Anne looked at him. "Hush, Timmie!" He saw tears in his mother's eyes and cried out, "Mama! Where're we goin'?"

Ewan covered Timmie's hands with his and whispered in his ear, "Laddie, I'm needin' help guidin' this horse. Would ye hold these reins an' watch for tree branches so we dinna get hit in th' face? Will ye do tha' for me?"

"Aye, Uncle Ewan, I'll keep a watch."

Evening fog covered them, but it also hid the path at the edge of the Trossach Mountains. They rode in single file. Janet considered the three lads whose lives had changed so drastically. *Th' wee ones will suffer. Daniel, Timmie, an' Mark ought to be playin' wi' toy soldiers instead of runnin' from 'em.*

In the last of the twilight, they stopped at a tree-sheltered place where a burn cascaded down the hillside, carrying water from the snowmelt far above. The water was cold and carried the taste and smell of peat. After eating bread and cheese, they dipped their hands into the stream and drank. Timothy and Daniel threw stones into the water, but Mark sat by his mother's side, clutching her hand as if for dear life.

"Anne," Janet asked, "How long will it take for ye to travel from th' abbey to yer father's lands?"

Anne said, "I'd say a day. Duncan and I visited my family once. Father was an absolute ass! Duncan did not take offense even when Father refused to sit at the same dinner table where he sat, let alone speak to him!" Anne nodded, "I will always cherish those sweet memories."

She wiped tears away and turned to Ewan. "Where will the three of you go after the lads and I travel on to England? You're welcome to come with me. Even though Father is a pain in the arse, still, he's not as difficult as he used to be."

Janet said, "I'm wonderin' th' same, Ewan, where will we go?"

"It's as I told ye earlier," he replied. "I'll keep my promise to Duncan. Then, when that's done, we'll decide wha' to do."

He looked at the three sleeping lads. "We're th' only family Daniel has, other than his mother's kin in Aberdeen. We won't be able to get word to 'em." Anne looked at Ewan. "Do you think the soldiers burned the broch with them inside? If it's possible, I'd like for Elizabeth and the lads to have a Christian burial."

"Aye, they were inside, Anne," Ewan responded. "We'll find a way to gi' 'em a decent burial."

"I'm willing to take Daniel with me. It's going to be very difficult in Scotland, and you've enough—""Nay, Anne, we'll care for Daniel. Ye ha' enough wi' yer two lads."

Quietly, Janet said, "I wish we'd brought Elizabeth an' th' bairns wi' us." She looked at Ewan. "Oh, I wish!"

"Lass, think about wha' yer sayin'. It was a close call we had wi' th' English soldiers. If we'd had four more, an' three of 'em little lads, wi' us, wha' do ye think would ha' happened?"

Janet nodded. They followed faint paths, close to woodlands. On the night of the fourth day, they reached the Scots-English borderlands, where the fires of English army camps glowed in the night sky.

"Anne," Ewan said softly, "Should we travel through th' forest or on th' moors?"

"Through the forest," Anne responded. "There's a path. I believe the troops are heading to the Highlands on the main roads. Let me lead, Ewan. At a bent tree, we'll turn east onto another path. Then it will be a three-hour ride to the abbey."

"Let th' lads stretch their legs." Ewan said as he helped Timothy, Daniel, and Mark down. "Be very quiet, lads."

"I've a plan that might save us should we be discovered." Anne looked from Ewan to Janet. "I am Lady Smallwood, daughter of His Lordship the Earl of Smallwood. I am traveling to my home in England with my servants and children."

Ewan shook his head. "Oh, I know, Ewan, but even a small chance would be better than none."

"Anne, it's more likely they'd kill us all an' then tell yer father it was accidental."

She shook her finger at Ewan. "My father is a personal friend of King George! I'd not be afraid to say so!"

"But tha' was in another time, Anne! Things are nay th' same now."

Daniel whined, "It's my turn to ride wi' Uncle Ewan."

"Daniel, I'm holdin' th' reins so our horse won't hit a tree. Ye dinna know how to do it!" Timothy responded.

Mark looked from one to the other; tears filled his eyes.

"Quiet, lads. Daniel, ye ride wi' Auntie Janet. Timothy, yer wi' me, an' Mark wi' yer mam."

It was after midnight when they reached the abbey. The door opened, and a priest greeted them. "Welcome!"

Ewan responded, "We're from th' Hielands an' ha' Anne Cameron an' her two lads wi' us. She must travel on to England where her family lives. May we rest for a while?"

"Aye, yer safe here. On th' morrow, Brother William will take baked goods across th' border to England to sell at market. Mistress Cameron an' th' lads can hide in th' back of th' wagon. When they reach England, they'll travel on wi' th' horse while Brother William barters fresh bread for the loan of a horse to bring him an' th' cart back."

"Aye," Ewan replied, "Tha' will do. Yer name, sir?"

"Father John. Yer safe here. We feed th' English soldiers an' allow 'em to bed down when needed, an' they leave us be."

"Father John, we're grateful to ye."

"Come along, all of ye. There's a kettle of stew on th' grate."

They sat down at a long table. A smiling monk brought stew in wooden bowls, loaves of bread, milk for the children, and ale for Ewan, Janet, and Anne. Father John sat at the head of the table. "Yer name?"

"Ewan Cameron. This is Janet, my wife, my cousin's wife, Anne, an' her sons, Mark an' Timothy. Th' little lad beside my wife is Daniel, my cousin's son. Father John, ha' ye heard about th' Hielands?"

"Aye, Lord Cumberland's regiment stopped here on their way to Edinburgh. Th' English won th' battle, an' th' duke ordered all royal army soldiers to wipe out th' Hielanders. They talked as we served a meal to 'em. They told of gold meant to buy guns for Stuarts' army tha' went elsewhere."

Everyone jumped when Ewan hit the table with his fist. "Ewan Cameron! It's nay my intention to anger ye."

"Father, I'm angry, but not wi' ye."

"Ewan, we offer sanctuary to any who ask. There may be English soldiers bedded in th' hall an' Scottish folk sleepin' in th' monks' quarters."

"I'd like a word wi' ye privately, Father," Ewan said.

"Follow me to th' cemetery; none will hear us there."

Ewan followed the priest into a courtyard. "Th' battle was a massacre! All of us heard about th' divine right to th' throne an' 'em sayin' that if a Stuart were king this'd be better an' that'd be different. But most of us dinna believe a Stuart would do any different than th' king we ha' now."

"Then," Father John said, "Why did th' Hielanders go to battle for th' Stuart?"

"Food an' money are short in th' Hielands. Some thought a Stuart king'd be more favorable to us. But we fought, lost, an' canna go back now. Young Daniel, th' lad travelin' wi' us, lost his da at Culloden's field. His mother an' brothers died in a fire set by th' king's soldiers. It burned down our broch."

Father John crossed himself. "Ewan, there's naught we can do about it. We'd best be thinkin' about here an' now. If ye leave tonight, th' light o'day'll find ye on th' bare moors, an' th' soldiers'll use ye to sight in their rifles. We heard 'em tell about it. Wha' are yer plans when you leave us?"

Ewan's shoulders sagged. "After we've been to th' ruins of our broch, we'll travel to Perthshire, where our son is with Janet's parents."

"Well, then, we'll fill yer knapsacks, enough to last should yer need to stay hidden a day or so. There's caves in th' hillsides not far from here."

Janet stood when the two men returned. "Ewan, we're weary. I dinna think we should leave now."

"Aye, we'll rest a bit."

Father John led them to a small room off the chapel. "It's my prayer room, quiet an' away from eyes an' ears tha' might interfere wi' my solitude. Rest, all of ye." He closed the door behind him. Father John knelt in the chapel and prayed. Later, when he heard the door open and close, he followed Ewan, Janet and Daniel to the courtyard. It was dark; clouds covered the sky. "Ewan, do ye ha' a pistol?"

"I did," Ewan said, "But I lost it in th' forest."

"Wait! Dinna leave!" Father John went to the abbey and returned with a wooden box. "See if this'll meet yer needs."

Ewan lifted the lid. Inside lay a pistol with lead balls and gunpowder. "Father John! How did ye come by it?"

Father John shook his head. "If I thought ye needed to know, I'd say so, but I dinna." He smiled at Ewan and Janet and patted Daniel on the head. "God be wi' ye."

Ewan saddled two horses and led them to the courtyard. "Father John, we'll leave th' other horse to pull th' cart tomorrow."

"Aye, Ewan. Dinna worry about th' lady an' her sons. We'll take care of 'em."

"Janet, ride ahead of me. If ye look back an' I'm hidden, dinna worry. If ye hear an owl's hoot, find a hidin' place!" Ewan hesitated. "If we're separated, make yer way to yer family. Travel by night, an' cover yer red hair! I don't ha' to tell ye what'll happen if th' English find ye."

Ewan handed her a leather pouch filled with gold and silver coins. "There's enough for ye, Duny, an' Daniel to leave Scotland, if it comes to it. I'd rest easier if I knew—nay, if it comes to tha', I'll be past restin' easy."

Janet listened as her husband spoke, but her mind raced ahead; it might come to her what their future held. She closed her eyes. *Why when I need to know I canna see anything, an' when I dinna want to know, I see things tha' I dinna want to?* Her head was aching, and her stomach cramped in a painful knot. *All my herbs are at home.*

Then she shook her head. *They're nay there, an' neither is home!* She shuddered at the thought.

Ewan reined in Prince while Janet's horse moved forward. She turned and waved at him. He blew her a kiss, which she caught and brought to her lips. The wind rustled through the leaves, and she thought she heard voices. She looked over her shoulder but did not see Ewan. She rode on through the forest, hoping Ewan was somewhere behind her. Then she heard an owl's hoot. Quickly, she guided the horse off the path, lifted Daniel down and they both hid.

Soon, a small troop of Redcoats passed by. Janet watched as Ewan, bound by rope to a saddle, walked behind the last soldier's horse. Daniel started to speak, but she put her hand over his mouth. She heard one soldier say to the other, "I'd say he'll go to Inverness and be shipped out to New Zealand. He'll make a good slave."

Barefoot, Ewan was almost running to keep up with the gait of the horse. She had to let him know she was nearby. She whistled the three-note trill of the mountain lark. She repeated it and then was silent. Far off in the distance, she heard the sound repeated; another lark answered her whistle. Ewan turned his head slightly and nodded. *He knows I'm here!* The troop marched on. Janet waited until she was sure the soldiers were well out of the forest before they returned to the path.

Janet pondered what to do. *They're takin' him to Inverness, an' I need to be there to free him.* She whispered to Daniel, "Dinna worry. There'll be a way to free yer Uncle Ewan!"

Daniel whimpered and looked into her face. His lower lip trembled, and tears filled his eyes. "Now, now, laddie"

"Wha' did they do to Uncle Ewan?"

Janet answered, "They've taken him prisoner. When they're not lookin', he'll escape." Janet hugged the little lad. "We dinna want 'em to find us too, so we'll travel a different direction. I'll take ye to meet a dear friend of mine. Her name is Auntie Mary, an' she always has bannock buns wi' jam an' milk."

Daniel looked up at his aunt and smiled. *Ah*, she thought, *to be a bairn an' smile at th' thought of a bun wi' jam.*

Janet smiled back at him. Daniel was very quiet; his fingers twisted the blanket corner into a knot. "Auntie, where's my mam an' brothers?"

Janet patted Daniel's shoulder. "I canna tell ye now." Daniel nodded his head and closed his eyes. She stopped the horse and stepped down, careful to not disturb the sleeping child. Her head ached, and her stomach was sour. In the knapsack was a flask of water and a small bag of sweets. She ate some of the candy and splashed water on her face. Then she remembered the pistol in the knapsack behind Prince's saddle. She knew Prince would come to Ewan and Thomas with a whistle, so she cupped her hands and whistled. At first there was no sound, but then she heard brush being pushed aside. What if another troop of soldiers was on the path and had heard her? Janet waited, hardly breathing. It was gloomy in the forest; perhaps they would not see her.

She heard heavy breathing and then a snort. A nose nudged her elbow. Prince stood by her side. He nudged her arm while she spoke to him. Prince could maneuver through rocks and ravines better than any other horse. He could trot at an even pace or run like the very wind. He nudged her again. "Let me see, where is yer grain?"

She opened the knapsack and found cheese, bread, and a flask of ale. A second knapsack held the box with the pistol and a bag of oats. Janet filled her hands and held them out to Prince. His ears were alert; if he stopped eating and raised his head, she would know something had caught his attention.

Janet moved the contents of her knapsacks to the larger ones fastened to Prince's saddle. She was glad to have Prince and the pistol. She opened the box. It also held gun powder and a bag of lead balls. She helped Daniel down from her horse, removed the saddle, hid it, and placed him on Prince. Could she find the way to

219

Mary's cottage? There were high mountains to cross or go around. After they reached Mary's cottage, there'd still be a ride to Inverness with English soldiers traveling the same path. When she reached Inverness, how could she find Ewan?

There was a fork in the path ahead; one way led downward, and the other went deeper into the forest. She choose the first way. When they reached the bottom of a ravine, she tethered Prince and spread a blanket on the ground. "Daniel, we'll rest here." She pulled her cloak around both of them, folded her arm under her head, and slept.

Several hours later, she sat up when Daniel shook her shoulder. "Auntie, where are we?" She whispered, "Daniel, lad, speak softly. I dinna know where we are. Let's wash our faces an' find somethin' to eat."

Janet rinsed her hands in the cold water of a burn and splashed some on her face. Daniel, watching her, did the same. Then she dried her face on her shirt; Daniel wiped his face on his sleeve. There was bread, cheese, and ale. When she handed Daniel his portion, he smiled and said, "Thank ye, Auntie. I'm very hungry."

"We'll make a marker wi' stones. Then, if we come this way again, we'll remember this day an' place."

While Janet marked out a square with a sharp stick, Daniel gathered stones. She showed him how to fill in the square with the stones. She thought of Duny. *Th' lad dinna know his da's a prisoner.'* Then she thought about Thomas, who was as her own brother. *We did'na say a proper good-bye. I should ha' told him to stay wi' his brother. Nay, he did wha' he had to do.*

Janet explained to Daniel why he must not make even a tiny sound. He nodded that he understood. Together, holding hands, with Prince following behind, they followed the burn until they climbed out of the ravine into the forest. At dark, if all was clear, they would ride north and west toward the high glens. "Daniel, help me watch for soldiers. They must not find us."

Daniel looked at his aunt's face. "Auntie, dinna be afraid. I'd throw rocks at a soldier an' knock him down. Dinna worry, Auntie. I'll take care of ye."

"Thank ye, Daniel. Yer a good lad."

Janet placed Daniel in the saddle astride Prince. She held the reins and began walking. It was always twilight in the ancient forest; very little light filtered through the great canopy of branches. It was quiet and peaceful here, almost a sanctuary. Janet asked for God's protection.

Chapter 30

Ewan's feet throbbed, but his arms ached even more. The rope tied around his neck was looped around the rope tied between his hands. If he lowered his arms, the rope around his neck tightened, and he was unable to breathe. He focused on moving his feet. *Must walk. Right foot, left foot, right, left, right.* When did he last sleep? Was it a night ago, two? His full bladder was painful, and he had no choice but to urinate as he walked. The urine left a trail in the dried blood on his legs and feet.

"You there, Highlander, did you piss yourself?"

Ewan raised his head. "It's about doing wha' ye ha' to do. Next I'll be shittin' unless ye let me go behind yonder tree. Ye'll think yer leadin' a chamber pot instead of a man."

The soldier looked around; he didn't see any harm in letting the man relieve himself. "I'll loosen the rope and hold the end while you go, Highlander. Get it done quickly, or I'll be hanging you from a tree limb. Then you'll be shitting your breeches for certain."

"Aye, from th' feel of my guts, it'll not take long."

The soldier dismounted, loosened the rope, and motioned for

Ewan to go to the tree. Ewan noticed the soldier was younger than the rest of the troops and seemed to be left out of conversations between the other soldiers. "I'm a Cameron—first name is Robert, an' yer can call me Rob." Ewan didn't know why he said that given name instead of his own.

"A Cameron, huh? My granny on my father's side was a Cameron. She married my grandpa Ball in Edinburgh. Granny Ball lived to be a hundred years old. Say, Rob, now that I'm in Scotland, I don't see any difference between it and England."

"Ah, there's a difference. Ye'll see wha' I mean."

"Lieutenant, sir! Might the troop take a rest?"

"Halt!" the lieutenant ordered. "We'll rest. Soldier Ball, tie the prisoner to a tree."

"Yes, sir!" With the rope around his neck loosened, Ewan sat with his legs and feet stretched out in front of him. His feet were bleeding, and he had bruises on his legs and arms. But other than that, he was in one piece. The young soldier sat a short distance from him, eating a meat-filled pastry. Ewan's mouth filled with saliva when he smelled the food.

"Soldier Ball, wha's yer first name?"

"William, but I'm called Willie. Here, take it." He handed Ewan half of the pastry and his flask of ale. Ewan stuffed the food in his mouth and washed it down with ale. "Thank ye, Willie."

"Rob, your feet are in bad shape. There's few rocks here in the woods, but out on the open path, rocks is all there are. They'll make a bloody mess of your feet. I'll see what I can do for you."

"Thank ye, Willie."

"You sound like my granny Ball, Highlander."

"Willie, how is it tha' yer a soldier?" Evan asked.

"It puts a few coins in my pocket, and I always have a place to sleep. Besides, I want to fight for our king. Rob, why'd you want to fight against a good king?"

"Ye ken yer granny Ball?" Ewan said. "She could tell ye why. Ye said ye dinna see any difference between England an' Scotland. I can tell ye th' difference. It's th' mist on th' mountains an' th' valleys. It's th' smell of heather an' gorse on th' glen an' th' wild weather that blows in from th' North Sea. It's th' people, laddie, th' ones tha' tend th' sheep an' bake th' bread. If I could only tell ye—but then, I'm no able to find th' right words."

Ewan closed his eyes and slept. Too soon, the rest ended. "Say, Rob, do you think we might be kin?"

"Aye, we're kin! All Camerons are kin. There's th' northern Camerons, th' Lochiel's Camerons, an' Camerons who've left Scotland. We all share th' same blood, an' as I'm lookin' at yer face, I see th' same crooked nose tha' I ha'. It's how we know we're Camerons."

Willie put his hand to his nose. "Why, you're right, my nose is crooked. Come to think on it, I look like Gran. Her nose was crooked too!"

The soldiers in front of Willie took no notice of Ewan and Willie talking. Ahead was the edge of the forest; soon they would be riding through prickly heather, gorse, and thistle-covered moors. "Willie, ahead is th' edge of th' woods. I'm dreadin' walkin' on th' moors wi'out boots. I'm sore a'feered yer lieutenant will lose patience an' shoot me."

"Rob, I've a pair of boots in my bag. We're issued two pairs, as there's no bootery repairs on the battlefield and a soldier can't fight barefooted. I've got a second set of uniforms too. They give us one when we sign up, and then money is held out of our pay for the second set. What do you get paid to fight in Scotland's army?"

"Paid?" Ewan said. "Yer mean money?"

Willie answered, "Yes, money."

"Ye might not believe it, Willie, but I get no pay for fightin' for Scotland an' my clan's rights. If ye've never heard of William Wallace an' Robert th' Bruce, I'll fill ye in on 'em. They're yer kin too. Yer Granny was a Scots lassie, an' ye are a Scots laddie. It's tha' ye was born on th' wrong side of th' border. Yer a Sassenach, but I think none th' less of ye for it."

"Soldier, catch up!" ordered the lieutenant, looking over his shoulder. "Move the prisoner along so we can keep an eye on the bugger. Don't coddle him. He's just a Highlander, and everyone knows they're like goats, wild, climb on rocks, have head bones hard as horns, and eat weeds. I've heard it said they have goat blood. I'd not put it past the lot. Who knows what goes on in those Highland pastures when the moon is full? This one may be going to New Zealand if he's lucky. If not, he'll be crow bait, dangling from the hangman's noose."

Willie jerked on Ewan's rope, speaking loud enough for the lieutenant to hear, "Hurry up, you sorry piece of shite. Don't fall behind, or you'll be shot."

Willie winked at Ewan and whispered, "You can't put the boots on until we stop. The lieutenant's been drinking ale all afternoon and will need to stop and piss before long. He won't notice if you're shod or not. Now, don't do nothing to give me away. It'd go badly for both of us."

"Aye, cousin, I'll be careful." Willie quickly turned away, but not before Ewan saw a hint of a smile on his lips and thought, *I'll escape if I ha' a chance. Willie will help me. They'll nay miss me for a while.* His legs throbbed; every low-growing thorny bush he ran through tore at the skin on his legs and ankles. Blood mixed with dirt on his feet until they resembled red clay.

"Sorry, Rob. It won't be much longer 'til we stop. Is this the Highlands? I've heard my granny talk about Scotland, but I don't think she'd been to the Highlands."

"I'll tell ye about it to get my mind off'n my aches an' pains." Willie turned to look at Ewan and saw his bloody feet, legs, and ankles and torn breeks that barely covered his buttocks. "My God, man, you'll have your banger an' balls torn off if we don't stop soon—and your feet! They look like fresh meat hanging in the butcher's shop."

"While we're travelin' I'll tell ye about Scotland's Hielands. Th' Hielands are nay like England. There's fewer villages an' people. We've all sorts of dwellin's, from castles to stone cottages."

The lieutenant held up his hand. "Halt! I'll scout ahead."

Willie dismounted, loosened the rope fastened to his saddle, and handed Ewan a flask of water. "My boots won't fit ye, Rob, your feet are too big."

"I'll tell ye more about Scotland. Th' Hielands ha' rivers, lochs, an' burns. Ye'd best be knowin' where yer goin', for there'll be none to ask yer way." Ewan struggled to stand as his mind became stronger than his pain. "I'll tell ye about th' Hielanders. We belong to a clan, wear kilts, an' speak Gaelic, a language tha' is understood only by another Hielander. Th' Scottish lowlander is more like th' English. Some lowlanders think we're savages."

Ewan chuckled in spite of his aches and pains. "But we look at th' lowlanders an' pity 'em 'cause they're like th' English, payin' homage to England's king, bowin' an' blowin' kisses to him. Some of us, called lairds, ha' land in our care. We raise cattle an' sheep an' grow oats an' barley. We make a fine malt whisky wi' th' barley, shear our sheep, weave our wool, an' fashion our clothes. Some of th' wool is so fine tha' it brings a high price at th' Edinburgh market. Then we ha' money to buy more sheep, cattle, an' things for our wives an' bairns. Cousin, ha' ye seen th' Hieland cattle?"

Willie shook his head.

"They're shaggy beasts wi' horns. See my cross? My wife made it wi' hair from my Hieland cattle. Here, Willie, take it. It'll remind ye of how we learned tha' we're related."

Willie took it and placed his hand on Ewan's shoulder. "Thank you, cousin. I'll put it away for safekeeping. Ah, damn, Rob, the lieutenant's back. Come along, now. There'll be no more stoppin' 'til we set up camp."

When the rope tightened around Ewan's neck, he began running behind Willie's horse. He stumbled but then regained his footing. "Rob, hold on a little longer."

Ewan began running and closed his eyes. He fell when his foot turned; the rope continued to pull him behind Willie's horse. Ewan called out when his head hit a large rock, but then he felt nothing as the rope pulled him up and over the rock. By the time Willie realized Ewan was no longer on foot, the horse had traveled over more rocks and through a burn. "Lieutenant! The prisoner is down!"

The lieutenant rode to the end of the line. "Is he breathing?"

Willie placed his hand on Ewan's chest. "Yes, he does."

"Soldier Ball, how did this happen?"

"Sir, I do not know."

The lieutenant shook his head and looked from Willie to Ewan. "There's no horse to carry him. I wonder who he is."

"Sir, his name is Rob Cameron."

"Cameron, you say? Well, then! He's guilty of treason! A shot to the head will save hanging him. Drag him off the path and then catch up."

"Yes, sir!" As William loaded his pistol, Ewan tried to sit up.

"Rob, don't move. I've been ordered to shoot you, but I won't. I can't shoot one of my family. I've put my spare coat, breeches, and boots in the knapsack. There's coins in the pocket of the breeches. I'll shoot into the ground, an' you stay here until you're sure we've gone."

He stood a short distance from Ewan, fired a shot into the ground, and moved Ewan away from the path deeper into the forest. He lifted Ewan's head and placed the knapsack underneath. "Rob, you hit your head when ye fell. I've left a flask of wine and some biscuits. Cousin, not all English soldiers are the bastards that Scotsmen think they are."

Chapter 31

"James." Abigail Dunsmuir smiled at her husband. "What say you to a trip to Perth? I need thread, ribbons, and fabric for a new gown. I never dress as a lady anymore. My satin slippers are dusty from lack of use, but my barn boots are near worn out!"

"So, my dear, yer wantin' new boots an' a gown? There'll be money for th' barn boots, but th' gown—well, we'll see."

"Keep it up, James dearest, and you'll be wearing your arse for a bonnet!"

"My, my, Abby, go put on yer breeks if yer goin' to speak as a barn lad." The two smiled at one another.

"Aye, it's time to get out an' about," James agreed as he steered Abby in the direction of the barn. "Let's take a look at Jamie's pony, Tanner. He's already trained to th' saddle an' bridle."

James walked with a cane, and Abby paced her steps to match his. "I'll be damned if he's not goin' to be ready to sell quicker than the rest!"

Then James lowered his voice and took Abby's hand. "When John brought Meghan home, he said th' uprisin' had started, but we've nay heard a thing since. It may be all th' fightin' is over or it dinna happen after all."

James paused to catch his breath. "Did Ewan an' Janet say they'd be comin' to get Duny after th' new year? It's near th' end of April, an' we've not seen hide nor hair of 'em. Course, we're glad for Duny's help, but still ... It's nay like 'em to leave him this long."

"James, they said they would be here after Christ's Mass, but I told them we were in no hurry for Duny to return home. I knew Jamie would need a hand with training the colts while your leg was mending. We'd have heard by now if there was something to hear."

"Aye, yer right." James returned to his favorite subject. "I'll tell ye, Abby, Jamie knows more about raisin' an' breedin' horses than I did when I was twice his age. Th' lad and I had a bit of a set-to when he wanted to bring in tha' Hieland mare an' stallion. But he did anyway, against my better judgment. I'm still shakin' my heid after seein' how strong an' healthy those animals are. They'll find grazin' when the pasture looks bare an' be healthy when other animals would be starvin'."

"I've seen the animals, James, but I didn't pay much attention to them. After hearing you fuss about Highland animals coming on the place, I thought they'd not be here long."

"Aw, well, I've learned a lesson. People will purchase Hieland animals. They're gentle, a good ridin' animal for th' ladies an' will take to th' bridle at least three months before other breeds. Besides, they do better in bitter weather. Our son has a heid on his shoulders!" James smiled. "Th' lads will manage well enough wi'out us for little while. Let's go to York!"

"Oh, James, I'd love that! England is beautiful in the spring, and the Dales is my favorite place. Then, James, when we return, we'll take Meghan home. She's a month or so from delivery, so there's time. I know she'd rather birth the babe in her own home, and I'd like to help her get things together."

James brought Abby back to reality. "Abby, if, I said if, things are bonny fine in Scotland, we'll take both Meghan an' Duny home. But there's somethin' askew. I dinna know wha'."

They held hands as they walked down the well-worn path to the carriage house. Abby heard James' concerns but then put them out of her mind. "Let's take the little carriage with the top. It pulls well behind one horse, and we can stop for the night in Edinburgh. James, I'm making do with mended and patched clothing! I've nothing to wear!"

James laughed. "Tsk, tsk, 'tis a shame about ye, my dear! We may ha' barn muck on our boots an' clothes, but we ha' coins a plenty in our pockets!"

Laughing, Abby nodded. "When will we leave?"

"Gi' me th' morrow, an' I'll be ready. There's some work to be done wi' th' yearlin' colts, an th' mares tha' will be foalin' need to be moved to the birthin' pastures. That'll keep th' lads busy for a fortnight, an' by then, we'll be back. I dinna want 'em huntin' while we're away. They'll end up in th' village tavern. I'll tell 'em to stay put an' out o' trouble.

James rubbed his right knee. There were times when it ached so badly that he sipped on barley malt whisky as the day went by. Abigail knew he was in pain most of the time, and she did most of the dealings with the buyers. On occasion, she encountered a buyer who did not appreciate the extent of her knowledge of horses. It usually did not take very long before he did. Jamie handled and trained all of the animals while Duny could speak with potential buyers about the bloodlines of every stallion and mare James owned. Duny, nearly as tall as his grandfather, had his mother's red hair and green eyes. He was a good-looking lad with the bony frame of a boy whose body was still growing. His first love was horses, and his second was reading books about geography and history. On long Sunday afternoons, he studied maps. He found a country called America where there were red-skinned people who used canoes on rivers. In a different direction was India, where brown-skinned people rode strange animals called elephants. When Duny slept, he would dream of these wonderful places. Other times he dreamed of places and saw things that frightened him; there was something very different about these dreams. After waking he pondered on them. One night, he dreamed his grandfather was dead and lying beneath a tree. Frightened by the dream, he did not speak to anyone about it.

On long evenings after supper, Jamie and Duny played chess. One night the game stalled while Jamie deliberated on his next move. During the long minutes it took for him to decide, Duny crunched fried salted potato slices. Jamie frowned. "Duny, ye dummy! Are ye trying to distract me wi' all yer chompin' so I'll make a wrong move?"

Duny looked up. "Aw, Jamie, if yer want some of my chips, ask for 'em!" Duny held out a plateful of the chips. "Here, Uncle Dunckle, ha' a bite. They're very tasty."

Jamie stood up, pushed his chair back from the table, and glared at Duny. James caught the withering look. "All right, lads. Tomorrow ye can pitch hay into th' barn loft, an' then when tha's done, ye'll pitch it back down again; mayhap it'll get rid of some of yer piss an' vinegar."

Abby smiled. She was knitting trim on a blanket for her grandchild. A village woman had gifted her with a square of soft woolen fabric. Abby admired the pale yellow color.. "How did you get such a beautiful color?" she asked.

"Milady, I used buttercups. It took many blossoms to dye th' yarn for this wee bit of wool. I do so love to see th' colors th' wool takes when it's soaked wi' different flowers. My favorite's a rose color, but this color will hold through many washin's while th' rose'll fade away after a while. Milady, if I may say so, when ye first came here, we all thought yer were royalty, wha' wi' yer fine ways an' all. But instead of lookin' down yer nose at us, ye treated us like we were not just common folks but a bit fine ourselves. Ye've been kind to us, an' I'd like to gift ye this fabric. It'll be nice for a babe."

"Our grandchild will be born soon. Meghan's expecting."

"Then, milady, God bless all of th' Dunsmuir family."

Abby thanked the woman and made a promise to herself to speak with some of the shopkeepers in Perth about purchasing woven fabric for resale. This could be a way for the villagers to add coins to their purses.

When she listened to Jamie and Duny arguing, Abby was thankful for James. He kept peace in the family. She dearly loved this man who was her husband, lover, and friend. Abby smiled when James looked at her.

He smiled back. "Milady, may I escort ye upstairs? It's bedtime, ye know."

Abby used the Scottish words she loved hearing from her husband. "Aye, let's see if we can get ye' up th' stairs, husband."

James grinned. "Lassie, if ye will but go ahead of me so I can see tha' lovely swing in yer behind, I'm sure I can make it just fine."

Jamie and Duny, hearing James teasing Abby, laughed. "Just think of it, Duny. One of these days, ye'll be talkin' to some lady like tha', an' she'll hit ye up th' side of th' heid wi' her shoe."

"Nay, nay! Uncle Jamie, I've learned from watchin' ye. I know to not put my hand down th' front of a lass's gown like yer did wi' Ellen—it got yer face slapped!"

"Shut yer trap, Duny, or I'll clout yer wi' my boot."

James, hearing the exchange of words, said, "Good night, lads. Would ye bank the fire for me? Jamie, best be careful about wha' ye do to Ellen. Her da is bigger than ye. He could use ye to sweep th' floor!"

Jamie gave Duny a fierce look. "Aye, sir, we'll bank th' fire."

Chapter 32

Death and The Dark One sat in a tree watching as the man's chest barely moved with each breath. "He'd be dead if not for that strong Highland heart," Death said.

The Dark One whispered, "He does not belong to me; I've heard him praying to his God." The Dark One held out his scaly hand. "Aren't humans interesting? They're told to love one another, but hatred is much easier for them. Master says there is a fine line between love and hate; he instructs all demons in ways to lead humans over the line. Ah, well, no point in waiting around here. We'll meet again later."

"Wait, Dark One," Death said. "I've seen a few who crossed the line you mentioned but then thought better of it and went back! What about those you lose?"

The Dark One threw back his head and howled; the sound was hideous. "Once they get a taste of what we have to offer when they do cross the line, it's easier the second time. I never give up, you see."

Death thought for a moment and looked down at the man who labored to breathe. "As you say, this one's not yours. There is no need for you to wait, and he is not ready for me either. In fact, it appears that the one he prays to is giving him strength to live even as we speak. Well, demon, can you overcome that?"

"No, but you won't hear me admit it elsewhere—and if you said I did, I'd call you a liar. It's true, I have no power to overcome what is happening here. I must never mention it, and neither does Master!" The Dark One spread his wings and flew away.

Ewan opened his eyes. His stomach forced bile into his throat; he tasted the bitterness and then drifted back into darkness. Hours later he opened his eyes again. A large bird stood by his left leg. Ewan lay very still; the bird pecked and pulled at his flesh. Helpless, Ewan watched as the bird pulled away a piece of skin and swallowed it. Ewan closed his eyes and opened them again when the bird flew away. A second, very large bird flew over him, and he caught a glimpse of chestnut, white, and black feathers. *I'll not be bait for ye yet,* he thought. He discovered he had feeling in his left hand and was able to move his right hand. He looked at his right foot, pleased when he was able to wiggle his toes. He had no feeling at all in his left leg or foot. He crawled to a tree and rested his back against it. He would stay upright even when he went back to sleep. As he closed his eyes, he wondered why he was under a tree in the forest.

Chapter 33

Daniel slept as he rode. The forest was behind them now; ahead was a wilderness of rocks, heather, and burns. Janet tested each step; a rock rolling down the hill might draw attention. When she quickened her pace, Prince responded to the tug on the reins. A sharp rock slipped beneath her boot, leaving a cut in the leather sole. She thought of Ewan walking without boots on a rocky path. He would suffer. Ahead, the path climbed upward; soon they would be at the foothills leading to the Great Glen. Daniel stirred. "Auntie, I need to pee."

As Janet helped him down, he looked around. "Where are we?"

"We're on our way to find Uncle Ewan, remember?"

Daniel thought for a minute. "Oh, aye, Auntie." He put his hand in his pocket. "I still ha' rocks in my pocket, Auntie. Dinna worry, I'll take care of ye."

"I know ye will, Daniel. Would ye like to walk wi' me instead of riding?"

"Aye. Auntie, my bum's tired of ridin'." Daniel's voice turned into a sorrowful whine. "I miss my pillie an' bed."

"Aye, me too," Janet replied. "We must be very careful tha' no one sees or hears us."

"I'll not make any noise, Auntie. See how quiet I am?" Daniel looked at Janet to be sure she was watching him walk on his tiptoes.

Janet felt a smile tugging at the corners of her mouth. "I know of no lads who are as quiet as ye, Daniel. Would ye like a bite to eat? Here's a flat rock we can sit on."

They sat together eating cheese, bread, and an oatcake each. Afterward, Janet gave Prince his grain. A light mist began falling. In the cool dampness, she wrapped her cloak around her shoulders and folded a blanket around Daniel's thin shoulders. Holding hands, they continued to climb.

Janet hoped to walk until daybreak. Then they would find a place to sleep. She and Daniel could find a sheltered spot, but Prince would be difficult to hide. She turned to the only place where she could find comfort. "Heavenly Father, I pray ye'll protect us an' be wi' Ewan. Yer word says 'Though I walk through th' valley of th' shadow of death, thou art wi' me.' I hold to tha', Father, tha' ye're here wi' me."

Janet could feel her worries lighten as she said the words, "In Jesus's name, amen." She squared her shoulders. "Now, laddie, let's put ye back on Prince, an' ye can nap for a while. I'll wake ye if I run into any soldiers."

Daniel ran to Prince's side and held his foot out for Janet to lift him up to the saddle. She wrapped the blanket around him and gave him a hug. Now she was alone with her thoughts. *There are at least three more nights of travel to reach Mary's cottage. When we pass Fort William, it's not far to Mary's. When I reach Inverness, where will Ewan be?* She caught her breath. *What if he's nay there, or been hanged? Heavenly Father, help me. I canna do this alone.*

Again, she felt fear leave her. *In Jesus's blessed name, I pray. Amen.* Janet thought of the cross she had given Ewan. She hoped he still had it. The mist lifted enough that she could see hills in the distance, and then the glens of the Highlands. The two of them had to travel through those glens without being found by the king's soldiers.

Chapter 34

James sat on the side of the bed and looked at his sleeping wife. He thought of their lovemaking the night before, at first gentle. Then as their passion became stronger, Abby knew that James could not make love to her in the usual way, so she made love to him. James leaned over to kiss her as she stirred and opened her eyes. "Not so fast, husband. Give me a proper hug, will you?"

James wrapped his arms around her and whispered in her ear, "We could start our trip late. Th' sun is just now coming up, an' we could ..."

"No, no, I'm anxious to be on our way." Abby jumped out of bed. "Everything is ready. There's food in the larder and work to be done by the lads. Bess will not need anything until we return."

Abby was dressed and downstairs before James got his boots on. He called after her, "I'll be at the barn hitchin' up th' horse an' loadin' the carriage; Farley can help me. Ye finish up wha' ye need to do, an' then we'll both be ready about th' same time."

As they bade good-bye to Meghan, Jamie, and Duny, Jamie said, "Da, we'll move th' yearlings into th' training arena. Duny'll bridle train 'em, an' I'll groom 'em. When ye get back, we'll ha' 'em ready to saddle. Dinna worry, I'll see to it tha' Duny stays in line." Duny looked at Jamie and frowned.

Abby kissed them both. Then she smoothed Meghan's hair back to kiss her forehead and told her to take care and rest as much as possible.

A carriage waited with a beautiful mare hitched to it. "Oh, I'm glad we're taking Bonnie. She's a proud horse, prancing and ready to go. Thank you, Farley, for combing and grooming her."

Farley tipped his cap. "Ha' a safe trip!"

As they left, Abby turned to look at the broch sitting on the hillside. "James, every time we ride through those gates, I remember the first time I saw our home. It was beautiful then, and it is even more beautiful now."

"Aye, lassie, it is."

They rode through the Perthshire countryside with lush grass and wild roses blooming on the hillsides. "This has to be the most beautiful place on God's earth, don't you think, James?"

"Aye, ye'll get no argument from me. I've traveled some in my horse tradin' business, an' I've never seen anyplace I'd rather call home. If ye'll notice, th' road is smoothed out, an' there're new bridges over some of th' rivers we've had to cross in th' past. That'll make our travels easier."

Abby enjoyed the countryside so much that she did not notice the small troop of English soldiers. "Halt!" A captain at the front held up his hand.

Abby saw rifles pointed at them, but she was not worried. James stepped out of the carriage. "Good mornin'. I'm James Dunsmuir. I see yer ridin' a horse or two tha' came from my farm. Wha' can I do for ye?"

"Get out of the cart!" The soldier nearest to them pointed his rifle at Abby. "Now!"

Abby looked at James. "What do ye mean, talkin' to my wife tha' way? I can see yer th' king's soldiers, but why ha' ye stopped us?"

"We follow orders from Lord Cumberland. Soldiers, take possession of this cart and horse; they are needed for His Majesty's service."

One of the soldiers pointed his rifle at James and said, "Hand over your money and the lady's jewelry."

"I'll nay be given' ye any money or her jewelry."

The soldier cocked the gun and shot at James's boots. James jumped and backed away. "Who are ye? Thieves waylaying people who are carryin' on wi' business? I'll be findin' a constable to arrest all of ye!"

One of the soldiers raised his pistol and pulled the trigger. The shot knocked James backward, and he fell to the ground, blood staining the front of his coat. Abby ran to him and pulled his coat aside. The lead ball had passed through and out his back. Blood pooled on the ground beneath him. Abby pulled his leather belt away from his breeks and wrapped it around his shoulder, close to the profusely bleeding wound. She tightened the belt and fastened the buckle underneath his arm. She stood and faced the soldiers.

"Leave us be! I am English and related to King George. I will see to it he knows of this, and there will be retribution, I promise you!"

"No, Madam," the captain replied. "It is fortunate for you I spent the night with a whore. Otherwise I would throw you in the dirt and take what I wanted from you. Kiss my hand and be grateful I am not ordering you to kiss my arse. The king's army won the battle at Culloden's moor, and the clans are no more!"

Abby looked at James, walked to the captain, bowed, and spoke softly. "Thank you for our lives. We did not know about the battle. We live in the country, and word of it has not reached us. We are at your mercy."

"Ah," the captain said to his men, "take their horse, let them go, and we'll move on."

When the soldiers unhitched the horse from the carriage, one of them held out his hand and motioned for Abby to take off her ring.

She slipped off the emerald ring James had given her and handed her gold wedding band to the soldier instead. Without looking, he put it in his pocket. They did not search James's pockets, where gold and silver coins were tucked into the blood-soaked pocket of his waistcoat.

Abby stood beside the carriage. "James, we must get you out of sight."

She helped him to his feet, led him to the rock wall, and helped him lower himself to the ground on the other side. Painfully, he said, "Abby, we'll need a horse to get home."

"Somewhere there will be one I can buy, beg, or borrow." Abby brought him a flask of whisky from the carriage. "Here, James, take a sip while I have a look at your shoulder."

The entry wound was barely seeping blood, but the exit wound on his back was a large, gaping hole, by far the most serious. "James, the bleeding has slowed. I know it's painful, but there does not seem to be too much damage."

"Abby! Unload th' carriage an' hide it, quick! I feel hoofbeats on th' ground!" Abby unloaded boxes, placed them beside James, and pulled the carriage across the road. She pushed it over the edge and hid just as a troop of soldiers rode by.

"Abby, ye cut it short gettin' off th' road. Listen to me." James spoke so low she could barely hear him. "It'd be best if ye find two horses, but take wha' ye can get."

James reached in his pocket and handed her a pouch of gold and silver coins. "Take this, but pay no more than a gold coin for a horse. See if ye can bargain—" James saw the look on his wife's face and stopped. "Sorry, Abby. Do wha' ye can. I'll be pleased wi' an ol' nag."

She had walked only a short distance when she realized her flimsy leather slippers were coming apart. *Who'd have thought I'd be walking on the road today? Mayhap James's injury is not as bad as it looks; if I can find a horse, we can reach home by morning.* In the distance she saw a cottage and several outbuildings. Then she felt hoofbeats on the hard-packed dirt road. Heart pounding, Abby hid in tall weeds at the side of the road as a score of soldiers rode by. James was right; this road was not safe to travel on. She remembered the captain mentioning a battle and the clans. What about Meghan, Jamie, and Duny? Then a terrible thought crossed her mind. What of Ewan, Thomas, and John? They likely fought in the battle. *No,* she thought, *I must think about what needs to be done now. Later, I'll worry about them.*

She could not stay on the road; there was nowhere to hide. She left the road and climbed over rock walls, one after another. Finally she reached the cottage and knocked on the door. The door opened, and a young man said, "Good day to ye."

"May I come in?" she asked. The man stepped aside and motioned for her to enter. "Sir, would ye know of James Dunsmuir, the horse trader?"

The man thought for a minute. "Aye, I do."

"He's my husband. Tell me, sir, do you befriend the English who travel by here?"

The young man gave her a questioning look. "Milady, I canna answer yer question. James Dunsmuir is a Scotsman, I believe?"

"Yes, he is. And if I may ask, is there a problem with knowing he is?"

"Nay! Your English accent gave me reason to be cautious in answering. I'm a Scotsman myself." The young man was thoughtful. "Ah, we're afraid to trust each other. Let me put yer mind at ease, Lady Dunsmuir. Yer safe here."

"Thank you. We were overtaken by English soldiers who shot my husband and took our horse. I want to take my husband home, and we need a horse—two if you have them." Abby stopped to catch her breath.

"Please sit down, I'll get ye a cup of water."

"Wait! Can you help me? I must know before I tarry any longer. If you cannot, I'll be on my way."

"Aye, I can. But I'm here for one reason only, an' that's to feed th' English soldiers an' their horses when they stop. Ye must nay be here if they are. They leave me be—at least, they ha' so far."

Abby gasped. "You are helping English soldiers? Why in the hell would you do such a thing when they're killing your kinsmen?" She stopped, "I must apologize for my words."

The man said, "Nay, it is I who should apologize, milady. I know wha' it appears to be, but tha' is not as it is. I'm listenin' to every word th' soldiers say while they're soppin' up whisky an' ale; then I pass th' information on to Lord Murray, who is doing everythin' he can for those who survived th' battle. Th' soldiers say th' prince is on th' run, an' all Hielanders are suspected of enablin' him to stay hidden."

"Then, sir," Abby said, "You are to be thanked. What is your name?"

"Brian Smith to all who ask, but my clan name is MacGregor."

"I'd think your Scottish brogue would be a giveaway. Surely they notice it?"

"Aye, they do, but I tell 'em it's 'cause I was raised by a Hieland granny."

"Brian, I wonder how long you'll get away with this. God watch over you, for it's a brave thing you're doing."

"Thank you, milady. If I'm able to get word to Lord George an' the life of even one is saved, it'll be worth it."

"You say you have a horse?" asked Abby.

"Aye, but for its use, I must ask a favor of ye. Wha' is your name, milady? I know your husband's name, but wha' is yours?"

"I'm Abigail, or Abby." She paused before she spoke again. "Brian, not all English people are murderers. Most are peace-loving folk who want nothing more than to live their lives without strife and trouble. I know how things are in the Highlands. Many are without a roof over their heads and food for their families. My daughter is married to a Highland laird, and she says there's rampant starvation, which will be even worse next winter because the seed grain set aside for spring planting was eaten last winter. I can understand why it seems the English are more fortunate than the families of Scotland."

"Aye," Brian said. "Th' English ha' th' blessing of their king while th' Scots dinna! It's th' high taxes th' Scots pay to England's damned King!"

Abby looked Brian in the eye. "While you are damning England and the King, please remember both France and Spain look upon these lands as an asset, and they covet them. Yet they do not attack solely because of their fear of England's ability to defend herself and Scotland. There is a price for this protection, and taxes are the price we must all pay."

Brian smiled. "Aye, it's true, but there's another side to th' story. Th' palace where King George lives is just one of many tha' belongs to him. He has th' means to purchase castles and palaces because he collects bloody high taxes from us!"

Abby knew young Brian did not fathom royalty. She chose her words carefully, hoping she could explain so he would understand. "Brian, he is entitled to everything he has. Royals are very wealthy, with ownership of a great deal of land, jewels of value beyond measure, castles, palaces, and all that he inherited when he became king. By taxing residents under his rule, he has funds to support the Royal Navy and British Army. It also is a means to measure the loyalty of his subjects. The king knows some of Scotland's people do not accept his authority, especially the clans, and he is making his presence known."

"Abby, th' people of Scotland are sufferin'! Everythin' bought an' sold in Scotland is taxed more than England, Wales, or Ireland!"

Abby frowned. "I see. I was not aware of that. "To be honest Brian, I'd fight too, if my family was without food or a roof over our heads. But for now, I need a horse and must ask you, what do you need in return?"

Brian motioned for Abby to sit down. "A'fore ye agree to it, ye need to know wha' I'm askin' of ye." He looked around the room. "Th'

English soldiers eat an' drink here. When they're too besotted to get on their horses, I offer 'em a bed while they sleep it off, an' a meal when they're on foot again. I listen while they brag' of how they've murdered women an' children, th' names of those who will be next, an' where they're going. Then I write it down for Lord Murray."

Brian brought out a leather bag. "These papers also ha' th' whereabouts of prisoners an' who is waitin' to be hung. I know about Charles Stuart's most trusted man an' how he had control of th' arms an' money meant for th' Stuart prince. Every gun an' box of ammunition for th' Jacobite army went to th' Redcoats. I dinna know where th' gold went; no one seems to know."

"Brian, our daughters' husbands likely fought in the battle, Ewan Cameron and John MacIntyre—do you know of them?"

"I know most of th' Camerons died on the battlefield, an' their brochs were burned. Th' English soldiers bragged about how they boarded th' doors an' windows, set th' house a'fire, an' then had target practice at any who tried to escape. It's said many o' th' MacIntyre clan were on horseback an' left th' battlefield. Unless ye know yer Cameron daughter an' family were elsewhere, it's likely they're dead. Abby, this is why ye must get this packet to Lord Murray. He's th' only one who is keepin' track of it all. I ha' a copy of a letter written by Lord George to Prince Charles Stuart, an' I want ye to read it. An army officer left it wi' me for Th' Duke of Cumberland to read."

Abby began reading. When she finished, she said, "Lord Murray understood what happened. He knew O'Sullivan sent the supplies elsewhere and named him as the culprit. Even though Lord Murray was respectful of Charles Stuart in his letter, he knew Charles was not a good leader."

Abby took the bundle, "Brian, I'll gladly deliver this packet. If you will be so kind as to provide a horse, I'll bring James here. We'll rest tonight, and then we'll be able to return home."

"Th' horse I ha' for ye will carry ye both. Abby, stay to th' pastures. Look to see if there's two lanterns hangin' from my gate;

if so, soldiers are here. It'll be best tha' ye take th' packet wi' ye now, should there be."

Brian handed the leather packet to Abby. She hugged him. "God be with you, Brian MacGregor."

"An' wi' ye, Abby Dunsmuir."

Abby pulled her cloak around her shoulders. The horrible day that had begun so pleasantly was nearly over. Was it possible they'd left home just this morning? Surely it'd been longer than that. The sun was nearly below the horizon as Abby guided the horse through fields, getting on and off the horse as she came to rock fences. When she caught sight of a horse and rider bearing the English flag, she reined in her horse and hid underneath an oak tree surrounded by briar bushes. A large troop of soldiers passed by; she knew there would be no rest for her and James at Brian's cottage tonight.

Chapter 35

Ewan opened his eyes and looked at himself; he was nearly naked from the waist down, with nothing from the waist up. A knapsack beside him held a pair of black breeches, a red coat, a shirt, boots, a tin of biscuits and a flask of wine. He ran his tongue around his mouth, *front tooth is loose. Most of th' hide on my left shoulder an' elbow is gone, an' my left leg dinna ha' any feelin'. I'd say it's broken, so it's as well I canna feel it. Mayhap I was tied to a rope, as there's burn marks on my wrists. I dinna know wha' happened.*

Ewan looked at his feet. *I've toenails missin' on my left foot.* He used a stick to lift himself to his knees. By leaning to the left he could place his right foot flat on the ground. Using the stick, he was able to use his right hand to straighten his left leg and place his left foot flat on the ground. He was standing!

Ewan looked at his surroundings. Pieces of bark and fir needles marked where he had been pulled through the forest. He followed the trail. *Wha' is my name?* he thought. *My name is ... my name is ... Willie Ball! It dinna sound right.*

His tongue felt thick. He remembered seeing a flask lying

on the ground. He slowly turned around, making his way back to where the flask lay. He filled his mouth with wine and swallowed. Finally he was able to move his tongue. "My namph ish Williee Balsh. My namph ish Willie Bash."

He repeated the name until he could say it fairly clearly. *But, he thought, it's not my name.*

Still holding on to the stick, he picked up the knapsack and hung the flask by its strap from his right wrist. *I'll find water an' think wha' to do.* Progress was slow; he had to put the boots on before he could travel very far. The path led to a snow-melt burn. He dipped water with the flask and splashed it on his face, and body. He felt the water's coolness on his right foot and leg, but his left leg and foot were numb. He forced the boot on his right foot; his left foot was swollen, and the boot was much too tight. He managed to get part of his left foot in the boot, but his heel rested on crumpled leather at the back. He left the shirt unbuttoned, fastened the top button on the pants, and slipped his right arm through the sleeve of the red coat. *If I stay on th' path an' walk toward th' light, I could reach the edge of these woods.*

After slowly walking a short distance with his left leg and foot dragging behind him, he stopped and smiled, pleased that he was able to think of two good things about his situation. *I dinna know where I'm goin', an' it won't matter which direction I take!*

Ewan slowly made his way down the path. Then he heard a shout. "Hold up, soldier. Halt!" He stopped and started to turn when his left leg folded beneath him and he sprawled flat on his face.

Chapter 36

Janet struggled to stay awake. She had to find a place where they could stop to rest and Prince would not be seen. She thought of Elizabeth and the bairns. She could almost see the broch burning from the roof down to the inside. Stone walls would stand without the timbered roof or inside wooden walls. Did Elizabeth and the lads feel the heat of the fire as it consumed them, or did they die trying to breathe in air that was nothing but heavy, dark smoke? It was unbearable to think about the suffering they endured. She was angry with men who killed innocent women and bairns.

When she stopped to wipe away tears, she realized she was looking at a second pathway that seemed to go around a corner and out of sight. Perhaps it would lead to a sheltered place where they could stop. Janet tethered Prince and walked down the path. It was just as she had hoped; after a short distance it turned and wound down and around the hillside. Prince would not be seen from the main path.

As she led Prince down the path, Daniel stirred. "Auntie, is there a drink, please?"

Janet lifted him off the horse and hugged his thin body, "Aye, little one. We'll stop an' rest. Are ye still tired, Daniel?"

"Oh aye, Auntie. I'm tired of sleepin' sittin' up. I want to sleep wi'out hearin' 'clop, clop, clop.' I want my bed to be still an' nay move when I get it back."

Janet had to smile. "I know, laddie. Being rocked for a little while is nice, but not all th' time."

She tethered Prince in a grassy spot and made sure he was out of sight. "Daniel, let's make another marker so we'll remember tha' we traveled this way. Ye gather stones, an' while yer doin' tha', I'll find somethin' to eat."

Janet found two oatcakes and a wedge of dry cheese, but nothing else. "Daniel, here's an oatcake an' cheese, an' if ye want, there's half of another oatcake."

"Auntie, ye ha' th' other oatcake. I'll ha' my oatcake an' a bite of cheese."

As she ate the remaining oatcake, she realized she was hungry, very hungry. Janet divided the cheese into two pieces. While they ate it, they agreed it was the best cheese they had ever eaten. Janet gave the last of the grain to Prince and led him to drink from a trickle of water flowing down the hillside. After filling her flask and looking once more to be sure they were alone, she spread the blanket, folded another blanket for a pillow, pulled her cloak around her and laid down. "Daniel, keep a watch if yer nay goin' to sleep. Wake me if there's a sound."

She was asleep before Daniel answered, "Aye, Auntie, dinna be afraid. I ha' rocks in my pocket."

Twilight faded, and Daniel watched as one star after another appeared. Suddenly he looked toward Prince, whose ears pricked up. Daniel heard a faint sound coming from the path; he waited, hardly breathing. He wrapped his fingers around a rock in his pocket. Something was moving toward them. First he saw a shadow and then a shape. Tiptoeing, Daniel approached the shape. A head loomed above him. Then he saw the outline of a stag's horns. The animal looked at him, curious and watchful. Daniel took a step forward. The stag did not move. He held out his hand; the stag stood still. Daniel took another step, and the animal looked down into his eyes. Both froze for a moment. Then the great animal slowly turned and majestically walked away.

Daniel watched until the stag was out of sight. "Auntie, Auntie, guess what I saw?"

She sat up. "Wha' did ye see?"

"A stag, Auntie. I looked at him, an' he looked at me, an' then he left."

"Daniel, it's very unusual for a wild animal to come so close to people, but mayhap he knew yer meant him no harm. It's a warnin', though. If a stag can come down th' path wi'out wakin' me, then so could a soldier!"

"Auntie, is there any to eat?" Daniel rubbed his belly.

She shook her head. "Nay, but there'll be somethin'." She had to find food—and soon. There had been very little for Daniel to eat for the past four days. He would sleep more and more as his body began to lose strength.

"Heavenly Father, ye know our needs. In Jesus's name, Amen." She said her prayer quietly while she folded the blanket. "Daniel, I'll put ye on Prince, an' ye can keep a watch out. If ye see somethin', give a tug on th' reins. I'll ha' 'em in my hand."

The narrow path wound around sharp curves, always moving upward. Daniel was asleep. Janet wrapped the blanket around his thin shoulders. "Daniel, we'll find food for ye, I promise," she whispered. At the thought of food, her belly rumbled.

Chapter 37

Abby led the horse to the place where she thought James was waiting, but she could see nothing familiar. Had she turned the wrong way when she left the cottage? Where did the carriage leave the road? She stumbled, turned her ankle, and fell. Painfully, she stood, *Abby Dunsmuir! There's nothing to be gained with tears. Later, I'll cry, but not now!* Then, she realized she was standing across the road from the place where the carriage left the road. She tethered the horse, climbed over the wall and woke her husband. "James, are you all right?"

"Aye. I see ye found a horse."

"I did." She was relieved to see no fresh blood on his clothing.

One of the boxes had bread, cheese, and whisky. As they ate she asked, "Are you in pain, James?"

"Aye, but not so much tha' I canna stand it."

"Sip the whisky; it'll dull the pain. James, I met a young man named Brian MacGregor. He has a cottage not far from here and serves English soldiers food and drink as they're traveling to the Highlands. While they're eating and drinking, Brian listens and writes it down for Lord Murray!" She pulled out the packet. "See this? It's to be delivered to Murray in Edinburgh as soon as we possibly can, in return for the horse."

James tried to stand. "Damn it to hell, Abby. If we're caught by th' English soldiers an' they find these papers on us, we'll be shot on the spot! Why dinna ye just gi' th' man coins for th' horse?"

"Listen, you big oaf, you'd have done the same had you heard Brian's story. If delivering these papers to Edinburgh will make a difference, then I'm glad to do so! I'll deliver them myself, and you can stay home. Besides, if English soldiers stop us, no matter if we have papers with us or not, they'll shoot! You discovered that the hard way.

James shook his head. "Abby, ye'll not be goin' anywhere wi'out me by yer side." Between bites of food James said, "Fetch th' horse, an' we'll start for home."

Abby helped James climb in the saddle. "Abby, ye say th' battle is over?"

"Yes, Brian said several of the clan chiefs and Charles Stuart survived, but only a few of th' Highlanders lived. The Duke of Cumberland, son of King George, has given orders to destroy them all, including their homes and animals!"

Abby led the horse across rock fences and pastures. At first, James tried to stay in the saddle as the horse jumped over fences, but after nearly falling off, he decided to crawl over each fence and then climb back on the horse to ride on to the next fence. "When we reach those trees we'll be able to ride together. We'll travel this night, and hope we're close to home by morning. If soldiers have been there, I hope Jamie, Meghan, and Duny let them take whatever they wanted, be it horses or whatever. All we can do for Janet, Ewan, and John is pray for their safety."

Chapter 38

J anet and Daniel stopped to rest in a sheltered spot on the trail. They slept sitting beneath a tree. Janet dreamed; she was at the top of a high glen looking down at a valley far below. She saw empty land, dark with smoke. There were no homes, bagpipes, tartans or people. She woke with a start and touched her face; it was wet with tears. Her empty stomach hurt, she would have thrown up if there had been something to throw up. *When was the last time I had my monthly?* She could not remember. In that quiet moment, she realized she was with child. Her heart was joyful, but her mind was in turmoil. They had no home, Ewan was the king's prisoner, and Duny might be safe or not. There was no food for Daniel or her. Then she thought of her mother and father.

They are not safe, she thought, not knowing how she knew it was so. *Heavenly Father, protect those who need yer lovin' touch. Help me find food for th' laddie. He's starvin' an' must be fed if he's to survive. In Jesus's name, I pray.*

Her eyes searched the valley below them. She caught the barest glimpse of a light, perhaps a crofter's fire or starlight reflecting from a burn. Mayhap she only imagined it. "Daniel, wake up! We must be goin'."

"Auntie, is there any oatcake left? I'd ha' only a bite."

"Nay, there's none, but we've water."

Daniel took the flask and drank. "Aye, Auntie, thank ye."

"Daniel, look where my finger is pointin'. Do ye see a light?"

"Aye, I do!"

"Let's see wha' it is." They followed the path as it turned downward toward a meadow. Janet caught a brief glimpse of the light before it disappeared again. Then she realized wind blowing through the low-growing grouse and heather caused the light to come and go. She stopped to catch her breath. *Could it be soldiers settling down for th' night, or a thief waitin' to snare a passin' traveler? I think not,* she thought. *It'll be a crofter on th' moors watchin' over his sheep.*

She handed Daniel the reins and held up her hand for him to wait while she moved closer. A man sat with his back to her. Beside him was a black and white dog. She crept closer and was startled when the man stood and turned toward her. "Halt, who goes there? Show yerself!"

The dog growled as Janet walked closer. She looked at a man dressed in the rough clothing of a crofter. She stumbled and would have fallen had he not reached out to grab her arm. "Steady, lass. Be ye well?"

"Aye, I am, but let me fetch th' laddie."

She walked to the edge of the field where Daniel and Prince were waiting. The crofter watched the woman, child, and horse approach. "Misses, will there be more of yer kin comin' along? If not, I'll share some of my food stash wi' ye, but if there be more, we may be a bit short."

Janet shook her head. "There's none but us. Sir, it's been several days since th' laddie's eaten, an' he's very hungry. Please, if ye will, share wi' him."

"Here, laddie, sit yerself down." The crofter handed him a piece of bread with fish and cheese.

Even though he was so hungry his stomach hurt, Daniel remembered his manners. "Thank ye, sir."

"Here's a cup of water for ye, laddie. Eat and drink slowly. Miss, there's food for ye as well."

"Thank ye, kind sir."

"Eat, an' then we'll talk." The man looked at both of them and shook his head. "I'm wonderin' who ye are an' why yer here on th' moors. It's a long way from any broch tha' I know of."

She was unsure what to tell this man. Between mouthfuls of food, she said, "Sir, wha' be ye doin' here yerself?"

The man refilled Daniel's cup, sat down beside him, pared an apple into slices, and held them to him. "I'm takin' yonder sheep to summer pastures in th' high glens. Wha' about ye, lass?"

Janet took a deep breath. "Do ye know wha' has happened in th' past several days?"

"I do," he said. "I know there was a battle, an' th' English won. I built a fire this evenin' to bake th' trout I caught, but if ye were drawn to th' light, then others might be as well." He began covering the coals with ashes.

She hesitated, but her concern for Daniel overcame any shame she felt. "Please, sir, if there's enough, could th' lad ha' an oatcake?"

"Aye, he can. Here's more cheese and oatcakes, an' some for ye too, mistress."

"Thank ye, sir."

The crofter sat back, waiting for them to finish eating. Prince, standing quietly, caught his attention. "What a fine animal! Would ye like some grain, my lad?"

Reaching in his coat pocket, he brought out a handful of barley and oats. Prince ate from his hand. He reached in his other pocket and brought out more. "I always ha' grain in my pockets to bring in th' stragglers when they get separated from th' flock," he said as he stroked Prince's head. "Yer a handsome fellow, ye are. I ha' more to gi' ye." He emptied a small bag of grain on the ground.

"Thank ye, sir. If I may ask, yer name?"

"Ian Douglas, th' laird of Greystone Broch."

Janet shook her head. "I dinna know th' name." Janet looked at him and his clothing. "Yer a laird, not a crofter?"

Ian smiled, removed his cap, and shook his head of black hair. "Ye, milady, are no washer woman yerself. Ye speak th' dialect of a Hieland lady. So, where is th' father of this young laddie, yer husband, assumin' tha' ye ha' one?"

"Aye, I do, an' tha' is th' problem." Janet hoped this man could be trusted. "My husband, Ewan Cameron, his brother Thomas, an' cousins were at Culloden's field where th' battle took place a fortnight ago."

"My God, then yer a widow!" the man exclaimed. "None survived!"

Janet did not refute him. "Milord, did ye not join in th' battle?"

Ian sighed. "It's a long story. Do ye ha' time to listen?"

Janet looked down at Daniel asleep by the fire. For the first time in days he had a full belly. Janet covered him with her cloak. "Poor laddie, he's glad to sleep on th' ground. He's used to sleepin' while ridin', ye see. Now, sir, ye ha' my attention!"

Ian brought out a flask of whisky, poured his cup full, and offered to fill Janet's cup. She held it out to him. "Ye know of th' MacLeods, of Skye an' th' outer Isles?"

"I know of 'em, but I've not met any. They dinna attend clan gatherin's, an' tha' is th' only way I'd know 'em."

"Yer right, they'd not be there. They tend to separate themselves from other clans. When it comes to bickerin', th' MacLeods dinna take part in it. They may knock heids wi' th' MacDonalds, but even tha' is short-lived. Wha' is yer name, milady?"

"Janet."

"Yer Janet Cameron?"

She nodded her head. "Aye. Might ye know of James Dunsmuir? He breeds an' sells horses. He's my father."

Ian thought for a minute. "I've heard of him. My father bought several mares from Master Dunsmuir a long time ago."

Janet was pleased he knew of her family. "Father sold horses to people from th' Western Isles."

"Father was not from th' Isles. He lived not far from here. It was my mother who was a MacLeod. She met Father when he traveled to th' island to buy sheep for his fold. He bred an' raised Leicester sheep while Mother's family raised th' Scottish Blackface or Hieland sheep, as they're commonly called. Th' Hieland sheep raise a good lamb crop, even when there's little forage, while th' Leicester animals have a long, full wool clip. Father thought th' two breeds mixed would produce a fine animal wi' th' best of both."

In spite of her backache and troubles, Janet found herself interested in the story. "An' did it go well?"

Ian pointed to a flock of animals. "They've black noses, an' their fleece is full an' fine! They're sturdy an' easy keepers. I'm sad to say Father died shortly after the first lambs were born."

"I'm sorry about yer father, Ian."

"Aye, lass, me too. He was alive an' well one day an' gone th' next evenin'. It was black fever that swept through th' village. Mother returned to Skye, takin' me an' my younger sister wi' her. I lived on th' isle 'til I decided to return to th' lands I inherited when Father died. Father's brother an' his wife were caretakers for th' broch an' animals, an' they still live close by."

Ian Douglas looked at Janet. "Ye asked why I dinna go wi' th' others to battle? My mam raised me to think for myself, not pledge fealty to someone who'd make decisions for me. She said Scotland is but a small part of a big world. Perhaps someday I'd travel to other places, an' I'd want freedom to do so. Ye see, Janet, Skye is under th' rule of an English king, but there's naught to draw kings to th' island. They travel elsewhere in their domain an' give little notice to th' residents of Skye. Some years a tacksman comes to collect rent an' taxes an' some years not."

"Did yer father agree wi' yer mother's thinkin'?" Janet asked.

"He did. Before he met her, he dinna feel obligated to take part in th' Douglas clan gatherings. He cared for his sheep, an' th' Douglas clan chieftain abided by it as Father owned his lands and payed his share of taxes when they were due. Th' land I inherited from him is at th' far northern edge of Clan Douglas lands, so there's few invites to mingle wi' th' rest of 'em. Besides, not havin' daughters wi' dowries or sons to go courtin', there's no neighbors comin' by. To answer yer unspoken question, I'm naught married." He chuckled. "Nor ha' I ever been married. An' th' next question, aye, I'm a man who visits th' ladies, but I've not yet met one I'd want ter bring' home wi' me. Lass, ye look as if yer could sleep sittin' up. Ye be tired?"

"Aye, even though yer tale is interestin', sir, I'm fightin' sleep. Would it trouble ye if I rested for a bit?"

"Nay, milady. Lie down by th' lad an' sleep. I'll sit here an' rest a bit myself. On th' morrow, if ye wish, yer can travel wi' me over those hills in th' distance, if it's where ye'll be goin'. I dinna know why yer travelin', but I'm at yer service."

"Thank ye." Janet lay down by Daniel and slept.

Ian Douglas reached in his pockets for his pipe and tobacco. He filled the bowl and lit it with a straw held over the last of the fire's coals. He thought about the lass and lad alone on the Glens. *It's nay safe, but she's survived so far.* He considered the things she spoke about. *It's likely her husband is dead. I wonder where she's going.*

Ian thought of the battle at Culloden. Many Douglas clan members fought in the uprising. He'd given consideration to his options if safety became a problem on the mainland. He could return to his mother's clan on Skye. Those living on the mainland were closely watched by the king's men, and Ian cherished the right to make his own decisions. He was not a coward, if it came to it, he would fight to protect his lands and home. He shook his head, *I'll be damned if I can see th' use of senseless dying' for th' sake of one king on th' throne over another! Once yer dead, that's th' end of it. Me, I'd rather live an' see what life has to offer day after th' morrow.* He looked at Janet and Daniel, sleeping soundly. They could stay at his broch, where they would be safe, at least for a while. *I could take th' sheep on to high pastures an' return to ask if they'd want to come wi' me.* He finished the last of the whisky, pulled his cap down over his eyes, and slept.

Chapter 39

"Captain! There's a soldier on the ground! He appears to be injured!" The soldier dismounted and spoke to Ewan. "On your feet, soldier."

Ewan struggled to lift his head. The soldier helped Ewan sit up. "My God, man, what happened? Where's the rest of your troop?"

Ewan shook his head but said nothing. The captain searched for identification papers in Ewan's knapsack. "Soldier," the captain asked, "what is your name and regiment?"

Ewan said "Willie Balsh."

The soldiers looked at one another. The captain spoke. "He's injured. Help him to his feet, and let's have a look."

They lifted him until he was standing and held him steady. "Soldier, what happened to you?" Ewan shook his head and kept his eyes focused on the ground, which at the moment was moving beneath his feet.

Captain Horatio Strong looked at Ewan as he tried to make sense of his condition and missing paperwork. "Somehow this man became separated from his troop. I suspect he was captured by the bloody Highlanders, beaten, and left to die. We'll get some food and drink in him and take him to the infirmary at Fort William. They'll get it sorted out."

The soldiers brought Ewan bread, meat, and ale. He had difficulty chewing but managed to get some of the food down. Ale helped his aching head. He was not an English soldier, but he knew he needed to be. Another soldier helped him mount a horse and rode beside him, straightening him in the saddle when necessary. In spite of being numb, the pain in his left foot was excruciating.

Ewan motioned to the soldier beside him to stop. "Captain, he wants to stop, perhaps to take a piss. I'll stay with him, and we'll catch up."

The soldier helped Ewan dismount. When he pointed to his left foot, the soldier worked the boot loose and looked at the swollen foot with three black toes. "I'll see if there's something to wrap your foot in." He returned with a white stocking and helped Ewan pull it over his foot and mount his horse.

"Than's," Ewan said.

The soldier looked at Ewan and asked, "Your name is Willie?" Ewan nodded.

Chapter 40

Abby could go no farther. James, astride the horse, was asleep with his head resting on the horse's neck. She knew she should wake him to look for bleeding, but it was better that he sleep than be awake and in pain. She eased the empty whisky bottle from his hand and arranged his tartan around his shoulders and neck. She felt his forehead and was relieved that it was not hot. Had she not been so tired, she would have noticed the clammy coolness of his skin.

Her thoughts turned to her own pains. *My ankle is swollen, and my slippers are impossible to walk in. I feel every stone I trod upon.* She sat on the ground, wrapped the horse's reins around her wrist, closed her eyes, and slept.

Sometime later, James opened his eyes. His heart labored, and he could hardly breathe. As darkness gathered around him, he fought to stay awake. *Nay! I must not go without Abby knowin'. Abby, Abby, where are ye, lass?* When he lost consciousness, he slipped off the horse and lay where he fell on the ground.

Death answered the call; another soul was ready to depart. Looking upward, James saw a dazzling light and heard the sound of beating wings. Death assisted as the soul of James Dunsmuir lifted from his injured body and was welcomed by Elight, who clasped his hands as they moved upward toward the light. Death never grew tired of watching the healing of bodies and spirits. "He will be made whole, but his beloved wife is left behind. She will miss him. Such is the way of humans; they make great attachments to each other and suffer when one must stay behind while the other goes on."

The Dark One traveled; there was much to do. His Master required more disciples, and there were many who were willing. He would visit services in great cathedrals and churches with tall steeples topped by crosses. Converts could pray reverently and often were extremely pious; none of this was any impediment to joining him. He would promise them great wealth, ownership of lands, and seductive physical relationships that could not be denied. Within a heartbeat, they were blinded to all but these things. *Wonderful trick,* he thought as he spread his arms. He too had wings, but unlike angels, his wings grew from his upper arms rather than his back. Under each arm the wings were attached to his body. When he was not in flight, his wings folded around him, and he rested by tucking his head under his wing. He knew he stank of darkness, dampness, and mold, all odors of the place from which he came. Master lived with great heat that radiated from his body. The Dark One preferred the coolness and dark of underground caverns; it was like a grave.

Abby opened her eyes when she felt the horse pull at the reins. James lay beside her. "James, James!"

She gathered him to her. She knew he was not breathing. The ground beneath him was soaked with blood. Abby lay down beside him and wept until she finally slept. She did not waken until a faint ray of sunshine touched her face. She sat up and said, "James, I must leave you to return home, but I will return for you as quickly as I can."

She kissed him and covered him with his tartan. Wrapping her cloak around her shoulders, Abby mounted the horse and noted that James lay in a protected spot in a copse of trees. Just past the trees, a wooden bridge crossed a burn. *I will remember this place*, she thought. *I leave my heart here*. She guided the horse to a path away from the road. At the top of a hill, she saw a church spire in a distant valley. As she rode in that direction she thought of James dying at the hands of her own countrymen. Her thoughts turned to Janet, Meghan, and Jamie. Abby closed her eyes. "Father in heaven, help me, for I cannot bear this loss alone. The one I left behind is now with you. I love him more than life itself and will always love him. I look forward to the day when we will be together again. In Jesus's name I pray, amen."

Abby became aware of a presence surrounding her, felt a light kiss on her forehead, and heard a whispered, "Abby, my darlin' wife, I'll love ye forever. Farewell, my dearest." She knew James's voice; the kiss was his. It was a parting gift from him. Now, she knew she could find her way home. If she could reach the church before dark, it might be a safe place to hide through the night.

The Dark One sat resting his head under his wing when he heard the spoken prayer. His eyes opened, and he raised his head to look around as he searched for the source. Finding her, he saw she was crying. "Why do they suffer so when one of them dies? They are so imperfectly made! They depend on one another to live their sad little lives. I'll ask Death his opinion, although lately, I think he has drifted over the line. Of course, I don't bring out the lights and strike up the band when a soul comes my way. But all the same, I am pleased. I can give humans much more in their earthly lives than the other one. I offer money, as much pleasure as one can manage, and everything anyone could ever want. Why, then, do some of them seek another way? My Master says God made a mistake when he fashioned them. I believe he is right."

Chapter 41

Just after midnight, Janet stirred and called out, "Da, dinna leave. Please, dinna go."

Ian covered her and sat back, watchful. *She must ha' been dreamin',* he thought. *Her eyes were closed all the time.* He slept for a short time, and when he woke he found Daniel standing beside him.

"Sit here beside me, Daniel. I'm Ian, do ye remember, lad?"

"Aye, I do, sir. I need to pee, sir. Excuse me." Daniel went behind the tree. He returned and sat down beside Ian.

"Did ye ha' yer fill last night, laddie, or are ye still hungry?"

"I'm only a wee bit hungry, sir. A bite of oatcake, if ye ha' one." Ian found one in his knapsack and handed it to Daniel.

"Thank ye, sir. Do I ha' just a bite?"

"Oh, no, laddie, ye may ha' it all." Ian smiled at Daniel. "Are ye always so polite, Daniel?"

"Aye, my mam taught me. She said there're two things next to bein' like God, th' first bein' clean an' th' second havin' manners."

"Yer mother is right, lad. How long ha' ye an' yer mam been travelin'?"

"Oh, sir." Daniel pointed at Janet. "She's not my mam. She's my auntie Janet. I dinna know wha' happened to my mam an' my brothers. I'm but a bairn, yer see, an' grownups dinna tell bairns things they're not to know. Do ye know how I know it?"

Ian shook his head. "Nay, lad, tell me how ye know."

Daniel settled himself on the ground. In between bites of oatcake he said, "Ha' ye seen how grownups are wi' bairns there?"

"Aye, I ha'," said Ian, wondering if Daniel thought of him as a grownup.

"If they're whisperin', ye'll be put to bed an' dinna know wha' for!"

Ian stifled a smile and said, "Ah, laddie, I know. I'm a grownup, but I remember how it is to be a bairn. Yer auntie may not know wha' happened to yer mam an' brothers. It's likely she'd tell ye if she could."

Daniel looked at the ground. "I've somethin' to tell ye, but ye canna tell!" Daniel peered into Ian's eyes.

"Aye, laddie, I won't."

"I saw a big stag. He came close, looked at me, bowed his head, an' then turned an' walked away. His eyes were nice. I wanted to touch him, but he left."

"That's a wonder, laddie. Those animals are usually very afraid of people. They know they'll be shot if they stand still for very long."

"That's wha' Auntie said. I ha' another secret to tell ye, an' ye hav'ta cross yer fingers on both hands an' let me see 'em."

Ian struggled to keep a smile from his lips. It'd been a very long time since he'd been told to cross his fingers, in fact so long ago that he would have been a small boy, about Daniel's age. "Here they are, laddie." Ian held out both hands with the second finger tucked under the middle finger.

Daniel solemnly looked at Ian's hands. "Very good, sir. Auntie an' me saw my uncle Ewan. He was tied to a horse tha' had a redcoated soldier ridin' it." Daniel searched for words. "Uncle Ewan was barefooted an' tied wi' a rope to a horse tha' was goin' too fast for him to keep up, so he was runnin, barefooted an' all, sir."

Daniel paused to catch his breath. "Auntie said we'll find him, an' I can help. Auntie an' I make markers when we stop so we'll know where we are."

Ah, Ian thought, *Th' lass is trackin' her husband. He's been taken prisoner.* "Tell me lad, was there one English soldier or more?"

"Oh, sir, more."

Ian thought, *Wi' th' bairn, she canna travel as fast. She's a long ways off th' path tha' most would travel to Fort William or Inverness, but tha' would be th' best. She dinna ha' time to gather provisions, or mayhap she's been travelin' long enough tha' she ran out.*

Ian mused to himself. Daniel interrupted his thoughts. "Sir, Auntie an' me were hungry when we saw yer light. Thank you for th' food, sir."

Daniel's dirt-streaked face looked up at him. *Ah, he's a braw laddie,* Ian thought. He hugged the little boy. "Yer welcome! Some day ye may need to share yer food wi' me, ye know! Yer did very well tellin' wha' happened. Mayhap one day ye'll be a bard an' a keeper of stories to tell around th' fire at night."

"Nay, sir! I want to play th' bagpipes. Th' sound bagpipes make is like a story. They can be happy, sad, or make me want to march. That's wha' I want to do, be a bagpiper!"

"Then speak wi' yer auntie about it, laddie."

The two sat side by side, company for one another. Ian wondered about Janet's cries in her sleep. Perhaps he could help her in some way. Her husband's capture was a serious thing. Did she have any idea where she was going?

Ian considered whether to leave Janet asleep or to wake her; she had the look of one who was very weary, with dark circles under her eyes. He wanted to talk with her more, but he was unsure as to what he could to do help. She was a very pretty lass, and even with her uncombed hair and plain clothing, he could see she was not a scullery maid or a common goodwife. *Somewhere's a Hielander who'll be missin' his beautiful wife. If he dinna find her, or her find him, I'd be glad to take his place,* Ian thought. "Laddie, ha' ye had enough to eat?"

"Aye, sir, I ha'."

"Here's more cheese an' oatcakes to share wi' yer auntie when she wakes. I must take th' sheep on to th' pastures. Now, dinna follow me or walk out on th' path. Wolves an' bears are here, an' ye'd be a tasty bite for 'em."

"Wolves an' bears, sir?"

"Aye. Stay close by yer auntie an' ye'll be safe."

"Aye, sir. I ha' stones in my pocket, an' I'd throw 'em at a wolf or bear. That'd scare 'em away! Auntie'll be safe. I'll watch out for her."

"Good lad." He put his hand on Daniel's shoulder and patted the small boy. "One day, ye'll be a fine bagpiper. I'll pay a pence to hear ye play a tune."

Daniel looked up and smiled. Ian walked a few steps up the path and disappeared into the mist. Daniel heard him call to his dog.

Daniel sat quietly, waiting. Janet stirred and sat up. "Daniel, yer alright?"

"Aye, Auntie. Ian went up th' path to take th' sheep to th' pasture. He said there's wolves an' bears. If I dinna stay still, they'll take a bite of me."

"Daniel, tha' was good advice he gave ye. We must be movin' on, laddie. Come, help me gather our things, an' we'll be on our way."

"He left oatcakes an' cheese, Auntie." Daniel held out a packet of food.

"Tha' was kind of him. We'll fill our flasks wi' water from yonder burn while Prince has a good, long drink."

"I like Ian, Auntie. I told him about th' stag an' Uncle Ewan."

Janet caught her breath. "Daniel, Ian is a Hielander, like yer Uncle Ewan—an' for tha' matter, ye an' I are both Hielanders too. But, laddie, be careful who ye tell who ye are or about yer Uncle Ewan bein' taken prisoner. Not all ye meet can be trusted. Th' less ye say, th' better."

Janet folded the blanket behind the saddle, led Prince to water, and held out one of the oatcakes in her hand, offering it to the horse after he drank. Prince ate all of the cake and nudged Janet's shoulder for more. "Nay, good fellow, we must keep what we ha', for we dinna know how long it'll be a'fore there's more."

"Daniel, this is a good time for ye to pee, for we'll not be stoppin' for a while."

Daniel nodded and left her side. The misty fog of the Glen would be good for traveling. Janet remembered Ewan's warning to keep her head covered, so she shook the twigs from her cloak and pulled the hood over her hair. She paused for a minute to say a quick prayer of thankfulness for the kindness of the laird who had fed and cared for them. *Mayhap one day I'll be able to return th' favor,* she thought, *but it's not likely our paths will cross again.* She helped Daniel to the saddle and began walking.

Chapter 42

Abby guided the horse to a fence-enclosed kirkyard beside a small chapel and a stone cottage. She tethered the horse and entered the chapel. A stained-glass window shed sparkles of blue, red, and green onto the walls and floor of the room. Abby stared at the stained-glass portrait of Mary, the mother of Jesus, standing beside the empty tomb with an angel lovingly watching over her. Abby felt the presence of God in this place and knelt at the altar. "Holy Father, how Jesus's mother must have suffered watching her beloved son die on the cross. Father, you know I am suffering with losing my beloved husband. It is only with your help that I can bear this burden. In Jesus's name I pray, amen."

Abby was not aware of another person in the chapel until she heard a voice. "My dear, may I help ye?"

Painfully, Abby stood and looked into the face of a nun who held her arms out to her. The woman was dressed in a black habit with a wooden cross hanging from a leather strap around her waist. Abby welcomed the embrace. "Yes, I'm in need of help."

"Come wi' me, an' we'll talk. But first, a cup o' tea might refresh ye."

"Thank you, sister."

The nun led Abby across the kirkyard to a cottage and inside to the kitchen. "I'm Sister Marie, an' ye are?"

"Abigail Dunsmuir. Please call me Abby."

"Do ye want a bit of honey an' cream in yer tea?"

"Yes, please." It seemed strange to be carrying on a polite conversation when James was lying cold on the ground. Abby shook her head when tears started.

The sister moved her chair beside Abby's chair and took her hand. "Now, my dear, wha' has happened?"

"Sister, my husband, James, died last night. We were returning to our home near Perthshire."

"Ye say he died. Was he ill?"

"No, James and I were stopped by a troop of English soldiers. They said Scotland's Highlanders lost the battle with King George's army. When James tried to explain we live in Scotland but are not Highlanders, one of the soldiers shot him in the chest. Abby reached in her pocket and found her emerald ring. How long ago was it that she placed that ring in her pocket and gave her gold wedding band to the soldier instead? She slipped the ring on her finger and said, "They took our horse and left us beside the road. I had to get James home and was fortunate to find another horse. We started home, but could not travel on the road as it was too risky with one regiment after another traveling the same way. We stayed in pastures and fields. I led the horse while James rode. Each time we came to a rock wall, he dismounted and crawled over. He did not say so, but the wound must have hurt terribly. Sister, the lead ball passed all the way through his chest and out his back."

Abby continued her story, nearly overwhelmed with sadness as she spoke. "Sometime during the night, I could go no further and slept sitting on the ground under a tree. While I was asleep,

James fell off the horse. When I woke, I found him lying on the ground beside me."

Abby sobbed. She stood and walked around the room. "I could not have done anything if I had been awake. The wound inside his body bled and I did not know! How he must have suffered! He said not a word."

"Ye've had a terrible thing happen. Abby, come sit down an' drink yer tea. Father Mathew will not be here 'til th' morrow, an' Sister Martha is visitin' her family." As she spoke, Sister Marie thought of how she could help Abby.

"Abby, after you've rested, we'll talk." Abby nodded, and Sister Marie handed her a cloth dipped in warmed water. "Wash yer face an' hands. We need to get these clothes off, clean ye up, an' then it's to bed. It's rest ye need now. There's some clothin' here tha' people give to th' chapel for those in need, an' there's no one in any greater need than ye."

As Sister Marie removed Abby's cloak, she saw dried blood stains that completely covered Abby's gown. Her hair had dried blood in the long strands, and even her chemise was blood-soaked.

Sister Marie looked at her in alarm. "My dear, are ye hurt? Yer covered in blood from th' top of yer head to th' bottom of yer gown."

Abby looked down and saw the dark stains. "No, I'm not hurt. This is blood from my husband where I lay beside and held him through the night."

"We'll get yer cleaned up, then ye'll feel better."

Sister Marie hurried to get a kettle on the kitchen fire. She helped Abby undress and wrapped a blanket around her. Picking up the gown and undergarments, she considered what to do with them. They could never be washed enough to remove the stains. Sister Marie put them in the parlor fireplace. When she returned to the kitchen, Abby was nearly asleep sitting at the table. Sister Marie placed a bucket in front of her, poured warm water over her head, and soaped, washed, and rinsed her hair.

273

"Come wi' me." Sister Marie pointed to a chair beside the parlor fire. She brushed Abby's hair until it was dry and then led her to a bed chamber where there was a bowl of warmed water and soap. Abby washed and dried with pieces of flannel. Sister Marie pointed to the bed with a comforter, and plump goose-down pillow. "Here's a gown tha' is too big for ye, but it's soft an' comfy. Dinna worry. Yer safe here."

Abby snuggled down in the warm bed, and Sister Marie covered the window so the room was dark. She closed the door and gave thought to Abby's situation as well as her own. *We won't be safe for long. This chapel is close to th' path th' soldiers will use.* Abby slept while day lengthened into night.

Sister Marie sorted through a box of discarded clothing and found a gown of dark green wool and a mended linen petticoat and chemise that would fit Abby. She tried to clean Abby's slippers, but they came apart and could not be repaired. She dampened the clothing, smoothed out the wrinkles, and hung everything by the fire to dry. *When she wakes, there's somethin' for her to wear.*

Then Sister Marie remembered the horse tied outside. *Poor thing, it's been waitin' wi'out food or water!* She hurried to place the horse in the stable, filled the water trough, gathered grain and hay, and put them in the manger. "There, there, I'm sorry I forgot ye," Sister Marie whispered to the horse.

Chapter 43

"Auntie, where we goin'?"

Janet looked up from the trail that was bare rocks in places where dirt had washed away.

"We're goin' to Stronabaw Glen. Last time I was there it was wi' yer Uncle Ewan an' Uncle Thomas, an' snow was on th' ground. It'll look different now. I'm hopin' Auntie Mary's cottage is where I think it is."

"Will Uncle Ewan be there?"

"Nay, Daniel. Remember th' soldiers said they'd be takin' him to Inverness? Daniel, I'll be leavin' ye wi' Auntie Mary while I'm travelin' to Inverness to find yer Uncle Ewan. It'll not take long, an' I'll be back."

"Auntie, do ye promise ye'll be back? Where's my mam an' da?"

Daniel covered his eyes with his hands, put his head down, and sobbed. Janet knew she had to tell the lad.

She lifted him from the saddle, found a place to sit, and held him close. "Laddie, there was a battle between Scotland's people an' England's people. Uncle Thomas, Uncle Duncan, an' yer Da died in th' battle. Because th' English soldiers are angry th' Scottish people fought wi' 'em, they want to punish us by burnin' all th' brochs in th' Hielands. Daniel, yer mother an' brothers lost their lives when our broch burned."

She held Daniel as he sobbed. Finally he dried his eyes, looked at Janet and asked, "Auntie, do ye think if I throwed rocks at th' soldiers, they'd stop?"

"Nay, Daniel, I dinna think so. Th' soldiers who did these things to yer family ha' yer Uncle Ewan now. This is why I must find him."

Daniel wiped his eyes and looked into her face. "I'm glad ye told me, Auntie." Janet held Daniel, smoothed his hair, and rocked back and forth.

She remembered the vision from last night. It was very real; she saw her father fall from his horse and die. Her mother cried as she cradled him in her arms. *Dha Shealladh*, the second sight, told the truth. Her father was dead, and her mother was with him when it happened. She was comforted by knowing her mother was still alive. She cried silently, aware that Daniel had lost his entire family. What would he remember of a Christ's Mass feast with gifts? Or, playing with his brothers and being safe? She considered taking Daniel to her parents' home, where Duny, Jamie, and Meghan were, instead of going to Inverness. Ewan might be on his way elsewhere.

Nay, she thought. *Duny is wi' family; they'll manage. Mother is strong, an' it's Ewan who needs my help now.*

"Laddie, are ye ready?"

"Aye. Auntie, do ye know how to write numbers an' letters? My mam said I'm old enough to learn an' she'd be teachin' me. If ye know how, would ye help me?"

"Aye, Daniel, I know how to write both letters an' numbers. I'll be happy to help ye learn to print letters so they make words an' sentences, an' numbers so ye can count things."

"I'd like tha'!" Daniel smiled at Janet as she placed him in the saddle and began leading Prince on the path through the Glens. A misty fog wrapped around them, bringing dampness to their clothing, but Janet was grateful that it provided a measure of cover.

Chapter 44

At the top of Stob Dubh Glen, Ian Douglas paused to gaze out over the great glens and valleys of Scotland. From his lofty perch he could see a glint of water from Loch Etive and the rivers that flowed into it. He searched for the path leading to the high valley between Stob Dubh Glen and Stob Na Brige Glen. A burn carrying the snowmelt from Stob Dubh cascaded down the glen to a valley, where it joined a second burn from Stob Na Brige. Then, farther on, the water joined other burns until it finally ran into the Etive River, which emptied into Loch Etive, a long, thin body of water that provided fresh water to most of the Highlands. There was an abundance of fescue, sweet vernal, and meadow grass in the high valley where Ian's sheep would stay the summer. Ian thought of his stone cottage. It would be the perfect place to stay when England and Scotland battled one another. Its remote location reminded him of the Isle of Skye where his mother lived: peaceful and almost inaccessible. If a body could gather enough provisions and wood to last through the long, bitter winter that always came to the High Glens, there would be no bother from anyone. A person could sit back on a cold winter's day and watch golden eagles glide through the sky on air currents that carried them from the lower valleys to the top of the glens. When Atlantic and North Sea storms clashed in the high glens, there would be dark days and long nights good for reading, writing and sitting by the fire, sipping barley malt whisky. He had some work yet to do, building a south-facing shelter for his sheep among other things.

Ian did not mind being alone. A long winter spent in the High Glens would be a good time to write a chronicle of his mother's family. The MacLeod clan had an interesting history of survival in the Scottish Isles. *I should return home an' spend time wi' Mother. When I was a bairn, I did'na understand the importance of listenin'. Now I do, an' I'd like to write down th' tales she told.*

One of his mother's stories had become a part of family history. Every MacLeod bairn could recite it word for word. Alexander MacLeod, Ian's great-grandfather several times removed, had a history of killing tacksmen, military officers, and those of that ilk who came to the island with the intention of collecting rent and tax monies thereby enforcing the laws of the land. When his mother told Alexander's story, everyone followed her to the library. There she selected the *Great Book* of the MacLeod clan, sat in her special chair, and began reading, marking the words with her finger. "Alexander MacLeod dwelleth in ye isles, whear ye officers of ye law dare not pass for hazard of their lives."

Then Ian's mother would speak to her audience. "Yer ancestors ha' lived on Skye for at least three centuries or more. They built this great castle, an' then other parts were added by another ancestor, Norseman Leod himself. Th' words about yer kin, Alexander MacLeod, are truthful, for th' officers of th' law do not yet today willingly come onto th' isle. Ye see, they be still afraid tha' wha' was done could be done again. Lads an' Lassies, dinna take it lightly tha' yer ancestor was so fearful tha' th' king's officers issued a declaration sayin', 'Dare not pass for hazard of your lives.'"

Everyone sat quietly, spellbound by the family history lesson.

When the family gathered together, the bard told stories of the clan. He always spoke of the MacLeod Fairy Flag said to possess the power to save the clan from disaster, but only for three times. It was told that two of the three times had been used up, once in 1490 and again in 1597. The flag was always carried with the MacLeod clan when they went into battle. There were many accounts of strange things happening when the Fairy Flag was present. Ian thought the tale about the flag protecting the castle and its inhabitants from harm on a stormy night long ago was his favorite. The Bard gathered all around, cups were filled with whisky and ale, and he began the story. A fire always burned in the fireplace in the great room, and Ian thought the flames leaped higher with the telling of the story. This was one tale he had to write down. Ian closed his eyes and remembered the story as the bard told it.

"All that day, th' sky had a strange green look, wi' clouds tha' reflected th' gray-green water of th' sea. Even th' gulls stayed hidden amongst th' rocks an' trees. Then, as th' sun went down, th' wind began blowin', first from th' west an' then from th' north. By nightfall, a terrible storm blew in from th' Atlantic Ocean. It met an icy gale from th' North Sea, an' th' winds mixed an' mingled, screamin' an' howlin' as even th' old ones had never heard. Icy rain lashed through th' trees, bringin' huge limbs crashin' to th' ground. The family gathered in this very room around a fire such as we're sittin' by now. Even with th' doors an' shutters closed, still th' wind came in an' put out th' candles an' lamps that are always burnin' within th' castle walls."

Ian and his cousins swore the candles and lamps flickered when this part of the story was told. "Th' sound of waves crashin' against th' high rocks could be heard from inside th' castle walls. Old John, th' oldest MacLeod, pointed to th' Fairy Flag in its place on th' wall in th' castle's great room. They all saw flames burning within th' flag. It was on tha' night that a great ship was destroyed as it tossed against th' rocks. Men with dark skins, slanted eyes, an' long mustaches, dressed in strange silk clothing, carryin' long curved swords with strange carvings of th' sun, moon, an' stars on th' handles, died in th' wreckage. Their bodies were found on th' rocks th' next mornin' after th' storm blew itself out."

The bard finished the story by saying the Fairy Flag brought on the storm to protect the castle and the MacLeods from an invasion by these strange people. Ian's memory of the story sent a shivery feeling up his spine, even now.

Ian's one-room cottage had a fireplace, a rope bed across one side, two chairs, a table, cabinets and a wash pan with running water. He had firewood left from last year, and the only thing missing was food. After sharing the contents of his knapsack with the lady and laddie, he'd need to snare a rabbit and roast it over the fire when he got hungry. He moved one of the chairs outside the door, filled his cup with cold water from the burn, and sat down. He had full view of his sheep grazing in grass up to their briskets. At his feet, yellow mountain violet and white heather blossoms were beginning to open. When he lifted his eyes to the sky there were patches of blue where there had been only gray clouds. Sunlight glinted on water rushing past in the burn. The air was chilly and always would be in the high glens. Even when the sun shone at summer's solstice, it would be cool here; a fire during a long evening and night would be welcome. In the early summer afternoon, the shadow of Stob Dubh placed the upper part of the valley in shade. This high glen also sheltered the valley from the worst of winter's storms. Ian thought he could stay here forever and not miss any of what was happening elsewhere. He thought of the beautiful lass and felt concern for her and the lad. He had hoped to find someone like her to wed; mayhap he was not much to look at, but he was honest, and that should mean something, he thought. He didn't think Janet and Daniel would be there when he returned. She would not stop until she either found her husband or knew what happened to him.

Lost in thought, he closed his eyes and slept. Dark clouds moved across the sun, and he woke to a deluge of cold rain, with lightening crashing down and thunder echoing through the glens. He went inside and started a fire using the tinderbox. He found a bit of bread and cheese in the bottom of his knapsack. A tot of whisky would be good in the dampness of the spring evening, but then he could get along without it; he was glad he'd shared the whisky he had with the red-haired lass. He selected a book from several he had in the knapsack, lit the lantern, and settled down for an evening of reading. *I'm nay a good Scotsman,* he thought. *A good Scotsman would ha' left th' books behind an' brought extra whisky.* He smiled to himself. *I'd rather ha' th' books. On a night like this, I'll ha' to admit a wee dram would chase away th' chilblains. Still, I'm glad I brought th' books.*

The fire crackled and snapped. Almost asleep, Ian rubbed his eyes and thought of his sheep. *I'd best take a look at the lambs. There's few wolves here, but still ...* The outside air was chilled; it would not be unusual for snow to fall even in May. Ian looked out over the valley. *I hope th' lass an' little fellow be safe.* The lambs were tucked in beside their mothers, and all were accounted for. He returned to the cottage, lay down on the bed, pulled his plaid around his shoulders, and slept.

Chapter 45

There were several paths leading to the High Glens; Janet considered one that circled Stob Dubh and went down the other side toward Glencoe. The Glencoe pass would not be safe, as it was the main way to Fort William. *Instead, we'll cross Glencoe at Altnafeadh. Mayhap I can purchase food there an' find a place to sleep.* Janet touched the coins she carried. *But a lone woman wi' a small lad, buyin' food an' spendin' coins, could draw attention. A church or chapel would be safe, an' if there's a kind priest, I might trade coins for food. I'll ask for th' way to Fort William, one tha' crofters use, an' we'll travel on.*

She thought about oats with cream and a cup of hot tea with a slice of pear tart with cream. "Auntie, why are ye smilin'?"

"Ah, lad, I'm just thinkin' how tasty a bite of pear tart would be. But it may be a while before we have any."

"I'm cold, Auntie."

"I'll tuck this blanket around ye, an' ye'll go to sleep." Janet patted him on the shoulder as he leaned forward to rest his head on Prince's neck.

"Prince is warm, Auntie."

She'd have to stop soon to rest. Her back ached, and she thought of the babe. When would he be born? His name would be Ewan James, or if there was a lassie, her name would be Abigail Beatrice.

Chapter 46

E wan remembered being bound by rope to a horse with a rider who wore a red coat. Then he remembered falling. He knew the man in the red coat was a soldier as were the ones he rode with now. He thought of the red coat he wore.

"I'm wearin' th' coat of a bloody English soldier!" Ewan spoke out loud and immediately realized his Scottish dialect would give him away. As long as Willie Ball stayed mute, they wouldn't know he wasn't one of them.

The captain called a halt. "We'll camp on the river bank tonight, and tomorrow will continue our search for Highlanders. If we capture a clan chief, we'll all receive silver coins from The Duke of Cumberland!"

The captain consulted his map. "We presently are on Cameron lands. Most of them live on the west side of River Lochy; on the east side are the Campbell and MacKenzy clans. We've heard Donald Cameron is in hiding and men from his clan are assisting him. Charles Stuart could be hiding with them. Lads, there's a thirty-thousand-pound reward for Charles Stuart's capture! I might send out a scout to look things over. Soldier, how is the injured man—any better?"

"Yes, sir, he is. Other than a swollen leg and ankle, he seems to be in good shape."

"Well, then, I'll have him scout for us. Soldier Ball, come forward."

Ewan rode to the front of the line. "Sir?"

"I'd like you to scout the area and report back to me. Perhaps there is a house with inhabitants and belongings we can dispose of. They may be carrying firearms, so be on guard."

One of the soldiers spoke. "Captain, Soldier Ball is unarmed. He cannot defend himself if need be."

"Soldier Ball, if there are clansmen in the area, you are to return for reinforcements!"

"Yes, sir." Ewan saluted.

Ewan knew where he was. *There's th' gate to my lands. My grandsire lived here, my father lived here, an' they're mine to gi' to my son!* He passed through another gate and then the last one. He tethered the horse, dismounted, and looked at the ruins. *Wha' happened to our broch?*

Then he remembered and began sobbing as grief overwhelmed him. "Elizabeth an' her lads died here! Oh! My God, why ha' ye forsaken us?" On the threshold where double doors once hung, Ewan found the remains of a large dog. "Bran?"

There was no sound other than the wind blowing through the ruins. He looked at ashes and pieces of charred timber covering the stone floor. In the kitchen, he found the remains of Elizabeth and her three children. The iron hook, where the great copper kettle once hung, had charred pieces of rope that had bound the mother and children together. When the rope burned through, they fell to the floor, still clinging to one another. The fire was so hot there was no flesh left on the bones. He remembered promising Anne they would have a Christian burial.

For the second time in a little more than a fortnight, Ewan prepared a grave for members of his family. He arranged the bones, covered them with dirt, and placed an iron spade over the grave for a marker. "Later, I'll make a proper marker wi' their names, so they'll not be forgotten."

After saying a prayer, he returned to the horse and mounted with difficulty. *When I return to camp, I'd best ha' somethin' to tell th' captain. If Gordon's broch is still standin', mayhap they'll be satisfied wi' burnin' it. I'll keep quiet so they'll nay know I'm a Hielander, or it'll be a quick death!"*

The captain was speaking to the men when Ewan rode into the campsite. "Ah, Soldier Ball, what did you find?"

Ewan picked up a stick and began drawing on the sandy river bank. He outlined the campsite and path leading through the forest to his house. He crossed the house with lines and drew flames coming from it. Then, he drew the number four and crossed it with lines. "Very good! You found a Cameron home that has been destroyed with four people who died. Excellent! Is there more?"

Ewan nodded and began drawing again. He drew the path to Gordon's lands with the outline of a house. It did not matter if it burned down, his life depended upon pleasing the captain.

"Very well! On the morrow, you'll lead us to that place." He noticed Ewan's foot and said, "You've festering wounds on that foot that needs care."

Ewan said "Yes, sir."

"We'll get you to the infirmary as quickly as we can."

The next morning the captain said, "Soldier Ball, ride point for us; you know where we're going." The day was beautiful, with a clear sky and warm sunshine. New leaves were budding, and the air smelled clean and fresh. Had it been any other day, Ewan would have been working in his fields. There would be lambs, calves, and foals with attentive mothers nearby. He and Thomas, together with the men from the village, would be clearing fence rows, mending rock fences, and tilling the fields, preparing them for the sewing of oat and barley seeds. It was a beautiful spring day in the Scottish Highlands.

As they rode north, Ewan hoped Gordon's broch was standing and there would be plunder for the troops. Then, the captain and men could brag about the win. His leg throbbed, but his foot no longer ached; it felt as if his leg was attached to a dead weight. The corporal in charge of food and drink gave him a flask of whisky, he sipped from it as he rode.

By early afternoon the troop passed through the gate to Gordon's broch. The captain shouted, "Surround the building, break down the door, and secure anyone inside. After we search the house for valuables, we'll burn it. Soldier Ball, no need for you to assist with this. How is your foot and leg today, any better?"

Ewan shook his head. "No? You've served your king well by leading us to this house! I will see the duke hears of it."

Ewan watched while the men destroyed the door and moved into the house armed with rifles and pistols. After they were convinced there was no one there, they would set fire to it. Only the outer stone walls would be standing when they finished. Ewan heard soldiers shouting "Burn it!" Burning haystacks spread to century-old oak timbers in the barn. Smoke filled the valley and mingled with mist from the Glens.

At dark, soldiers gathered to sort the plunder. "Here's crates of whiskey and ale," said one soldier. "I found jewelry and coins," said another.

"I have a gold timepiece, a set of silver spoons and a silver bowl."

After the captain selected the gold pocket watch and coins for himself, they spread everything out and began dividing them. Captain Strong handed Ewan a bottle of whisky and several silver coins. "Soldier Ball, you've earned this. You seemed to know the location of this house. Have you traveled this country before?"

"No, sir, I've not." Willie Ball accepted the bottle.

"Thanks to you, Soldier Ball, we have items of value that we'll take to Fort William, as well as the news that we've destroyed another traitor's home."

"Very good, sir." Willie held the bottle high and waved it. The captain did not notice the tears running down his face. Light from the blazing house and barn did not reach as far as the rock wall where Ewan sat, holding the bottle to his mouth.

Chapter 47

Abby was awake, but she did not want to open her eyes. If she did, it meant she had to face the day without James. "My dear, there's a poached egg on toasted bread an' a bun wi' jam for ye. Do ye want milk or tea?"

"Tea, please, sister, thank you."

Sister Marie pulled out a chair, and Abby sat down. "Ye slept all afternoon an' night. I prayed ye would. It's th' best thing when th' body an' spirit ha' been wounded."

Abby stood and gasped, "Oh, my feet hurt!"

"It's nay a wonder. Yer slippers were worn completely through, an' ye were walkin' on th' soles of yer feet! Ye were ridin' when ye got here. Did ye walk part o' th' way?"

"James rode, and I walked. It was not until after—well, after James died—that I rode."

Sister Marie poured tea for Abby and a cup for herself. "Eat, Abby, an' then we'll talk. There's no hurry. Take yer time."

Abby was famished; the egg on buttered toast was delicious. She had a second bannock bun with jam and drank her tea. Sister Marie poured her a second cup and looked at her bruised feet. "We'll soak yer sore feet in a pan of warm water wi' some lavender soap. When yer ready, I've a good wool gown wi' a blouse an' undergarments laid out on the bed. There's boots, but yer feet are too bruised to put 'em on. Come along, Abby. I'll help ye get dressed."

Sister Marie held out the gown for her. "Sister, I wore clothing like this when I attended school at the castle."

"Ye went to school at th' castle? My goodness, yer royalty?"

"No, I'm not, although my mother was a cousin to Queen Anne. She served the queen as her lady-in-waiting. I was the only child raised in the royal nursery, and the queen was my auntie. I did not realize how special my childhood was until after I married."

"Tell me about yer James, Abby."

Abby smiled. "He came to the royal stables to purchase horses from Queen Anne, and soon James and I were talking about the animals while we shared each other's company. When he proposed, I accepted with the queen's blessing."

Abby laughed as she remembered, "It was a shock to the court when the queen announced James and I both were related to her through the Stuart lineage. After our wedding in the palace chapel, we left the next day for James's home in Perthshire. Oh! We've had a wonderful life!"

Abby smiled. "I'm not so sad now," she said, surprised at her feelings. "Talking about our lives together makes me happy, not sad. James and I have two beautiful grown daughters and a son who will follow in his father's footsteps."

"Aye, Abby, one survives losing someone they love by remembering the good times."

Abby suddenly remembered the packet of papers. "Sister, where is the horse?" "In th' stable. He's been fed an' watered an' is in good shape."

"Did you notice a knapsack tied to the saddle?"

"Aye, I did. Shall I get it for ye?"

"Oh, yes, please. That knapsack holds a packet of important papers. I'll tell you all about it."

As Sister Marie hurried out, she said, "Try on yer garb to see if it fits." The jumper fit well over the chemise and underskirt. Abby looked at the boots, but her feet were too sore to wear them. Sister Marie returned with the knapsack.

With a sigh of relief, Abby retrieved the bundle of papers. "Sister Marie, you know about our encounter with the English soldiers, and it's sad ending. However, it is only a small part of what is happening in the Highlands. Charles Stuart promised the clan chieftains weapons for the Jacobite army, but when the time came, there were no guns or ammunition. He also promised provisions, but the men had nothing to eat for days before the battle." Abby stopped to catch her breath. "It's no wonder the battle was lost!"

"Abby, as yer speaking, things tha' I dinna understand before are beginnin' to make sense. I believe I know where Father Matthew is, an' I dinna think he'll be back. I'll get a pot o' tea, an' we'll talk about it." Sister Marie was deep in thought as she filled the teapot with hot water. She spooned in leaf tea, covered the teapot with a cozy, and placed it, together with a pitcher of cream, a sugar bowl, and a plate of ginger biscuits, on a tray. She carried the tray to a table beside the fireplace and pulled two chairs close by.

"Abby, I believe our chapel priest had a part in a scheme to send weapons meant for Charles Stuart to th' royal army instead. Men brought wooden crates here an' left 'em. I believe those crates contained th' guns yer talkin' about tha' should've gone to th' Highlanders. About three weeks ago, a very large man visited here. He told th' father to get word to Lord Cumberland tha' Charles was in Inverness waitin' for a shipment from Ireland. He also said Charles would be waitin' for a long while! Abby, th' Hielanders had no weapons because they were waylaid an' went to th' king's army instead! It wasn't 'til ye spoke of th' Hielanders goin' into battle wi'out weapons tha' it began to make sense. To think I prayed for Father Matthew's safety! Wheesht! He's an English spy!"

"I wondered why a priest from London would come to a tiny village like this. Th' rat was away most of the time! Sister Martha an' I visited th' sick an' made arrangements for weddings, burials, an' th' like."

Abby interrupted, "You did not question his absences, sister?"

"Nay," Sister Marie said. "A nun never questions a priest. If I'd known then wha' I know now, I would ha' though! It's prayer time. Abby, will ye come to th' chapel wi' me?"

The two women walked to the chapel, one supporting the other. "Sister Marie, please consider coming with me. I do not want to leave you here."

Sister Marie patted Abby on the shoulder. "Abby, if ye ha' not asked, I would ha' asked ye. It'll naught be long a'fore th' soldiers reach this church. I'm ready to leave. After prayers I'll gather a few things, an' we'll be on our way."

Each woman prayed silently, one tearfully after losing a beloved husband and the other because her quiet life was about to disrupt. As they left the chapel, Abby said, "Sister, is there a horse for you?"

"Aye. Usually Father Matthew takes him, but there was a loaded cart to pull, an' he borrowed a stronger horse from a parishioner. No question wha' was in th' cart, is there, Abby?"

"No question, Sister Marie. Would you have breeks and a cloak that I can wear?'

"Aye, I do, an' I'll find some slippers for ye 'til yer feet ha' healed enough to wear boots." Sister Marie handed Abby a black wool cloak, black breeks, and knit slippers with soft leather soles. Sister Marie removed her habit, folded it, and placed it in a knapsack. She fastened a pair of brown breeches around her waist, buttoned a linen tunic, and tucked it into the waistband.

"Sister, do we have any weapons?"

"Let's take a look at wha' th' imposter left behind." Sister Marie cocked her head to one side and said, "No wonder he had trouble wi' th' sacraments!"

She opened the door to a room with a bed, a wooden box at the foot, a few clothes hanging on nails, and a chest under the bed. Abby opened the wooden box; inside was priest's clothing and a small knife in a leather case. The chest contained another knife with a bone handle. Abby held out the knife in the leather case to Sister Marie. "There's one for each of us."

"Abby, ye gather grain for th' horses, an' I'll ready our food."

The night was bright, with a full moon and no clouds. The two women held hands as Sister Marie said a quick prayer, turned to Abby, and said, "From now on, I'm Marie."

"Yes, we're kin traveling to our home in Perthshire. Marie, I've only a few coins. I didn't think to bring what James had."

"I've enough for both of us." Marie opened a leather purse and held it for Abby to see. "This money was given by parish members. They'd be pleased to know it'll not be squandered on men barterin' guns."

Marie led the way to a path. "This way is little traveled. Th' king's army won't use it, as it doesn't go anywhere they'd want to be."

As they rode Abby said, "Marie, I've directions for you. Should something happen to me, you must follow them!"

"I give ye my word, Abby, I will."

"The horse I'm riding was provided by a young Highlander named Brian. He's risking his life to gather information for a man named Lord George Murray who led the Highland troops into battle on Culloden's moor. Lord George is a highly skilled military man who wrote a letter to Charles Edward Stuart after the battle was over, stating how mismanaged it was and reasons why it should have been delayed until there was sufficient arms and provisions. I personally—" Abby spoke louder than she meant to—"will never forgive Charles Edward Stuart! Never!"

"I understand why ye feel as ye do, Abby. Lower yer voice an' tell me more about th' papers yer carryin'."

"The papers in this knapsack," Abby said, patting the leather bag, "describe England's plans to destroy the Highland clans and enforce English rule in Scotland."

Abby looked at the woman who rode beside her. "Marie, I am glad you are with me, but the danger is great. Should we be captured and the papers found, we'll be guilty of high treason! You're a gentlewoman, Marie, and cannot imagine what a troop of English soldiers could do to prolong your misery before they kill you. If we're found, you must save yourself! Do not be concerned about me. Marie, you must get away, find Lord Murray, and deliver these papers to him. If for some reason, I am unable to return home, I've a favor to ask of you. Please tell Jamie Dunsmuir, Meghan MacIntyre, and Duny Cameron the circumstances leading to James's death and explain why I am not with you. If you cannot do what I've asked of you, do not feel badly."

Abby shrugged and managed a small laugh, "I promise I'll not come back to haunt you. Should haunting be possible, I'll search out Lord Cumberland, Charles Stuart, and the soldier who shot and killed my husband! I'll be around every corner, at the top of every staircase, and at the bottom of every hill they must go around, climb, or descend. I'll be the most horrible banshee they've ever seen or heard!"

Marie smiled. "I'd not want ye hauntin' me, I wouldn't!" She gently chided Abby, "Let's nay borrow trouble. We've said our prayers an' asked th' Lord to protect us, an' he will."

"Abby, yer family situation is far more serious than mine. My kin are safe in Edinburgh, an' they'll be at home where they've always been. Since we've a long night ahead of us, I might as well tell ye a bit about my family. Mam and Da were employed by th' royals at Edinburgh Castle. I'd wait for 'em to come home in th' evenin' so they could tell me about their day. Oh, th' things royalty would say an' do—one never knew wha' would happen next!"

Chapter 48

"Soldiers, we'll reach Fort William today. Soldier Ball's discovery of a Cameron dwelling will bring honors for our regiment. Perhaps the fort's physician can determine what can be done for him."

As the Captain spoke, heavy, dark clouds gathered around the tops of the High Glens known as the Glen Nevis. Thunder rumbled through the valleys; lightning struck bare rocks on the peaks, causing explosions of white-hot sparks. Each strike flamed in bushes that quickly turned into bright fires that were doused as rain moved across the glens. A small regiment of men bearing the king's flag rode toward the group. At the front, a black stallion carried The Duke of Cumberland.

"My God!" Captain Strong exclaimed. "The Duke of Cumberland! Attention, men! Your Royal Highness! We're on our way to the fort to celebrate a success in destroying a Cameron dwelling. It is a triumph for Your Highness and your father, God save the king!"

"Thank you, Captain. I am pleased! When you reach the fort, ask General Canady to reward your men with an extra ration of whisky."

Speaking only to the captain, Lord Cumberland asked, "Tell me, captain, whose orders do you follow?"

"Sir, my orders come directly from you. We are to destroy all Highlanders, including their properties and animals."

The duke smiled. "Excellent! My orders are being implemented as intended." Then he paused and looked at Ewan. "You, there! What is your name?"

Ewan spoke with the barest hint of a Highland accent. "Willie Ball, sir."

The duke frowned. "Is this a bloody Scot in our midst? Is he?"

"No, no!" the captain said, shaking his head emphatically. "Your Highness, no, of course not. He has suffered injuries to his head and cannot speak clearly. I believe his troop did not realize he'd fallen by the wayside, and they moved on. It may be that when we reach the fort, someone there will know him. He has no identification papers; however, that's not unusual for troops who have been in the field for a while."

The duke listened carefully. "No identification, you say? His commanding officer will have a roster, if we can find the fellow. How long has he been with you, Captain?"

"Over a week, Your Highness. When we found him, he was in better shape than he is now. The man deserves recognition. He led our regiment to a Cameron home, where we were able to restock our food supply as well as taking booty. Sir, let me present you with a fine gold watch; it keeps excellent time."

Ewan watched as the duke took the timepiece from the captain's hand. "Remarkable! Tell me, how would a Highlander acquire a beautiful watch such as this one? I would not expect to see something so valuable in the possession of a commoner, unless it was stolen."

Ewan raised his head, eyes flashing. "Nay, tis a lie!"

The duke smiled at him. "I detect an accent that does not belong to an English soldier."

The captain spoke quickly. "Sir, this man is very ill. At times we can hardly understand what he is saying. He has been talking nonsense for the past several days. We're taking him to the fort for treatment."

The duke continued to look at Ewan, who, under his piercing gaze, felt a painful burning in the middle of his chest. "Who are you? Your captain says you assisted with locating a Cameron castle. How is it that you would know where one could be found? Even I, with my maps, have to search for these places. Who are you, soldier? Answer me! Are you spying on the king's army? I suspect you are hiding behind the disguise of being an injured English soldier!"

"Your Highness," the captain hoped to redirect his attention, "Please forgive me for interrupting. We have, in our possession, many bottles of exceptionally well-made malt whisky. I know Your Highness enjoys Scottish whisky. May I offer you a flask?"

The duke turned his attention to the captain. "Yes, it is a favorite of mine. Let's rest for a few minutes and enjoy the fruits of our labors, shall we?"

The captain quickly found a bottle. "Sir, allow me to pour a cup for you."

Moving quickly, the captain motioned for Ewan and the two soldiers beside him to separate themselves from the rest of the troop. Speaking quietly, he ordered, "Take him to the fort and see what the physician says. You may need to transport him on to the infirmary. I'll inform the duke you've left because Soldier Ball was too ill to stay here any longer." To himself he thought, *I'll tell the duke after he's had several drinks.*

Ewan was barely conscious, but pain kept him awake. He held out an empty whisky bottle; someone handed him a full one. A soldier riding beside Ewan wrinkled his nose, "Something smells rank. What is it?"

Ewan replied, "Foot rottin'." His foot, still in the filthy stocking, was twice its normal size. He was dying; it was his due for leaving

Culloden's battlefield. Ewan drank enough to sleep. Soldiers on either side of him led his horse through Glencoe pass. He did not see purple flowering heather on the hills before they became the High Glens. He could not see yellow flowering grouse or white and purple violets blooming in the high meadows. He was unable to take deep breaths of crisp, clean air, and the scent of the Highlands did not tickle his nostrils. On a different day Ewan would have smiled and thought of how this country was as much a part of him as he was it. None of those things mattered now. Ewan Cameron was dying. He would not die the quick, patriotic death of a soldier on the battlefield, but he would die a good Scotsman, one who told stories of great Scottish accomplishments in the ancient Gaelic and who was gentle to his wife, a loving father to his son, and loyal to his clan. He would die without honor. Yet he fought a battle the same as did his cousins on Culloden's moor. His horse carried him forward; he slept, waking only long enough to take another drink from the bottle.

"Very fine whisky, Captain. I should like several bottles to take with me."

"Of course, sir. Please allow me to refill your cup. May I offer you cheese and bread?"

"Thank you, yes. I find the taste of malt whisky is complementary to food, and I look forward to sharing it with the king. He prefers wine with his dinner, but I believe this whisky will capture his interest."

As he was speaking, the duke's eyes searched the soldiers. He looked for one man in particular. "Captain, where is the soldier I spoke to earlier? I do not see him."

The captain cleared his throat. "Sir, he has a terrible odor about him. I did not want you to be offended, especially while you are eating, and I've sent him on to the fort with an escort."

The duke frowned and fixed his gaze on the captain. "Are you defending the man, Captain?"

"No, no, Your Highness. I'm only thinking of your comfort and well-being."

The duke smiled. "I shall find him; he has the look of a Highlander about him. They have a way of looking down their noses at all but themselves."

William Augustus continued to speak in a quiet, controlled voice, "I hope to locate Donald Cameron while we are in the area. The man is hardly worth the powder it would take to blow his arse away; however, I suppose I could come up with a reward for the person who reports his whereabouts." Cumberland smiled. "This malt whisky has an exceptional flavor. Perhaps it is in the aging process."

Thoughtfully choosing his words, the duke asked, "Will Soldier Ball and his escorts go directly to Fort William, or will they be traveling on to the infirmary?"

"Your Highness, they will take him to Fort William."

"Captain, Soldier Willie Ball is not the man you think he is."

"Sir, in no way would I question you. However, I personally did not see anything untoward about the man that would cause me to question his loyalty to the king or to you, sir."

"Good point, Captain; there is nothing to be seen that you would take exception to." The duke paused, eyes staring into the distance. "It is the unseen I find fascinating about the man. Why is he afraid?"

"Afraid, sir? I sent him on a mission by himself to search the countryside. We knew there were Cameron homes in the area, and, following your orders, did not want to leave until we were sure they were destroyed. Soldier Ball was gone most of the day. When he returned, he reported one destroyed Cameron home and found one that was still standing. We would not have found it without his help. Your Highness, not once did he falter in following my orders."

Cumberland rubbed both hands together, thought for a minute, and then spoke. "It is interesting that Soldier Ball knew where to find the Cameron houses. An English soldier would have no idea where to look. Think about it, Captain. You said yourself you would never have found the second Cameron property had it not been for Soldier Ball."

Against his better judgment, the captain defended Willie Ball again. "Sir, why would he lead us directly to the home? Would it not make better sense for him to lead us away?"

"You might think so. However, I can see through his plot, even if you cannot!" William's face took on a color that almost matched the red of his satin sash.

"My loyal captain." William Augustus spoke with heavy sarcasm. "It is remarkable that you and your men were not ambushed! Make no mistake about it: if the Highlander could have completed his task, you and the king's soldiers would be dead!"

The duke began pacing the floor. "There's no question in my mind! He's a Scottish Highlander, Captain! Now, because of your incompetence, he knows exactly where you are and understands your plans for tomorrow and the next day as well. He is a spy, Captain, a spy! He must be dealt with before he delivers more information to one of his fellow Camerons, who will pass it on. I shall take great pleasure in finding and punishing the louse!

Captain, my men will join you as you travel on to Fort William, and I will search for Willie Ball—or whomever he is."

The captain hesitated before speaking further. "Your Highness, I doubt the man will live long enough to reach Fort William. He is very ill."

"Captain, my concern is with those he will come into contact with between here and there. If you will, Captain, I'd like to have several bottles of the whisky you served me earlier.

"Of course, sir. I will mark the rest of the bottles with your name; they will be waiting for you at the fort."

"Thank you for your hospitality, Captain. My regards to your men." He mounted his horse and urged him forward.

The duke's men mingled with the other soldiers as they gathered wood, lit a fire, and sat down with ale and food. During their meal, they talked. "The duke—we've heard tales of him, that one! We've heard he sprouts wings and can fly. Is it true?"

The duke's men laughed among themselves. One of them said, "I was with him in Nairn, the night before the battle. He told us about Charles Stuart and made predictions about the battle at Culloden. He told how it would be, and that was exactly the way it was."

The soldier looked around at the group. "He drank whisky along with us, and while most of us were too drunk to stand up, he was sober as could be. Another thing: he didn't have anything to do with the ladies. I don't think he seeks the company of men either. He seemed to enjoy watching others having their pleasure, but he didn't join in."

Chapter 49

William Augustus looked at the night sky. When William was a child, his tutor was Edmond Halley, the famous atheist who excelled at astronomy and was a noted geophysicist, mathematician, and physicist. William Augustus thought about the man who had a profound influence on him. As a young child, William was taught about God, who was completely in charge, required obedience to his laws, and dealt out punishment for all who disobeyed. William admired the military aspect of a God who punished those who failed to follow his orders. Like his mother, Caroline of Ansbach, William was interested in everything. Caroline's surrogate mother was the queen of Prussia, Sophia Charlotte, well known for her intelligence, strong character, and liberal court. Caroline grew up in Berlin, had many suitors, and received an offer of marriage from the Catholic archduke, Charles of Austria. She declined the offer, saying she would not convert to Catholicism. In June 1705, Caroline's first cousin, George Augustus, a prince of Hanover, Germany, visited her disguised as a Spanish shipbuilder; he wanted to look her over prior to proposing marriage. George Augustus was completely taken with beautiful Caroline, who immediately saw through his ruse and found herself laughing at her suitor, who clearly was German and not from Spain after all.

She found George attractive, and, more importantly, this handsome young man might one day find himself in England, wearing the king's crown. Caroline planned her wedding with the thought that one day she might be queen of England. Then, when the currently unmarried George I, Caroline's husband's father, was crowned king of England, the entire family moved to London. Caroline's and George Augustus's first son, Frederick, preferred to stay with family in Germany. When their second son, William Augustus, was born in 1721, he became his grandfather's favorite grandson. Frederick was absent from the royal family and went unnoticed until the king died and Frederick's father, George II, was crowned king. Then Frederick arrived in England to claim the title of Prince of Wales as King George II's first son.

As with many royal families, the use and misuse of power led to anger and jealousy. George I and his son, George II, were constantly at war with each other. Two separate courts developed with strong differences; George I wanted only a German court, with advisors who spoke German. But his son separated himself and his family from his father's German preferences and developed his own court of wealthy English nobles. This led to young George gaining popularity with the British people; he spoke their language because it was his language as well. Political opposition to George I gradually became focused around young George and his beautiful, gracious wife, Caroline. England's people, both the aristocracy and commoners, observed that George II was adept at conducting public and private appearances for the sake of the country, and, he spoke English fluently. Therefore, he was far better qualified to be king of England than his father. King George, angry that his son and daughter-in-law were favored by his subjects, placed

George and Caroline under a cruel and debilitating house arrest at St. James Palace. Their children were taken away from them and placed with their grandfather in the king's castle.

Not yet five years old, little William Augustus knew his grandfather hated his father. When William was six years old, his grandfather gave him the title, "The Duke of Cumberland." William was beginning to understand the importance of power. He had his own servants, a suite of rooms in the palace, and a stable of horses. He learned to respond to his grandfather when he was asked in German who he preferred, his father or his grandfather. Speaking in a clear voice, William always chose his grandfather. Patting his grandson on the head, King George I would say, "Gut, gut." In 1727 when the old king died, William was the only one who wept. When his father became King George II, William, unsure of his future with a father who constantly found fault with him, was pleased to be placed with a tutor instead of living in the castle. His mother, seeking the nation's best scholars as tutors for her son, was interested in finding a teacher who would take the boy and provide an education along with bed and board. Caroline truly loved her son and justified fostering him as she felt a superior education was the best thing she could give him. Wisely, she surmised that having the youngster educated away from his critical father would be in his best interests.

One spring morning, twelve year old William sat at his desk reading about the planets, moon, sun, and stars. He questioned his tutor; "Teacher, how did we—I mean, humans, sir, not the planets or sun—come to be?"

Edmond Halley smiled at the handsome boy and patted his shoulder. "We are an accident of nature, William, an accident! Nothing more, nothing less. Thousands of years ago, there was the right mixture of chemicals, oxygen, heat, and cold. Because of that perfect blend, a spark of life happened by pure chance. I speculated in one of my scientific papers that a lightning bolt may have been the very thing that brought life into being. Every living creature on our planet—humans, animals, birds, and fish— came from that single spark. Does that answer your question?"

"Almost, sir. How do you compensate for the Bible, which says God created our world in six days and man in his image?"

Teacher Halley stroked his goatee and sat down in a chair beside his young pupil. He knew he had William's attention; this would be his best opportunity to introduce the child to a secular viewpoint. "It's a story, William, created by men. I admit, it is interesting reading. But really now, who could believe that a God could fashion life from dust and a woman from the rib of a man?" Edmond smiled at his young pupil. "Not I. However, according to the Bible, it happened! I find the entire tale of Biblical creation unbelievable, and being a thinking man, I am unable to accept it! While we are discussing this subject, there have been many gods worshiped by different cultures. The Egyptians, for example, were one of the world's oldest civilizations. They worshipped a Sun God. It makes sense, you see: We are dependent upon the sun to come up every morning to warm the earth so that plants can grow and provide Earth's inhabitants with food. That is why they worshiped a Sun God, or Ra, as the Egyptians called him. I personally know of people who worship a God called Gautama Buddha. William, there have been, and still are, many Gods."

"Then, sir, you are saying you believe the Bible is not true and God does not exist?"

"Correct, William, nor do I believe in his counterpart, Satan. The Bible is a collection of stories handed down and added to from one generation to another. We are all free to make our own choices and do what we will with our lives. There is no one greater than we are to bring us to task for it. William, you are a very bright boy. The next time you enter a church, look around. You'll see it's no more than a stone edifice with statues of martyrs who lived long ago, if they lived at all."

Teacher folded his arms across his chest and smiled at the child who sat next to him. "Tell me, William, can you see God? Can you reach out and touch God, as you do me or your mother? No! Of course you can't. At least the Egyptians could look up and see their Sun God as they worshiped him."

Sir Edmond placed his hand on William's arm. "In time, you will learn that among intelligent and educated people, each one can have his or her own belief and still manage to discuss many topics with respect for one another."

The child thought about his teacher's words. A small part of him was disappointed that there was no God, but his tutor's words did make more sense than those he had heard in church. He said, "No, sir, I cannot see or touch God. Thank you for helping me understand."

The sun was shining; it was a lovely spring day, but The Dark One took no pleasure in it. However, he was greatly pleased for another reason. A child, who would grow into a strong and powerful man, had just accepted one of his best lies! The seed of disbelief in God had been planted and would take root. Now his task was to carefully nurture the child along so he would be in the right places at the right times. The Dark One recalled the child's father, who was critical of his son and rarely found any good in what the child said or did.

Excellent, he said to himself. *The child will grow up angry and hostile as long as he is raised away from his mother's influence. When he is grown, he will lead a battle for the English, against the people of Scotland! Ah! It is a fine day after all!*

William remembered tucking a book in his pocket to read when he attended church while visiting his family. As he read about great battles and how they were won, time spent in the cold, stone building passed quickly. He was pleased when his mother, who wished to travel throughout Europe, told him that Sir Edmond had invited him to stay with him and his family for a year. William looked forward to not attending church services; he had outgrown fairy tales. Now, William Augustus focused all of his anger and hatred on the Highlander who had managed to elude him. *I'll stop at the fort and inform the general of the Highland spy who fooled one of our best captains and nearly cost the king an entire regiment of men.*

Chapter 50

The general listened as the soldiers explained how Willie came to be a part of their troop and what little they knew of the cause of his injuries. "Many a king's soldier has fallen by the wayside and survived, even with extensive injuries. Take Soldier Ball to the infirmary and ask the physician to look at him. It may be he can apply treatments which will ease the soldier's pain until he can be taken on to Stronabaw."

The general wrinkled his nose and pulled out his handkerchief. "General, sir, Soldier Ball smells God-awful."

"Yes, he does, but we'll tend to that." Holding a scented handkerchief over his mouth and nose, the general took one look at Ewan and knew he would not live. Gangrene was in his left foot and leg. His right leg had dark spots, and the toes on that foot were black. The man's flesh was rotting while he was still alive. The pain must have been excruciating. He was placed on a bed.

"Whisky, whisky." Ewan spoke in a faint voice.

"Give him what he wants, as much as he wants."

The general returned to his desk and began preparing

paperwork for Soldier Ball's treatment. In the space showing the patient's assigned troop, full name, and date of birth, General Shannon Canady wrote, "unknown, William Ball, unknown."

The fort's physician, Doctor Smythe, completed his examination of the patient and spoke to his assistant. "Give him sufficient opium to put him to sleep. He has no feeling whatsoever in his left foot and leg and the right foot and leg has very little. I'll remove both legs above the knees. If he survives, the nurse at Stronabaw can treat him."

The physician gave instructions for Ewan's clothing to be removed. The filthy stocking fell apart with pieces of flesh clinging to it. "Stop there," ordered the physician. "No need to do anything more with his legs; both of them will be removed. We're making an effort to save his life; apparently, he's something of a hero."

A golden liquid was spooned into Ewan's mouth and washed down with whisky. Under the influence of the opium, he slept. The physician's knife, a saw-toothed instrument with a heavy handle, was placed beside a bucket of water on the table next to Ewan's bed. Tourniquets were applied to both legs. When the physician made the first cut halfway between the knee and hip, a thick dark liquid oozed from the incision. The stench was overpowering. He continued to apply pressure on the knife, bringing it back and forth across the bone. When it was severed, he cut through the flesh on the back of the leg.

Ewan stirred. "Janet, Janet, where be ye?"

The physician directed his assistant to give Ewan more opium. When the surgery was finished, flannel pads were placed over the stumps. The physician shook his head. "We'll not save this one, the poison is in his body. Give him more opium so he can be taken on to Stronabaw. Find the two men who brought him and get him away from here. We've done all we can."

General Canady sat at his desk, reading a stack of papers. *The fourth regiment of the king's army has been assigned detail to search for*

Charles Stuart. I'm willing to bet they'll not find him. He has supporters who will hide him at all costs. It will be futile to look any further— there was a knock on the General's door. Without waiting for a response, a Captain opened the door. "General Canady, His Highness, The Duke of Cumberland is here to see you."

"The duke! Bring him into the dining room."

The general welcomed Cumberland with a bow and salute. "An honor, Your Highness; how may I be of service to you?"

"I can always count on you to offer your services, general, and it is most appreciated! I am looking for a man who is a Scottish spy and likely has been brought here, or at least passed through here on his way to another hospital north of the fort. It's said he is ill and may not live. He must be put to death; the man nearly managed a massacre of the king's army! Under the guise of being an English soldier, he rode with our men, ate our food, and drank our whisky. I spoke with him face to face. He feigned a head injury that was blamed for his inability to speak; however, when he did speak, there was no doubt that he's a Highlander. I suspect he knows where his clan chief, Donald of Lochiel, is, and perhaps Charles Edward Stuart."

The duke looked at the general. "Do you have him here?"

"Your Highness, I believe he may be the one who was brought in several hours ago. If so, he is undergoing surgery as we speak."

The general paused as he considered how to extend hospitality to the duke. "Sir, may I persuade you to join me for a meal? Then, by the time we finish, the patient might be awake and able to speak with us."

"Yes, thank you, General. A meal at a table would be most enjoyable. You do recall how it is in the field, trying to eat a morsel as one is riding?"

"By all means, Your Highness. I've had many a meal astride my horse." Both men nodded.

The general led the way to the dining table, pulled a chair back, and waited for the duke to sit. "You will be very pleased to know I've received several crates marked with your name. They were brought by courier this morning. I am most curious about the contents. Your Highness, here is one of the bottles."

The duke smiled as he sat down. "Yes, I am very pleased! If you will join me; I can promise you a delightful experience." He poured two glasses of the light amber liquid. "A toast, General, to your health."

"And to yours, Your Highness." The general agreed with the duke that the whisky was delicious and asked where he might purchase several bottles for himself. The duke responded that this particular whisky came from a traitor's home which had been destroyed; however, in appreciation for the general's loyalty, he would gift a bottle to him.

Then the conversation turned to the battle at Culloden. "Sir, I am impressed; you trained your men well, and experience was on your side. Also, there's the fact that your soldiers were well armed with artillery provided by this fort. I believe the Jacobite insurgents have been laid to rest! If I may, sir, a toast to our king, God save the king, and to you, our highly esteemed leader!"

William smiled in acknowledgment of the fealty. Then he raised his glass, drank deeply, and held it out to be refilled.

"Your Highness, it's said Edinburgh's citizens cheered and welcomed English leadership back into their city. A justice who sits in the city court's highest chair told one of our men his conversation with Charles Stuart was similar to one he would have with a lad still in knickers."

The general knew Cumberland would enjoy hearing the news he had to share. "Charles's closest adviser told of Charles selecting fabric from Italy for his coronation robes and even choosing members of his court! It can be said he assumed he would win the battle."

The duke smiled. "You say he had chosen his coronation clothing? What a farce when you consider that Charles was so overwhelmed on the battlefield he was unable to call for the first shot! Instead of moving to the rear of the field as the battle progressed, he left completely! I believe him to be cowardly."

The general nodded his head in agreement. "Your Highness, I've ordered dinner for us."

"General, please call your physician in to speak with me concerning the spy he is treating. I want to hear his opinion of the man's condition."

"Of course, Your Highness." The general spoke to his adjutant. "Captain, bring Doctor Smythe as quickly as possible. The duke wishes to speak with him. We'll have dinner after we've spoken with the doctor."

The captain escorted Doctor Smythe into the dining room. The Doctor wore the same clothing he had on during surgery; the smell was overpowering. "Sir, you asked to see me?"

The general answered, "His Highness The Duke of Cumberland has an interest, Doctor Smythe, in our patient William Ball. I believe you are treating him. Is that correct?"

"Yes, General, I am."

The duke leaned forward in his chair. "If I may, General?"

"Certainly, Your Highness."

"Doctor Smythe, what is William Ball's current condition?"

Doctor Smythe looked directly into Cumberland's eyes and then lowered his gaze to the floor. "Sir, I have amputated both of his legs above the knees. I found advanced gangrene in the left leg, which has spread to his right leg and his lower body and organs as well. He will not last the night. I've given him opium sufficient to deaden the pain."

"Ah, so the man did have injuries! Interesting. What do you suppose caused these injuries?"

"Difficult to say, sir. He may have been in combat, left for dead, and yet somehow managed to survive. When gangrene set in, his foot should have been amputated; it might have saved his life."

"Did he speak to you, Doctor Smythe?"

"No. He did mumble a bit; however, as the opium began its work, he slept and did not talk."

"He said nothing at all?"

The doctor paused for a moment. "Yes, he did say something. Let me think. He said, 'Janet, Janet.'"

"Janet, would that be his wife?"

"I have no idea, sir."

"Take me to him. I would have a word with him."

"Sir, he is on his way to the infirmary in Stronabaw. He is heavily medicated and would not be able to respond to you. I sent him on because we needed his bed for a soldier that we could treat. Soldier Ball is beyond any help I could give him."

"Damnation and curses upon you, doctor! I've finally caught up with the man, and you've set him free!"

Doctor Smythe stared at the duke in astonishment. "Your Highness, I am very sorry." The doctor spoke with genuine concern. "I can honestly say the soldier known as William Ball in all probability is dead by now. He was barely alive when he left here with his two escorts."

The duke angrily paced the floor. "You do not understand! He is not, nor has he ever been, the king's soldier, William Ball! He is a Jacobite spy and will find a way to get to his Cameron clan if possible. He was able to take the king's regiment to several Cameron houses when even I could not find them on the map. The jackass of a captain who sent him scouting was not suspicious when he returned and then led the regiment to the Cameron homes. It was meant to be an ambush, with Cameron Jacobites waiting to kill our soldiers, but by hell, they did not get it done!"

"Sir, he has only stumps and cannot mount a horse—or dismount, for that matter. He is under the influence of opium and will not know who or where he is."

The duke continued to pace. "I do not believe it; he is still capable of telling his clan members what course our plans will take.

He can speak, and you have confirmed that. You said he called out to 'Janet?"

"Yes, sir, he did."

"His wife, no doubt. Perhaps I can find her before he does."

No one spoke for a few minutes. Then the general said, "Doctor Smythe, will you join us for dinner? It is but a simple repast. Had I known we would be honored with Your Highness's presence, I would have a more elaborate meal to offer."

The doctor looked from one man to the other and thought of how he would rather not join them. However, he knew the choice was not his to make. "Thank you, General. I consider it an honor; please excuse me while I make myself more presentable. I'll have a change of clothing and return in a few minutes."

"Of course, doctor."

The general was pleased there would be a third person at the table. He thought about the duke's anger when he realized the soldier, or spy, was gone. Having the doctor join them might take some of the focus away from him. "Your Highness, is there any way I can be of assistance to you as you search for Charles Stuart? I personally believe, from what I hear, that he may be on his way to France."

William Augustus stirred in his chair and spoke emphatically. "I do not believe Charles will return to France, General. He failed to gain the throne. He made a promise to King Louis that he could not keep. I doubt the King of France would welcome his return. I certainly would not if I were he!" The duke continued, "I have received word that a full regiment has been assigned the task of searching for Stuart."

The three men sat at a table where a platter containing sliced roasted meat, cheese, and bread was passed to each one along with glasses of wine. The General responded, "Yes, Your Highness. In fact, we will be supplying horses and the latest maps, so surely they will be successful!" .

"General, you have an important task as commander of this fort, and I ask no more of you than what you are already doing. Thank you for your hospitality." The duke turned to Doctor Smythe, "Doctor, I beg your forgiveness for being outspoken about the Scotsman. My father, the king, has directed me to find and eliminate traitors and, of course, I am intent upon following his orders."

The doctor replied, "Your Highness, it is my pleasure to serve in your father's army."

The duke nodded, accepting the fealty. "I thank both of you for your loyalty to the king. I shall be on my way. I understand the hospital at Stronabaw is north of the Fort?"

"Yes, Your Highness. Look for the first cottage on your left after you pass the village. The old woman there speaks with a Scottish accent, but her father was a royal physician. She is caring for our wounded soldiers from Culloden. We sent them to her to heal after we patched their wounds. I've not met her, but I hear she can work miracles with tea and some herbs."

"My appreciation to you General, and Doctor Smythe." William mounted his horse and considered the options. 'I shall find the spy and force him to answer questions. After I kill him, I will learn who Janet is, and find her. She will compensate for the disloyalty of the Highlanders."

Chapter 51

"Aye, Lass, I'll ride along wi' ye, at least part of the way. It's nay safe for ye an' th' lad to be by yerselves—too many Johnnie Redcoats out an' about," Edward said.

"Thank ye, sir. It is most appreciated, but wha' of yer family?"

"My good wife an' bairns are wi' her family on Skye. She's a MacLeod from th' Isles, an' they've not had any part of th' goin's-on here."

Janet studied the man standing in front of her. "Mam, I'm nay a Jacobite, but I'm no' a traitor to Scotland either. I dinna believe a new king'd make enough difference to be worth th' fight. I'm a freeman in my thinkin' an' a Stewart by birth. I earn my livin' keeping peace in th' village an' dinna need to gi' loyalty to a clan chief to keep th' roof over my head or food on th' table. There're naught many Hielanders able to say so."

"Yer a Stuart?"

"I'm Edward Stewart, a different spellin' of th' name, an' no relation to Charles Edward Stuart. Unlike some who'd gladly claim kinship wi' th' prince, I'd nay claim him if we were related! Mam,

316

ye'll be as safe wi' me as if ye were wi' yer kin."

"Thank ye, Mr. Stewart. I'm pleased to know ye. I'm Janet Cameron. Yon sleepy lad an' I need of a bit of rest. Would it be possible to rest here?"

"Aye, an' I've a spot where ye'll be safe." Edward led Janet, Daniel, and Prince to stables behind the constable's quarters. He pointed to a large loft. "Ye an' th' laddie can pull th' ladder up, an' none will think to look over their heids. When did ye last eat?"

"Yesterday morn. Food would be most appreciated."

Janet led Prince to hay in the stable. "Daniel, we're safe here."

"Auntie, I'm hungry." He smiled when the constable brought in a tray with oatcakes, cups of stew, and a jug of milk. "I'm Daniel, an' I'm six years old. Wha' is yer name?"

"I'm Mr. Stewart. Pleased to meet ye, Daniel."

Janet noticed a pan with water, soap, and squares of soft flannel. "Thank ye for th' food, Mr. Stewart. We'll wash up, eat, an' rest a bit. We must be on our way before daylight. Wha' would be th' less-traveled way to reach a place to th' north of Fort William?"

"I'd say th' western Hieland path. It's a crofter's trail an' likely will be washed out by snowmelt. I'll travel wi' ye, as far as Kinlochleven. Then yer can travel 'round Fort William an' find yer way from there."

"Mr. Stewart, thank ye. My husband has been captured by a troop of th' king's soldiers. I overheard their plans to take him to Inverness. They said he's bound for New Zealand. The last we saw of him, he was barefoot an' walkin' behind a horse. I ha' to find him."

"Ah, ye've troubles. I'll help if I can. Ye an' the lad rest. We'll leave a'fore daybreak."

"I'm grateful to ye. Mayhap there'll be a way to return yer kindness."

Edward shook his head. "It's me who's doin' a kindness already done for mine."

Janet smoothed the hay, folded a blanket underneath Daniel's head, and they slept.

It seemed only minutes until she heard, "Miss Cameron, it'll be another hour a'fore th' sun rises. We need to be leavin'."

Janet woke Daniel and helped him down the ladder. "Good morning, Mr. Stewart. We slept well!"

Edward handed her a brown woolen coat and knitted cap. "They belong to Kate, my good wife. I've been thinkin', if ye'll tuck yer hair inside th' cap, ye might ha' a chance of 'em thinkin' yer a lad."

Janet smiled and said, "Thank you! Wi' my breeks an' brogans, I'll do well for th' rest of th' trip."

She pointed to Daniel. "Th' lad's breeks ha' several torn places. Would yer bairns ha' somethin' he might wear? I'd pay ye for 'em, an' th' coat."

Daniel was hopping on one foot and then the other. "Daniel, go to the privy a'fore ye let go wi'out meanin' to. It's outside th' stable door."

"Aye, Auntie. I liked sleepin' in a place wi' no rocks under my heid. Thank ye, Mr. Stewart, for th' loan of yer hay. I'll hurry, Auntie!" The boy was talking as he ran out the stable door.

Janet turned to Edward. "Sir, th' lad has lost his family; his father died at Culloden, an' his mother an' brothers died in a burnin' broch at th' orders of th' royal army."

"Ah, th' poor wee laddie! I'll see wha' I can find for him." Mr. Stewart returned with breeches, a cap, scarf, and mittens. "My Angus would be glad to share wi' th' lad."

He also had a small wooden pony fastened to a stand with four wheels. "It belongs to Angus, but he won't mind."

Daniel ran into the stable. "Auntie, I'd like to walk instead of ridin', please."

"Aye, laddie, ye may. Mr. Stewart will be goin' wi' us for part of th' way."

"Miss, my name is Edward."

"Aye, Edward, an' I'm Janet."

"Wha's yer name, little fellow?"

"Daniel, an' I'm th' oldest brother." Daniel stood on his tiptoes. "I'm th' biggest one too."

"Aye, tha' ye are, laddie. Now, see wha' I ha' for ye?" Edward handed Daniel the wooden toy.

"Thank ye, Mr. Stewart. Thank ye, sir!"

"Daniel, Mr. Stewart brought a cap, scarf, an' mittens for ye."

"I canna wait 'til Brian sees wha' I got!" Then he shook his head. "Nay, Auntie, Brian won't see, will he?"

Janet shook her head. "Aye, child, he won't."

"Daniel, Janet, be careful on this path! Some of it has washed away. A horse'll get through it better than we will. They're used to watchin' out for their footin'. Say, Daniel, how'd ye like to ha' four feet, instead of two?"

Daniel grinned. "I dinna know, sir. I fall down wi' two feet. If I had two more, mayhap I wouldn't fall down so much! I've never seen a horse fall down; I'd like to ha' four feet!"

Edward smiled. "Aye, laddie, I dinna think of it tha' way. Tell me, how many fingers do ye ha'? Can ye count?"

Daniel looked at his fingers. "I want to learn, sir."

"Good! I'll teach ye. Hold up yer right hand an' count like this." He started with his thumb. "One, two, three, four, five. Now, Daniel, ye count."

Daniel counted. "Laddie, yer just counted to five! Now do th' same thing wi' yer left hand.

"One, two, three, four, five. I did it, Mr. Stewart!"

"Good lad! We'd best watch th' path, laddie. When we stop, I'll show ye more countin'. Miss Janet, up ahead—" Edward pointed ahead to the path—"there'll be a burn alongside th' path, an' th' goin' gets rough. If we run into a troop of soldiers. I'll tell 'em ye an' th' lad are in my care, an' I'm takin' ye to yer family an' show 'em my constable's badge. Keep yer heid down, miss, an' Daniel, say not a word! I believe we could fool 'em.

Chapter 52

"Abby, do ye know where we are?"

"I think so. The river is in the distance, and this path leads to it. We don't want to cross it at night, or during the day for that matter; it's deeper than it looks. There's a bridge on the main road. Dare we travel over it? If so, we could be on the other side before daylight. Should we?"

Marie nodded her head. "Th' Bible says, 'Fear not, for I am wi' ye,' so I say th' bridge!"

"Agreed! Ahead is the gate to the road. Once we're through it, there'll be nowhere to hide until we're over the bridge. If we're separated, make your way to Perth. Ask for directions to James Dunsmuir's broch. If it's standing, then we've been spared. If not, go on to Edinburgh and seek Lord Murray."

"Aye, I will if need be, but I ha' faith."

They reached the gate, opened it, and passed through. Abby was right: the road was flat, and both sides were clear of brush and trees. "How far is the bridge, Abby? I'd like to know before we start."

"Marie, I do not know and can't even guess."

"Then we'll take it as it comes, an' th' De'il take th' hindmost!"

Marie and Abby nudged their horses into a gallop. They rode down the road, crossed the bridge, and did not stop until they could leave the road to rest.

Late that afternoon, they turned onto a path. Abby motioned for Marie to rein in her horse. "We did it, Marie!"

"Aye, but the difficult part is still ahead." A light mist wrapped them in cool air as they rode through the first pasture. It was nearly dark when they crossed the bridge leading to the courtyard's stables.

Abby called out, "Anyone here?"

A lad answered, "Aye! I'll take yer horse an' cart."

"There's only two horses. Is everyone inside?" "Aye, but for Farley and Bess, who's visitin' kin."

Abby took Marie's arm and led her up the stone walkway to the front door. Taking a deep breath, she opened the door and walked in. Abby motioned for Marie to follow her to the library, where she found Duny asleep with a book in his lap. Jamie was stretched out on his bed, snoring.

Meghan, propped up in Abby and James's bed, opened her eyes when Abby walked into the room. "Mother, you're home early!"

"Yes, Meghan, I am."

Megan looked at her mother. "Mother, what is the matter? You're as pale as a jug of milk!"

"Oh, Meghan, I've much to tell."

"Who is this with you?"

"A dear friend."

Meghan looked from her mother to the woman standing quietly beside her. "Mother! Something terrible has happened."

"Yes, it has. Give me a few minutes, and then I'll share my news with the three of you."

"Don't tell without me!" Meghan said as she dressed.

Abby called, "Come to the kitchen, lads. I'll make tea and see what there is to eat."

When Duny walked in, he smiled at his grandmother and said, "Gran, Jamie cooked some charred oatcakes. They're nay browned, they're burned! I dinna eat 'em, so there's plenty left."

Jamie spoke as he pulled on his boots, "I say they're nicely browned, Duny!"

"Hoot! They're burnt, tha's wha'!" Duny said, buttoning his shirt.

Marie stirred the peat coals and put another peat brick on the grate. Abby filled the teapot with hot water from the iron kettle, placed tea leaves in the pot, and covered it. She sliced potatoes and ham into a pot, added water, and put it on the grate. Tears filled her eyes. James was not here to take his place at the table. He would never do so again. Abby squared her shoulders, wiped her eyes, and stirred the food.

Jamie, Megan, and Duny sat at the table. "My dear children, first we'll eat, and then I'll tell you everything."

"Nay, Mother," Jamie said. "Yer very troubled. We need to know wha' has happened. Now, tell us."

"Yes, you do need to know. Let me introduce you to a dear friend. I've not known her a long time, but she has cared for me the same as family would. While she's not dressed as a nun, she is one, and her name is Marie."

Abby looked into each beloved face and felt profound sorrow. "Dear ones, James is dead." They listened quietly as Abby described how she and James were stopped by a troop of the king's royal army and one of the soldiers fired at James, hitting him in the shoulder.

"I thought the wound would heal, but he was hurt internally and died from loss of blood. I had to leave him lying there. It was the most difficult thing I've ever done." She spoke of Brian MacGregor providing a horse, as theirs had been taken by the soldiers. She described his request that she deliver messages to Edinburgh and how she promised she would do so. Abby explained she found the chapel and Marie provided a safe place for her to rest. Her family gathered her in their arms and sobbed.

Through tears, Jamie said, "I'll bring Da home for a decent burial. I'll not ha' him torn to bits by animals or defiled by one who stumbles on him."

"I knew you'd feel that way, Jamie." Abby looked at her son, whose expression was so much like his father's. "I'm so sorry I could not bring him home myself."

"Mother, I'm thankful ye had th' good sense to not try."

Duny was thoughtful. He remembered the dream he had about his grandfather lying still on the ground. How could he have dreamed of something before it happened?

"Mother," Meghan said, "John said there would be a bad time after the battle. Is this it?"

"Yes, it is. In the Highlands, complete destruction is taking place. You have no idea how relieved I am to find you all alive and the house still here."

Abby looked at them. "We know why the battle was lost. The weapons that were meant for the Highlanders were sold to the English Army. The priest at the chapel where I found Marie was a spy for the English; he smuggled crates of artillery across the border to England. When Brian MacGregor spoke of unarmed Highlanders who were killed on Culloden's moor, I began asking why they did not have weapons! I could not think of John or Ewan, either one, going into battle unarmed."

Megan spoke. "John had his pistol with him."

Duny agreed, "Father always carried a pistol. He wouldn't go to battle wi'out being armed."

Abby nodded her head. "Both Ewan and John have good sense. All we can do now is pray they are safe, wherever they are. After we've eaten, we'll discuss what to do."

She placed plates of potatoes, ham, and cheese on the table and handed each one a bowl of crumbled oatcakes with cream and honey. Jamie, Meghan, and Duny looked at one another. Finally Jamie spoke. "Mother, wi' ye holdin' up as well as ye are, we'll follow yer example. After all ye ha' been through, it's th' least we can do."

Megan asked, "Is there any word of John, Ewan, or Janet?"

"No, it could be weeks before we hear anything." Abby talked as she filled everyone's cups. "Jamie, bringing James home will be very, very difficult, and we must think about the risks. English troops are moving through the borders to the Highlands by the thousands. Bringing James home ..."

Abby paused and shook her head. She could not finish the sentence. "Also, there's messages from Brian MacGregor which must be delivered to Lord George Murray in Edinburgh. Marie's family may be able to help with this."

Marie spoke. "My family are nay Jacobites, but I canna say they're safe."

Abby turned to Duny and put her arm around him. "Duny, lad, it breaks my heart to not know about your mother and father, but we cannot lose any more of our family trying to find out."

She knew he wanted nothing more than to saddle his horse and ride as fast and hard as he could toward home. Abby looked at each one. "I expect each one of you to honor James Dunsmuir's memory by respecting my request that none of you will go to the Highlands to search for Ewan, Janet, or John! Will you give me your word that you won't?"

"Aye, mother, there are other things tha' must be taken care of."

"Thank you, Jamie. Now, what shall we do, and how do we go about it?"

"First, we must bring Father home an' lay him to rest," Jamie said. "How long will it take to reach him?"

"A full day, a night, and most of a second day's ride. You must travel on the most remote paths." Abby took a deep breath and continued, "Marie can draw a map from here to the chapel, and I'll prepare one from the chapel to where your Father is."

Jamie looked at his mother with eyes full of unshed tears. "I'll prepare a coffin for him, an' late this evening, I'll go."

"Jamie, you must understand the risks. Scotland's border country is full of soldiers on their way to the Highlands."

Duny thought of Jamie's task of bringing James home. "I'd like to come wi' ye, Jamie."

"I'll gi' it thought, Duny."

"He's my grandfather, ye know!" Duny replied, afraid Jamie would refuse.

"Aye, I know! But, there's th' danger of both of us goin'. Mother, speaking of danger, ye've been handin' out orders; I ha' one too. I dinna want ye an' Marie to start out for Edinburgh 'til I'm here to go wi' ye. Ye still speak as an English-bred lady. I'm wonderin' if we could pass for English gentry, take th' biggest cart wi' our matched pair of Shire horses, an' ride on th' road as if we're on our way to visit our English relatives who reside in Edinburgh?"

Jamie turned to Meghan. "Could ye travel? We won't go wi'out ye."

"Aye, I can, but be thinkin' of how we can get word to John of where we will be."

"Jamie." Abby rested her hand on his shoulder. "Your idea could be successful, but if we're stopped by soldiers, you must be silent. Your father's Scottish accent angered the soldiers. They seemed to calm down when I spoke. I'm too tired to think clearly, but I think it might be the answer."

She continued, speaking softly, "There's no need for a coffin for James; a shroud will suffice. Jamie, you'll need to take along crushed lime and look in your father's waist coat for a leather pouch with coins. I suppose it's still there."

"Aye, Mother. I'd already thought of th' lime, but I dinna want to say so. I'll look in his pockets, all of 'em."

Jamie turned to Duny. "Do ye think ye can manage this?"

"I can, an' besides, ye'll need help watchin' out for th' bloody Redcoats."

"Aye, then get th' knapsacks ready wi' food an' water, Mother, ye an' Marie draw out th' map. Meghan, if ye will, stitch together th' edges an' bottom of a linen bed cover. I'll saddle th' horses an' clean an' load our pistols. At dark, th' English soldiers will be in camp for th' night. Wi' any luck, early in th' morn we'll cross th' bridge. Now, dinna fash yerselves if we're not back for several days. Duny, ye'll take Tanner, an' I'll ride Leather."

Abby looked up. "Leather? Which horse is that?"

"I've been trainin' him myself. He's Lady Love's foal. Like Tanner, he's a purebred Highland pony. Their sire is Light Foot, an' those two ponies can run as fast as th' wind can blow. If we had to journey to th' Hielands, those two horses would get us there an' back. Mother, dinna gi' me tha' look. I only made a passin' remark."

Chapter 53

Ewan lifted his head. He knew where he was. Through the veil of whisky, opium and sickness, he remembered. Janet and Duny were riding beside him; Bran trotted between the horses. It was time to leave them; he could go no farther. Before he closed his eyes for the last time, he looked once more at his beloved wife and son. His spirit, longing to be free of pain, began the separation process.

Soldiers riding on either side of Ewan thought he was asleep and tied the reins around his waist.

"Good evening, men. I am The Duke of Cumberland. Is this the soldier known as William Ball?"

"Yes, Your Highness," both men answered. "He's sleeping, sir. He had both legs removed a few hours ago."

"Ah, he is the one I seek. Step aside!" The duke dismounted. "Soldier Ball, I order you to sit up, now!"

The duke grabbed the horse's reins and the animal reared, throwing Ewan to the ground. The soldiers looked at the pitiful remains of the man lying there. "Aw, Willie's passed on. He was a good soldier, he was."

"A good soldier, my ass! The bastard was a damned Cameron Highlander! He and his clan fought to rob my father of his kingship! I find you both guilty of high treason. You have provided protection for a Jacobite!"

The duke drew his sword and ran it through the first soldier. The second soldier began running, but the duke shot him. He placed Ewan's body on one of the horses and roped it to the saddle. Before kicking the soldiers' bodies off the road, he stripped off their uniforms. Naked, they would be unknown thieves, set upon by other thieves.

When he reached the infirmary cottage, he pulled Ewan's body to the front door and kicked it open. Several soldiers were lying on blankets spread on the floor. He placed the body beside a sleeping man. "Who goes there? Dinna be kickin' my door! I'll be throwin' scaldin' hot water on yer tail as ye go back out. Now, wha' is this great lump on my floor?"

Bowing low, William Augustus said, "Madam, this is Willie Ball, one of the king's soldiers. He's passed out from too much drink. It's best to let him sleep it off. He's lost both legs to battle injuries. Whatever needs to be done for him is to be done."

"Well, leave him, an' I'll look to him when I can."

Mary covered the man with a blanket and turned to the one who brought him. "Yer did yer duty. I'm nay entertainin' company, so be gone wi' ye!"

"Why, you sharp-tongued old bitch!" Angry, the duke lifted his hand. Then he remembered the general saying the old woman was a healer and her father had been physician to the king.

He lowered his arm and said, "I apologize. I am very tired and need a place to rest. I have a few coins I could give you if you can find room."

"I dinna want it said I turned a body away. Find yerself a spot in the corner, an' I'll fetch ye a bun an' water in a while."

One of the men stirred and coughed. "Now, laddie, I'll bring ye a

328

cup of tea wi' a little somethin' in it to help wi' th' cough. Martha, make tea an' put some honey in it. Bring it along, an' ... Oh! My dear God!"

Mary fell to her knees. "My dearest laddie, Ewan, it canna be ye. Nay, nay! Not him!"

Mary touched his face; it was cool. "This canna be. How can my dear Ewan be wearin' th' red coat of an English soldier? Could it be someone who looks like him? Martha, fetch th' lamp!"

"Mary, wha' ye goin' on fer? He's just another soldier tha' ha' gone on to his heavenly reward. We'll gi' him a lift to th' shed, an'—"

"Nay! He's not a Johnnie Redcoat! He's a Cameron, a fine Hielander! I dinna know why he's wearing th' red an' brass o' th' king's army, but I tell ye, he's nay one o' 'em."

The duke swore under his breath. Feigning sleep, he listened.

"He smells of rotted flesh. Oh! His legs ha' been amputated."

Mary pulled away the flannel pads and turned aside, holding her apron to her nose. "Ahh, how th' laddie suffered! I'd say he left us only a few hours ago."

Angry, Mary said, "This God-awful, terrible battlin' must stop. I'm sick to death tryin' to mend bodies tha' ha' been torn apart because some bloody fool wants to sit his arse on th' golden throne in England. I dinna care if he shits silver an' gold, it's not worth this!"

"Now, now, Mary, we'll get ye a tot of whisky." Martha steadied Mary while leading her to the kitchen, where she sat down.

Martha placed a cup of whisky in front of her. "If I drink all this, ye'll be pitchin' me in th' bed, an' there're others tha' need doctorin' between now an' mornin'. I'd best get my head cleared an' get on wi' wha's to be done. Come along, an' we'll get wha's left of th' dear laddie to th' shed."

Martha helped Mary wrap Ewan in a blanket, and together they carried the body through the shed door. "Put him in th' far corner," Mary said, "Away from th' rest of 'em."

They returned to the cottage and began scrubbing stains on the floor. "Oh! I wonder wha' happened to Janet an' their laddie."

The man sitting in the corner of the room heard the name he wanted to hear. The old woman knew her. He pulled his black cloak around his shoulders, over his head, and melted into the shadows.

Death was waiting for Ewan. "Ewan Cameron, come with me. I'll keep you company until ... ah, Elight has arrived."

The angel took Ewan's hand. He looked at his legs and feet shimmering in a soft golden light. He felt wonderful, but could not leave until he said good-bye. "I ha' one request. Please, may I tell my wife good-bye?"

Elight smiled. "Yes, and she will hear you, Ewan. I promise."

Chapter 54

Janet felt a hand resting lightly on her shoulder. A voice whispered in her ear, "My darlin' wife, I'll love ye forever. I must leave ye now. Tell our lad an' lassie tha' their da loves 'em."

She felt a soft kiss on her cheek. Then the voice and touch were gone. Dizzy, Janet stumbled.

"Auntie, watch th' path!"

"Daniel, did ye hear someone speakin?"

"Nay, Auntie."

Then Janet knew Ewan had said good-bye. "Miss Janet, are ye nay feelin' well? We can stop if need be."

"Edward, I need to sit down for a minute. May I ha' a drink of water an' a bite?"

Edward brought her a flask of watered wine with an oatcake.

"Mr. Stewart," Daniel asked, "May I ha' somethin' to eat too?"

"Here, lad, it's a bit of treacle candy. It'll melt in yer mouth. Ha' ye tasted treacle candy a'fore?"

"Oh, aye, Mr. Stewart. My mam made it for me an' my brothers. She said to eat it before it melts."

"Tha's a good lad, Best to eat it before it melts."

Janet thought of Ewan's words to her. *He asked me to take care of our lad and lassie. I'm carryin' a sister for Duny!* Janet placed her hand on her belly, knowing that a bit of herself and Ewan was there, safe from harm.

"Edward, I'm feeling better now. Daniel, do ye want to ride for a while?"

"Nay, Auntie, ye ride. I'll walk wi' Mr. Stewart. He's goin' to teach me more about countin'. Will ye, Mr. Stewart?"

"Aye, laddie, I will." The two counted as they walked down the path. Janet swayed with the movements of the horse. She closed her eyes and thought about Ewan's touch and kiss. As they climbed upward, heavy, dark clouds moved across the sky. Ahead, mountain peaks towered above the ancient Mamore Forest where massive oaks grew. They traveled on a path through high pastures with sheep grazing on spring grass. For a brief moment, sunlight shone through the clouds. Then the scattered rays dimmed and disappeared, leaving behind a bit of warmth which diminished as a sharp, cold wind blew rain into their faces.

Daniel stumbled. "Laddie, yer sleepy?"

"Aye, sir." Daniel shivered. "An' I'm cold."

Janet dismounted, lifted Daniel into the saddle, and tucked a blanket around him. Ahead was the West Highland trail that would take them through the lonely moors to Fort William.

Edward considered Janet as she walked beside him. *I canna leave her to go th' rest of th' way alone. She'll not get past th' fort wi'out runnin' into soldiers. I dinna believe her husband is still alive. His Cameron chieftain was a Jacobite, a sure death sentence.* Edward tamped tobacco into his pipe. As he prepared flint to light it, he thought of his wife and sons on Skye. After seeing that Janet and Daniel were safe, he'd travel there.

In the shadows of the High Glens, darkness came early. In the distance, the highest peak in the Glens, Blara Chaorann, towered over the foothills. After reaching it, they would begin the downward descent to the Nevis Forest, where they'd cross the Nevis River. The king's army rarely traveled this path, but one had to be watchful.

"Edward, where are we?"

"We're north of Kinlochleven not far from th' Nevis Forest. I'll stay wi' ye, missus, 'til we reach where yer goin'."

"Edward, thank ye for yer kindness."

As they climbed Blara Chaorann, Janet thought it felt as if she was at the very top of the world and could touch the sky if she tried.

Chapter 55

Abby walked to the barn where restless horses were stamping and whinnying. She checked the hay mangers. They were full, and the trough had plenty of water. For some reason, they all were uneasy. Abby decided they should put out the lights in the broch and dampen down the fires, with only the peat kitchen fire burning just enough to give a little light and warmth.

Marie met her at the door. "It's too dark to finish my knittin', and we're all on edge. Even th' house cat's hidin'! Did ye see or hear anythin' outside?"

"No. However, the horses are not settling down either. Marie, help me pull these shutters together."

"Let's take turns wi' a night watch, Abby," Marie said, pulling her shawl around her shoulders. "I'm nay expectin' trouble, but ... well ..."

Abby interrupted, "I know why we're restless. Jamie and Duny should be home before the night is over. Marie, think about it. The master of the house is on his way home! It's the last trip he'll make."

Abby found Meghan in the kitchen eating bread with jam. "How are you feeling?"

"I'm miserable, Mama. My back's paining so much that I can't sit still. When I get up, I pee myself. There's a puddle in the floor and on my slippers."

Abby hugged Meghan. "You do know your water will break before th' bairn is born?"

"Aye, I know. I wish John could be here. I can't sit still, and I don't feel like sleeping either."

"Poor dear. I promise when the babe is born, you'll forget all of this. Your father was so proud of the three of you. He carried each one of you to the barn to see the horses when you were only days old!"

Abby's voice broke, and she wiped her eyes. "I never took the time to realize how much I'd miss him if something happened. I thought he'd always be here."

She spooned tea leaves in the teapot, poured hot water over them, and set out the china cups and a tin of biscuits from the cupboard. They sat together in darkness, drinking tea and listening to the wind blowing tree branches against the windows.

"'Tis an ill wind tha' blows no good," Marie said as she came into the kitchen. "I can't sleep. I've gone to bed twice. I close my eyes, an' then I'm wide awake. I heard th' clock chime nine times an' decided I'd come downstairs. Are th' two of ye keepin' one another company an' a third would be one too many?"

"No, of course not. Do you want a cup of tea, or mayhap something a bit stronger?"

"Aye, is there a spot of brandy?"

"Yes." Abby went to the china cabinet. "There's brandy, sweet mead, last year's malt whisky, and claret. James buys the brandy, claret, and mead, but the whisky is made here."

"Let's bring it all out an' see wha' strikes our fancy, shall we?" Marie said as she moved the bottles to the kitchen table. "I usually ha' only a tot, but this evenin', well, we'll see."

Abby poured Marie a cup of brandy and a cup for herself. "Meghan, will you have something?"

"Yes, Mama, watered wine, please."

"Meghan, you and I are alike, while Janet and Jamie are like your Father. You know the story of how your father spoke with the queen for my hand?"

"Yes, Mama, I do, an' I think Jamie's idea of us being a fine English family traveling to Edinburgh to visit our English relatives, is likely the only way we'd get by."

"Hmmm, we might be able to carry it off. Instead of hiding, going through brush and bramble, we ride in our best carriage with the matched Shire horses, dressed in our finest gloves, hats, and parasols, holding our heads high. Now, let me think. Who would we be visitin' in Edinburgh?"

Marie spoke. "I'm not too proud of it, bein' Scottish myself, but I ha' an auntie by marriage who is a distant kin of th' Hanoverian King George. Auntie is from Osnabruck, Germany. I wonder ..." Marie did not finish her sentence.

Abby said, "I think that would be the best way, Marie. Jamie and Duny could be our men-at-arms, and Marie, you and I'd be relatives of your auntie and uncle. What are their names?"

"Margaret an' Robert Wakefield; Rob's a barrister in th' Edinburgh High Court. He's a fine fellow, dressed in his robes an' powdered wig. It's rumored he'll be th' next judge of th' High Court."

"Would we dare give it a try?" Abby poured another cup of brandy for herself and Marie.

"Why not?" Marie said. "Might as well be shot for bein' a thoroughbred as a jackass, I'd say!"

They all giggled. "Sorry, Abby, tha' was a poor choice of words."

"No, Marie, hatching this plan is keeping my mind busy. I must deliver those messages to Lord Murray, and we'll manage it one way or the other. Excellent brandy, Marie. Pass your cap—er, cup—and we'll have another."

They continued planning while the hours passed. Just after midnight, two riders approached; Jamie and Duny were back with the remains of James Dunsmuir. They placed the shrouded body in a sheltered place inside the barn, turned the restless horses out to pasture, and went inside where Abby, Megan, and Marie sat waiting.

Abby greeted them. "Lads, we're glad you're home. We're planning a trip to Edinburgh, to visit our English and German relatives. Our dear cousin Marie here, is visiting us and wishes to return to her home in Edinburgh, We'll accompany her and visit our relatives who live there as well.

Abby stood and gestured with her hands toward Marie and Meghan. She swept around the room, holding her skirt off the floor and her nose in the air. "Of course, we're all relatives by marriage to King George, who, of course, is related to all of us—by marriage, of course."

"Mother." Jamie shook his head. "I'm havin a hard time keepin' up wi' yer reasonin'. Do I understand tha' we're goin' to Edinburgh to return Marie, who is related to King George? Is this true?"

Abby nodded. "Of course! That is what I said, exactly! We'll work out the rest of the details later. Now, Jamie, where is your father?"

"In the barn. It's just as ye said; we'll need to bury him on th' morrow. Is there someone who can say th' blessin'?"

"We'll ask Marie to read from scripture and say the Lord's Prayer. Later, when we can, we'll have a proper headstone engraved. We'll lay him to rest beside his mother and father. Lads, tell us about the trip. Are you hungry? There's boiled eggs and bread. Anyone care to join me?"

Everyone nodded. She poured ale into flasks and set the kitchen table for a meal, saying, "It'll be a while before I can set at the high board without James beside me."

"Mother, after wha' Duny an' I ha' seen, we're very fortunate to be sittin' here in our broch."

Abby nodded. "Yes, th' Scotland we're used to is no more. I don't understand why the king's army have been ordered to destroy families and homes. Your father was a peaceful man and I will never understand why he was killed. In the meantime, Jamie, we'll want to let the villagers know. They thought well of him and will want to be at the service."

"I'll go to the village in th' mornin'. We'll ha' th' burial at noon an' tell 'em afterward to seek safety wherever they can."

Jamie lowered his voice and turned to Marie. "We passed th' chapel yer described, but there's no windows or spire. They even upended th' headstones in th' kirkyard."

Jamie looked at his mother. "Wha' about th' horses? It'd be better to sell 'em than th' English takin' 'em."

Abby said, "Jamie, your father would like it if we gave the animals to the people who worked with him for so long."

"Aye, he would, Mother." Abby hugged her son as he wiped tears from his eyes.

"I forgot to tell ye we met Brian McGregor. He ga' me another packet an' asked me to gi' ye his condolences." Jamie sat beside his mother and put his arm around her. "Brian said tha' none of th' Cameron clan on th' front line survived. An English soldier told him so."

Abby asked, "We'd not know for certain, would we?"

"Nay, we won't. It'll be a while before we do. Meghan, th' news is better concerning John. Brian said tha' most of th' MacIntyre clan were spared as they were on horseback an' off th' battlefield when th' end came. I dinna know where John is, but I'll wager wherever he is, he'd rather be here."

"I hope it is so, Jamie," Megan said.

Abby filled the cups with brandy. "We'll sort through things and bury what we cannot take with us. Two days from now, we'll leave with our dear cousin Marie, who is related to His Royal Highness King George."

Abby took a big gulp of brandy. "We're going to stay with our relatives in Edinburgh until things calm down. You never know about people. Those who are nearly royalty, such as ourselves, cannot be too careful, of course." For the first time since she returned home, Abby smiled.

The next morning, the villagers and family gathered in the chapel. After the service, the group walked to the cemetery, where a wooden cross carved with "James Dunsmuir, b. 1689 d. 1746" marked the place where he lay. Sister Marie read scripture, and James Dunsmuir's family and friends bade husband, father, grandfather, and friend good-bye. On the way back to the broch, Meghan clutched her mother's arm and cried out, "Mother, help me."

"Jamie, get her to the house and up the stairs to the big bed. Duny, go to the attic, find the cradle, and bring it downstairs. Marie, in the storage room in a trunk by the window are linen pads, nappies, and gowns. I should have been paying more attention, Meghan. I'm sorry I'm not better prepared, but it won't take long. Jamie, I need you to put water on for tea, and bring the rocking chair up from the kitchen, will you?"

Abby, the midwife, felt Meghan's belly. "Just as it should be, firm and laboring to be rid of its precious burden."

Abby propped her daughter's knees open and placed pillows under each one. "Now, Meghan, you have some very, very hard pains yet to come, and you'll truly understand why they call this 'labor.' When you feel like pushing down, push as hard as you can."

"Abby," Marie said, "It'll be a while a'fore I'm needed. I'll be in th' kitchen makin' supper."

Marie passed Duny and Jamie on the staircase, one with the chair and the other with a cradle. As Abby said, the pains increased, and Meghan began bearing down. "Mother! The babe is—"

"Meghan, push as hard as you can. Then take a deep breath and push again and again."

"Oh, my God, Mother! I'll never again lie wi' a man—" The words stopped while she screamed.

"Meghan, your babe's head is here, and I'm easing the shoulders out. Here's an arm, and another, and, oh, how wonderful! Meghan, you and John have a fine laddie!"

Abby cleaned the mucus from the babe's mouth, which brought a loud, protesting cry. Then the cry turned into a yelp as the newborn was held up for all to see.

"Marie, could you please help me?" Abby called from the top of the stairs.

"Aye, wha' can I do?"

"Bathe the babe. Then wrap him in a blanket while I help Meghan finish the birthing."

As soon as the afterbirth was received, inspected, and wrapped in a cloth to be buried, Abby carefully cleansed Meghan and changed the pads underneath her. Marie helped Meghan sit up and put the babe in her arms. The little lad's mouth found its way to the plump softness.

"It's a fine job yer ha' done, an' I'm proud of ye, Meghan," Marie said. "I've heard it said tha' a cup of ale is good for a nursin' mother an' th' one who aids in th' birthin'. Abby, if ye'd rather, I'll bring ye a dram of whisky instead."

"No, Marie, my imbibing last night has caused me more than a little discomfort today. I'll have a cup of tea instead, thank you.

"Marie, we laid our dear James to rest today. But, praise God, we've added a fine grandson to the family. James would be so proud! Meghan, have you thought of a name for your little laddie?"

"Aye, Mother. John and I decided on John's father's name, Aaron George MacIntyre. Are you terribly disappointed that he's not named after Father?"

"No, Meghan. You must honor John's wishes for his firstborn son."

Abby looked at her new grandson. "Ah, what a darling babe you are! Meghan, he's perfect!"

Abby laid the newborn on a soft blanket in the crib and moved it beside the bed. The little lad slept with his mother's hand touching him. "Marie, Megan needs rest now. When she's ready, we'll give thanks and christen this babe. Jamie'll be Aaron's godfather. Marie, will you help with a christening?"

"Aye, I believe I can manage an acceptable one."

"Now we can begin planning for the trip to Edinburgh. Be thinking about it."

"I already ha', Abby. I'll be yer lady-in-waitin' an' nurse to th' wee lad."

"Good, excellent! Keep your mouth shut. The first time you said a word it'd be done for us."

"Bosh an' bother! Fine English ladies often ha' Scottish maids!" Marie smiled at Abby.

Chapter 56

"Edward, I'll take my turn walkin'."

"Nay, I came alon' fer th' walk!" Edward smiled at Janet, "I think I've placed where we're goin. Would there be a cottage sittin' alon' side a sheep shed?"

"Aye, there is, Edward. How do ye know of it?"

"I've taken more than one fellow ter th' lady for treatment of a wound."

"Mary's known far an' wide for her healin' skills. I stayed wi' her several days learnin' from her. I could've stayed for weeks an' still not know all she does. Edward, my husband is not alive, but I know no more than tha'."

Edward shook his head. "I dinna think he lived, but I knew yer believed otherwise."

"He told me farewell."

"Ah, he did! Missus, he'd naught rest easy 'til he did. We'll rest an' ha' a bite."

"Edward, does this road lead to Stronabaw?"

"Nay, we'll come to a crossroads an' turn to th' right, goin' north. We're close to Fort William, and I'm expectin' to meet a troop of soldiers. At the crossroads, Daniel will ride, an' I'll walk beside ye."

Janet nodded and shivered as she thought about meeting English soldiers on the road. She did not frighten easily, but after Ewan's capture, she knew they were not safe anywhere in Scotland.

Now there was no need for her to travel to Inverness. How fortunate they were that Edward helped them. She thought of Laird Ian Douglas, who depended on no one to tell him what he had to do or not do. *If I could, that's how I'd be, like him an' Edward. I'd make up my own mind an' not be bound to anyone.*

At Mary's cottage she'd sleep in a bed and sit in the rocking chair by the fire. *Dear Lord, I'd like to know how Ewan died an' where he lies. I dinna know where to start lookin', an' I place my trust in ye. Father, thank ye for keepin' us safe. In Jesus's name, I pray. Amen.*

Several hours passed before the crossroads sign came into view. "Janet, a'fore we move into th' open, I'll ha' a look see." Soon he returned. "If we're stopped, I'm th' constable an' ye an' th' laddie are my charges to deliver to Inverness. Dinna say a word, an' keep yer heid down." Before long, a uniformed soldier stopped them.

"Disembark and identify yourselves."

"Sir, I'm Constable Stewart overseeing th' legal transfer of two lads to their family in Inverness. Their father, a soldier in th' king's army, has been sent to Germany an' their mother is deceased."

"Are you or the lads in any way connected to the Jacobites, or the uprising?"

"I am not. They are but young lads."

"Do you have the lawful order transferring them?" "I do. Lads rest by th' tree there while I get the papers." Edward rummaged in his knapsack and brought out papers which he handed to the soldier who looked them over carefully. "Constable, all appears to be in order. Proceed on then."

"Aye, Sir."

They continued on their way.

"Edward, I canna tell ye wha' was goin' through my mind! Wha' papers did the soldier see an' where did ye get 'em?" Edward smiled.

"Miss, I made 'em up a'fore we left. Best to take no chances. I did th' same for Katie an' th' bairns when I took 'em to Skye."

"I'm still shakin'. Edward, thank ye for bein' prepared. I'd nay ha' thought of papers."

Several hours later, they traveled through the village near Mary's cottage. "Edward, there's Mary's cottage. They tied Prince to the front gate and walked up the path.

Janet knocked on the front door; Mary called out, "Hold on, I'm gettin' there."

When she opened the door, Janet stepped into the room and hugged her. "Oh, my word! Come in, come in!"

Janet stopped when she saw men covered with blankets lying on the floor. She touched Mary's shoulder. "Mary, Edward traveled wi' me. An' here is Daniel, Gordon's son. I've much to tell ye."

Mary pointed to Edward. "I remember ye, sir. Ye ha' been to my cottage a'fore, ha' ye not?"

"Aye, this time I dinna bring a man for ye to patch up."

"Is yer name Stewart?" Mary paused and looked at Edward. "Aye, yer a Stewart. There's th' fair hair wi' a bit of red cast an' blue eyes, an', if ye'll pardon me for sayin', a long, pointy nose."

Edward smiled in spite of himself. "Aye, madam, it's Edward Stewart, an' this is Missus Cameron's nephew, young Daniel. He's a bonny fine lad an' has learned to count to twenty."

Daniel looked at Mary, "I'll show ye!" Daniel counted to twenty.

Mary smiled. "I'm proud of ye, laddie. I've some biscuits tha' need to be eaten, an' ye look like th' one ter do it. Come wi' me."

Mary sat Daniel at the table with a cup of milk and a plate of ginger biscuits. A dark shape in the corner of the room stirred and arranged his cloak so he could see. He saw the old woman and caught a glimpse of red hair and fair skin.

344

Mary motioned for Janet and Edward to follow her. She opened the door and led the way outside to the shed. "Janet, it'll be a shock to ye, an' it pains me more than ye'll ever know to tell ye this—"

"Mary! Do ye ha' Ewan's body here?"

Mary grabbed Janet's arm. "Aye, I do. I canna tell ye how it's so, but he's wearin' a king's army uniform. Now, I must tell ye a'fore ye see him, he died from gangrene. He had an injury to his legs, an' that's where it started. Janet, love, I'll understand if ye choose to not see him." Mary stopped with a startled look. "How did ye know he'd died?"

"Oh, dear one, ye know how I am. Ewan came to me a day ago an' said good-bye. I dinna know where I'd find him, but I knew he was no longer alive."

Mary opened the shed door and led Janet through a row of bodies waiting for burial. Janet shuddered. She remembered this experience. It was exactly as she had seen it: bodies on the floor, the smell of death. Mary gently pulled a blanket back. Janet looked down at Ewan's face. He wore a filthy Redcoat with brass buttons. The stench was overwhelming. She stifled a cry and then reached down and pulled the blanket up, leaving only his face uncovered. She smoothed his hair, touched his mouth, kissed his cheek, pulled the blanket over him, and stood.

"Janet, he died a'fore he was brought here. He must ha' suffered terribly, wi' his flesh dyin' little by little an' th' poison movin' through his body." Mary wiped away a tear.

"Ah, Mary, it dinna touch his spirit, for he bade me farewell. Only I heard his voice,", .

"Come, sit down. I ha' things to tell ye." Mary led Janet to the kitchen, where she cleared the table and filled three cups with whisky. "Edward, ye might as well hear this. Sit yerself down."

In the corner, darkness watched the three at the table. "I'll tell ye wha' I know of Ewan an' his last days. He went by th' name of Willie Ball. He was well thought of enough tha' they sent him here. If he'd been nobody, they'd not cared one way or th' other. Th' question is, why was Ewan Cameron wearin' th' red coat of an English soldier? I'm thinkin' he had nay a choice. Tell me about th' rest of th' Cameron kin. I hear th' Hielanders marched to their graves at Culloden."

"Aye, Ewan buried Thomas, Gordon, and Duncan there. Gordon's wife an' their three lads died when th' English soldiers burned Glen Lochy. Ewan was captured as we were on th' way back from takin' Anne an' her bairns to th' borders. I dinna know wha' happened after tha'. I knew I'd find him. Gordon's son—" Janet nodded toward Daniel—"is th' last of his family. Edward, yer wife an' bairns are safe on Skye. I know naught of my family." Janet covered her face with both hands.

"An, my dear, yer carryin' a babe, aren't ye?"

Janet looked into Mary's eyes. "Aye, how did ye know?"

"I knew when I looked at yer face. Best for ye to come to bed. Yer past bein' tired."

Edward placed Daniel on the bed beside Janet. Mary covered them with a comforter and closed the door. Edward slept on the floor, and Mary slept in her chair.

In the darkness he did not sleep. When the fire burned down, he made his way to the door, opened it, and walked out. Edward woke when he felt a chill wind blow over him. He looked out the tiny window and shivered when he saw footprints leading from the cottage into darkness. William Augustus crossed the field to a tree where his horse was tied. In the top of the tree a large bird roosted with his head tucked under his wing. "Clamhan, awaken. I have need of your eyes."

The bird's head slowly appeared; its eyes focused on the man standing below him. "I am at your service, sir. What is it you wish to see?"

"I have need for a lone cottage that will not attract attention."

The great bird spread his wings and soon was over the

Highland moors which reached to the sea. "Sir, will this meet your needs?"

With closed eyes, William stood by the tree listening to the whispery voice in his ears. Now he could see the same sight the bird did. "Ah, yes, an empty shepherd's croft is perfect, Clamhan."

"Then I will return and wait for you. When will you need me, sir?"

"It will be several days. Clamhan, what must I do to not be observed by those in the cottage?"

"Sir, you need only to cover yourself with your cloak. It will be all the protection you need."

"Will another be unseen if close to me?"

"Yes, but be sure all is covered."

Mary spoke quietly with Janet about readying Ewan's body for burial. "Love, there's nay much we'll do other than sew a seam on th' blanket coverin' him."

"Mary, would you look in his pockets to see if there's anything?"

"Aye, I will."

"He was wearin' a cross around his neck when he was taken. Please see if it's still there. It's time I tell Daniel about him."

Janet sat in the rocking chair with Daniel on her lap. She struggled to explain Ewan's death. Because she knew so little, she simply said that he was no longer alive. Daniel did not cry. He held Janet's hand and looked into her eyes with sad eyes of his own. Late that afternoon, Ewan Cameron was laid to rest on the gentle slopes of Aonach Mor Glen. Edward said the Lord's Prayer, and Janet placed a flower of the Scottish thistle on the grave. Daniel stood between Mary and Janet, clutching their hands. None of them shed tears; they could not. While they were burying Ewan, The Duke of Cumberland wrapped his cloak around himself and sat in a chair by the fire. They returned to Mary's cottage, taking no notice of him there. William smiled to himself, relishing the protection he had.

When they returned to the cottage, Martha had tea and biscuits ready. "A courier from th' fort stopped by. He asked about th' two soldiers who escorted Ewan an' said they did'na return to th' fort. He asked about Willie Ball. I hold him tha' Willie died an' we buried him because of th' shape he was in. The soldier said tha' no one knew anythin' about Willie other than his name. The courier also said tha' Mary's cottage will be spared because of nursin' th' king's soldiers. He took th' rest of th' bodies in th' shed, an' the place is empty now."

Mary sniffed the air. "My dears, I caught a whiff of th' smell when a lightnin' bolt strikes. Do ye smell it, Janet?"

Janet sniffed and shook her head. "Mary, yer smellin' damp peat. Here, let's stoke th' fire an' make Daniel a bowl of porridge. Are ye hungry, lad?"

"Aye. I'd like honey wi' it, please?" Mary stirred honey into the porridge and filled a bowl for Daniel.

Edward motioned for Janet and Mary to follow him into the front room. "I'll leave on the morrow an' travel to Skye, where Kate's family lives. Janet, if yer willin', I'll take both ye an' the lad wi' me where ye'll be safe. Mary, if ye'd like to join us, ye'll be welcome. It's nay my intention to frighten ye, but ye live in th' Hielands, an' I fear those who dinna know yer value will ha' no respect for ye. Think about it an' let me know."

Mary looked at Janet. "I'll not leave, but ye've a babe an' th' little lad to think about."

"Mary, I've already decided. I'll go wi' Edward. It's still Scotland, but is removed from th' strife an' troubles here. I'll worry about ye. If they depend on ye ter heal their injured, they might leave ye alone."

"Aye. I'll fix an' mend their bodies, but while I do, I can think anythin' I want! Besides, I believe I'll stay it out to see wha' happens. Ye never know wha' turn things'll take, now do ye?"

Janet took Mary's hands in her own. "Mary, yer doin' wha' ye know's right for ye."

Janet poured a cup of tea, added a pinch of dried mint, and

stood in front of the fire sipping from her cup. "I'll mend Daniel's stockin's an' breeks."

"Well, then I'll pack th' knapsacks. Bring 'em to th' kitchen, an' I'll get started."

They would leave at dawn the next morning.

Chapter 57

In the night, darkness gathered and moved to the bed chamber where Janet slept. He picked her up in his arms and wrapped the black cloak around both of them. Asleep, she did not waken. The night was still with a new moon, no stars and deep shadows. The duke mounted his horse with her in his arms. *She is with child, a Highland Cameron child. I will shackle her and sit her in a cart pulled behind my horse as I complete my duties here. Perhaps the people of this sodden country will begin to understand the power of England, my father, and me. Her hair loose and tangled, torn, ragged clothing, and the belly of a breeding woman—let them look at her and know that once she belonged with them, but now she belongs to me.*

Janet opened her eyes. There were strong odors of sweat and horse. She forced her body to stay limp. After a very long time, the horse stopped, and the rider dismounted, still holding her enveloped in darkness. He kicked open a door and threw her onto a hard, damp floor. When she opened her eyes, he said, "Ah, you are awake. I apologize for the roughness of this hovel, but then, we are not here for comfort. Do you know who I am?"

Janet sat up and looked at him. She knew who he was. He was the one who led the king's army against the Highlanders. He watched as she looked at the rough rock walls and dirt floor. "I am a patient man, but I expect an answer to my question. Would you like to know why you are here? I can explain it so even a simple wench such as yourself can understand."

William reached for her arm and pulled her up until she was standing. He was surprised when she looked him straight in the eyes. "Do you not fear me, madam?"

Janet did not answer. William grabbed her arm and shook her. "I said, do you not fear me, wench? Answer me when I talk to you!" Quietly, Janet stood looking at him.

"I'll tell you who I am and why you are here. I am The Duke of Cumberland!" He walked away and then turned toward her with his fist clenched. "You are a Jacobite! I abhor you along with your husband and all of his fellow Highlanders and their families. I want them to know I have, in my possession, the Cameron wife of a Highlander."

He stood in front of her, gathered saliva in his mouth, and spat in her face. She did not flinch but gathered the hem of her nightgown to wipe the spittle away. It was very cold in the cottage, and she had only her cambric gown to cover her nakedness. She watched as he arranged logs in the cottage's fire pit. Somehow, a tiny yellow flame appeared and spread until the logs began burning, the smoke writhing toward the hole in the ceiling. He spoke softly as he took a bottle of whisky from a large knapsack. "We will share this while we learn more about each other."

He tipped the bottle up and drank deeply, wiping his mouth on his sleeve. He offered the bottle to her. She took it but did not drink. She considered what would happen if she threw some of the liquid in the fire. Would it be enough of a distraction to allow her to escape? Nay, she'd have to listen to and talk with him; it would be the only way to deal with this very dangerous man.

Wind blew through empty window openings. Feeling the cold, Janet moved closer to the warmth of the fire. "Come drink with me. I believe you will enjoy this fine whisky, which, if I am not mistaken, came from a Cameron house. I suppose it could even have been your own, my dear."

He searched in his knapsack and brought out two wooden cups, bread, and cheese wrapped in paper. "Please fill the cups while I prepare the rest of our meal. Fruit would go well with our bread and cheese. However, I must apologize; there is none."

Janet poured a small amount of whisky in one cup and filled the other to the brim. William placed cheese and bread on the paper and sat down. "Come, sit. I want to talk to you."

Janet handed him the full cup and sat down.

"Shall we talk about loyalty to the king of Scotland and England? The failure of Scotland's ragged army to defeat my father's royal army? The price that must be paid for a costly and futile battle?"

He drank deeply from his cup. "But what would you, a common wench, understand of royalty or, loyalty? You are simple-minded and, like most of your sex, good only for breeding. You are somewhat fair to look upon, although past your prime."

Janet looked into his eyes, "I understand royalty, and loyalty, sir. Ye are th' king's son, a prince. I am th' daughter of a man who breeds an' sells fine horses. Perhaps ye ha' heard of him, James Dunsmuir? His stables are near Perth."

William recalled the name. "James Dunsmuir—yes, the horse I ride was purchased from him. He is a knowledgeable man, even if he is a Scot."

"Sir, ye would ha' met my mother. She almost always is wi' Father when buyers make a purchase an' invites them to share a meal."

"Your mother? Why would I remember the woman? I am not one to pay attention to women. I find their whining mannerisms irritating, especially those who have no education and are dull-witted as well."

Janet thought of the only possible thing William might listen to. "Ye are speakin' of yer kin, Your Highness. Th' woman, my mother, ye called dull-witted is Queen Anne's niece. She was raised in th' queen's nursery, an' her education was provided by th' finest tutors in England. My mother taught all of her children to read, write, do mathematics, an' display polite manners when speakin' to others!"

Janet watched William's face, looking for a clue to his thoughts. He stared at her. Janet continued speaking. "Sir, it was durin' Queen Anne's rule tha' th' Act of Union was signed bringin' together England an' Scotland as one country wi' one king. Wi' all respect, it's because of my beloved Auntie Queen tha' ye ha' th' right to fight for yer father's kingship in Scotland! Had it not been so, Scotland would ha' her own king an' England a different one."

No longer frightened, Janet continued. "Queen Anne was a Protestant Stuart. Yer from th' Protestant Hanover family. Your Highness, my mother an' yer father share a common ancestor, King James. Your Highness, we are cousins several times removed, an' not only that, both you and I are related to th' Bonnie Prince!"

Janet stood and held out both hands. "Of course, I do not wish to claim him as kin, an' it is doubtful tha' you do, My Lord."

William raised his hand as if to strike her and then dropped it. "Do not dally with me," he shouted. Janet knew her revelation had taken him by surprise. He sat on the bench and drank from the cup.

"Your name is Janet Cameron?"

"Aye, it is, sir."

"Come and sit beside me, Janet. I would converse with you." He emptied the cup and held it out for her to fill. "One reason I do not care for women is that I detest their weaknesses. You, for instance: why do you not glance away when I look at you? Most women do."

"I am not afraid of ye, William Augustus. I hear tha' yer a cruel an' unkind man. Are ye?"

William looked sharply at Janet, eyes glaring, "I tell you the truth; there is anger in me. I don't know where it comes from. My father is known to be forceful and always has his way, but my mother had many friends and was well thought of by both commoners and royalty." William emptied his cup and held it out for more.

"Father and I wondered who would be leading the Jacobites in their rebellion. We were not surprised when Charles Stuart arrived in Scotland with one ship and a few guns. It is remarkable that he and his rebel followers were able to reach England, but they did! When Charles retreated to Scotland, we knew we could bring him and his army down, once and for all. It was just as Father and his advisors hoped it would be."

Janet shook her head. "Are ye sayin' th' English wanted th' uprising to take place?"

"Of course! When our spies reported Charles was begging for money in France and the pope gave Charles his blessing to proceed with the rebellion, we knew it was time to destroy the ownership the Jacobites and clan chieftains had on the king's subjects in Scotland. It was no surprise to us when Charles Stuart lost the battle!"

Janet listened to his statements and remembered that Duncan, Gordon, Thomas, Elizabeth, her bairns, and Ewan were all dead, but Charles Edward Stuart was alive. William smiled and continued, "The *coup de grace* was that most, if not all, of the ammunition and artillery meant for the Highlanders became available to our royal army! There is a thirty-thousand-pound reward on Charles Stuart's head, and we believe someone will come forward to claim the reward."

"Sir, earlier ye spoke of yer anger. Th' battle has been won, an' yer father is th' victor. Are ye still angry?"

"I am, because Scotland is a lawless land whose people disobey their king. If peace is ever to be possible in Scotland, the barbaric ways of the clans must stop. The Culloden battle was both the end and the beginning of a new way of life for Scotland and her people.

Those who supported the old ways and continue to resist the new ways will die." William emptied the cup, uncorked a second bottle, and handed the cup to Janet to be filled.

"Sir, Charles Stuart did not have my support, nor tha' of my husband, who was ordered to go to battle by th' Lochiel. My husband an' his kin were threatened wi' losin' their homes an' lands if they failed to do so. Many Hieland men fought but did'na believe Scotland would win."

"Janet, when I lead the king's army into battle, it is to protect England, Wales, Ireland, and Scotland from invasion by those who would do far worse things to our homeland and people than King George would ever be guilty of doing.

When Charles Stuart led the clans out on Culloden's field, he led them to their deaths. This battle was between the king's people fighting one another. A battle between the residents of two countries who share a king and have laws to protect that king is hardly an uprising. It is treachery and treason against the king and is punishable by death."

"Sir, Ewan was not on th' battlefield at Culloden. He returned to Inverness to obtain food for th' Hielanders who were starvin'. No one knows yet wha' became of the food tha' was intended for th' men. Do ye know of this?"

The duke smiled and said, "I do not. However, Charles's closest adviser might know. He's capable of such a deed. I've had dealings with him myself."

"Sir, ye brought Ewan to Mary's cottage, did ye not?"

"Yes, I did."

"There are many things about his death tha' are yet a mystery to me. Would ye be so kind as to enlighten me?"

Cumberland responded, "There's little to tell. One of my regiments found him lying injured on the ground. He wore the clothing of a king's soldier. When questioned, he stated that his name was Willie Ball. He seemed to have some knowledge of the countryside, and his captain sent him to seek Cameron properties to be destroyed. The more I heard about soldier Willie Ball, the more I was convinced he was a spy and would get word to his clan if at all possible. My captain strongly vouched for Soldier Ball and said that during his search he reported one Cameron home had been destroyed, while another further on was still standing. I felt certain it was meant to be an ambush and Willie Ball planned to lead my men into a massacre."

"He was called Willie Ball! I dinna understand why he had tha' name, or why he wore th' uniform of an English soldier. I ha' many questions, some ye may ha' th' answer for. Were ye wi' him when he died?"

"No," the duke responded. "He was dead when I found him."

"Surely he was not alone?"

"There were two soldiers accompanying him. I sent them on their way; transported him to the cottage, and you know the rest."

"How did he lose both legs?"

"His legs were amputated at Fort William because of gangrene."

Janet sat with her hands folded in her lap. Then she realized there was one more thing she could say to him. "Sir, you hold me captive, but I'm not yer enemy. I did'na fight on th' battlefield. I am not a Jacobite or a commoner. You'd nay do harm to yer own kin. I would pray to God tha' ye'd nay do so."

William glared at Janet. "There is no God!"

Janet returned his glare. "Ye, sir, speak blasphemy. I shall pray for th' salvation of yer soul."

"Woman, you know nothing of what you speak!"

Quietly, Janet said, "Come, sit down. I wish to learn more about ye." She looked at the man who sat beside her on the bench. "Were ye born in Germany?"

"No, I was born in Charring, Middlesex, England."

"Do ye ha' brothers, sisters?"

"My older brother, Frederick, the prince of Wales, will gain the throne when Father dies. I have three older sisters. Another son, George, died. After I was born, two more sisters followed."

"Sir, I ha' learned from Mother about th' succession of royalty to th' throne. It is true th' prince of Wales will gain th' kingship unless yer father names you as his successor. Why would he not prefer ye, William? After all, ye ha' defeated th' Jacobites and strengthened th' union between England an' Scotland."

William looked at the woman who sat beside him, green eyes looking straight into his own. She was undaunted by him. "Father sees me as headstrong and quick to temper; these are both qualities he has himself and yet finds fault with in me. I am in his good graces because I train soldiers well and have sufficient courage to lead them into battle."

"Sir, yer father used wisdom when he placed ye where ye are. Could it be he sees you as th' son who'll keep him on th' throne? Yer older brother, Frederick, may be more yer foe than yer father. Frederick is jealous of ye, William! He must stay close to th' king while ye are free to travel. Would ye rather sit inside th' castle while someone else leads th' king's army into battle? I think not!"

Other than his mother, she was the first woman he had spoken with who made sense of things. Janet folded bread around a piece of cheese and handed it to him. He ate the food, but as he lifted the cup to his mouth, his hand shook, and the contents spilled on the floor. "Damn, damn, damn! Fill my cup again," he shouted.

She refilled the cup and handed it to him. "There's no need for anger, Your Highness. We are sharin' th' food ye brought, an' we can speak between th' two of us, aye?"

He nodded and said quietly, "Milady, it is my wish that you come with me to England. You see, I am unable to converse with any woman, other than Mother, as I can with you. When she died, I lost more than I can say. With you by my side, Father might consider bestowing the kingship to me. You would be my queen!"

357

William stood and paced back and forth. As he paced, he ran his fingers through his hair until it stood on end, giving shadows on the wall the appearance of a wild man with horns dancing around the room. "A wife! The Duke of Cumberland with a wife! If I had a wife, Father would be forced to consider me for the throne. He knows Frederick is unfit to rule!"

She took the cup from his hand; it was nearly empty, as was the bottle. He reached in his knapsack for another bottle and handed it to her. "It is understood the prince of Wales will become king when Father dies. However, father prefers me over Frederick and openly says so. It is logical that I should be king. With you by my side, it will be even more so. Father can order you to marry me!"

Janet struggled to remain calm; she was completely at his mercy. "William, think of yer mother. She came from a royal family, one that yer father's family approved of before he married her. While I ha' a bit of royal blood, still, I did not grow up in a castle, as yer mother did.

"It will not matter whether you lived in a castle or not. You remind me of my mother who was a woman of character and intelligence. She always saw the best in Father; it is my hope that you will do the same with me."

Janet studied William; he was "The Butcher," known far and wide for his barbarous way of disposing of his enemies "I must rest, my dear. I will shackle you to me while I sleep. I prefer to think you would not leave. If you do, I shall find you!"

"Sir, I am not foolish. I know I'd not get far. William, lie down an' sleep. It'll ease yer weary soul."

The duke placed a rope around Janet's waist and secured it to his wrist. Then he lay down by the fire and closed his eyes. Janet covered him with his cloak and marveled at how it blended with the darkness of the dirt and stone floor. She lay down on the floor beside a man who frightened and fascinated her, both at the same time.

Janet felt tiny flutterings of life moving within her. *Oh, my little one, I'm so fearful for ye. Wha' does th' future hold for us, my lassie?* If she managed to escape, there were caves, ravines, and valleys to hide in for as long as necessary. She reasoned that William would soon return to London to receive recognition after winning the battle. She must protect her babe, be watchful, and hope he would not insist on taking her to England with him. She looked at his face. With his eyes closed, William did not seem so fearful. The fire burned down to coals, and finally she slept.

At daybreak, he stirred. "Ah, you are awake. Do you agree with my proposal?"

"Your Highness, there are many things to be considered. First, there's a length of rope connectin' us! It's not a bond tha' holds us together but a restraint! I am your prisoner. What would my fate be if I were yer wife? Will ye keep me bound to yer side always? I'll say this, I'd not stay tied to ye for long! I cannot marry you, sir. I carry my husband's child an' am not a free woman to marry."

"Madam! You are a widow. Your husband is dead and buried. I will claim your child as my own, and both you and the child will have the very best England has to offer."

Janet moved as far away as the rope would allow. "William, I believe a younger woman would better suit ye. My son is fifteen years old, an' yer only ten years older than he is."

She faced William and cringed when he enclosed her in a crushing embrace. "I am not the monster people portray me to be. I loved my mother while she was alive, tolerate my father, and am considered to be a man who has preserved peace for the United Kingdom. You will be honoring your mother and grandmother by returning to the same castle where they once lived. Our children will be born there. Name what you desire, and you shall have it!"

Janet shook her head. "Sir, the king will not allow you to stay in England wi' a wife. Frederick certainly cannot be captain general of th' king's royal army!"

William Augustus looked at her. "Yes, what you say is true. Until I met you, I had not given marriage a thought. Last night I spoke under the influence of whisky, but today I am sober. I will introduce you to Father and ask for permission to wed you. Then he will gift us properties of our own, perhaps a residence at Holyrood where you and our children can reside while I travel.

For now, I will return you to the cottage, where you must stay. Your child will be born, and then we will travel to London, where we will be welcomed as the king's son and his betrothed. There are yet some tasks here in Scotland that I must complete before I can return to London."

William waited while Janet gathered her thoughts. "Sir, I am honored by yer kindness." Janet thought about returning to Mary's cottage. She could stay hidden long enough for him to forget about her. William saddled the horse and helped Janet into the saddle. He rode behind her, holding her in his arms.

He asked, "How can I be of assistance to you in finding your family? Your father no longer sells horses?"

"Nay, he is not well."

"I will ask about James Dunsmuir and his wife. If I hear of them, I will send word to you."

Clamhan and The Dark One perched together in a tree outside Mary's cottage. "Clamhan!" The Dark One said, "He's in love with the woman! She will distract him from my intentions for him. He is not to seek her further, and if he does, we will intervene."

"Sir, he is quite smitten with her and will not discourage easily. What shall I do?"

"You will end it. I do not care how."

At the gate of Mary's cottage, William reined in the horse. "I shall leave you here, my love."

He dismounted and extended his hand to her. As he helped her down, he realized she was shivering and placed his cloak around her shoulders. "It will keep you warm and remind you of me when you wear it."

"Thank you, sir." When she looked into his eyes he felt sadness, an emotion he had not experienced since his mother died.

"Your Highness, please order your soldiers to halt th' killin' of Scotland's people."

He shook his head. "The king's generals, captains, and lieutenants must establish their authority here. You must not leave the cottage! If you do, you will be treated as any other Highlander. By the time I return you will have delivered your child. We will travel to London, where we will be married."

"Sir, I thank ye for yer kindness."

William put his arms around her and kissed her. "I do not understand this sadness I feel. I always look forward to new challenges, but I am reluctant to say good-bye to you. We have been together for only a short while, and yet I feel that my life has changed." He looked into her eyes. "Good-bye, my love. I leave with a great longing for you to be my wife. I shall return for you!"

Janet opened the cottage door. Mary looked up from her mending. "Wha' be ye doin' comin' in th' door in yer night clothes?"

"Mary, th' man who brought Ewan to ye was William Augustus, Th' Duke of Cumberland! He's been here th' whole time! In th' night he took me away to a crofter's cottage on th' moors." Janet reached for a chair to steady herself. "I kept him talkin' an' drinkin', an' finally he slept."

"Oh, dear God! Did ye kill th' bastard?"

"Nay, he's like some of yer patients who ha' troubles in their heids, yet he's a bit of a gentleman. It took him by surprise when I told him we're distant cousins. He said he wanted to marry me so his father would choose him over his older brother to be king. All this came about after he'd emptied three bottles of whisky!"

"Ah, marry ye! Indeed, yer a comely lass—a bit on th' thin side, even though ye do ha' a nicely rounded belly! But marry ye? I canna think of it!"

"Mary, at first I was a'feared of him. He spit in my face. But I thought about him bein' no more than a man like all th' rest, so I spoke up, an' then we talked as if we'd known one another fer years. He told me about bein' a little lad, an' I could see him tryin' to do his best tha' was never good enough for his father. He said he'd ha' his father, th' king, order me to marry him, but then he seemed to think better of it when I told him I'm still grievin' for my husband. He said he'll return after he's completed th' king's orders an' we'll be wed!"

Mary peered closely at Janet's pale face. "I wisht ye'd banged him on th' heid! We dinna want him to come back an' find ye here."

Edward came into the room. "I heard all ye said. Yer unharmed?"

"Aye, I suffered no harm." Edward patted her on the shoulder. "Ye stood up to him, aye?"

"Aye, I did. He bade me to stay here, but I won't."

Mary looked at Edward. "I bought a horse from my nephew an' ye might as well ride him to Skye. I'll nay be usin' th' beast; he's in th' pasture. Get on wi' saddlin' th' horses." "Thank ye Mary. I'll bring him back to ye, might be a while."

"Dinna fash yerself about it Edward. Daniel, there's cheese, oatcakes, an' a treacle tart in yer knapsack."

"Mary, William ga' me his cloak, but I dinna want it. Here, take it."

Mary picked it up, smelled it, and held it out. "Take a whiff, it smells of sulfur. This is wha' I've been smellin' all along!"

"Aye, it does!"

"It's charmed, it is, an' ye've been wearin' it! Go wash yerself wi' lye soap an' throw yer nightgown in th' fire. I'll bury th' cloak. It won't burn. Where it's from, th' fires be as hot as hell," Mary muttered to herself.

Chapter 58

Janet rode Prince; Daniel sat with Edward on Mary's horse. "Janet, we'll take th' long way to Skye. If I traveled alone, it'd be th' shorter way, but it's too risky for th' three of us."

"Edward, is Skye like Scotland?"

"Aye, wi' fewer people. 'Tis very lovely, lass. When we reach th' island, we'll be lookin' over one shoulder instead o' both. We'll still be watchin', but there's less risk."

"Edward, where'll my bairn be born?"

Edward replied, "My lady wife is a kind an' lovin' lass who'll gather ye into th' family. Ye'll ha' family wi' a different name an' in a different place, but still ye'll be wi' people who'll care for ye. We're all Scots! Yer babe'll be born as all babes should, loved an' cared for." Edward paused to search for a path. "Here it is. We'll follow this path to th' edge of th' forest an' rest when we can."

Janet thought about the night before, when she sat on the dirt floor of a cottage with a rope binding her to the duke. "I'm thankful to be wi' ye, Edward, instead of William Augustus."

Edward shook his head, "God watched over ye, lass. From wha'

I've heard o' th' duke, him bein' Th' Butcher an' all, it's a miracle ye got away."

They rested beneath an ancient fir tree whose lower branches brushed the needle-covered forest floor. Janet held Daniel while Edward spoke of Skye. "On th' island, th' closest neighbors are th' MacDonalds."

"Where'll Daniel and I live, Edward?"

"Lass, there'll be a place, dinna worry. My wife's mother married a man from the mainland, but he died from the plague. After he was gone, she brought her little lad and lassie home to Dunvegan where they grew up. Later, when her son was grown, he returned to the mainland where his father's family live. He inherited lands an' a broch, and as far as I know he still lives there an' raises a special breed of sheep. My wife an' her brother were very close when they were bairns. This brings me to wonderin' abou' him. I'd like to take word of him home to his mother an' sister. Would ye mind if we went a wee bit south to find him?"

"Nay, I dinna mind. I'm wonderin' how yer wife'll feel about ye travelin' wi' a widow an' a wee laddie?"

Edward smiled at Janet. "She knows she's dear to me an' will not fash about it one bit."

Janet rested against the tree and slept. Edward, always watchful, napped, opening his eyes at every sound. The sun slowly moved across the sky. Daniel woke and nudged his aunt's shoulder.

"Auntie, I need to pee, can I?"

"Aye, Daniel. Go behind tha' tree."

"Can we find rocks an' mark this place?"

"Aye, we can." Together they found pebbles and piled them into a small mound.

"Now we can find it, Auntie'"

"Aye, Daniel, we can."

They rode south, along the Highland path. "Janet, how do ye feel about comin' wi' me to Skye?"

"I'm grateful to ye, Edward. I hope I can help those on th' isle who need doctorin'. It'd be a way to repay kindness. Are we travelin' back th' way we came?"

"Aye, we'll pass through Glencoe and then turn south of Stob Dubn, where my wife's brother lives."

Janet was deep in thought. "Edward, I met a man somewhere close to Stob Dubn. He's a laird, an' now tha' I think about it, he told of his mother who was a MacLeod. Ian Douglas is his name. Would ye know of him?"

Edward crossed himself. "Do I know him? Aye, he's my wife's brother! Ye say ye met him?"

"Aye, we did. He fed Daniel an' me when we were near starvin'. Edward, yer wife's brother is a very kind man."

"Aye, tha's th' way of th' MacLeods."

"We ate every crumb of food he had, an' I dinna ha' a chance to thank him before he went on to move his flock to the high pastures. We'll be glad to see him."

"Ye didn't see th' Douglas broch?"

"Nay, he was camped at th' foothills of th' High Glens."

"Ah, then, ye'll see wha' amounts to a small castle. Ian is a fine man. He takes well to th' lassies, but he never found one he liked enough to bring home."

Janet laughed. "He told me th' same."

"His uncle an' auntie live close by, an' they help him wi' carin' for the sheep an' all. Ian may be wi' th' sheep in th' high pastures. He stays in a small cottage tha' he built in th' High Glens. It's beautiful there, especially in th' evenin' when th' sun is settin' an' th' sky is all gold an' pink."

Janet wished for a brush to smooth out the tangles in her hair. She thought how unbecoming her clothing must be. She shook her head, *Wha' am I thinkin' of? My husband, father of my son an' yet-to-be-born babe, was buried only three days ago.* Janet, angry with herself, blushed.

Several days later, Edward turned onto a path and Janet caught her breath when she saw a tall castle with a water-filled moat. "Edward, would there be a flag flyin' if Ian was here?"

"Nay, he'd not care if others knew he was here."

"How is it th' English ha' not plundered it?" Janet asked.

"I canna say tha' they won't, but Ian dinna take part in th' clan doin's, an' he's nay a Jacobite. His da owned several ships tha' carried fleece an' processed wool to markets abroad. When he died, Ian's mother sold th' ships an' put th' money away for Ian, sayin' it was his inheritance, along wi' th' castle. Ian's father bred sheep 'til he was satisfied he had th' best fleece-producing animals anyone could ha'. Instead of shippin' th' wool to England, Ian sells to buyers in Edinburgh for markets in France, Spain, an' even Italy."

"When Daniel an' I met Ian, he wore patched breeks, leather boots tha' ha' seen better days, an' an ol' leather vest. I thought he was a sheep crofter!"

Edward laughed. "Aye, tha' would be Ian! He has fine clothin' tha' could be worn at th' king's court, but he dinna care one whit for those doin's. He'd rather be dressed as ye say, herdin' sheep up th' hillside."

They rode into the courtyard, where a man-of-arms met them. "Good day, Mr. Stewart, and greetings to ye, milady. May I tell th' laird who ye be?"

"Tell him Janet Cameron an' her nephew Daniel are here."

"Aye, sir."

Edward lifted Daniel down. Daniel looked at the castle with its turrets shrouded in mist. "Are we lost, Auntie?"

"Daniel, ye know a man who lives here."

Janet waited for his response. Daniel looked up at the massive building. "I think a king lives here. I dinna know any king."

The man-at-arms appeared. "Th' laird welcomes ye."

The timbered doors opened, and Ian Douglas rushed out. "Edward! How good to see ye. Wha' of Kate an' th' bairns?"

"They're safe on Skye. I took 'em there a'fore th' battle."

He turned to Janet just as Daniel recognized him. "Ian, Ian, I do know ye! I told yer about th' stag I saw, and ..."

"Aye, laddie." Ian picked him up and swung him around. "I'm glad to see ye. Janet, my dear, how're ye? I've thought of ye many times an' hoped ye'd be safe. Come in, come in. Will ye stay for th' evenin' meal an' perhaps longer?"

Ian looked from one face to the other. "How it is tha' ye three traveled to my broch together? It's a mystery!"

Edward shook his head. "Ian, it's bad, do ye know?"

"I know, Edward. I knew ye'd see to it Kate an' th' bairns were out of danger."

"Ian, if I may—" Janet gathered Daniel close to her. "Again, I'm askin' ye for Daniel's sake. He needs somethin' to eat an' a place to lay his heid."

Ian apologized. "I'm forgettin' my manners. Please, allow me to offer ye supper an' a bed. Th' laddie needs a good night's sleep, an' so do th' rest of ye."

He called out, "Auntie Meg, there's someone I want ye to meet."

A smiling, gray-haired woman appeared. "Edward, be ye well? Likely not, wi' all th' upheaval."

Ian explained, "Auntie, Katherine an' th' bairns are at Dunvegan, wi' Mother. It's th' best place for 'em. This is Janet Cameron an' her nephew Daniel. We've met before, but I'd be hard pressed to explain why they're travelin' wi' Edward. We'll get it sorted out. For now, young Daniel needs somethin' to eat. His auntie says he needs a place to sleep, so I've invited 'em to stay th' night, or longer if need be. So, it'll be off to bed after he's eaten an' had a bath."

"Aye, sir. I'm hungry, but I dinna need a bath. Listen, an' I'll count to twenty. Hold up yer fingers while I count." Daniel started counting as Ian held up a finger for each number.

"Excellent! Daniel, I ha' somethin' for ye." Ian handed him a smooth stone. "See a seashell embedded in th' stone?"

Daniel examined the stone carefully. "I see it. How'd it get stuck in th' stone?"

"Interesting story! After ye ha' yer bath an' go to bed, I'll come up an' tell ye about it."

"But, sir, I'll eat my supper an' go to bed. I dinna need a bath, sir."

"Oh, ye do, Daniel. Auntie Janet will come wi' ye to th' kitchen an' eat wi' ye, an' then ye'll be havin' a bath to soak off some of th' dirt on yer neck!"

Meg beckoned for Janet and Daniel to follow her to the kitchen. They sat down to bowls of stew, cheese, and bread. Janet smiled at Meg through tears.

"Oh, my dear." Meg patted her shoulder. "It's good to ha' ye an' th' lad wi' us."

Ian led Edward into the great room and motioned for him to sit. He poured Edward and himself cups of whisky. "Edward, before ye speak, I'll tell ye tha' Janet Cameron has been on my mind since our paths crossed several weeks ago. I know she has, or had, a husband. For her to be wi' ye, I canna even guess at th' circumstances."

Ian rubbed his chin and continued, "Then there's th' little lad. She's been caring for him since th' English captured her husband. One has to wonder how they've managed to survive. When they stumbled into my camp, both were near starvin'. Daniel told me how he saw his Uncle Ewan walkin' barefooted behind a horse. Th' way Daniel described it, his uncle was tied by a rope to th' horse's saddle. I know Janet was searchin' for him, but tha' is all I know. Do ye think she found him? How did th' two of you come to be travelin' together?"

"It's a long story, Ian. When Janet an' Daniel stopped at my place to ask directions to Inverness, I thought of Kate an' th' bairns an' knew I needed to help her. I fed 'em an' knowin' it's too risky for 'em to travel where th' king's army is, I offered to escort her an' th' little lad at least part of th' way.

"Ian, her husband is dead. He died a miserable death, but we dinna know how. He was wearin' th' red coat of an English soldier when he died. We buried him two days ago. We'll never know wha' happened. There's no answer tha' makes sense."

"Edward, I could guess at wha' happened, but mind ye, it's only a guess. Daniel said his uncle was walkin' behind a horse, wi'out boots. It's a common way for th' English to move a prisoner. Then, when th' prisoner is unable to keep up, they shoot 'em. Did he die of a gunshot wound?"

"Dinna know, both of his legs were gone. Poor lass, it was a shockin' thin' for her to see wha' was left of him. We buried him th' next day.

It's brutal wha' is happenin' in th' Hielands. Brochs burned wi' families inside. I'm glad Katie an' the bairns are on Skye. Janet's a strong one, she is. When Th' Duke of Cumberland took her to a crofter's cottage out on th' moors, th' lass was able to talk her way out of wha'ever th' duke ha' planned to do wi' her. He brought her back to th' cottage unharmed. She's a'feared he'll find her again."

Ian was stunned. "It's a wonder she's alive!"

"Aye, an' there's one more thin' to tell ye. It'd be best if she told ye herself, but I dinna know if she will. After tellin' me how ye feel about her, ye need to know tha' she's wi' child. Th' babe must ha' been conceived just before her husband went to Culloden. Ian, she's a fine lassie, wi' pride an' spirit."

"Aye, I saw tha' too. I must keep my promise to the little lad. I'll be back in a while."

Meg smiled as Ian came into the kitchen. "They're upstairs, Ian. Janet's a lovely person."

"Aye, Auntie, she is. I met her a'fore, an' I'll tell ye about it later."

Ian bounded up the staircase. He stopped at the first bedroom, where Janet was tucking Daniel in bed. Candlelight shone on the red and gold curls on her head.

"Lass, ye cut yer hair. Why?"

"It's best tha' I pass for a laddie. Same for my clothin'."

"Aye, tha' makes sense. Daniel, where's th' stone I ga' ye?"

Daniel held out his hand. "It's here, Ian."

Ian pulled up a small rocking chair for Janet and sat on the bed beside Daniel. "Laddie, here at one time, there was a big ocean, wi' water all th' way up to yer bed."

"My bed? Ye mean all th' way from th' ground to my bed?"

"Aye. Th' shell, pressed from th' weight of all of tha' water into th' stone, was at th' very bottom of th' ocean."

"I want a box to keep it in."

"We'll find ye one, Daniel. Now, lie back an' close yer eyes. In th' morning, there'll be somethin' good to eat waitin' for ye."

"Thank ye, sir, an' good night!"

Ian smoothed the little lad's hair and pulled the covers around him. Daniel, snuggled down in the bed with a soft pillow and blankets, was asleep before they left the room. Ian offered his arm to Janet. Together they walked down the stairs to the kitchen.

"Janet, my dear, would ye like a cup of tea, or something wi' a bit more strength to it?"

"Aye, a cup of tea would be most appreciated, Meg."

"Sit by th' fire, then. I'll bring ye a cup."

Ian led her into the great room and drew two chairs close by the fire. "Even in th' warmth of summer days, we always keep a bit of a fire goin'. Th' evenin's get chilly here in th' Glens. I like to sit by th' fire an' read a bit before I retire for th' evenin'."

Ian pointed to floor-to-ceiling bookcases filled with books across one end of the room. "Books are my one weakness. I canna pass by a bookstore in Inverness, Glasgow, or Edinburgh wi'out stoppin' in to see wha' is new."

He selected a small book bound in red leather with gold lettering. "*Crustaceans' Shells from the Sea* by Samuel Bates. Here's a book Daniel'll enjoy. There's a drawin' of th' same shell I ga' him. Can th' lad read?"

"Edward has spent a little time wi' him goin' over numbers, an' he was very proud to share wha' he's learned wi' ye, Ian, but he's not learned his letters yet. His mam was to begin teachin' him this spring, but—" Janet paused, "It was not meant to be."

Meg brought in a tray with teapot, cups, and a plate of ginger biscuits. "Thank ye, Auntie," Ian said. "Edward an' I ha' not eaten, an' those biscuits look tasty."

Meg leaned toward him and whispered, "There's a big tin of 'em on th' shelf above th' peat basket." Ian smiled and nodded.

Meg said, "Good night to all. Janet, yer company is most welcome, an' it's good to ha' a child in th' house. He's a fine little lad—an' wha' manners! Good night. I'll be over in th' morn to get th' meal."

Janet finished her tea, and Ian poured whisky in her cup. He disappeared into the kitchen and returned with bannock buns, cheese, and the tin of biscuits. As he prepared buns and cheese for himself and Edward, he said, "Janet, Edward's told me wha' happened to ye an' th' lad. I'm so sorry about yer husband. Wha' a shock it must ha' been to ye. An' yet, I know ye were prepared for th' worst."

"Aye, there's no words to tell how I felt when I saw him lying there. He suffered so much. I curse those who failed to get help for him in time to save his life." Janet placed her hand on Edward's arm. "Ian, just as ye fed us when we were near starvin', Edward was wi' me when we buried Ewan. I had no way of knowin' th' two of ye are kin, but I might ha' known tha' ye'd be from th' kindness ye both ha' shared wi' Daniel an' me. Th' Duke of Cumberland brought Ewan's body to Mary's cottage. He said he thought Ewan was a spy for Scotland, an' he made it clear th' king's troops are to kill all Hielanders."

Ian frowned. "Yer family, Janet, do ye know of 'em?"

She shook her head. "My son is wi' my mother, brother, an' sister in th' south o' Scotland. When I can, I'll search for my family.

Edward's asked us to travel wi' him to Skye, where yer mother an' sister are. My son will be worryin' about us, but I ha' Daniel to look after, for tha' an' another reason, it's best tha' we go wi' Edward to Skye."

"Hum," Ian spoke. "I've been plannin' a visit to see Mother an' th' kin. If ye'll allow me to accompany ye, we'll leave in several days. I've been meanin' to spend time wi' Mother, as I want to set down a chronicle of th' family history. Mother is one of the few remainin' MacLeods who knows th' entire history."

"I'll welcome ye to travel along wi' us," Edward said. "Janet, wha' say ye?"

"I'll be travelin' wi' my closest friends," she said through tears.

"Lass." Ian knelt beside her chair. "It's been a terrible time for ye. From now on, let me help wi' th' little lad. Ye ha' cared for him well, but Edward tells me tha' yer wi' child, an' now ye must take care of yerself an' yer babe. When do ye expect th' babe to be born?"

"After Christ's Mass, at th' new year. I thought I'd never ha' another bairn, but now ..." She covered her face with her hands.

"Come along. We'll get ye upstairs an' bring th' tub so ye can ha' a warm bath an' then to bed." Ian helped her to her feet and steadied her with his arm. "Edward, please put a kettle of water on th' kitchen fire an' fetch it up when it's hot. Also, fill th' two wooden buckets wi' warm water an' bring 'em too. We'll get this lassie a bath an' then put her to bed."

Together they started up the stairs. "Ye'll sleep in th' bed chamber next to Daniel. There's a door between th' two rooms, if he wakes, it'll be a comfort for him wi' ye nearby."

Ian opened the door to the bed chamber and led Janet to a chair by the fireplace. He struck flint to dry shavings underneath logs, and soon a fire was burning. He brought in the wooden tub just as Edward arrived with a bucket of water. He emptied it into the tub and then went downstairs for more.

"While yer bathin' I'll fetch a nightshirt for ye."

She was at least three months with child, but painfully thin and pale. Ian placed a nightshirt on the bed and stepped out of the room. He went downstairs, added hot water to a cup of wine and wrapped a hot brick in a cloth. "Ha' ye finished yer bath, lass?"

"Aye, I'm done an' dressed," she replied as she opened the door.

"I've a warmed brick for yer bed and a cup o' toddy for ye." He plumped the pillows, put the flannel-wrapped brick at the foot of the bed under the covers, and motioned for her to get into bed. He handed her the wine. "Drink this, lass, and then it's to sleep for ye."

"Ian, I need to speak wi' ye. Daniel an' I ha' been on th' run for I dinna know how long, an' now, in two days we'll be runnin' again." She held out her hand. "Will it ever stop?"

"Nay, it won't, for a long while. I knew a year ago th' uprisin' was comin' an' how it'd turn out. Yer too weary to hear th' tale?"

"I've been livin' th' tale, Ian! Tell me!"

"About a year ago, I was in Inverness an' stopped in a tavern for a bite. I sat by a man who said he was Prince Charles Edward Stuart's personal secretary. He spoke about rallyin' th' clans to support th' Stuart who'd be takin' the throne back from King George. Men agreed wi' him about th' high taxes we pay England's king an' how he controls wha' we can sell. I agreed, but I knew it'd be a lost cause. Even if all th' men o' Scotland went to battle against th' king's army an' fought a good fight, there'd not be enough to win. After th' man left, some said they'd nay fight for a Catholic Stuart, but others said they would. I came home wi' th' idea to make myself scarce when th' time came. Aye, lass, we'll be runnin', but it'll not be as it was when ye an' th' little lad was on yer own. We'll be travelin' only three or four days, an' I'll take full responsibility for ye an' th' laddie. Edward's done well by both of ye. It'll be my turn now."

"Thank ye, Ian." She settled back on the pillows and closed her eyes. He sat quietly, not ready to leave her. He worried that she had not had enough food for the babe to be healthy. He knew a bit about ewes birthing lambs. A starved ewe would not bear a healthy lamb, and many times the ewe died giving birth. Janet nestled down in the bed and sighed in her sleep.

Ian straightened the coverlet over her and thought, *For a second time, ye ha' been given to me to watch over, care for, an' love, an' I'll vow to ye tha' to th' end of my days, I'll do so, if ye'll but let me.* He put more wood on the fire and went to his bed chamber. On the morrow, they'd begin preparations to leave.

Ian was up early the next morning. He stoked the kitchen fire and put a peat brick on the coals. He filled the teakettle and sat it on the grate. This was home to him, as was the cottage by the burn in the high valley and even the castle on the far western shore of Skye, where he had grown up. His thoughts were interrupted when a small hand patted his arm. "Ian, sir, see wha' I ha'? It's th' sea shell, an' I put it in this box. I'll keep it in my pocket, an' I can look at it when I want to."

"Very good, Daniel! Now, lad, are ye hungry?"

"Aye. Wha' do ye ha' to eat, sir?"

The kitchen door opened, and Meg came in with a basket. "Ah, my two favorite laddies. Sit yer selves down. I made flat cakes wi' honey syrup."

She put a stack of hot buttered cakes on each wooden plate and then poured syrup over. "Daniel, this is Hugh's favorite. Try it an' see wha' ye think."

Daniel ate a piece of his hotcake. "Oh, it's th' best I ever had! I'll eat 'em all an' get more?"

"Of course, laddie. Ian, I came over earlier an' brought Janet clean clothin' an' a few things I think she can wear."

Janet came into the room, wearing the same breeches she had worn the day before, but with a clean chemise and blouse. "Thank ye, Meg, for washin' my clothes for me."

"Yer welcome. Now, sit yerself down, an' here's yer tea. Yer so thin tha' I can almost see through ye, an' those breeks, they're about to fall down!" Meg smiled. "I've brought some things tha' will fit ye. Here's a plate of cakes."

Janet ate several bites. "Wha' is this syrup? It's very tasty an' tastes a bit like honey."

"I knew ye'd like it. I make it by warmin' honey in a kettle an' then addin' a beaten egg, cinnamon, an' a pinch of salt. Then when it bubbles up, I take it off th' fire, add butter, and stir it 'til it's light."

"I'll remember tha', Meg. I ha' never had anythin' quite as good, an' even th' tea tastes special."

Daniel waited patiently until Meg and Janet were through talking. Then he said, "Ian, I dreamed my bed was floatin' on th' sea, an' when I woke up all th' water was gone, an' th' sun was shinin'."

Ian smiled at Daniel. "Scotland has water ever'where, an' I believe all of it was underwater a very, very long time ago." Ian placed Daniel on his lap; the two were deep in conversation.

A bouquet of fragrant red and pink roses sat in the middle of the kitchen table. Windows were bright with sunshine. A door to the kitchen garden stood open and a purring tabby cat wound around everyone's legs. Janet said, "Meg, I do so love th' flowers."

Meg gave Janet a hug. "As do I, lass."

A tall man with white hair and a beard and mustache to match walked into the kitchen carrying two rabbits and a pheasant. "Here's supper, Meg. I'll get 'em cleaned an' ready for th' pot after breakfast."

"Uncle Hugh, let me introduce ye to our guests. Ye already know Edward. This is Janet an' Daniel Cameron. Janet, Daniel, this is my father's youngest brother, Hugh Douglas. Come join us, an' we'll share plans for th' day."

Everyone gathered around the table. After looking at each one, Ian said, "We'll leave in two days. It'll be risky wi' th' king's army on th' lookout for Charles Stuart."

Meg took Daniel's hand. "Come along, laddie. I ha' toys tha' were Ian's when he was yer age: a toy boat tha' floats, an' a whistle tha' plays a tune ..."

The two went upstairs. Ian said, "We'll leave th' broch appearin' to be in ruin. Everythin' will be packed an' stored in Uncle Hugh's barn. Uncle, if ye'll take th' sheep to yer place an' look after th' ones in th' high pastures, I'll be back by fall. I'm not certain how things'll be then, but—"

"Nay, Ian," Hugh interrupted. "Dinna come back 'til things are better."

"But ye'll need help movin' th' sheep down from th' high pastures a'fore winter sets in."

"Why take a chance, Ian? Ye could be leadin' soldiers right to our doorstep!"

Janet, listening to the conversation between the two, had her own concerns. "Hugh, how is it ye an' Meg will be safe?"

"Our cottage is tucked away in th' woods. If yer standin' a few feet away, ye'd miss it. Same for th' garden an' barn."

Ian smiled at Janet, "It's true. Wait 'til ye see it. Tomorrow, we'll take th' household goods an' furniture there for storage. Janet, ye can pack th' kitchen things in crates. Most everythin' will be put away by this evening. My books will be stacked in empty wooden barrels tha' I usually keep ale an' mead in. They'll ha' a wonderful aroma tha' I'll enjoy while I'm readin'!"

Janet looked at Ian and then Edward. "I dinna want to say so, but ... I'm very fearful of goin' to Skye. I know, Ian." She caught his look. "Yer thinkin' I'm daft."

Janet hesitated as she struggled with words. "I've lost my husband an' most of his family, includin' three children. If I see so much as one English soldier, there's no way of knowin' wha' I'll do!"

"Lass, we'll not let anythin' happen to ye an' Daniel. Th' king's army are searchin' for Charlie Stuart on Skye, but they're lookin' more on th' eastern side rather than th' western side. My Mother, Katie, an' th' bairns are at Dunvegan Castle, on th' far western coast. It's naught but empty land there."

The day passed quickly. Janet wrapped china, silver platters, cups, copper pans, and kettles in kitchen linens and packed them in crates and barrels. She thought of the things hidden behind the fireplace stone at Glen Lochy. *Will they still be there?* She wiped away tears. *Duny'll ha' his inheritance. I'll be seein' to it!*

Then she remembered Ewan promising Anne that Elizabeth and her bairns would have a Christian burial. *I can't think how that can happen now.* To get her thoughts away from that sadness, she began packing Ian's books. History, geography, and nonfiction books made up the largest part of the collection. She stopped only long enough to move a full crate to make room for another.

Wincing when she felt a sharp twinge in her back, she went upstairs and lay down. She slept and dreamed of a well-traveled road to Edinburgh. On the road was a carriage with her mother, sister, and a woman she did not know. Jamie held the reins, and Duny sat beside him. Her sister carried a tiny babe in her arms. In her sleep, Janet smiled and did not waken when Ian placed an extra quilt over her and gently kissed her.

The next day, Ian and Edward dismantled the kitchen table and loaded barrels of books and crates of cutlery and china; the kitchen and great room were bare. The pantry and cellar were emptied. Barrels of fall wine and ale, together with last year's barley malt, went to the wagon along with crates of vegetables. Beds were dismantled; the rooms were bare. Sounds echoed from one room to another, upstairs to downstairs.

Before climbing into the wagon, Janet paused for a moment and pointed toward the western sky heavy with black storm clouds. "We'll be travelin' in tha' direction?"

"Aye, we will."

"Wha' is yet to do?"

"Th' broch must appear to ha' gone to ruin an' fool a soldier ridin' by.

Ian loosened the front doors from their hinges. With the glass windowpanes removed, wind howled through the openings, blowing leaves in from outside. Two sides of the barn were knocked down, and the roof was propped up by its center supports.

Edward shook his head at the sight of the derelict castle. "I'd not give it a second look! It'll take some doin' to get it right again, but if it keeps th' bastards away, then it's worth it!"

Ian took Janet's arm. "Wait 'til ye see th' cottage, if ye can find it! When ye do find it, it'll melt into th' forest a'fore yer very eyes."

Ian helped her to the bench across the front of the wagon. "Daniel's havin' a jolly time. Uncle Hugh's teachin' him to play a game of marbles wi' a set tha' belonged to my grandfather. Auntie mended his breeks an' made a pattern for two more pairs for him. Then she knitted th' lad two pairs of stockings. Dinna look at me tha' way, Janet. I dinna know how she does it. She must'a been up all night long."

Janet smiled. "Likely she did stay up, half of th' night anyway. Ian, I ha' a question, why did yer father build a castle? It's very big for a family wi' two bairns."

"Father wanted Mother to be happy, an' she was homesick for Dunvegan. This is wha' ye see, a bit of Dunvegan Castle. It's a small bit, for th' castle itself is much larger. The inside is very beautiful, wi' carved wooden walls, a grand staircase, an' so many rooms, a person could get lost. Mother is th' clan historian. If yer not mindful, she'll trap ye in th' library, an' ye'll be there for days." Ian laughed. "Our family history includes th' settlin' of Skye by Vikings an' Norsemen."

When the wagon entered the forest, Janet began looking for a cottage. Ian tethered the horse at the bottom of a hill, and they walked through the woods. He finally stopped and pointed to a cottage that seemed to vanish in the mist amongst the trees. Ian pointed out the nearly invisible barn.

"They'll not find this place!" Janet said, pleased with the cleverly hidden cottage.

David ran out to meet them, grabbed his aunt's hand, and said, "Auntie, come see!"

Inside the cottage, a large braided rug covered most of the split log floor. Lanterns hung from iron hooks. A pair of chairs with curved rockers and a long bench with cushions sat beside and in front of a rock fireplace. Another braided rug covered the kitchen floor. A table with chairs sat in front of windows. The cottage had windows across the back; however, the front had no windows at all.

"It's beautiful!" Janet exclaimed.

"Come along to th' upstairs." Meg took Janet's arm and led her to the second floor, where there were two bed chambers and one large room where Meg kept her loom, spinning wheel, and skeins of yarn arranged on shelves. The downstairs fireplace rock wall extended through this room and out the roof. "Meg, this room will stay warm from th' fireplace wall!"

"Aye, an' it's lovely to work in all winter long, even in bitter weather. I spend many a winter's day here, sewin', braidin' rugs, an' workin' up th' fleece. Now, let me show ye the cellar. It's where Hugh keeps his collection."

Janet followed Meg to the kitchen, where she pulled back the rug, grasped an iron ring fitted into the floor, and raised it. "Hugh balanced this with weights so I can raise an' lower it easily."

Janet was amazed. "I've never seen anythin' as clever as this, Meg."

"Aye, I'm proud of my Hugh. Th' Douglas family are all tha' way."

They went down the stairs. The cellar was underground on three sides; a doorway leading outside was on the fourth side. Massive logs buried deep into the pounded dirt floor supported the two top floors. Shelves with boxes of dried fruit and vegetables filled the cellar walls. One wall was full with barrels of whisky, ale, and wine resting on their sides in wooden cradles. A wooden cabinet held a small stock of rifles, pistols, and ammunition.

Janet looked around. "Meg, where's Ian's things?"

"In th' barn."

"I wondered how ye'd manage to find room for it here."

Meg laughed. "Th' books alone'd fill this place, all three floors of it. Durin' th' winter months, Ian an' Hugh stay busy wi' readin' an' sharin' wha' they've read. Yer may not know it, lass, Ian graduated from Glasgow University. He's one o' th' first to complete their engineerin' course."

She opened an outside door, and Janet stepped out onto flat rocks covering the ground. Split logs held side dirt walls in place. "I've never seen anythin' like this!"

Meg nodded. "Aye, Hugh's a man ahead of his time. Ian's th' same, always findin' a better way of doin' things. His cottage in th' High Glens has runnin' water in th' kitchen!"

"Meg, yer just as wise. Ian said ye'd made Daniel new breeks an' stockings. He surely does need 'em, but how'd ye find th' time?"

"Oh, I'd started Hugh's winter breeks an' socks. I trimmed 'em down a bit. Janet, Edward tells me yer a healer, so ye ha' abilities too. I ha' respect for anyone who can help sick folk. Let's go upstairs an' ha' a cup of tea"

Daniel sat on the floor playing with a box of toys. "Auntie Meg, I can play a song wi' this whistle. Listen!" He played a few notes. "This is my bagpipes. It did'na sound like bagpipes, but I did'na care."

"Well, my fine laddie, it's a good start at playin' th pipes. I like th' sound of th' whistle. It's just right for playin' in th' cottage, while pipes'd be much too loud. Daniel," she called as she motioned for Janet to follow her into the kitchen, "Play another tune for me."

Meg placed two chairs by the fire and set two teacups and a pot of tea on the table. Janet sat back in the chair with its plump cushions and footstool. She put her feet up and sighed. Meg sipped from her cup and lowered her voice. "Janet, Hugh an' I talked about this last night. If ye'd leave Daniel wi' us, we'll take good care of him. He wants to learn to read an' do his numbers. Hugh worked wi' him last night usin' th' slate an a piece of chalk. Th' lad is smart, an' it won't take long a'fore he's able to write his name an' read. I know th' two of ye ha' been through many things together, an' to spare yer life an' tha' of yer unborn babe, ye must leave th' Hielands. If ye can leave him, Daniel'll be safe wi' us. We'll understand, wha' ever ye decide."

Janet looked at Meg and smiled, blinking away tears. "I want only one thin', an' tha' is for Daniel to ha' a bed to sleep in, enough to eat, an' somethin' to look forward to. There's been no time for him to be a little lad. He needs ..." "Janet, Ian an' Edward ha' told me much of wha' happened to ye an' Daniel."

"Our travels were hard on Daniel. Many days there was little or none to eat, an' tha' is nay good for a growin' bairn."

"Or for a mother carryin' a babe, my dear. Yer too thin an' need more flesh on yer bones."

"Meg, th' trip to Skye frightens me. If Daniel stays wi' ye, I'll know he'll be safe."

"Janet, ask Daniel how he feels about it."

"Aye, I will."

Daniel came into the room blowing the whistle. "I'm playin' tunes, Auntie Janet!"

"Aye, ye are, Daniel. Ye'll be readin' a'fore long. Ye know we're leavin' tomorrow?"

"Aye, Auntie, I know. Yer goin' up in th' sky?"

"Daniel, it's an island called Skye."

"Oh! Skye is its name."

"Aye. Daniel, would ye be happy stayin' here wi' Uncle Hugh an' Auntie Meg while I go wi' Ian an' Edward, or would ye rather come wi' us to Skye an' stay there 'til we can come back? Think about it a'fore ye answer."

Daniel put away his whistle and climbed into Janet's lap. She smoothed his hair as they rocked. "Auntie Janet," he said in a soft voice, "Would ye be sad if I stay here? Uncle Hugh showed me how to make numbers, an' I can print th' ABCs. Next I'll learn to read books!"

He looked into Janet's face, his eyes searching hers. "Auntie, I'm tired of sleepin' on a horse an bein' hungry."

"Daniel, it won't be as it was when we were by ourselves."

"I missed my pillie an' bed, an' Auntie Meg has a pillie an' bed like mine at home."

"Then yer sayin' ye want to stay here?"

"Be ye sad, Auntie?"

"I want wha' is best for ye, lad."

"I'll help Uncle Hugh wi' th' sheep an' learn to read."

"If it's wha' ye want, then, I'm nay sad about it."

"Auntie Meg, can I ha' a dog?"

"I'll ask Uncle Hugh about it. Ye can ha' one if there's one to be had."

Daniel smiled and snuggled down in Janet's arms. She continued rocking until he was asleep. "Poor wee bairn. Even when there was naught to eat, he dinna whine. This is th' first time he's said a word about it."

Janet looked at Meg. "Had it not been for Ian, we'd not be alive. When he shared wha' he had wi' us, we were able to go on."

"Hugh says there's yet th' worst o' times comin' for Scotland, Janet. He says England has turned against us, an' th' king'll hold all of us to task for th' uprisin', whether we agreed wi' it or not. Ah, well, th' lad is tired. Bedtime for him."

Meg carried Daniel upstairs with Janet following. She placed him in bed and tucked the comforter around him. "It'll be a joy for Hugh an' me to care for th' little lad."

Janet smiled. "Meg, did ye an' Hugh not ha' any children?"

"I had two stillborns, an' I dinna conceive again. Some of us are blessed an' others not. Hugh worries about who we'll leave this place to. We hoped tha' Ian would find a wife, but ..."

"Ewan an' I had one laddie an' a good marriage. He died so horribly. It dinna make sense to me tha' he died in th' uniform of a English soldier."

Janet was close to tears. Meg held her arm as they went downstairs. She pointed to a chair. "Sit down, put yer feet up, an' I'll get supper ready. Won't take but a little while." Meg continued talking, but Janet was asleep.

Chapter 59

Hugh carried in wood for the fire. Behind him Edward and Ian brought peat bricks. "It's goin' to storm tonight. Auntie Meg, is there tea?" Ian asked.

Meg held her finger to her mouth and pointed to Janet asleep in the chair. Ian nodded. "Ah, she needs sleep. While they traveled, she walked so Daniel could ride. Meg, ha' ye seen Janet's horse? He's a bonny fine animal an' is gentle as can be. She calls him Prince, an' that animal obeys her as if he understands wha' she's sayin. I'd not want to sell him short by sayin' tha' he dinna."

Meg poured hot tea into cups for each one. "I've seen her horse. If I understand

rightly, her Da raises and sells fine animals. Is tha' right, Ian?"

"Aye, he does, or did. I dinn't know about now. Janet's Da is a fine man an' well-known." "Is there a biscuit?" Ian looked around.

"We'll be eatin' soon, an' ye can wait along wi' the rest of us." Meg patted Ian's arm. "I've a nice meat pie bakin'. Drink yer tea, an' by th' time it's gone, supper'll be done."

"Ah, the smell of peat burnin' is just wha' a kitchen should smell like."

"I hate to spoil yer idea of wha' a kitchen should smell like, Ian, but wha' yer smellin' is my pie."

"Auntie, I know th' difference between pie an' peat!"

"Dinna get too smarty, lad!"

"Th' wind's comin' up," Hugh said. "I'll take a look at th' lambs an' close up the barn. Will one of ye help wi' feedin' th' horses?"

"Aye, Hugh, I will." Edward followed him out the door.

After the door closed behind them, Meg turned to Ian. "Daniel'll stay wi' us when ye leave. Janet spoke wi' him about it, an' he asked if he could stay. She told me she'll rest easier wi' him stayin' here."

Wind blew the kitchen door against the wall as Hugh walked in. "Edward'll be stayin' in th' barn wi' th' animals tonight. It's goin' to be a bad storm."

Lightning filled the room. "Tha' one hit close!" Daniel called. "Auntie, Auntie!"

Janet ran to his room with Meg close behind. Janet picked him up, held him, and then handed him to Meg. In pain, she sat down on the bed. Meg spoke quietly to the little boy. "Wheesht, child, ye heard th' wind blowin'. Did'na be afraid."

"But, Auntie, I heard somethin' outside."

"We'll take a look." Meg pulled the curtain back just as a fiery bolt of lightning struck.

She closed her eyes, and Daniel squirmed down. "Auntie Janet, did ye fall?"

Meg shouted, "Hugh, Ian, come quickly!"

Ian was first to reach the room. "Wha' happened?"

"I dinna know. Daniel was frightened, an' I was trying to quieten th' lad. Next thin' I knew, she was on th' floor."

Ian lifted Janet, and Meg caught her breath; underneath her the floor was stained with blood. "Oh! Ian, put her on the bed."

She waved the men out and began removing Janet's blood-soaked clothing.

"Meg, I'm losing th' babe. Oh, Meg, I'm hurtin' so."

"Aye, lass, ye are."

Janet cried, "Why, why?"

"We dinna know why. There's naught to do but get through it."

The storm became a howling gale with lightening crashing around the cottage. Ian stepped into the room. "Auntie, Uncle Hugh needs help wi' Daniel. He won't stop cryin'."

After she left the room, Ian looked at Janet and thought of the lifting and packing he'd asked her to do. *Wha' was I thinkin' of?* He whispered, "Ah, lass, 'tis not fair."

Janet stirred and opened her eyes. "Ian, I'm so cold." He covered her with another blanket and settled in the rocking chair.

Meg returned with Daniel. "He's had a bite to eat, an' I'll put him to bed. He's ready to sleep now. Ian, come downstairs wi' me."

"Meg, is she goin' to be all right?"

"Aye, but she canna travel now. Yer in love wi' her?"

"Aye, Auntie. I've loved Janet since I first saw her. She was desperate for food for Daniel, but she held her head high. Auntie, she's th' one I thought I'd never find."

"Well, then, she's goin' to need some patience from ye. She canna love again 'til she's over losin' her husband an' now th' babe. Are ye understandin' wha' I'm sayin'?"

"Yer sayin' to bide my time?"

"Aye, I am. Edward might as well go on to Skye. It may take a while a'fore Janet is up to travelin'."

Ian paced the floor, "When it comes to women an' bairns, I'm a dunce! Now, with sheep it's different! I'd know exactly wha' to do."

Meg looked at Ian and shook her head. "This is th' first time ye've been faced wi' needin' to know th' business of how a woman carries a bairn, an' yer learnin' th' hard way."

Meg rubbed her arms. "Feel tha' chill in th' air? A hot toddy'd go down well. I'll put some water on, an' ye put whisky in th' cups an' a dab of honey. It'd be good for Janet too."

A flash of lightning hit so close that it shook the cottage; thunder boomed overhead. "If yer needin' advice about how a man and woman get together to make a bairn to begin wi', I'll be sendin' ye to yer Uncle Hugh."

"Auntie!" Ian pointed his finger at her.

Meg smiled. "I've heard a bit about ye from th' village doxies. If—" She looked at Ian's face. "Oh, fash it, I'm teasin' ye, Ian."

Ian bounded up the stairs, two at a time. Janet sat up in bed. "Ian, did it hit th' cottage?"

"Nay, but it was close." Meg brought a tray with cups of whisky to Janet's room. Lightning crashed around the cottage.

"This storm'll be batterin' us th' rest of th' night. Meg, go on to bed. I'll sit here wi' Janet. Is Daniel asleep?"

"Aye, he is. Wake me if ye need to."

"Janet, Edward will be leavin' for Skye on th' morrow," Ian said.

Janet closed her eyes and struggled to keep from crying. "I'm grateful to him for his help. He risked his life for us, an' I'll want to wish him a safe journey."

At the first light of dawn, Ian woke to a cold room. Janet was asleep and warm with a down comforter over her. Downstairs, Meg handed him a cup of hot tea. "Auntie, I'll stoke up th' fire. It's a mite brisk this morn'. Uncle Hugh up an' about?"

"Aye, he's at the barn. Th' storm brought in a change of weather. Now tha' I think of it, we had snow on th' Glens in late August last year. Hmmm," Meg said. "Mayhap if th' king's soldiers had ter stand in snow up to their arses, they'd go back to England!"

Ian grinned. "May I join ye?" Janet asked as she came down the stairs.

"Ye should not be up, lass. But then, I dinna stay abed either. Would ye like tea?"

"Thank ye, Meg."

Janet sat down at the table. "I'm thinkin' wha' to do now tha' things ha' changed. I want to find my son an' th' rest of my family."

Ian looked at her. "Janet, is it worth th' risk?"

Janet shook her head, and tears filled her eyes. "I did'na know."

"Then lass," Ian said in a soft voice, "Take time to think through wha' is best for ye. I'd say nay to goin' any direction other than to th' Western Isles. First, lass, you must gain yer strength. Tha' comes before anything else. Ye need a little time."

"Aye, I know, Ian. When I can, I'd like to return to Glen Lochy. There'll be nothin' left but stone walls. I'm hopin' Duny's inheritance is still there." Janet covered her face with her hands.

"Now, lassie." Ian's voice was soft and soothing. "*Tha mi duilich, chan a' tuigsinn.*" (I'm sorry, I understand.)

"Ye speak th' Gaelic?"

"Lass, ye'll be hearin' naught but Gaelic on Skye. It's one reason th' king's tacksmen dinna go there. They dinna understand a word of it."

Ian put his arm around Janet's shoulders as she shook with silent sobs.

"Here, lass." Meg handed her a bowl of porridge with cream and honey. "Eat, an' then go upstairs an' climb into yer warm bed. Ian, eat yer porridge. Then ye can help our lass up th' stairs."

"Nay, I'll walk by myself!"

"Oh! Well, then. Ian can walk alon' aside ye?"

"Aye, he can. But, Ian, Meg, I'm ashamed tha' I cried. I'm not th' only one who's suffered. Gordon died, an' Elizabeth an' th' bairns are dead. Duncan's dead, an' mayhap Anne an' the bairns made it to England, mayhap not. Ewan's dead an' buried, an now, our babe's gone ..."

Meg and Ian looked at each other. "Come along, lass. It's to bed for ye."

Meg took Janet by the arm and led her upstairs with Ian close behind. Janet pulled the covers up and closed her eyes.

Ian turned to Meg. "How has she survived, Auntie?"

Meg replied, "I wonder th' same myself."

Later that morning, while Ian, Hugh, and Edward surveyed the storm's damage, Ian told them about Janet losing the babe. Edward nodded. "Aye, th' shock of it all caught up wi' her. I dinna know how she's gotten alon' this far. I do know her an' Daniel were near starvin' most of th' time. I'm glad she was here wi' Meg when it happened."

"Edward, I'm concerned about Kate an' th' bairns. Ye might as well go on to Skye to be wi' 'em."

"Aye, I'll leave a'fore winter weather sets in. Ian, same for ye an' Janet."

"It'll depend on how she mends. Edward, find a MacLeod to take ye over th' water to Skye. Tell 'em who ye are. They'll find a way to get ye home safe."

Edward left in the late afternoon but returned before nightfall. He rode to the barn, his horse lathered and panting. Hugh looked up from feeding the animals when Edward led his horse inside. "Edward! Wha' happened?"

"Hugh, let's go to th' cottage so I hav'ta tell th' tale only once."

Hugh opened the kitchen door. Ian, Meg, and Janet sat at the table. "Th' king's army is camped inside yer south boundary, Ian. I rode a big circle 'round 'em an' passed by where Lewis Douglas's broch used ter be. It's been burned to th' ground. Lewis an' his family are lyin' on th' ground. They've all been shot in th' heid."

"My God!" Ian was visibly shaken.

Janet nodded. "Aye, it was th' same wi' Elizabeth an' her bairns!"

"It's a warnin'," Ian said. "I'll stock th' cave at th' top o' th' hill if we needed to hide for several days."

"Ian," Edward said, "I'll make another try at it an' this time I'll ride far enough around their camp to miss 'em."

"Aye, then. When ye reach Skye, explain things to Mother an' Kate for me."

Edward left on a cold August evening. That night, Ian walked through the forest to his southern border. He saw many tents, men, and a corral of horses.

A week later, Hugh and Ian walked to the same site, where they found the remains of an abandoned camp. "They've gone. We've not been found, but tha' dinna mean we're safe," Hugh said.

Chapter 60

One frosty morning while hunting, Hugh and Ian walked to the western edge of their lands. Hugh had two rabbits in his bag. Ian aimed at a cock pheasant taking flight. When his arrow found its target, the bird fell to the ground. As Ian pushed aside grouse and heather to find the bird, he caught the stench of death. The smell became stronger as he waded through a patch of bramble bushes. He found Edward where he had fallen, shot through the head. Ian dropped to his knees and cried out. "Damn, damn! He dinna make it! Th' bastards got him! How'll we get word to th' family?"

"Ian, we won't." Hugh looked around. "We dinna know they were this close. I'm thankful we dinna find out th' hard way. For now, we'll be sad he's gone an' glad we're alive."

Hugh picked up the pheasant and added it to his bag. "Ian, there's trout to be caught an' this meat to clean. Come alon', lad, an' we'll get on wi' it."

Meg and Janet sat at the table drinking tea. "Ah, th' lads ha' come home wi' th'—" Meg saw Hugh's face and stopped short. "Hugh, ye look like ye've seen a ghost."

"Meg, we found Edward in th' ravine, shot through th' heid. Th' English ha' been wi' in rock-throwin' distance of th' cottage. They've gone, but not before Edward crossed their path."

Ian heard Janet sob. "Lass, I'm so sorry. I wish he'd waited. I did'na ha' a good feelin' about it."

"Ian." Meg stood and put her hand on his shoulder. "I'm thankful ye an' Hugh found th' body. At least we can bury him an' know wha' happened."

Janet wrapped her arms around Ian and Meg. "Please, dear God, no more! I dinna want to lose anyone else!"

"If only he'd waited a day," Ian said, "He'd still be alive."

"Ah, Ian," Hugh said, "Edward was in the wrong place at th' wrong time, an' it could ha' been ye or me."

Meg led Janet back to the table. "Wipe yer eyes, lass, an' we'll get th' meat ready to cure." She spread a layer of finely ground salt on the table, rolled a piece of meat in it, and handed the meat to Janet together with a wooden mallet. "Here, love, pound th' salt into th' meat."

Janet picked up the mallet and hit the meat so hard that it landed on the floor. "Well, dear, do yer feel better now?"

"Aye, gi' me another piece."

"When we finish wi' th' meat, we'll start th' winter's candles an' soap. Th' early turn to cold weather has reminded me tha' it needs to be done."

"I've made candles an' soap both," Janet said.

"Good! Then we'll get started. I'd like rose petals for scent, or we can use a bit of pine sap. Hugh, remember th' honey tree ye found last spring?"

"Aye, an' I know wha' ye'll be needin'. Ian, ye come wi' me, an' we'll gather in honey an' beeswax for th' ladies."

"Meg," Janet said, "Mayhap I can find a bit of bog myrtle, feverfew, an' rose berries. I've dried herbs in my knapsack, but not enough to last th' winter."

"Hugh, here's a piece of linen, enough for a shroud."

"We'll get things ready and return before sunset." Hugh and Ian prepared Edward's grave, wrapped his body in the linen shroud, and laid him to rest in the spot where he had fallen. The next morning they gathered at the site. Hugh read scripture, and they mourned the loss of a dear friend and kin. They would always remember Edward's stories, his smiles, and the good things he did for everyone. Daniel, quiet and somber, told about the horse with wheels that Edward gave him.

The next day, clouds covered the sky. That night, the wind whistled around the tree tops and blew chimney smoke to the ground. The next morning a snowfall covered the fields. "It seems too early for snow. Come along, Daniel, bring yer toys. Janet, fetch a pot of tea, an' we'll spin yarn to make Daniel a nice sweater to wear wi' his breeks. There's yarn for socks an' a scarf for Ian an' Hugh. If ye feel like it, Janet, ye can get started on 'em."

"Hugh, I'm wonderin' about a mixture they use in Glasgow called concrete. It's a thick gray substance tha' hardens into th' shape of th' mold they pour it in. I'd like to try formin' a mold tha' would hold concrete to harden into troughs to carry water for th' cottage." The two men spent the rest of the afternoon in the storage room at the back of the barn, selecting books to bring to the cottage.

That night for supper they had baked trout, roasted potatoes, carrots, and onions, along with baked apples with sweet cream. There was fresh bread, butter, and slices of yellow cheese.

After the meal, Hugh cleared off the table and set out blocks of wood. "Daniel, we'll make ye a barn an' animals for ye to play wi'. First we'll whittle out a couple of sheep, then lambs, an' then maybe a horse."

"Could we make a dog, Uncle Hugh?"

"Aye, laddie, I'll see wha' I can do. Do ye want a big dog or a little dog?"

"A big dog, please, Uncle Hugh."

Janet sat by the fire knitting socks. She thought of past winter evenings at Glen Lochy when she was warm and safe by the fire knitting socks for Ewan and Duny. Overwhelming sadness flowed over her. Now, her life was starting over, and she would make her own decisions.

She smiled when she remembered Mary saying, "Men are needed to lift heavy things, keep th' larder stocked, an' sire bairns. In return, they need their clothin' mended, socks knitted, a good meal cookin', an' a bit of strokin' here an' there—then they'll be happy." Janet smiled to herself. *It's a wonder Ian's not found a wife. He's quite handsome wi' his dark hair an' blue eyes.*

She looked at him as he helped Daniel sort through the blocks of wood. *He'll be a good father an' husband, but he'd want a young woman who'll bear him bairns. Ah, well,* she sighed. *I'm th' widow Cameron, an' I'll make my own way. If folks know tha' I can treat th' sick an' injured, I might be able to bring in enough coins to not ha' to beg for a bite or a stick of wood for my fire.*

Janet was surprised when she looked at the stocking hanging from her needles; she had completed the first of a pair of socks, and she was able to think about her future without tears. Next morning Hugh and Ian brought in two deer and a boar. The hides and fat were for later use; nothing was wasted. Some of the meat was cured with salt and honey boiled down to sugar; the rest would stay frozen in an outside shed.

"Janet, th' sun is shinin'. Do ye feel like takin' a walk?" Ian asked.

"I'd like tha' very much."

Janet took Ian's arm, and they walked through the woods to the castle. Janet looked at the massive structure. " Ian, it's difficult to see it as it now, knowin' how it was before." She smiled at Ian, "Ye lived here alone. Ye did'na marry, Ian?"

The question hung in the air. "I've kept to my plans. I went to th' university for two years, an' then I decided to learn ways to improve Father's flock to bring th' best price for high quality fleece. I traveled to France an' Italy to talk wi' buyers so I'd know wha' they were lookin' for."

Ian's excitement was evident. "Now, I'm researchin' horticulture so I can plant a more productive grain crop. I've not had time to find a wife, an' I've been in no hurry. I'd rather have th' right one than settle for just anybody."

"Aye, I'm thinkin' about my future as well. Now tha' I'm a widow, both poor an' past my prime—" Janet paused. "I'll not depend on Duny to care for me. If he'd inherited Ewan's family's lands, he would've lived there, just as his father an' grandfather did. But King George will grant those lands to others who'll pay taxes to him instead of th' clan chieftain. It's never goin' to be th' same, an' there's naught to be done about it. I'm hopin' I can make my own way wi' my herbs an' medicines. I dinna know where I'll go, but there'll be somewhere I can call home."

"Janet." Ian cleared his throat. "Yer a lovely lass as well as very pleasant to be wi'."

"Oh, Ian, thank ye for th' kind words."

"Nay, I said those words because they're true! I've thought many times about ye since th' first time we met. It's true, th' Scotland as we know it, is no longer. I've prepared for five or more years of very lean times. Only th' strong will survive. Th' English king can take away our clans, tartans, pipes, an' freedom, but he'll never take away our love for bonny Scotland. She's in our blood, an' survival is wha' we'll live for."

Ian held his hand out to her. "Janet, I'd like to offer ye marriage, if ye'll ha' me. I've been waitin' for ye all my life. Meg says I should not speak so to ye just yet, but ye need not say anythin'. I love ye lass, an' someday I hope tha' ye'll find tha' ye care for me. Until then, I'll bide my time."

Janet could hardly breathe. "Ian, I'm honored tha' ye seem to be speakin' from yer heart. I canna think but for today. Th' past is still real to me, an' I've not yet separated myself from it. But th' past is also one where ye fed Daniel an' me. I knew then yer a decent man, an' I was not wrong. I'll need some time, Ian."

"Aye, lass, I'll wait. Come to me. I want to hold an' comfort ye."

"It's not sympathy I need, Ian. It's strength."

Ian took her hand and started to speak, but she placed a finger on his mouth and said, "I believe my family is well, Ian, but I must know for certain. I intend to go to Edinburgh when I can to search for 'em."

"Yer sayin' ye'll be goin' alone? Surely after all ye've been through ye'd not set out alone? I'll nay ha' it. Nay, Janet."

"Ian, ye should go to Skye an' tell' yer sister about Edward's death. She'll need to know. When Daniel an' I came from th' borders to where Edward joined us, I made our way, an' I can do so again! I know it's best for Daniel to stay here, so I'll be travelin' alone. Do as ye will, Ian, but if ye come wi' me, there can be no ties between us. I canna yet care for another. Ian, I cry when I dinna want to."

Ian thought for a few minutes and said, "I accept yer terms. We'll go when yer ready. Now, may I share a little of my strength wi' ye?"

Janet walked into his arms when he held them out to her. "I'll need one week, Ian, an' then I must go to Glen Lochy."

"Janet, love, nay. Glen Lochy lies to th' north, an' it's thick wi' soldiers lookin' for Charles Stuart. We could travel to Glen Lochy on our way back. We'll travel at night, just as ye an' Daniel did. Lass, I can sleep in a haystack, but ye may need a bed an' a pillow."

"Nay, I'm not expectin' comfort. It's safety I'll seek."

"You believe your family is in Edinburgh?"

"Aye, sometime, I'll explain how I know. Mother, my sister Meghan MacIntyre, my brother Jamie, and my son Duny Cameron are there."

"I dinna know ye knew that, lass. We'll prepare for th' trip, then. I'm thinkin' ye'll need a cloak, breeks, boots, an' a woolen shirt."

"I'll gather some of my medicines an' salves to take wi' us. It's a blessin' to not worry about Daniel. But, let me say tha' anywhere else, I'd not leave him behind."

Janet knew she had to tell Ian about her encounter with William Augustus. As time went by, it seemed as a dream; sometimes, she wondered if it was. "Ian, I tell ye this only because ye need to know. When Th' Duke of Cumberland took me to th' crofter's cottage, he said he planned to display me to th' Hielanders an' tell 'em tha' I was part of th' booty he an' his army took from 'em. But later, he asked me about myself. I told him of my mother bein' related to Queen Anne an' how she was raised in th' queen's castle. Then he said he wanted to marry me, an' he understood tha' I was carryin' a babe an' not yet over th' loss of my husband. He did me no harm an' took me back to Mary's cottage, but he said he'd come for me when he was through wi' his obligations in Scotland. He told me he'd ask his father, th' king, to write an decree of marriage! I'd ha' no choice but to marry him!"

"Well, lass, how do ye feel about it?"

"I thought of only one thin', to get away wi'out bein' hurt. He's very frightenin', yet other than threats, he dinna harm me."

"I know of William. Dinna worry, lass. He'll not find us. We'll be like animals of th' night, leavin' no trail behind us an' nowhere to be found in daylight."

The great bird's wings extended to their fullest as they caught the north wind and carried him far above the peaks of the High Glens. "Sir, I have flown over every hill and moor of Scotland. Only once did I locate a trace of her in the Highlands. It was during a storm. I heard her cry out, but then I lost the sound. I found your soldiers camped not far from a ruined castle, but there was no sign of her. I will continue to search, sir. What are your plans, sir, should I need to communicate with you?"

"I will be in London and then on to the Continent near Maastricht. Janet is here, but she stays hidden. When she is ready

397

she will make herself known. Listen and watch for her, Clamhan. When you hear her voice, contact me. I shall reward you for your efforts."

"William Augustus, I have been promised a thing of great value if my services are pleasing to you. I shall do everything within my power to obtain this promise."

"Who made such a promise to you, Clamhan?"

"The one who made it possible for me to help you on Culloden's battlefield. Will you say I am worthy?"

"I cannot say. Only the one who sent you can say so. I have only one request, Clamhan. Find her and advise me. Then I shall personally carry the message to your master that you are more than worthy."

"I shall do so, sir." Clamhan could not disobey his master, and yet he had not been released from service to this man. He would not find the woman; it was not what his master wanted.

Chapter 61

The week passed quickly. When all was ready, they left. Janet rode Prince carrying food, watered wine, and clothing in knapsacks. Ian's horse carried firearms and bedding. The first night, they rode only a short distance before they had to dismount and hide while troops of Redcoats passed by.

At sunrise they found a deserted crofter's cottage at the eastern edge of the Trossach Forest. "Ian, will we be safe here?"

"We should be. We'll take turns watchin' an' keep th' horses inside." Janet measured out grain for the horses and set out flasks of wine and pastries for herself and Ian. They sat on the floor eating and talking.

Ian said, "Last night we saw th' fires of th' king's army camps."

"Nay, Ian, those fires were high as th' trees. They're burnin' broch's! Where will we be after we travel tonight?"

"On th' eastern side of Loch Lomond. Then we'll turn south an' be at th' edge of th' Garadhban Forest. If all is well, we'll pass through th' forest an' follow a path tha' will take us to Strathblane."

"How far will we be from Edinburgh then?"

"Many things could happen between here an' there. I'm leavin' time to change th' plans if needed."

"Another week, then?"

"Aye, likely."

Janet could not sleep. She was tired of riding, tired of running, and tired of sadness. She stepped outside and stood in the bright sunlight. She knew the risk of being found, but she loved the warmth of the sun. She knew her father was dead, but she also knew her mother, sister, brother, and son were alive. *I want to see Glen Lochy,* she thought. *I'll lay Elizabeth an' th' bairns to rest, an' I want to take Duny's inheritance to him before it's forever lost. Poor laddie, he dinna know his da is dead.* She wiped away tears, went inside, lay down, and slept.

That evening, before they left, she shared her thoughts with Ian. "I'm not yet thinkin' straight. Th' things I put away at Glen Lochy will help Duny, but only if he has 'em. I know th' danger of goin' there, but I feel I must do so. Ian, if ye wish, ye can return home."

Ian sat quietly for a few minutes. "Janet, I canna tell ye th' risk we'll be takin'. It's th' Hielands an' Cameron country! Th' Redcoats are as thick as thieves lookin' for Charles Stuart. Edward said th' king put a bounty on Charles's heid, an' it's said he may be wi' th' Cameron chieftain in hidin'. I can't talk ye out of goin', but if we do, we'll be hidin' more than we'll be travelin'."

"There's th' same risk goin' to Edinburgh. Ye said so yerself!"

"Aye, I did."

"My mind is made up, an' I know where I'm headin'. Yer can make th' choice tha' is best for ye."

"There's nay choice for me to make. I'll be beside ye."

They mounted their horses and turned north toward Cameron lands. The night sky was tinged with a red glow.

"Master, the woman is traveling with a man. What would you have me do?"

The Dark One responded, "She is of no use to me. I care not what becomes of her. If the duke returns to Scotland looking for her, he'll be wasting his time."

"Master, do you wish me to cease services to William Augustus?"

"You've served my purpose for now Clamhan." The demon's fangs appeared. "He thinks you will find her, but you will not."

"And if he insists?"

"You will not find her. She will disappear."

"Very well, sir. It is an honor to be of service to you."

Author's Note

In the aftermath of the battle, families were left without husbands and fathers. Those Highlanders who did not die at Culloden or were killed by order of The Duke of Cumberland, were taken as prisoners and sent to other countries, where they would become slaves.

Mothers frantically sold meager belongings to provide for their children. While it was not known at the time, the worst was yet to come.

Sources of Information used in Survival of the Blood

Publications, including *The Highlander, Scotland Magazine,* and *Scottish Life.*

Charles Edward Stuart: The Life and Times of Bonnie Prince Charlie, by David Daiches

William Augustus, The Duke of Cumberland: A Life, by Rex Whitworth

The Visitor's Center, Culloden, Scotland

CPSIA information can be obtained
at www.ICGtesting.com
Printed in the USA
LVHW091446010322
712329LV00003B/37